HEART
OF
CRUELTY

HEART OF CRUELTY

MAYBELLE WALLIS

POOLBEG

This book is a work of fiction. The names, characters, places, businesses, organisations and incidents portrayed in it are either the product of the author's imagination or are used fictitiously. Any resemblance to actual persons, living or dead, events or locales is entirely coincidental.

Published 2020
by Poolbeg Press Ltd.
123 Grange Hill, Baldoyle,
Dublin 13, Ireland
Email: poolbeg@poolbeg.com

A catalogue record for this book is available from the British Library.

ISBN 978178199-735-2

www.poolbeg.com

Dedication

To Eve and Sam

1: In the Workhouse Yard

5th March 1840, Birmingham

The pile of waste bones from the slaughterhouse had been dumped in the yard and lain uncovered and stinking for days. As we sunk our hands into it, brown rats swarmed out and I gasped, fearing they would bite me, but they fled to their burrows in the workhouse walls. We dropped the bones in the ramming-bin and between us both worked the heavy iron rammer up and down, grinding the bones into meal. We went on for hour after hour.

The kinds of labour that bore little profit for much effort, not enough to support life, were given to those who existed by the feeblest of margins in the workhouse, under the control of the Guardians of the Poor. The bone-crushing work, normally given to the men, was meant to punish Clara and me, for we had both offended by complaining of Reverend Glyde, the workhouse chaplain.

Siviter, the workhouse master, watched us as we slowed, jeering at what he called our idleness and swishing his cane. Rows of small windows peered down from the high black walls: on one side the loathsome dormitories and the workshops, on the other the infirmary and morgue. Before us was the chapel with its cross; behind us rose the boundary wall.

The fragmenting bones squirted putrid marrow up at us. Sweat soaked the armpits of my dress; my shoulders were burning, my hands blistering. The bone-meal had to be shovelled into sacks and a new load of bones fetched. It had been just after six o'clock in the morning when we had started; now the chapel bell was striking ten.

'Are yer hungry in yer bellies now, yer idle bitches?' Siviter demanded. 'There'll be nought for yer today, no bread nor water, only work. Let yer lying tongues go dry, teach yer a lesson.'

It was the day after Ash Wednesday, when we had already endured a fast, but we made no reply, and kept on banging the iron rammer down, its thuds reverberating in the stone enclosure.

'Idlers like you get a night in the lock-up,' gloated Siviter.

I had been in there once before, for some infringement of rules I had not understood, hungry, thirsty and alone in the fetid gloom behind the iron door. And not only that: we had already been condemned to the ordeal of the Sunday Penances, administered by Reverend Glyde. It was unjust.

'I won't.' I let go the rammer and stood doubled over, my hands dropping to my thighs. 'It's not right.'

'Get back on the job, yer!' Siviter lashed out with his cane. 'I'll kill yer, lazy drab!'

The blow jarred my spine and cold needles of pain shot down into my legs. I heard a man shout. As I tried to straighten up, another whack of Siviter's cane caught my head and knocked off my cap.

'Jane!' Clara cried out, but she did not come to me.

The pain was immense. I put my hand to my head; it came away wet, and red. I knew Siviter had not finished. I was overwhelmed by fear, and by the grotesqueness of the scene: the hideous walls of the workhouse yard, the fetid reek of the bones, the blood filling my palm. His next blow sent me crumpling forward so that I lay curling my arms over my throbbing head, my face to the slimy cobbles, one eye open to the red rivulet of blood that trickled between them.

As I heard Siviter's cane whistle again through the air, there came another shout from across the yard.

Siviter stopped.

'Coroner Doughty, sir, good morning, sir!' he called out, and to Clara and me he muttered that we should get back to work.

I could not move.

'Mr Siviter!' A cold, clear voice came closer to where I lay. 'Mr Siviter!'

'Good morning to yer, sir, Dr Doughty, sir, a fine morning too.'

Then I saw darkness and heard nothing.

After a time I smelt a gentleman's cologne, and found I was lying on my side. My head throbbed as something pressed it down against the cobblestones.

My first sight of Doughty was of his wrist emerging from a white shirt-cuff, of his black coat sleeve, and the corner of his handkerchief. He was kneeling beside me on the filthy cobbles of the workhouse courtyard, applying pressure to my wound. As he lifted the handkerchief, I raised my eyes to his: wide-open, dark, intent on mine. His face was close and as I looked up I could see the dark hairs inside his nostrils and the tiny black dots left by his cleanshaven beard. A frown creased his forehead.

'She's conscious again, but still losing blood.' He pressed the handkerchief to the side of my head again. 'Speak to me. What's your name, m'dear?'

'Jane.'

'Jane what?'

'Verity.' I closed my eyes again.

'Well, Jane Verity, you must go to the infirmary. Are you able to get up?'

Doughty grasped my upper arm, trying to raise me with one hand while still holding the handkerchief to my head with the other. I opened my eyes but, as I lifted my head and shoulders, the darkness came back. I leaned into the handkerchief, drooping my head against his hand with a sigh. The scent of his cologne revived me a little.

'Malingering, sir.' Siviter was still close by.

'Get help!' snapped Doughty.

Siviter sent Clara to find his wife, the matron.

If I made no effort it would count against me later, so I heaved myself up and around, resting on hands and knees like an animal. My breath came fast and shallow, hindered by the pain in my back. The coroner cursed, for his handkerchief was dislodged by my movement and my blood dripped on the ground beneath. I was dizzy and wanted to sag down again to the stones.

'You've already given me sufficient work for one day, Mr Siviter. I have one inquest to hear in this place and have no need of more.' Doughty pressed the handkerchief back into place with a hand either side of my head.

Clara had not returned but Siviter called out to a couple of male inmates who came across the yard and, laying hold of me, hoisted me upright. I winced at their grasp and felt I might faint again. Doughty gave up his handkerchief, placing the hand of one of the men to where he had been applying pressure, and standing away.

He turned to Siviter. 'Put her in the infirmary with a proper binding on the head wound, and a milk diet until she's healed.'

I closed my eyes.

'Filthy drab, full of disease,' muttered Siviter.

But, as the men lugged me away, Doughty said: 'My inquests have only four possible verdicts: natural death, accidental death, temporary insanity – that means suicide – and the fourth verdict is wilful murder. What verdict, in this young woman's case, shall I recommend to my jury?'

I was brought to the workhouse infirmary and dumped on a bed, where I lay for some time, half in a swoon. To my relief Mrs Siviter did not come to tend me. It fell to Clara instead, who brought a bucket of water and an old nightgown to tear up for bandages. There were no dressings or medicines in the infirmary, only two rows of iron beds on which the sick lay coughing and crying out. I was lucky to have a bed to myself.

'That gentleman liked the look of you, I'd say.' Clara smiled at me. She had beautiful diction, having learned a cut-glass accent at an early age from her clients. 'He might have been tending your wound but his eyes were all over you like a rash.'

'You're mad, Clara.' My breath came easier now. 'In that state, and me, to quote Mr Siviter, a filthy drab?' Workhouse girls were considered ignorant and loose.

'But wouldn't you fancy a man with kind hands, darling?' Clara arched a fine, dark eyebrow.

'There's no such creature.'

'Did you not notice his gentleness, and how he pressed his handkerchief to you?' Clara lowered her voice a couple of octaves and drooped her eyelids with feigned passion. *'What's your name, m'dear?'*

I levered myself up to sit on the edge of the bed. The workhouse stench was powerful here: the odour of the paupers, whose clothes were never washed but merely heated in the stoving room to supposedly kill lice. Added to that were the vapours of bad food and worse digestions, of greasy heads, of sores and sweat, all mingled in an atmosphere tainted by the effluvia of the cesspit and the mortuary.

'What was he doing here, Clara? He said he had an inquest. Who's died?'

Clara did not reply. Her smile faded and she busied herself tearing the nightgown into strips.

It was not the routine for the coroner to be summoned. The last time had been several weeks ago when an old man had fallen into the hot water in the laundry copper and half his skin had scalded off. Usually if a pauper died there would be a swift burial, and no concern over the reason why, as long as there was one less burden on the so-called Guardians of the Poor. Reverend Glyde might recite an extra prayer at Evensong, although I knew that he never concerned himself over the babies who, as had befallen my poor Nathan, died unbaptised and were put into the cesspit.

'Who's died, Clara?' Perhaps someone on the outside had reported a concern of ill-treatment.

Clara, no longer able to maintain her teasing demeanour, detached Doughty's handkerchief from my wound and said she didn't know. She was a poor liar, yet it was often hard to make her speak the truth.

'Look at this,' she said, showing me the blood-soaked cloth. 'Fine linen, such dainty hemstitching – you might wash it with some salt and get a ha'penny for it at a clothier's. A penny if you unpicked his initials.'

'You do know something,' I said. 'Tell me.'

'Or you might use it as a clout for your monthlies,' said Clara, casting it aside, then taking a remnant of the nightgown and dipping it in the bucket. 'He'd be glad of that, I should think.'

I winced as she dabbed at my wound, but I would not give up.

'They must be holding an inquest. You heard the coroner. He said that Siviter had already given him enough work.' I stared at her haunted pallor, the dark shadows beneath her eyes. 'Yes, you know something horrible. I can see it in your face ...'

Clara wound a mass of calico over my hair. Her hands were unsteady. Then she lowered her voice. 'Pious Betty told me that a girl was found hanging in the laundry this morning. But I don't know ...'

'Pious Betty! Well, she has not the wit to lie.' I hated her, even though she was simple, because Nathan, only nine days old, had died in her care. She had by heart the Psalms, and the Proverbs, and the Beatitudes, and recited them often and endlessly in her toneless voice yet knew not enough to keep a baby alive. 'In any case, I imagine that a suicide would have brought the coroner.'

Then it occurred to me. My heart lurched.

Theresa Curran had been the origin of our trouble. As she often did, she had followed Reverend Glyde out of our dormitory during the night, as I shrank, terrified, under my blanket. On this occasion she had not returned by the morning, when Mrs Siviter had come to wake us as usual. We complained to her, but she brought us to her husband's office straight away. She boxed our ears for what she termed our '*filthy talk*', and the two of them judged us with faces of iron. She said that the Reverend would be informed and would see us for the Sunday Penances. We had gone there with hopes of justice and now we were utterly dismayed. Leaving that fear to worm its way through our souls, Mr Siviter added that in the meantime, hard work and empty bellies would start us on the path of correction. We had been sent straight out to crush the bones.

'Theresa – have you seen her yet?'

Clara stopped what she was doing, and her eyes met mine. 'I know. I imagine they found her while we were in the yard.'

'It couldn't be …' I could hardly bring myself to say it. 'Oh … not her. Surely to God, she was but a child. Twelve? Thirteen?'

I did not ask Clara anything else. Although my mind recoiled from the thought, I could have predicted it. Theresa had been wasting away, ignoring her meagre rations until they were snatched away by others, unhealed wounds multiplying on her skin. Quietly, she had almost ceased to exist; her death had been written in her eyes. She was sent to Reverend Glyde every Sunday for Penances that she did not deserve. On the nights when she followed him out of the dormitory she had returned after an hour or two, creeping silently back to her place. Once I thought I heard her weeping, but when I whispered her name there was silence. During the day, if I approached her, she turned her face away in shame.

'What good will the coroner do?' Clara tucked in the end of the bandage; the thing was starting to slide down over my eyes already. 'What's he to do if Theresa … if she made away with herself? Why get a doctor to look at her when she's already dead?'

I lay back down on the dirty blankets. I would reapply the bandage later, myself.

'He might not be a medical doctor, Clara. He might be a Doctor of Law.'

'And what do you know of Doctors of Law, Jane?' Clara said with a smile.

'More than you realise, Clara,' I retorted. I had never told anyone in the workhouse of my background, feeling ashamed that I had once possessed far more advantages than they and in my folly, in the blindness of passion, had cast them aside. 'In any case, what if he sees the state she was in? The marks on her body? He saw Siviter beating me: perhaps he will realise what this place truly is. Our suffering should be revealed: the cruelty, the Sunday Penances. It might get into the newspaper. People should know. The whole place should be torn down.'

'Gentlemen look after one another.' Clara fixed me with her pretty eyes. 'The coroner is Glyde's brother-in-law. And the Reverend Vernon Glyde is not just our chaplain but the Chairman of the Board of Guardians of the Poor, the Rector of St Michael's and a Magistrate of the Bench.'

'And you, what do you know of Magistrates of the Bench, Clara?'

'More than you realise, Jane.' Her lips curved into a smirk. Clara knew far too many gentlemen. She would have had no need of the workhouse but for a dose of a certain illness that had prevented her from plying her trade.

'They're all keeping things quiet for each other,' she continued. 'Look at Mr Madden. Two offices in the same person. Relieving Officer of the Parish Union, supposedly paying to feed us paupers, and at the same time as the Registrar of Deaths he sends us off to be buried. Dr Wright, the workhouse doctor? I've barely seen him, and you know how often I've had to help in this so-called infirmary. He only comes when someone dies, writes a certificate without even looking at them, and Mrs Siviter takes it to Mr Madden to get it registered. That's all. If you died tomorrow, there'd be no mention of your head wound.'

We learned nothing of the coroner's inquest, and I supposed that Theresa was sent to the burial grounds in one of the coffins from the basement, for even her small body would have been too large for the cesspit.

After that I lay for some days in the infirmary, fearing that my back was broken and that my throbbing wound would turn septic. I asked where was my milk diet; there was never any milk, they said, only gruel. I feared that Dr Doughty would soon return for my inquest. What would his verdict be? As I felt close to death, I pondered my past like an old woman, wondering if I could have had a better life. I thought of my mother and saw her again in our parlour at home, in her dove-grey silk, correcting me with precision as I practised at the piano. And my father: how high-minded he was, and how he had campaigned for the abolition of the slave trade. What would he think now of his disinherited daughter, gone from being a theatre-company piano-player to forced labour in the Birmingham Parish Union Workhouse? They would never learn of Nathan's brief life, too shameful to be told.

More often I dreamed of Edmond in all his flamboyant glory, of his fair hair and his powerful voice, of his passionate avowals. I prayed to him as though to a golden god, that he would return to me. I conjured up his profile and the shape of his lips and tightened my arms around myself as though he held me again to his chest. I pictured his lithe limbs moving with my music across the stage. He had not intended to leave me to this, I reminded myself. I would live for him, for his peerless love beside which all else became insignificant.

I did not die, nor was I sent to the Sunday Penances. I recovered, with the resilience of youth. My wound started to heal and after a few days Mrs Siviter came to the infirmary in the early morning and informed me that the coroner and Mrs Doughty had requested me as a domestic servant, at ninepence a week, although she had no idea why they would have chosen me, and thought that ninepence was far too much.

This meant the end of my time in the workhouse. I thanked her, hoping that I had the strength for it, and that the coroner had acted out of charity. It had been the sight of my blood that had drawn his notice, and at that time his motive thus appeared to be honourable. Yet it was also possible that my degraded state had excited his interest.

'Get dressed, then.'

I got up hastily, expecting her to berate me for being slow. She merely dropped a pile of clothing on the floor. 'I'll send Clara Scattergood to help you. I suppose we'll get you back when you prove to be unsuitable.'

With that, she left. The pile contained a mobcap, a black stuff dress, black woollen stockings, and an old pair of boots. There was a small bundle with a few things I had brought into the workhouse with me: a brass ring, which I did not put on, a tea-token from the shop on Navigation Street, a nightgown, an ivory comb. Of my reticule, of the clothes I had on when I came in – a well-made walking-dress and shawl – and of the layette I had bought for Nathan, there was no sign.

Clara came to unwind the bandage. I covered the scab on my head with the mobcap, hoping my raggedly shorn hair might soon grow back.

'You're being sent out, then,' said Clara, 'at Dr Doughty's request. I told you he'd taken an interest in you.'

'I'm sure they must be a respectable family.' I remembered Doughty's white shirt-cuff, his professional manner, and his fine handkerchief.

Clara snorted. 'Oh, they'll think themselves respectable – far enough above you that they can treat you as they want. You're to do as you're told. You'll be drudging, day and night. If you don't work enough, they'll whip you, and when the gentleman wants you he'll have you, and when his lady wife finds you at it, you're out on the street. After that, there's only one way to survive. If you haven't done it before, then stay away from the cribs is my advice. Go to Mrs Graham's on Suffolk Street. Else it's back to the workhouse.'

'Well, I shan't be coming back to the workhouse. And I shan't be drudging forever, for that matter.'

Clara smiled at me. 'What, are you to be a girl of the game then? And I thought you so straitlaced.'

'Don't be foolish, Clara. I shall find Edmond. He promised to come back.'

'You must look forward, Jane, into the future.' She put out her hands and held mine in them. 'Don't be looking back all the time, to what no longer exists.'

The Beadle came for me then, and there was no time to argue with her. I gave her a hasty embrace. Her words remained with me, even though I was certain that she was wrong.

2: A Respectable Employment

I followed the Beadle through the centre of Birmingham. The bells of St Michael's rang the hour; it was eight o'clock in the morning. We were late and I was slow; he grasped my arm to hasten me.

Like the finest of its residents, the town had an appearance of gentility. The newly incorporated Borough was on rising ground beside the River Rea. Visitors arriving by the stagecoach or by the railway might avail of a hansom cab to one of the hotels in the upper town. Here they would appreciate the ordered geometry of long brick terraces, the tree-lined squares, the fine churches, the Town Hall, the theatres, the library, the superior shops of a civilised society. But should they stray to lower levels they would encounter the industrial areas: the manufactories of the Gun Quarter and the Jewellery Quarter, the canal basin with its wharves and gasworks, the slums, the institutions. Steam-engines and forges consumed coal by the cartload, their black penumbra velveting everything with soot. Decaying by the river was the mediaeval underbelly, with the beastly squalor of its meat market, its tanneries, its half-timbered tenements listing across cobbled streets and its effluvious burial grounds.

We were making our way now towards the upper town. There were a few drops of rain, and then a heavy shower. Water ran off the Beadle's gold-braided greatcoat but soaked though my dress and flattened my mobcap to my head. The Beadle steered me along Colmore Row, past the churchyard known as Pigeon Park. It gave my heart a jolt to see theatre playbills everywhere, but none bore Edmond's name. If I could only find him, I could write to him.

From Colmore Row, Newhall Street ran down the hill away from the town. Number 49 was at the far end of a terrace of tall, flat-fronted houses. It seemed at the bounds of gentility, for the next building, across a side turning, was a wireworks. Further down by the canal bridge were the smoking chimneystacks of the manufactories amongst the tenements of their workers. The thump of machinery shook the ground and the air, still teeming with rain, smelt of coal.

I hesitated in front of the house, unsure where to go. Railings guarded a small area in front, with steps leading down to a puddle in front of a tradesman's entrance. A doorway in the side wall must have led to a backyard. Three steps led up to the front door, which had a shallow portico with a white stucco column on either side, affording a little shelter from the rain. The window-frames were peeling and cobwebbed. I wondered what kind of family lived within; the house was far smaller and shabbier than my parents' house had been.

'Behave yourself, now, Verity, or I'll be fetching you back.' The Beadle nudged me forward up the steps. 'You'll be at Penances on Sunday with Reverend Glyde.'

I lifted and let fall the iron doorknocker, its dull note echoing in the house. There was no answer. I turned to glance at the Beadle, who stood waiting, rain dripping off his cocked hat. I knocked again, afraid lest the house proved empty, for no servant came to answer and no lights could be seen within. But eventually the door was opened.

I looked up from the doorstep into the coroner's face while he hesitated, as if considering me and doubting his decision. This was Glyde's brother-in-law, according to Clara, but also the man who had rescued me. His eyes, intelligent and curious, were belied by the mouth, which seemed soft and exposed amidst clean-shaven skin. He had a straight and narrow nose, and his wavy black hair had not yet begun to recede, although there was a little grey in his sideburns. He had a tendency to form a furrow between his heavy eyebrows, as though concentrating all the darkness in his face at that point. I imagined that in anger his features would be startling in their severity.

Behind me the rain splashed in the street as a horse-and-cart trundled past.

'You sent for me to come from the workhouse.' I was shivering with cold, conscious of my shabbiness, and the wet dress that clung heavily to my frame.

The Beadle took a letter from his pocket and passed it up.

'Miss Verity.' Doughty glanced at it and pocketed it without breaking the seal. 'Jane Verity. I was hoping that you would have arrived earlier.' He was already dressed as though to go out, in a coat of fine black cloth and polished boots.

He dismissed the Beadle and motioned me to follow him inside.

The hallway was narrow, and I closed the door behind me and stood dripping on the doormat. There was a row of coats on hooks, a worn-out hall-runner, and an iron hallstand bristling with umbrellas and walking-canes. The light from a tall window on the back landing filtered through dust. A long-case clock ticked dolefully by the foot of the stairs.

Its pendulum skittered as Doughty strode past it into the shadows. He was a well-built man, lean and long-limbed.

'I must go out shortly, but I'll show you the house.' He spoke over his shoulder, and there was something of the North in his accent. 'Mrs Doughty's not yet up.'

I followed him along the passageway and down the back stairs to the basement kitchen. It was well furnished, and equipped with a modern cast-iron range, but filthy, fetid with damp and the odour of stale food. Dirty crockery was stacked on the kitchen table. The scullery beyond was piled with washing and the fire was out under the copper, even though the coal store was full. On the pantry floor was a bare mattress with its striped ticking blotched with brown stains. A couple of cockroaches scuttled away.

I looked at Doughty in dismay.

'My housekeeper has left,' he said, 'and my wife is ill, so I've had to do the best I can. I expect you'll set the place straight. I hope you're fully recovered from your injury.'

'Yes, sir. Thank you.'

'Reverend Glyde informs me that you have become accustomed to hard work and stern discipline.'

I replied that I would try my best.

With my head starting to ache, I lagged behind as we returned to the ground floor. He had brought a picture into my mind of Glyde and his fleshy lips, haranguing us at Evensong, or plying his switch at the Sunday Penances. For a moment my fear returned, but I resolved to dispel it, telling myself that now I would be safe.

The parlour with its cottage piano and hard-looking sofas was connected by a large folding door to a back parlour. Woolly drifts lay alongside the skirting boards. The furniture was scuffed, and its style out of date, but I cast a longing glance at the piano and ran a finger along its dusty lid.

Doughty frowned at the trail I left. 'I'm sure you'll find plenty to do.'

Across the hall were the dining room and his study, again much in need of dusting. There was a broad mahogany desk, with an inkstand and a chaos of papers; the longest wall was lined with shelves of books and ledgers, and by the window was a side table piled high with newspapers and journals.

On the first-floor landing were four more doors.

'This is Mrs Doughty's room,' he said, 'with her dressing room beside it.' He tapped briefly at the door, then opened it and intruded his head into the darkness beyond. 'Harriet, my dear? Harriet, the new servant has arrived.'

He took the letter from his pocket and went in. There was a low murmur from within, and then he emerged, scowling, and closed the door.

'She is indisposed and will ring later for her medicines. Take her a glass of fresh water when she does.'

Further round the landing were Doughty's room, and his dressing room. I stayed back on the landing as he pushed the doors ajar.

'I require hot water at seven in the morning,' he said, indicating a bowl and a jug on the marble-topped washstand. 'Breakfast at eight. I'm usually out of the house by half past.'

'Are you a medical doctor?' I ventured.

'What other sort should I be?' He closed the dressing-room door and regarded me with a half-smile.

'There are doctors of law, and philosophy,' I said.

'*Hm.*' He raised an eyebrow. 'Do you imagine that a doctor of law would have staunched your wound?'

I apologised, conscious that I must remember my place.

He seemed a little amused, and merely shrugged as he continued up the stairs.

'These rooms are not in use,' he said as we passed more closed doors on the next landing and went on up.

On the top floor were lumber-rooms, and a servant's room.

'Mrs Eddam slept in the pantry. She didn't like the stairs. But you can sleep here, if you prefer.'

He held the door open for me and I went inside. Under a skylight were a narrow bed and a chest of drawers furred with dust.

'Yes, sir.' I brightened. 'I might perhaps dispose of Mrs Eddam's mattress? The one in the kitchen?'

Doughty paused in the doorway, sombre in his black coat. The little room had filled with the scent of his cologne.

'How old are you?' His eyes passed over my servant's dress, which was still wet and muddy, noted my waist and my bosom, and then held my gaze.

'Twenty, sir.' I felt myself blush, and should have looked away, but I could not read his expression.

He stared past me at the bed, sliding his hand down the edge of the door until his fingers encountered the key. He slipped it out of the keyhole and held it out to me.

'Lock your door,' he said, turning away.

'Thank you, sir.' I remembered that I owed him a debt for rescuing me from Siviter. 'I must thank you also for troubling to help me when I was injured, and for fetching me out of that dreadful place.'

'It was my professional duty.' He walked across the landing and paused with his hand on the banister, held his back straight and spoke into the void above the stairs. 'As a medical doctor, I could have done nothing else.'

I pulled the door to, and locked it, dropping the key into my skirt pocket and reflecting that Clara had probably been right about him. I followed him downstairs but paused on the second-floor landing; one of the doors was slightly ajar.

I glanced inside. The shutters were closed at the dormer window and the dim interior was heavily cobwebbed, but under a dusty blanket was a crib. So, he too had his grief: a dead infant, a sick wife. I could not linger there. I heard Doughty's footsteps on the floor below. He cleared his throat impatiently.

I closed the door and hastened down the narrow stairway.

'What ails your wife, sir?' I asked.

'I am informed that she suffers from melancholia.' He lowered his voice to a murmur as we passed her room. 'In my view, her illnesses are compounded by the attentions of her physician.'

'Can you not treat her yourself?'

He gave a short laugh as he continued downstairs. 'I am not sufficiently skilled as a medical doctor. She would have passed beyond hope before she might benefit from my services.' He was in the hall now, putting on his tall hat to go out, adjusting it with a grimace into the mirror. 'Good day, Jane Verity.'

He went out without waiting for my reply.

I closed the front door behind him, wondering what kind of man he was. He seemed to be a gentleman, and almost certainly had saved my life, yet I wondered how professional his motive in helping me had been, and whether removing me to his house was really part of the duties of a medical doctor. Furthermore, if I must lock my door, was it safe for me to go through the house at night? And if he encountered me in the corridor, or if I left my door unlocked and he came in, would it mean that any consequences were not his fault?

3: Dressing Mrs Doughty

There was work to be done, in any case. My first action was to drag the malodorous old mattress out across the back yard to the side gate. I stood it outside the wall. Even though soaked with rain, scavengers would soon remove it. Then I filled the copper with fresh water from the pump, emptied cinders from its firebox and started it up with fresh coal. Harriet would need hot water to wash. I cleaned the range and prepared it to be lit.

Needing to rest, I sat for a moment at the kitchen table, turning the chair aside from the dirty crocks. I looked at my blackened fingernails, and marvelled that a year ago I would not have known how to do this. As a child, I had been drawn to the kitchen, enjoying the warmth of the range, the gleam of the pans, and what fragments of servants' gossip I could overhear. I had read *The Housekeeper's Guide* and helped Cook and Martha with the baking. My mother had approved, thinking I would one day learn to supervise staff. But I never saw how they rose a good two hours before their employers to prepare for the day. It was in my cheap lodgings at Duddeston, after Edmond left, that I learned to work a range, and light a copper.

As my thoughts strayed back to Edmond my hopes returned. I must write to him, as soon as I could. And as for the time before Edmond, my parents, and our house on Bedford Street, that memory had smudged like a pastel drawing into a cloud in my mind. Sometimes their talk surprised me by arising in my speech: my father's legal language, my mother's moralising. Apart from that, they must be forgotten; I was no longer their daughter.

The long-case clock struck the hour: ten o'clock. It was time to start cleaning the house.

The first object I dusted down was the piano. It was a lovely thing: a Broadwood, in polished walnut, with a fine marquetry inlay. I shook the dust off the sheet music in the piano rack: all hymns and requiems. I lingered, picking drips of wax from the candle sconces, then succumbed to temptation and lifted the fall, which swung easily back on its long brass hinges. The black and white keys were so invitingly smooth. I touched the middle C; it sang out true. My fingers itched to play the lively modern pieces that had accompanied Mr Davenant's theatrical productions, but that would never have done. I played a couple of chords, and an arpeggio. As the last notes faded, I listened, but the house was totally quiet, so I dared to sit for a moment on the piano stool. My hands were stiff, but from memory I tried Mendelssohn's first piano sonata. It reminded me of happier times, and for a moment the notes climbed cheerfully into the air, but then I hit a wrong key, and startled as the ceiling creaked above. I waited to hear if Mrs Doughty would ring, but there was only silence. I hastily finished cleaning the parlour and continued on upstairs.

Dr Doughty's room was sparely furnished: a dressing

table with a speckled mirror, a tall wing-chair, a run of shelves with a closet at either end, and a divan-bed placed in front of them as though it were a temporary accommodation, although the rectangle of dust beneath it told me it had been there for some time. The wainscoting and shelves had once been painted cream but were dunned by time to brown and scuffed at the corners. The red-damask curtain had faded to pink along its folds, the bolster at the bedhead was darkened with grease, and the counterpane of olive-green silk had worn thin where he had tucked it in to his neck or his armpit. Only his toiletries were expensive: that Cologne water was from Robert Low & Son, The Strand, London, by Royal Appointment. His night reading was piled on the shelf next to the bedhead. You can know a man, my father once said, by the quality of his library.

I perched on Doughty's unmade divan, its springs creaking, and looked at the titles. I had never heard of *The Works of the Right Honourable John, Earl of Rochester*, *Satyricon* or *The Memoirs of a Woman of Pleasure*. Their covers were worn. The first book fell open at a bookmark of ribbon and a few words caught my eye – *whore* – *lechery* – *wanton*. I snapped it shut and got up.

I straightened the bedclothes, then gathered discarded linen from the floor and took it down to the scullery. The scent of Low's Cologne rose from the crumpled shirts in my arms as I thought of how he had stared at my bed. Clara had guessed right, and he must have intended to seduce me by bringing me here. Yet, he had given me my own key, and I thought I had discerned that there was something in him that was honourable, that joined him to the standards of his profession and fought against his baser instincts. I might after all have died in the workhouse had he not challenged Siviter.

By eleven o'clock, Mrs Doughty still had not rung for me.

I had in any case got a large jug of hot water ready in her dressing room. I fetched a glass of water upstairs for her medicines and paused on the landing. There was silence in Mrs Doughty's room. I knocked softly, then opened the door and peered around it. There was the stifling odour of a sickroom and a little light filtered around the edge of the curtains.

Mrs Doughty lay face up in bed, eyes open.

'Mrs Eddam,' she muttered. 'Where is Mrs Eddam?'

'I am Jane Verity, madam, the new servant.'

There was a silence, and Mrs Doughty blinked. Tears ran back from her eyes and disappeared into the fair hair that was strewn across her pillow.

'Madam,' I tried again, 'I am Jane Verity, the new servant. Mrs Eddam was the previous servant, and I was sent to replace her.'

I went and opened the curtains. The walls of the room were arsenic green, and the newly intruding daylight lit Mrs Doughty's face: an elegant oval, her complexion as downy as a child's, and her staring eyes like violet-blue marbles. This then, was Glyde's sister.

'My medicines. Time for my medicines.' She wore a nightdress twice her size, fountaining with layers and lace.

'In a minute, madam.'

I put the glass down on the dressing table, helped Mrs Doughty into a sitting position and plumped her pillows. Under the damp nightdress there was a tremor in the wasted shoulders.

'My medicine, my medicine,' Mrs Doughty repeated breathlessly, 'I want my medicine.' She outstretched a wavering finger, directing me through the interconnecting door to her dressing room.

Scores of medicine bottles were crowded on a shelf that ran the length of the room, enough to fill a druggist's shop.

It was a confusion of glass jars and bottles of different shapes and sizes and colours, amber-brown, dark sapphire-blue, emerald-green, ruby-red, bottles with little droppers inset into the tops, or with ground-glass stoppers. Mucilages and decoctions, infusions and ferments, all bearing the name of their patent holder: Hervey's, Skinforth's, Yeoman's, Murdleston's. I had hoped that my new mistress's ailments were temporary, but at once I could see that this was not to be the case. No wonder her husband could not cure her.

The cry came again: *'My medicine! Bring me my medicine!'*

'Which one, madam?' I hesitated in the doorway.

'The laudanum!' She was panting, open-mouthed. 'The laudanum in the violet flask. Twelve drops.'

The violet flask was fitted with a dropper. Mrs Doughty protruded her tongue for the dose and swallowed it with a grimace. She closed her eyes, leaning back against her pillows with her face tilted up to the ceiling and her teeth clenched. Her breaths came in short whimpers.

I asked if she was in pain but she did not reply. I waited, watching her, wondering if she was going to suffer some sort of seizure. A blood vessel pulsed frantically amongst the emaciated lines of her throat. After a while it slowed, and her breathlessness started to subside.

'My dressing gown …' She looked up at my face. 'Who did you say you were?'

'Jane Verity, madam.'

'Verity. Well, Verity, I want my dressing gown.' She turned onto her side and swivelled her legs out of the bed, the nightdress billowing in excess around her.

I stooped to turn her beaded silk slippers around to meet her feet.

Her dressing gown was cream quilted silk, trimmed with swansdown, and I helped her to stand up and get her thin arms into the sleeves and drag the weight of it to her dressing table, where she sat and stared at my reflection in the mirror. Then she turned around.

'You are from the workhouse, you say?'

'Yes, madam. There was a letter.'

Dr Doughty had left it on the nightstand. His wife examined it closely, her eyes becoming sharper, her lips slowly forming a smile as she studied the writing on the envelope.

'This is my dear brother's hand. Is it not elegant?'

Her grin was like her brother's. She opened the letter and read the contents.

Studying me for the first time, she said, 'How beautiful his writing, how precise his choice of words! His good nature, his kindness to me! He says that you are to work hard and be kept under close control.'

I felt sick and said nothing.

Her smile faded as she read on. 'You have been reformed from a shameful past by the strict regime of the workhouse and, if you require any further discipline, are to be returned there, whereupon he will administer it himself.'

'Yes, madam.' I kept my face still, while fear and resentment rose up in my throat, as if I had been once again in the workhouse chapel.

They had sent me for the Sunday Penances. I had knelt in line with the others facing the altar, our knees aching against the stone floor as a grinning Glyde lectured us. Moving along the line, examining each of us in turn, the chaplain had grasped my face and turned it up to him between his palms, the heels of his hands pressing my jaws open. I had kept myself completely still, not even daring to tremble, and avoided his eyes. With a chuckle he had let go and moved on. The Penances were this: after we had prayed we were made to hold our hands out – then he moved slowly back and forth along the line and, at random, slashed at our palms with a switch. There was one young boy who could not bear to do this. Glyde had mocked him for his cowardice, called him a miserable sinner, and, still grinning, whipped him about his head and shoulders. In terror, I fixed my eyes on the figure of the dying Christ that hung above the altar, wishing I could close my ears to the swish and slap of the switch and the cries of poor Patrick until he crumpled sobbing to the floor.

'My brother shoulders a weighty burden.' Mrs Doughty pressed the folded letter to her breast. 'The workhouse, the parish, the magistrates' court. His many charities and good works. He is a muscular Christian, who, by his devotion and his earthly sacrifices, has built himself a treasure in Heaven.'

'Yes, madam.'

Glyde's muscularity had made my left hand barely usable for four days. I could only listen in silence as Mrs Doughty described at length her brother's good works, his visits to the sick, his contributions to charity, his selfless endeavours for his flock. Were it not for him, it seemed, the town itself would be engulfed by fire and brimstone. His credit was so high at the Gates of Heaven that he could spend the remainder of his life in sin and still be admitted to heavenly bliss.

I remembered holding out my burning hands, squeezing tears behind my eyelids, knowing that Glyde could deliver another blow, whenever he chose, and that I could do nothing even to help myself endure it.

Mrs Doughty was still babbling about her brother. I poured out her hot water, then to my relief was asked to withdraw and wait on the landing while she performed her ablutions. I stood outside her door and looked down the stairs and through the back window at the empty washing lines in the yard. It had stopped raining. I would hang out Doughty's shirts. Below me the long-case clock rumbled and whirred into a chime for the half-hour.

The memory of the Sunday Penances continued to intrude. Glyde had made us all kneel in line for a long time after the whipping, with our bruised hands pressed together as he recited prayers. He had then dismissed everyone but Theresa. Later at Evensong, he had preached of sin and shame and degradation, bellowing about stains being washed away by blood. Theresa had been beside me, blank-faced and rigid, as pale as if her stains had been washed so much that all her blood was gone. I said nothing to her afterwards. I had learned to ask her no questions, for they seemed to add to her misery and I never received replies.

Mrs Doughty rang me back in. I noticed a little brass handbell on her dressing table, amongst the jumble of boxes and jars. She wanted me to help her now. I opened bottles greasy with stale perfume. A dab of this here, a drop of that there; every wrinkle and every pimple had its own particular salve. Then brush her hair two hundred times, and dress it with Lemur Brand Macassar Oil, imported from Madagascar. Its jasmine scent lay heavy in the air.

'My hair,' she murmured. 'How my hair is growing thin …'

There were handfuls of it in the hairbrush. I did not reply, and braided the pale hair, dividing the front into loops, some dropping over the shoulders and others curving upwards on each side to join a bun at the back. I presumed the style was still in fashion.

Mrs Doughty, gazing into her mirror, seemed oblivious.

'I can see that Death is coming to me. We live upon death in this house.'

I was loath to reply.

'Have you entered my husband's study? Have you seen

the coroner's records, of deaths that came too early, of the unquiet spirits that have come to gather in our house? Even to touch those ledgers might bring a curse upon your head. As for him, he spends morning, noon and night in the company of the dead. Death fills his heart and his soul, it haunts his eyes, it clings about his clothes and his person.'

'Surely Dr Doughty is only performing the professional duties to which he was appointed?' I used bandoline to fix strands of hair across gaps where her white scalp showed through.

'Did you not see our nursery? My little Agnes's crib. We are cursed, invaded by death.' She turned and surveyed the room, as if death might be in the curtains, or the bed hangings, or waiting in the wardrobe.

'I hope you're satisfied with your hair, madam.' I wished she would speak of something else.

Mrs Doughty turned back towards her mirror and gazed into its depths, as though searching for phantoms.

'But my dear brother says that I must not be afraid of death, only fear God, and obey the Church. Death is then eternal life.'

Her talk of death made me think again of Theresa, and suddenly it was as if I saw her clearly, alone in the laundry at dawn, tearing up sheets, splitting the fabric between desperate fingers, weeping silently as she plaited a rope and fashioned a makeshift noose. I closed my eyes. I was ashamed to think of how grateful I had been at that Sunday Penance, that it was Theresa and not I who had been kept back to the last.

'Are you discreet, Verity?'

'I beg your pardon?' The question seemed unconnected. I was unsure if I'd heard aright.

'Are you discreet? My brother says that a maid must be

quiet, and go about her duties, not wasting her time in tattling to the neighbours' servants.'

I muttered a reassurance and then it was time for Mrs Doughty's corset. My months in the workhouse had given me strong hands and, as I pulled the laces through, Mrs Doughty gasped that I was better than Mrs Eddam. Mrs Doughty's habit of tightlacing had clearly shifted her internal organs; her waist contained little more than her spine and might have been encircled by two hands.

A deeply crinolined gown in green satin completed Mrs Doughty's preparations and, declining breakfast, she allowed me to settle her in a chair in the drawing room with her embroidery.

The laudanum rendered Mrs Doughty calm and docile, and her breathing became slow and shallow. Her pupils became black pinpoints through which she could barely see her stitches; I thought she might sew no more than a square inch in a whole day. She had bread and milk at lunchtime, and ate only a couple of spoonfuls, accompanied by another twelve drops from the violet flask.

Mrs Doughty's comments about her husband's ledgers remained in my mind. By the early evening I had managed to get her to take a piece of buttered toast and a cup of milky tea, after which she had me get her ready for bed. The work was little more than dressing and undressing a doll. Another mouthful of laudanum lulled her to sleep. Dr Doughty was not yet home and I determined I would trace the report of Theresa's inquest.

In Doughty's study, behind the massive desk were the shelves of black ledgers, textbooks of medical jurisprudence, and then the *Encyclopaedia Britannica, The System of Geography,* Dryden's *Fables,* Milton's *Poetical Works,* Polehampton's *Gallery of Nature and Art,* the *Quarterly*

Review, the *Yearly Journal of Trade* … It was over a year since I had been amongst books. I glanced at the piled newspapers. He took *The Lancet*, *Aris's Birmingham Gazette*, and *Bell's Life in London*. I felt a leap of hope: Edmond's notices would be in the newspapers, I might write to the theatre and, if only he received my letter, surely he must come back for me?

I returned to the ledgers: inquest reports and Coroner's Rolls. Here were the records of the sudden deaths of Birmingham's citizens. The moments they faded unexpectedly from life were chronicled, one after another. One day they flourished, the next they were in procession to the next world with their grim companions, and the day after that their mortal remains were inspected by Dr Doughty, his Beadle, his clerk, and a jury of fifteen respectable men.

I did not believe Mrs Doughty's superstitions, yet I looked up, wondering if I was alone. The long-case clock ticked but nothing else stirred in the house, from the empty crib in the nursery, to the shadowed bed-hangings around Mrs Doughty in her drugged slumber, to the fading coals beneath the copper. As I listened to my surroundings, I heard the distant throb of the factories, but otherwise the dusk was undisturbed. If there was anything evil in the house, it was quiescent. I lit the oil lamp on Doughty's desk.

I rested my hands on the back of his chair and imagined him working in the yellow circle of light beneath the lamp on his desk, late at night, with all around him still. His writing hand would be animated by the grievous memories of the dead: their starvations, their sufferings, the neglect of their protectors, the cruelties of their tormentors. The ink would flow along the lines like a thin stream of black blood, accurate and elegant, summarising the putrefaction of corpses, the dissections of internal organs, and the testimony of witnesses.

On Doughty's desk were a pile of reports; but all within the last few days. A sheaf of paper marked a place in a ledger, but it was dated the 20th of February. A silver-handled ivory nose-pick lay across a pile of tradesmen's bills. Then I saw that I would not need to examine his ledger further, for the inquest was on the front page of the *Birmingham Gazette*.

4: Coroner's Inquest – Death by Hanging

From the *Birmingham Gazette*

An inquest was held on Thursday 6th March at the Birmingham Parish Union Workhouse, Lichfield Street, before Dr Doughty, and a respectable jury, to inquire into the death of Theresa Curran, an inmate. The coroner having sworn the jurymen, they proceeded to view the body. The deceased had been found hanged by pieces of a sheet which she had evidently tied to a roof-beam whilst alone in the laundry.

Mrs Violet Siviter, Matron of the Workhouse, stated that Theresa Curran, about 17 years of age, was in the workhouse for over a year. The deceased was of Irish extraction and her parents, poor immigrants, had departed this life leaving her to fend for herself. As a result her morals were completely corrupted, and it had been impossible to send her to any respectable employment, due to her profane language.

She was a vile individual. Not right in the head, there was no virtue in her. Despite having been admitted from the most degraded of circumstances and given refuge in the workhouse, and the opportunity of reform, she had rejected the very hands that were attempting to drag her from the mire of corruption into which she had sunk. She made vile and baseless accusations against the Workhouse Guardians. The officials of the institution had made unceasing efforts to correct her over a period of more than a year's duration, but regrettably the strict discipline of the workhouse failed to deflect her downward course, and in her despair she destroyed herself.

At reveille she had been missed, and at first thought to have escaped, but when the girls went into the laundry first thing in the morning, they found her hanging amongst the drying linen. She clearly exploited the opportunity of being alone, to consume herself with her own evil.

Dr Doughty observed that the deceased exhibited an emaciated condition with numerous injuries upon her skin and enquired how this had arisen. Mrs Siviter remarked that the deceased had been in the habit of mutilating herself during violent outbursts. She further assured the jury that the deceased had been provided with the same rations as those issued to all other inmates but was contrary and refused her food.

Dr Doughty's view was that the injuries could not have been sustained in the manner described and requested that the jury agree to a post-mortem examination.

A discussion ensued in which it was put to Dr Doughty by members of the jury that a post-mortem examination would not materially alter the verdict.

He insisted, however, that the jurymen had a duty to discover not merely how the unfortunate deceased had died, but why she had died, so that if any irregularities were discovered that had led to the death there would be an opportunity for these to be corrected to avoid a similar misfortune in the future. He asked them to consider their actions if this poor wretch, who had no-one to speak for her, had been their own daughter, or sister, or other member of their family, who had fallen into adversity.

A post-mortem was carried out by Mr Graves, who testified to the marks of severe and repeated corporal punishment, which could not have been self-inflicted.

Mrs Siviter, being questioned further about these injuries, stated that as the deceased had been of an extremely violent and offensive temperament, it had from time to time been necessary to chastise her for uttering obscenities or threatening to cause harm to other inmates. It had been her (Mrs S) Christian duty to do so, following the Regulations, as authorised by the Board of Governors. The birch was a most efficient minister, and a few cuts would deliver more religion than fifty sermons. Indeed, after numerous repetitions, it was thought that the deceased might have reformed. But clearly the Devil had been reluctant to relinquish his hold on her soul and tempted her to self-murder. 'The Scriptures tell us it is the greatest crime of all,' Mrs Siviter said.

Coroner Doughty asked whether the deceased's suffering had driven her to end her life.

Mr Huntly, Foreman of the Jury, speaking on behalf of his brother jurors, opined that these were matters for the Board of Workhouse Guardians, and not for an inquest jury, for whom the verdict was clear, and indeed had been so all along.

Mrs Siviter repeated that she had often had no option but to punish the girl, according to the Regulations. She was rebellious and insubordinate. Only the previous day she had grossly insulted, and even made wild and baseless accusations against the workhouse chaplain himself. Her behaviour had been intolerable.

Mr Huntly, as Foreman of the Jury, said that there was no time to further examine the behaviour of the deceased. He repeated that the post-mortem would not alter the verdict and observed that waiting for Mr Graves to perform his dissection and deliver his report had consumed the time of the fifteen jurymen who were present; indeed the duration of the inquest had been prolonged to half past eight in the evening.

The jury withdrew for only five minutes before pronouncing: 'Verdict – Self Murder – Temporary Insanity.'

5: A Life in the Theatre

Mrs Siviter had lied then: I had never seen Theresa raving or violent. I had barely heard her speak, much less swear. I had never seen her mutilate herself. They had tormented her – the Siviters, and Glyde – and had concealed the truth. Mrs Siviter had not admitted to birching Theresa until after the post-mortem report was read. And what of the 'wild and baseless accusations against the workhouse chaplain'? Had Theresa complained of Glyde to Mrs Siviter and been received, as we had been, with cruel disregard? In her shame and despair, unable to bear further torment, she must have felt driven to end her life.

Evidently Doughty had not been completely deceived. He had seen something amiss and had insisted upon a post-mortem examination against some resistance by the jury. But Theresa's injuries had in the end proven nothing, and Mrs Siviter's change of story had passed unremarked, perhaps due to the lateness of the proceedings. I wondered if he understood that the jury had made a gross error. Or, had he thought to protect his brother-in-law after all? Where did his sympathies lie? I thought of his bedside library, and of the stories that Clara had told me. A coroner and a jury of righteous men might even be titillated by whip-marks on young and wayward flesh.

It made me angry to think that Glyde had come through it all unscathed. If I could have struck him down dead by the force of my thoughts, if I could have put a curse on him, an evil prayer that would have slowly poisoned him, I would have been glad. But my mother always taught me that such malice destroys no-one but its originator. In time, she would have said, he will suffer the consequences of his actions.

What other recourse did I have against Glyde? I might have Doughty's ear, if his seeming attraction towards me proved stronger than his loyalty to his brother-in-law. But it was risky. I had already been penalised by the Siviters for speaking out and I feared being dismissed back to the workhouse. My life might then become what Theresa's had been.

I could not see how I could succeed, and the more I reflected, the more I longed to escape the corrupt penumbra of the workhouse and the officials and their hangers-on who ran the institutions of the town. I had eloped with Edmond to seek a life in the theatre. Now I could return to him, and perhaps to the theatre company. After all, we had not parted in anger.

The Imprisoned Contessa had been a great success with the citizens of Birmingham. Maud Frith had played a helpless young woman whose wicked guardian, played by Edmond, imprisoned her until she promised to surrender to him. She threw herself night after night from the battlements of the ruined castle to preserve her virtue. Edmond's evil passions would have the ladies fluttering their fans while the young hero, played by Martin Hellbronn, brought them to tears as he cradled the dying body of his inamorata to my piano accompaniment.

The production had run in Birmingham until after the Christmas of 1839. Edmond found a lodging in a fashionable street beside the Town Hall, and I grew familiar with the centre of Birmingham, much of which had been built recently to serve its growing industries. There had been a huge civic pride, which I had never encountered in London, a sense that the place was creating itself like a phoenix from the fires of industry. There were no cotton mills or coalmines here; metalworking was the basis of most trades. The directory listed all kinds of skilled craftsmen: gunmakers and button-makers, silversmiths and penmakers, furniture-makers, carriage-works and wireworks. Edmond ordered me a piano from a local maker so that I could keep in practice when, with my pregnancy advancing, I was no longer performing. He encouraged me to browse the shops in Bull Street that carried goods from all around the world: Russian furs and African perfumes, cosmetics from France and silks from Turkey.

But in January, once the merriments of Christmas were over, the attendances at the theatre started to decline. There were only so many people, after all, who could be expected to go and see *The Imprisoned Contessa*. Davenant started to write to the other provincial theatres and eventually announced that the company would travel to Liverpool. By now my belly was becoming heavy and I was feeling exhausted.

'We'll only be in Liverpool a few weeks,' said Edmond. 'Then Davenant's talking about either Glasgow or Leeds. 1840's going to be a busy year, I'm afraid. Still, it helps to pay the bills.'

At that point a great weariness had defeated me – the desire to build a nest and settle in it.

'I'll stay here,' I said. 'Until you can send for me, of course. I don't think I can keep moving like that.'

Edmond agreed readily. 'I'll send you money every week for the rent.'

He seemed calm and cheerful as he took one of the trunks and packed his clothes in it.

'Perhaps, when you get back to London, you could find a lodging and send for me,' I said. 'I'll bring the furniture and the silverware, and we could set up a little home. A cottage on Highgate Hill or in Camden Town, something like that.'

He said it would be capital, quite the thing, then he kissed me, not in farewell, but as if he were going out to a performance and would be back in a few hours. I detained him a moment in my arms, thinking that his face, and his blue eyes, and his golden hair, were the most radiant vision of my whole life. A hansom cab arrived, and I watched him load the trunk and be driven away. He had not even taken all his clothes.

The first remittance had arrived after a week, and the second after a month. I dismissed the maid and economised on food and candles to pay the rent. After that I had to sell the piano and the sheet music that went with it, then the silverware, then our clothes, leaving until the very last my rose silk, the one I had worn on the opening night of *The Imprisoned Contessa* and at the party afterwards, when I had hung on Edmond's arm with all eyes drawn to me.

The pawnbroker had rubbed the rose-silk fabric between finger and thumb.

'Nine shillings.'

'But it cost ten guineas,' I gasped.

There were people queuing up behind me in the pawnshop. I heard them muttering. I was wasting time.

'Well, it's not worth ten guineas now. I shall be lucky to get a sovereign for it. I have to make something. I can't just stand here handing out money because people don't know the value of things. Ten shillings, my final word. And it'll be fifteen shillings if you come back for it.'

Mr Parkes had come the next day, to take what I owed in rent, and the payment for the next week.

'I see you've sold your silverware,' he said. 'Have you heard from your ... your husband?'

'Not yet.' I felt for my ring and twisted it around my finger. I had been cleaning out the fireplace and my fingernails were broken and dirty.

Mr Parkes noticed my hands, and he inclined his head towards the ring. 'My son makes them. Birmingham brass, the best in the world. He turns them out by the thousand. You need to shine it up a bit, though, eh?'

'I think the theatre company will be moving to Glasgow,' I said. 'Edmond is very busy.' I had seen a favourable review of the play in the newspaper. They had already moved on to Manchester, selling out all their performances at the new concert hall at St Peter's Fields.

'Will he send for you, do you think?' Mr Parkes glanced briefly at my belly, and then his eyes searched my face, waiting for me to reply. He turned and looked out of the window at the Town Hall. 'I've a cheaper lodging becoming vacant, over towards Duddeston. A shilling a week. If you can be out by next Friday, it would help me. There's a new tenant ready to move in here. A respectable family, regular payers. They want to be settled in quick.'

'Next Friday?' I felt weak. The baby shifted in my womb. 'I'll never be ready in time. And how would my husband find me?'

'Can you not write to him?' asked Mr Parkes.

I could not answer. I had written to all the theatres, and to Mr Davenant himself.

'But what would I do with the furniture?' I said.

'You might want to sell up, miss,' said Mr Parkes, still dubiously eyeing my brass wedding ring. 'Broomhead's is the nearest auction house. The other lodging is quite a bit smaller, you see, though it should be adequate. A furnished room, decent size, mind, and the use of a washhouse. And you could enquire at Howe's, on Deritend High Street, regarding a removal.'

'Edmond will think I have deserted him,' I blurted out.

Mr Parkes did not reply for a moment, looking at the sideboard with his lips pursed together, and I saw the empty circles in the dust where the silverware had been, and that I was the one who had been deserted.

'You could find yourself a position, miss,' he said. 'If you can find someone to care for your child. You could maybe try Mrs Standlye's agency for domestic service, begging your pardon. Could you let me know regarding the Duddeston place in the next couple of days? Send me a note, care of the land agency office.'

I wrote to Edmond in Manchester with the new address in Duddeston but, as my time drew near, there was still no reply to my letters. I could no longer even afford the rent for the tiny room. I called at our old lodgings, but there was nothing for me. Perhaps Mr Davenant had moved the company again. I saw that Mr Parkes was right and I would have to find some means, after the baby was born, to support myself, until Edmond came back for me.

An advertisement in the *Gazette* had given an address in Crown Alley, where, for five guineas, a *'gentlewoman'* could be *'delivered of her baby in comfort and safety, given the dignity appropriate to her station, and the infant placed with experienced nurses'*. With no other choice, I sold my few remaining possessions, and having received almost six pounds, bought a layette of baby linen on Bull Street. My child would be sheltered. I would find work, in a factory perhaps. It would not be for long, in any case.

I was weary, my pains starting, when I reached Crown

Alley. Even though it was within ten minutes' walk of the great banking establishments of Colmore Row, it was narrow and filthy. The smell of Smithfield Market, of stale blood and meat and refuse, tainted the air. Ragged children played beside the open sewers that ran down the middle of the street and the houses wore an air of neglect with broken and boarded-up windows and grass and weeds growing in the gutters. But my time was close and a pang shot across my belly.

I reached for the rusty knocker and rapped on the door.

There was at first no reply, then as my knocking grew ever more desperate, the door was opened by an old woman. She had slack greasy hair and her hands were like brown claws. I shuddered and held out the advertisement.

'Is this ...?' I steadied myself against the doorjamb as another pang took my breath away.

She gave me a cold smile. 'You're in luck, love. The undertakers have took the last one away just an hour ago and the room's clear.'

I looked down the street, wondering if I should try elsewhere, whether I would be refused at the workhouse if they found out I was from London. As I hesitated, I was gripped by a stronger pain.

'You'd best come in,' said the midwife. 'Have you got the five guineas?'

I took the money out of my reticule and handed it over, and followed her into the front room, in which a woman had but lately died. I wondered how many others had entered the house and never left alive. The floor, it seemed, had been mopped, and there was an iron bedstead with a damp mattress, a chamber pot beneath it, a dresser, and nothing else. Dusty shutters occluded the windows. The room smelt of blood.

'Open the window,' I gasped, sitting on the chair as yet

another pang took hold of me. 'For the love of God, open the window! I can't breathe!'

'Calm yourself, girl,' replied the midwife, unlatching the shutters with her dirty hands and raising the sash an inch.

The sounds of the city came in, the grinding and groaning of horse-carts and the whinnies of the horses and the shouts of the children playing in the gutter outside. Was this the world to which I was to abandon my child? The thought of saying farewell to the small life inside appalled me. And now in between contractions I felt his vigorous movements. I had grown so used to his small company, in the last few weeks I had noticed how he would startle at loud noises and might be calmed by a little patting or by the sound of my voice.

I had thought that he would be taken care of until I could reclaim him. But this was not what I had expected. I was afraid that the care that had been advertised in the newspaper was nothing more than the gin bottle and certain death.

The midwife took a blanket from the dresser and spread it out on the bed.

'I'm frightened,' I said.

I sat down on the edge of the mattress, curved forward over my belly, my hands braced against my knees. Moisture seeped into my skirts, but I could not leave my child with this woman.

I forced myself to stand. I gathered up my bundle of baby linen but she refused to give me back my money. Now the workhouse was the only other place. By the time I had dragged myself there I was so far gone that they could not refuse me: Nathan was born in the receiving room and Pious Betty cut the cord. His miserable death, nine days later, had left me with a deep core of bitter memories, too painful to disturb.

Although I dreaded telling Edmond the bitter news, I

constantly assured myself that he would forgive me, that he must still care for me and our separation had been accidental.

Now, at least I was free of the workhouse.

Doughty's newspapers lay in the study. I would find the theatre notices and write to Edmond as soon as I could discover where the company was playing.

6: Mr Graves

I found that running the house in Newhall Street was not difficult. It was not large, and, unlike at my parents' home, there was no one but me to regret the rim of dust on the window-frames or the unswept hairs on the floor. Nevertheless, I washed the kitchen and pantry thoroughly and dusted and swept the rest of the house, apart from the deserted nursery, which I left untouched. I had a fair amount of laundry to do and made sure to hang it out on sunny days in the yard. It was hard work but a vast improvement on the workhouse. Once I had caught up with the house, I intended to spend more time caring for Mrs Doughty. If she found that I was educated she might accept me as a companion, and perhaps allow me to play the piano.

Doughty was always busy: one inquest followed another through the day so that he was often out of the house from the early morning until the late evening, and even the Sunday seemed to bring him little rest. He did not seem to attend church, which surprised me, preferring to work in his study, and he often dined out. Presumably he found the local hostelries, where a meat pie and a pint of porter could be had quickly and cheaply, more to his taste than watching his wife toy interminably with her food at the dinner table. I made up a stockpot with leftover food, which I kept at a constant simmer on the range, and this more than sufficed for my meals.

Due to Mrs Doughty's frailty and her husband's long hours they did not receive visits from friends. The people who came to the door were the Beadle, looking for Doughty with news of a case requiring inquest, and tradesmen seeking payment for invoices or with deliveries of supplies. I saw and heard nothing of the neighbours although, if I went out on errands, I had the sense of being watched from behind their half-shuttered windows.

After I had been at Newhall Street nearly a week, a gentleman called in the early evening with a foolscap envelope hugged tight under his arm, looking for Dr Doughty. I recognised his name from the inquest report in the newspaper. Mr Graves was the surgeon who had carried out Theresa's post-mortem examination. He had a round bespectacled face, a neat black beard and moustache, and spoke with a soft Irish brogue.

'You could leave the envelope on his desk,' I offered, as Doughty was still not home, but Mr Graves shook his head.

'I believe he'll be back shortly. He told me that the afternoon's cases would not take long. A man struck down by a runaway cart, and so on.'

He gave me his hat and coat, went into the front parlour and sat in an armchair, keeping the envelope in his hands. I pressed him to take tea and fetched the tray from downstairs. As I poured for him, he pushed the envelope behind the chair cushion. He watched me closely.

'You're after coming from the workhouse, I heard?' He

took his spectacles off and folded them into his waistcoat pocket: a dandified waistcoat of bright green tartan. 'William – Dr Doughty – told me about it.'

'Yes, sir.' I passed him his cup and saucer.

His white hands were scrubbed clean. I imagined him incising skin with a scalpel, his hands lifting and weighing internal organs like a butcher handling offal. How he must have worked on his hands afterwards with soap, to remove the human grease.

'Now, there is, if you'll permit me, something I should like to ask you about the workhouse.' He indicated that I should sit, facing him across the room.

I perched reluctantly on the edge of the chair.

'For how long were you there?' He leaned a little forward with his bearded chin jutting out, intent on my reply.

'From the ninth of February to the eleventh of this month.' I wondered where this was leading.

'And how did they treat you?' His voice was quiet, his tone calm, almost languid.

'I have no complaints to make, sir.' I found that I was rolling the edge of my apron between my fingers, conscious of his scrutiny. Whatever I said might be reported to others.

'To be sure.' He took a sip of tea, his blue eyes twinkling at me over the rim of the cup, missing nothing. 'William, I think, treated you for a head injury during which you sustained a significant loss of blood.'

'It is all quite healed up now, thank you for asking, sir.'

'So, tell me. How did you come to sustain such a serious injury?'

'I can't quite remember.' I wondered how much Doughty had told him about Mr Siviter. 'The head wound … well, I lost consciousness. Perhaps I had fallen and hit my head.'

He rested the cup and saucer in his lap and pursed his lips.

'You should realise that there's no need for you to be afraid of speaking to me.'

'No, sir.' I attempted a smile, shifting on the armchair, feeling my body prickling with sweat inside my stays, but offering no further information.

'And you were treated well there? You were aware of nothing untoward? Of any improper behaviour?'

'I would prefer not to speak of it, sir, if you please.' I averted my gaze. Outside the window a cart went past in the street. I wondered how soon Doughty would return and put an end to this inquisition. 'What if I am sent back there?'

'If you had been well treated, then you would not be so afraid to return.'

I studied the tartan of his waistcoat, wondering if it was safe to mention the Sunday Penances, or the lock-up, or how the slightest of faults produced the most fearsome of punishments. I was also aware of a deep shame. I could not admit to my humiliation, the moment when Glyde had grasped my face, or how helpless I had felt, waiting for the cut of the switch. Instead, to fill the silence I explained that I was reluctant to return to the workhouse as the work in Dr Doughty's household was far more to my liking and that I could make no comment about my treatment in the workhouse as my memory of it was very sketchy, owing to my head injury.

'Now, I think that Dr Doughty will not send you back to the workhouse. He speaks of you very highly. He suspects that you have had an education.'

'I've no idea how he arrived at that conclusion.' I saw my chance to change the subject.

Mr Graves smiled. 'It is obvious in your speech, my dear. William says that he has observed a weighty tome – *The Housekeeper's Companion* – lifted down from its shelf and open to be studied upon the kitchen table. And he suspects that his papers have been disturbed on more than one occasion.'

'I have only been dusting ...'

'But you are capable of far more than that, are you not?'

'I can play the piano,' I offered.

'A most unusual skill in a workhouse inmate. Most of them cannot read the printed word, let alone the musical stave.' Mr Graves rested back in his chair with a peacable look in his eye. 'Do go on. Explain.'

'I once had a piano teacher. And a governess. My mother was very musical. My father was – is – a barrister at Gray's Inn.' It could not harm me for him to know that. 'But we are no longer in contact. I committed an indiscretion and my parents have cut me off.'

I felt my homesickness returning. I could remember every detail of the house where I had lived for eighteen years: the black and white tiles in the hall, the mahogany chest in my bedroom, the aroma of beeswax polish. I had not acknowledged how much my home meant to me, in the madness of my elopement with Edmond. I had been too in love with him to care about anything else. After we parted I yearned only for him. Now I felt myself crumple within: at this point I knew I would never see my parents again. My eyes ached.

Mr Graves kept up his benevolent inquisition, to which I returned answers about my past, at first brief and then in more detail – about my home, about Edmond, about the theatre. How Edmond had got me an audition with Mr Davenant who took me on as a piano accompanist. Edmond would alternately encourage me to practise and then divert me with dresses and parties. After a while there had been no need for me to work, for Edmond, a rising star, had been paid handsomely. I did not directly mention my pregnancy, but I explained that Edmond had moved on with the theatre company, promising to send me money.

'*Hm.*' Mr Graves looked down at his empty teacup and sighed.

'Would you like some more tea?' I asked. 'I expect Dr Doughty will be back soon.'

Mr Graves shook his head and put his cup aside.

'So, during your time in the workhouse, did you become aware of anything improper occurring towards Theresa Curran?' Now he peered at me as though, having thoroughly prepared his patient, he was about to make a surgical incision. 'You may speak in complete confidence.'

I had told Graves so much about my past that my claim of having a poor memory was looking thin. I opened and closed my mouth, inhaled and exhaled. My first thought was that Theresa deserved justice. Here was a gentle girl abused and bullied to the point at which her life had become intolerable, and all the newspaper could print was that she was wild, blasphemous, and could not be controlled. But I reflected that Theresa was dead and would derive no benefit from the improvement to her reputation, whereas I, by causing an embarrassment to the powers that ran the workhouse, one of whom was the brother-in-law of my employer, might find myself in trouble. I was certain that anything I said to Mr Graves would be repeated to Doughty, and what if he dismissed me? I would return to the workhouse to face certain retribution.

'I am very sorry,' I said, hating myself. 'I am not familiar with the name.' I could see that Mr Graves did not believe me, for he opened his mouth to protest, but at that point Doughty came home.

I leapt up and busied myself by taking his hat and coat, offering him tea, and asking him what he would like for supper and whether he would like to go in and greet Mr Graves, who was still in the drawing room, or if he would prefer that I showed Mr Graves into the study.

Instead of answering, Doughty paused and eyed me. He still had a way of sweeping his eyes over my body before resting them on my face. An amused wrinkle deepened at one corner of his mouth.

'You're flustered, Jane. What's the matter?' He went into the parlour and I followed. 'Has Mr Graves been flirting? If he's so much as laid a finger on you, I'll fight him hand-to-hand.'

Mr Graves, chuckling, stood up to shake his friend's hand.

'It's you she lives in fear of, Coroner Doughty. She does not dare to say anything in case you send her away.'

Doughty had noticed the envelope that stood behind the cushion and grew serious.

'Is that ...?'

'Yes. If you will excuse us, miss –' Mr Graves made a gesture of dismissal.

'Verity,' said Doughty. 'Jane Verity'. He pronounced my name carefully, his voice lingering on its syllables.

'Verity,' repeated Mr Graves. 'Your name obliges you to speak the truth, so.'

'Thank you, Jane.' Doughty dismissed me before I could think of a reply.

I had some silver to clean and sat with it downstairs at the kitchen table, pondering as I worked. Mr Graves must have found something else in his post-mortem examination that gave him unease, or he would not have asked me those questions. He had mentioned impropriety. Had he discovered something that pertained to Glyde and his habit of summoning Theresa at night? An injury that matched with her 'wild and baseless allegations'? I wondered if Mr Graves was relaying his concerns to Doughty, who might now be minded to ask me the same questions himself.

After half an hour or so I heard Mr Graves leaving. I finished the silverware and scrubbed the black off my nails in the scullery. When I went up to get the tea tray, I found that the envelope had gone, Doughty having presumably taken it into his study. He did not ring for me until another hour had gone by. I had already been up to check on Mrs Doughty and had returned to the kitchen to prepare supper.

I went into the study and stood facing him across the desk. He had tidied it up so that the loose papers were in a precise stack on the side-table. Only one ledger, which was closed, rested in front of him. Mr Graves' envelope was in the wastepaper basket, its contents presumably filed away somewhere.

Doughty was hunched in his chair, with an elbow upon the chair-arm and his chin propped on his finger and thumb. He wore an unhappy expression, his eyes intent on mine.

'You're aware, Jane, of my responsibilities as Borough Coroner?'

I said that I was.

'And Mr Graves tells me that you have an education, indeed something of a legal background, and presumably some understanding of these matters.' He paused, bringing his fingers down to rest on the cover of his ledger. 'All my papers are confidential. You are not to pry into them, or spy upon me, or disturb anything in any way. You realise that, I hope?'

'Certainly, Dr Doughty, I have no wish to.'

'And you realise, I hope, that the consequences of any infraction will be extremely severe.'

I nodded, expecting that he would threaten me with a return to the workhouse.

But he continued, looking down at his ledger with a flush suffusing his features: 'I was advised, by Reverend Glyde, that it is essential to use corporal punishment amongst the young women at the workhouse, to regulate their behaviour.'

I could hardly deny it. He had already seen me with my head split open by Siviter. Nor was this the ideal time to challenge Glyde's methods.

'He urged me to continue it, here, even for the most trivial of faults, to keep you in check. I argued against him, but he convinced me that I was too lenient. He has, after all, the experience of administering the workhouse over a number of years.' Doughty heaved a sigh. 'And now I notice that my papers have been disturbed, which I cannot tolerate.'

I saw then that he had brought his walking-cane into the study and leant it up against the desk. Yet the hands that rested on the ledger trembled, and found each other, the right thumbnail worrying at the left.

Appearing cowed at this point would not have served me well. I remained calm and polite. I replied that I had no intention of prying into his private papers, but had cleaned his study, as I had the other rooms, and that I hoped that the standard of my work in his house was such as to deserve praise, and indeed remuneration, rather than physical harm.

He shrank a little further into his chair at that and his eye fell upon his carefully dusted shelves. It was true that I had made the house a far more pleasant place. I had been punctual with his hot water in the mornings, his shirts and smallclothes were washed and ironed, and the only room that had not been thoroughly cleaned was the nursery. Moreover he had yet to pay my wages: the nine-pence a week that I had been promised.

'You have been very good in the house, Jane. And I have also noted your attentions to my wife, which have greatly reduced the burden on me.' He studied his hands, as if noticing their inability to perpetrate violence. 'Nor am I unaware that I have a duty to treat you fairly. You will indeed be paid, at the end of the month. But I'm certain that my desk has been disturbed. You really must not touch my papers, and it would be better if you refrained from cleaning the study unless I am actually in it, and desire it to be cleaned.'

The more that I reassured him of my cooperation, the more the opposite intention formed in my mind. Clearly he wished to conceal the contents of Graves' envelope. But it would have to wait. Theresa was dead in any case, and there was no helping her. Eventually he was satisfied with my replies.

He had made a stack of waste on the floor and I said that I would be grateful to have his newspapers to read, if he had done with them. He assented readily. His manner had become gentle, appreciative, almost as if he would rather caress me than beat me.

In the kitchen I put an armful of old newspapers on the table. The *Birmingham Gazette* was uppermost. I took it to the window and studied the tiny print. Nothing much had happened in Birmingham, beyond a meeting of the Street Commissioners. Mr Wright was appearing in *The Wood Demon* at the Theatre Royal. I refolded it, and opened *Bell's Life in London*. How far I had been from the world! An assassination attempt had been made on the Queen. Incendiaries had been at work in Tiverton; a girl had died of a vitriol ointment applied to her scalp; ships had sailed for Madras, Calcutta and Wellington; the Thames Tunnel, its workings lit with gas, had advanced to within fifty feet of Wapping.

I quickly found what I sought.

7: Theatre Notice

From *Bell's Life in London & Sporting Chronicle,*
Saturday 7th March 1840

Mr G Davenant presents THE PURPLE ROBE. Mr E Verity, Miss M Frith, Miss V Rainforth, Mr T Nisbett. Highly Acclaimed and in its 2nd week by Overwhelming Public Demand at the Theatre Royal, Drury Lane. Performances at 7 p.m.

8: Invoice

16th March 1840
To the Birmingham Magistrates, at the Court of Petty Sessions, Bull Street

In respect of Coroner's Inquests of the 4th & 5th instant:

The Sum of Two Guineas. Plus Two Guineas per Inquest, in regard of Surgeon's Fees & Post-mortem Reports (viz. Receipts attached). No Travelling Expenses claimed. Total Six Guineas.

In respect of which Payment, Sirs, I hold myself your Faithful Servant, & sincerely assure you of my deepest Obligations &c.

Her Majesty's Coroner, Dr William Doughty, MB BS.

9: From the Birmingham Magistrates, at the Court of Petty Sessions

Friday 27th March 1840
Bull Street
Birmingham

To: Dr William Doughty, Esq., Coroner for Birmingham, 34 Newhall Street

Sir,

You are hereby summoned to appear before the Court of Petty Sessions, Bull Street, on Friday 10th April at half past 9 o'clock.

As you may already be aware, in consequence of the case of Rutter v. Chapman, there is currently a dispute in the Court of the Exchequer Chamber in London, which calls into question the legal status of the Borough of Birmingham. As a result, the churchwardens are unable to collect the rates and the town is heavily encumbered in its finances.

Since you were appointed to your position, the

expenditure on the Coroner's Courts and in particular on post-mortem examinations has doubled.

You are required therefore to make a full justification of your invoices and fees before the Magistrates of the Bench may authorise any payment.

Yours etc.,
Thomas Pountney, Kt., Chief of the Bench

10: Edmond

I read the theatre notice over again. On the day that I had left the workhouse, Edmond had been due to perform in the second week of a new play. I did not know what I missed more: his company, or the opportunity to be there playing the piano, perhaps in a new silk gown, glancing up from the orchestra pit as he strode the stage. At least I now knew where he was, and I determined to write to him as soon as I could obtain pen and paper.

On the last day of March Doughty paid my salary, but I lacked the opportunity to go out to obtain the means with which to write, and to go into the study was now forbidden to me. Instead, as I went about my chores, I composed and reworded the letter in my mind.

49 Newhall Street, Birmingham. Friday, 3rd April 1840

My dear Edmond,

I hoped that you would return for me, and that you had

not forgotten your Jane, to whom you once, less than a year ago, swore eternal love. I have so longed to write to you, but have been unable, due to my desperate circumstances, which I will presently …

But I did not want to sound too much like a lawyer's daughter, despite the difficulty of my situation. Surely, we were still in love.

'I'm giddy with love, as though walking around myself.'

Edmond had said that. I remembered his face close up, the warmth of his breath, the miracle that such a handsome, desirable man should be in love with me.

I cradled my face in my hands, for my lips still dreamt of his: of that evening party at Litchfield House, my head floating with Tokay, his blue eyes that were hazed with passion. He had lounged at the piano as I played, making my heart flutter with his compliments. He would recommend me to Mr Davenant; my music would enrapture the public. I had laughed at his threats to carry me off. But we disappeared from my mother's gaze amongst the throng on the ballroom floor, through the French windows onto the terrace and he drew me out of the circle of their light. In the shadows beyond the terrace wall he kissed me ferociously. I was cold and trembling, the thrill heightened by fear. My satin slippers were muddy. I protested about my parents, and what my mother would say.

'Do you live for your ancestors, or for yourself? This is your moment: Jane, a perfect love is yours. You must seize it, or it will forever fade beyond your grasp.'

He might have been quoting from a play, but all that possessed me at that moment was a hypnotic desire. I was swept away by the emotion in his voice.

He gripped me powerfully, his hand cupped the back of

my head, and clamping his mouth again to mine he seemed to empty the breath from my lungs.

I felt his fingers in my hair, then with a swift movement he pulled a pin from it and it collapsed around my shoulders. I broke away from him with a gasp. The elaborate confection was in ruins; a hank of false hair tumbled to the ground.

'You can't go back in, not now. They'll know what you've been about. Come here, adorable angel!'

His hands encircled my waist and he drew me back, kissing away my protests. I sighed as his hot tongue slid down my neck.

'You shan't go back,' he breathed as his lips crossed my collarbone, 'nor do you wish to.'

It was true; I was helpless.

He took me to his rooms at the Adelphi in a cab, and there I stayed. It was a fashionable residence where apartments were rented by theatrical and artistic types and by down-at-heel aristocrats. I joined him in a mad existence of parties and debt and sleeping all day after late nights. Mr Davenant agreed, as a favour to Edmond, to take me on as a piano accompanist, and I had my first experience of public applause.

I was not yet nineteen. My father, a London lawyer, was a Unitarian and held strong religious principles. My mother was equally scandalised by my behaviour, having expected that I would marry into the *'noblesse du robe'* that regulated London: the lawyers and bankers and professional men. An actor was so far beyond the pale that the fact that we were unmarried was almost irrelevant. I had been taught to play the piano in order to be an ornament to my household, not to perform in public, for payment. That I was their only child merely served to make the situation worse.

Their door was forever closed to me and when I sent a letter asking if I could collect my clothes, it was returned unopened. Edmond shrugged and sent for a fashionable dressmaker. My new gowns were made to his taste. They were cut low across the bust and shoulders and in the gaudiest of colours: Paris green satin, rose silk taffeta, Prussian blue velvet, trimmed with lace and gilded ribbons and embroidered with flowers. I had changed irreversibly, but had no regrets, and indeed could barely visualise my past life. Edmond's love was an intense light that threw everything else into shadow.

Oh Edmond! I carry my love with me wherever I toil, the love that finds no release, the love that is without a mouth, that is closed up as though behind prison walls. Do you think I have no desires? None that you will fulfil now, as you are oblivious to me, weeping in agony, alone in the hell where you abandoned me, grieving for the loss of our dear son …

I was too ashamed to contemplate writing it down. I could not imagine telling Edmond what had befallen Nathan. Perhaps it was as well that I lacked ink and paper, and in any case, I was much occupied.

In the last few days Mrs Doughty's needs had increased, so that her bell would ring out at any time of the day or night, and she would reproach me if I was slow to respond. It got so that, even when I was not needed, I could not be at ease, in case she were to ring.

When I did go to her, I could not see how to help her. It was never a simple thing: find my wrapper, do my hair, or the like. She seemed to have entered a rapid decline, and would be prostrated by pain, breathlessness, nausea. Her fear was so strong that I felt it in my own heart, as if she were actually dying. Yet she recovered every time and I could not understand what ailed her: one day her chest, another day her head, the next day her stomach. She might be unable to lift her arms at one moment and then at the next moment be fending me away.

Her medications helped her, although she seemed to consume a great deal of laudanum.

But she drew most comfort from the thought of her brother.

'Vernon,' she would sigh. 'Oh, Vernon!' Just as I had sighed for Edmond.

And then one morning: 'Oh, I wish Vernon would visit! Oh, lighten me of the darkness!'

'Darkness, madam?' I drew back her curtains. It was late morning and the sun was shining in the street outside.

'Yes, Jane, it comes in. You must keep the window shut, lest they fly in. The things that fly past in the darkness.'

'Bats, madam?' I supposed that was what she meant. 'Why, they are harmless. Nought but tiny furry things with wings as thin as silk. I found a dead one once that had struck our carriage, and it was as light as a feather to pick up. It couldn't harm you ...'

'No. Not bats. Creatures, spirits, dark formless things with hidden eyes, screaming and screaming from their dead throats. At night I hear the drum, a gigantic drum beaten with a human bone.'

I tried to reassure her that she was simply hearing the sound of the manufactories further down the hill.

'A wireworks, madam, and foundries –'

'But I hear the beating through the evening, and at dead of night, when Godfearing men and women sleep. Then the monsters come, and they beat the ground, and dance.'

'The manufactories are lit by gas, madam, and run through the night.'

'The sound throbs in my head, there is no relief. Sometimes

I think I would gladly die, only to be able to sleep, to be at peace.'

I was alarmed. 'Do not speak of that, madam. There must be something I can do to help you. In truth, I often don't know what it is that you require. Perhaps I could play the piano for you? The music might calm you.'

She was surprised at that.

'Servants do not play the piano. I should not like to listen to the mangling of my Broadwood at your hands.'

I looked down at my fingers, red and coarse with work. But I had no doubt that I could still play well. I told her that I had once played in the theatre.

'I was taught the piano as a child, and was for a short time a professional pianist, madam,' I assured her.

She did not approve of the theatre but, as we followed her morning routine, I drew her out to talk about her own musical tastes and persuaded her to allow me to play for her. I coaxed her downstairs into the parlour, settled her by the window with her embroidery, and seated myself at the piano.

She preferred church music so I worked through the dusty sheets of processionals and recessionals, and a hymn – Vernon's favourite, she informed me – to which she sang the words from memory. She had a sweet singing voice, and I told her so.

After that, much to my delight, she drank a cup of tea and ate an entire ham sandwich. Her spirits seemed to have improved. Then she scribbled a note at her escritoire, sealed it and sent me out with it to the Rectory, saying I was to wait for her brother's reply.

At last this was a chance to leave the house and obtain writing materials. With Harriet settled for an afternoon nap, I also had time to divert past the Town Hall and check at my old lodgings that there were no letters from Edmond.

A disdainful housemaid said that there were not. I said that I would ask again in a week.

'You needn't trouble yourself,' she said.

Clearly she had no intention of keeping any mail for me, and I half hoped that Edmond was no longer sending remittances.

From there I went on along Waterloo Street and skirted the neat grass plot of St Michael's Churchyard, which people here called Pigeon Park. The Rectory was a tall handsome house with a walled garden, beside the Blue Coat School.

A young housemaid answered the door and took the note. I told her that I hoped the Reverend Glyde was in, as I was to wait for his reply. She nodded. I noticed that the hand that held the letter was puffy.

'Do you want to wait downstairs?'

She led me down to the kitchen, where she showed the letter to an older woman who stood in front of the range, stirring a pot.

'Hetty,' she said, 'can I watch that and you take this up to the guv'nor?'

'Take it up yerself, Mary,' replied Hetty, turning back to her work. 'Yer got legs, ain't yer?'

'I'll do all your fireplaces,' Mary pleaded.

'Get gone.'

Mary went back up with the letter, her pretty face creased by a frown.

I leant against the doorjamb, wondering how long I would have to wait.

Hetty chopped vegetables at the kitchen table and added them to the pot without a word to me.

The frown was still crumpling Mary's face when she returned.

'He'll visit at eleven o'clock next Thursday morning,

you're to tell your mistress. I'll show you out.'

I followed her out through the scullery door. The yard was enclosed by a high wall and she struggled to open the side-gate.

'Can you …?'

There were tears in her eyes: the latch was stiff and her swollen hands trembled at the lever. I helped her. Then I glimpsed the same purple welts that I once had on my own palms, before she closed her fist. I took her hand briefly before she snatched it away.

'It's nothing.'

'I've had the same,' I said.

She turned wary eyes to mine. 'You watch yourself,' she whispered.

I had already been watching myself, conscious that Doughty was attracted to me – although after warning me about his study, he had made every effort to behave honourably. I did not relish the thought of Glyde coming to the house and filling the Doughtys' heads with his ideas about corporal punishment.

I hurried back to Newhall Street, stopping at a stationer's shop for writing necessities on the way. Then I went up to Mrs Doughty's room with Glyde's reply, together with a cup of tea and the bread and broth she liked for supper. While she exulted in the news of her brother's visit, I was determined that by Friday my letter would be in Edmond's hand.

After I had dosed her with her laudanum and she had lain back in fresh linen and fallen asleep, I took my purchases up to my room. Dr Doughty was still out.

If I wrote to Edmond at the Theatre Royal in the Haymarket, someone would give him the letter. I saw the auditorium again: the gilded plaster ceilings, the red plush of the banquettes, Mr E Verity's voice filling the air. He would be a seducer, a liar, a murderer, in irresistible style, brilliant beneath the gas-lit chandeliers – his voice, his bearing, and his presence adored by his audience. But I knew another Edmond, boyish, warm-hearted and tender, and I would write still cherishing that image in my mind.

It had been a destructive passion, sweeping my old life away, destroying every vestige of security. I compared myself with other women who had made good marriages, setting my travails and losses against their lives of ease. They were cheerful with their husbands, mutually delighting in the pleasures of the home, in the companionship of their family and neighbours, and the upbringing of their children. It led me to wonder whether I had sought out my downfall, and if what was security to them was merely confinement to me. The wildfire of destruction had brought with it the hope that from the ashes would rise the phoenix of a new life.

I lit a candle in the dusk and spread a sheet of writing paper on my chest of drawers. I had bought a steel pen, a bottle of ink, and sealing wax, but to my disgust the inkbottle was dry and a layer of unusable black residue had congealed in the bottom.

I had to write to Edmond. My thoughts and emotions, pent up over the last few weeks, now demanded release. It was surely still two hours before Doughty would return, and it would take me only a few minutes to make use of his inkstand.

I took my candle downstairs with me, not daring to light the lamp on his desk.

I sat down in his chair and dipped my pen in the pewter inkwell.

11: My Letter to Edmond

Friday 3rd April, 1840

49, Newhall Street
Birmingham

My Dearest Edmond,

You must wonder why I have been so long in writing, and I fear that if you had returned to Birmingham, you might have been dismayed at the loss of your rooms, and your furniture and plate.

In truth, I did not know what to do, for you cannot have received my letters, and as you sent no money I was reduced to desperate circumstances. I could not find work in my delicate state and, in the end, to my shame and despair, I gave birth in the workhouse. You had a son, Nathan. It is almost impossible, dear heart, for me to impart this information on paper, and I beg that you will forgive me for writing in this way, but it is important that you should know what befell us.

Nathan was born on the 9th of February, but sadly lived only nine days. It gives me constant anguish that, when he was all that I had of you, I could not preserve his life. In the workhouse he was taken from me and given into the care of another inmate, on account of her piety. Knowing no better, she bathed him in cold water and it killed him.

I too suffered grievously in the workhouse, but now employment has been found for me. I am a domestic servant in the house of a doctor and his wife, at the above address. They are quite respectable. Dr Doughty is somewhat advanced in years and no longer practises medicine, being fully occupied as the Borough Coroner.

I know not if you have sought me and been unable to find me, for whilst I was in the workhouse for a period of several weeks I had no knowledge of the outside world, nor could you have any way of finding me. Perhaps you believed I had deserted you for another. But I have remained faithful. You are constantly in my thoughts and my love for you is a flame that never burns out, as devoted as it ever has been.

Now that I know that you are back in London and enjoying good fortune, I am praying that someone at the Theatre Royal will be kind enough to make sure you receive this. If only you can return to Birmingham, you may come for me, for I hope to remain at this address for now.

Kindly remember me to Mr Davenant. If he is ever in need of a pianist, either for rehearsals or for public performances, I should be delighted if he would reconsider me.

I beg you to be assured of my constant love and adoration and my fondest hope for your return.

With my most sincere and undying affection,
– Your Jane

12: In the Study

I had been slow in composing my letter, mourning my losses, sighing for Edmond and grieving for my lost son. I had hesitated, wondering how best to impart the manner of Nathan's death. In the end I had written the bare minimum, telling myself that Edmond would not question my explanation. The ink was still drying and I was searching for sealing wax, having left mine upstairs, when I heard Doughty at the front door, turning his key in the lock. Straight away I snuffed out the candle and shoved the desk drawer shut – the wretched thing kept sticking – then hastily folded the letter and tucked it into the bib of my apron. But I was too slow. The street door opened.

I came out of the study and he was already in the hall. I could smell alcohol on his breath.

'What are you doing there in the dark?' he demanded.

He was in a vile mood.

I said I had heard a noise and come downstairs. Then he went straight into the study. I followed him in. Candle smoke hung in the air.

'You were in here.' He turned round, close to me, and I drew back.

'I thought I heard a noise at the back.' The study gave onto the back yard.

'Why did you put your candle out?' He laid his walking cane on the desk and put his hat beside it. 'What were you doing in here?'

'I was afraid.' I stood watching while he lit the oil lamp on his desk.

'If I find you in here again, I'll give you something to be afraid of! Do you understand me?' He glowered over the documents that lay on the desk.

I knew I had not moved anything.

'Yes, sir.'

'Vernon's right – I've been remiss.' He glanced at the walking cane: polished ebony, with a brass ferrule. 'Tell me the truth. What were you doing in here?'

'I thought I heard a sound.' I retreated towards the hall.

'Heard a sound!'

Grasping my wrist, he wrenched me back and closed the door.

'You've disobeyed me. I made it clear that I cannot permit you in here. This study is private. My papers are confidential. And yet I return home to find your unwarranted intrusion. What were you looking for?'

Although he had been drinking his hand was steady, and his eyes bored into mine. I saw the thickness of his arm and the breadth of his shoulders: he was capable of doing me a deal of harm. But I met his stare with my own.

'I have not touched your papers, sir.' I did not really believe that he wanted to hurt me.

'Don't be impertinent!'

'Look, nothing has been disturbed.'

He stared down at the desk. His pen was lying on the blotter. Mine was in the inkwell, but he did not notice.

'Then what were you doing in here?'

I was silent and strained away from him, but he held my arm and pulled me up close.

'*Answer me.*' His voice was low in my ear. 'I should do what Vernon told me: raise your skirts and beat you until your pretty skin turns red. Draw blood, he said, bloody the chemise!'

'I did nothing wrong!'

'Better a short lesson in pain than a lifetime of depravity, Jane Verity.' He was breathing fast, the scent of whisky mingled with his cologne. 'Isn't that what Reverend Glyde teaches us?'

A memory tingled in my hands: the Sunday Penances.

'He is the one that's depraved!' I was against his chest and raised my face to his. 'You have no idea of the cruelty of the man. He has a heart of cruelty. How can he claim to be a follower of Christ? What right does he have to preach to us?'

'How dare you?' For all his talk, his face betrayed him. Holding me up close, his eyes became plaintive and his mouth as soft as a girl's. 'Reverend Glyde is a pillar of the community … he's … how can you, in your position, question him?'

'Jesus taught forgiveness! He taught humility. He taught mercy. Yet do you know – do you know what Glyde did to us?' I started to wrestle my arm out of Doughty's grasp – we were close enough to have kissed each other. 'Did he tell you about the Sunday Penances? How he tortured us? He kept Theresa Curran to the last. It does not befit you to copy his methods. I believe you to be a better man than that.'

He released me, and I backed away from him and stood rubbing my shoulder. He regarded me ruefully.

'You girls,' he muttered. 'Workhouse girls.'

'Did you think that the truth came out at your inquest?'

I had ceased to be cautious. 'I read the newspaper. It was lies! She was picked on, bullied, abused for no reason, until she lost the will to live. Your inquest did not arrive at the truth.'

He looked as though I had poured cold water over his head. My chest was heaving, and he watched the rise and fall of it. You've done it now, I thought, but as he looked into my face his anger seemed to have gone. He leant on the edge of his desk, supporting himself with his hands. It seemed as though he was digesting what I had said, although he had found a way to diminish it by the time he recovered his voice.

'Well, I cannot expect you to speak well of the workhouse regime. After all, I saw how you fell foul of it. But can you not see, Jane, that such a regime is necessary? I have spoken to Reverend Glyde about it. He informed me that there are upwards of four hundred paupers in a workhouse built for two hundred and fifty: idle, feckless, insane. How are the Siviters to keep order alone? A system of penalties is needed, the higher penalties more rigorous than the lower ones, in case the lower ones are ineffective. He assured me that Theresa Curran was uncontrollable –'

'If you think so badly of paupers, of "workhouse girls", you will never find the truth. She was not what they said. She suffered in silence.' I could see that he doubted me. 'I did not *once* hear her raise her voice. I could not understand how you permitted your jury to arrive at that verdict.'

'The coroner may not overrule the jury.'

'But did they understand the case? Did they recognise the importance of the post-mortem?'

He eased himself into a sitting position on his desk and sighed, looking down at the floor.

'They are laymen, tradesmen: a bootmaker, a landlord, a gunmaker, and so forth. They know nothing of forensic science, of medical jurisprudence. It is my role to guide them but I often find myself unequal to the task. I told my jury that to understand the root cause of this suicide might help defend the paupers, who have no redress but the coroner. Yet they were unanimous that the post-mortem did not alter their verdict.'

'And tell me this,' I said, 'why did Mr Graves ask me about impropriety? That was the exact word he used: was I aware of *"anything improper occurring towards Theresa Curran?"*'

Instead of replying to the question, Doughty's suspicions grew. He stared up at me again.

'So, was that what drew you in here – to find his report of her post-mortem? Was that it? Tell the truth. Were you prying into my reports?'

'No. I have only read what was in the newspaper. I do realise that your papers are private.'

'But you were in here with a candle, in defiance of my express instructions. You put it out when you heard me come in.' The furrow deepened between his eyebrows.

I realised that I would have to tell the truth.

'I was not reading, sir, but writing. I bought my own ink out of my wages, but the bottle was dry. Look, my pen is in your inkwell.'

He glared, and I felt ashamed for using his things behind his back. I reached under my apron and drew out my letter to Edmond.

'You have a surprisingly elegant hand,' he said as he unfolded the letter. He frowned as he read. I wondered what he would think about Nathan.

'Advanced in years!' he exclaimed. 'I'm only thirty-nine! I'm the youngest coroner in the whole of England!'

I went red. Dr Doughty was a fine-looking man in the prime of life. But I had written that so Edmond would not think there could be anything untoward, the sort of thing that Clara had mentioned, the release of what I had seen captive in Doughty's eyes.

He saw my confusion.

'I suppose,' he said, making a face, 'to a young girl like you, that is how I must appear?'

I mumbled an apology. He glanced at the letter again.

'Graves told me about your actor friend,' he said. 'You honestly think he'll return?'

'We meant to marry,' I said, 'but there was not time to make the arrangements. Then I had to give up our rooms. He did not know I was in the workhouse. This is my first chance to tell him where I am … and of my … our … of Nathan.'

I could not say more, and watched his face grow sombre as he studied the letter further.

'I am sorry for your loss.' He looked sadly at me. 'But you can't send this.'

'Are you to stop me? Am I a prisoner here, barred from the world outside?'

He shook his head. 'Your situation is a common occurrence, Jane. I encounter it frequently in the course of my work.'

'Sir?'

'I speak of my inquests. My doleful duties as Borough Coroner. Of beautiful young girls like you who, finding themselves deserted, make an end to their lives. Found drowned in canals, or hanged, or poisoned. "Temporary Insanity." I will say no more. I am sure you know as much of that situation as I do myself.'

'I still love him. He said he'd come back for me.' My hand went to my eyes as I felt them pricking with tears.

'I'd advise you, for your own sake, not to contact him.' He refolded the letter and paused with it between his fingers, as though he thought that he should tear it up. 'It will lead only to false hopes, destroyed illusions, despair …'

'But I must write to him. We promised each other …'

He tapped the letter against the knuckles of his left hand. 'It will bring you either misfortune, or nothing at all.'

'I must take my chances, sir. It's my only hope for the future. Please.'

He frowned, pressing his lips together. Then a muscle twitched at the corner of his mouth – almost a smile. He passed me the letter with a weary sigh.

'Here. You may learn the truth for yourself.'

I thanked him sincerely, but he just muttered that he hoped that would be an end to it, and I was not to presume to use his study in that fashion again. I was to sweep and dust, in his presence, and no more. In particular, I was not to disturb any of his papers or reports.

I promised I would do exactly as he wished, thanked him over again and left the room before he had the chance to change his mind.

But I now was certain that he was guarding Mr Graves' post-mortem report on Theresa Curran.

13: Glyde Is to Visit

'You must help me prepare for Vernon's visit,' said Harriet, even though it was three days' hence.

To me, his mere name was abhorrent, but for her it seemed that he constantly occupied her mind. She could not settle to listen to the piano. It was as though an addiction had been reawakened by the sending of the letter, a craving that only his presence could satisfy.

I reminded her of her embroidery and, with her anxieties dulled with laudanum, she sat on her green-silk boudoir chair, stitching slowly as I listened to her meandering talk.

'Mama would scold me if I pricked my finger … Vernon always praised my embroidery, even when I was little and my stitches were still large and clumsy.'

She was making a church kneeler in Berlin wool-work, rendering from point-paper a pattern in gold, red and blue: a grid of bars with crosses at their intersections, reminiscent of a religious gaol. Confined in an oval at its centre two cherubs bore what looked like a crucifix.

'It was for him that I laboured, making his handkerchiefs,

his shirts, with ever finer stitches, so that the seams would not chafe his tender skin. He said that I was the best little needlewoman.'

It seemed she'd had a miserable childhood, growing up in a large, cold house in Yorkshire, subject to strict discipline. It had been Glyde who had borne the brunt of their father's freezing rages, of punishments that went on for hours or days. He had often been beaten for having dared to defend his sister. He had turned to Christ for courage and had come to believe that suffering brought purity and strength.

'My dear brother was always my guiding light. If I had been sinful and earned our father's wrath, he would correct me and show me how to behave in future.'

Glyde, ten years Harriet's senior, had been more than a brother to her: he was everything. His wishes had become her wishes, and all her principles and moral standards were according to his dictates. She had not a thought of her own. He was a brilliant churchman and had progressed from curate to rector in a short space of time. 'Vernon says …' was the refrain, often followed by a babble of High Church prating, as if Harriet's depression of spirits made her own thoughts intolerable.

It vexed me to listen to Glyde's words in Harriet's voice, for I could not dare to tell her of how I feared his cruelty.

I remembered that I had once seen inside his office, when I had been sent to mop the floor of the workhouse chapel. The chapel was too small for the expanding workhouse population and was no longer used for general worship; services were held in the refectory, and the chapel's sole use was the administration of the Sunday Penances. The enormous Bible was undisturbed, its gilt-edged pages in perfect line.

As I worked in the silence I kept glancing up to where, high up behind the altar a plaster Christ seemed to writhe upon the Cross, his flesh painted greyish-pink, limbs contorted in pain, and His eyes, half-closed, cast upwards to Heaven. His hands and feet had been torn by the crucifying nails, the crown of thorns hammered into His skull so that deep wounds dripped blood, the gash in His chest gaped to show a rip in the scarlet surface of the lung. A tasselled, gilded cord dangled beneath the cross, secured by the iron bolt that held the foot to the wall.

The air smelled faintly of vomit. Beneath this image of torture the wall and floor were splashed with it. As I swabbed it with fresh water I noticed a dark crust on the gilded cord and reached up to wipe it clean – and when I rinsed the cloth a reddish-brown stain oozed into the water as though Christ's blood had run down it from His feet.

In the wall on the right of the altar table was a door and, wondering if I should clean in there, I knocked at it. There was no reply. I turned the doorknob – the door was unlocked. Behind it was a small office, swelteringly hot, and silent apart from a faint clicking from the cooling stove. I presumed it belonged to Glyde. Vestments hung ghost-like on a hook behind the door, the apparatus of administering the Communion lay on a shelf, and there was the switch with which he had whipped our hands, soaking in a bucket of brine. He had a desk there, and a couch.

A journal bound in black leather lay upon the desk. It was open. I saw a sketch made with crude gashes of a pen. At the foot of a cross was a naked girl, half-kneeling, with her hands joined above her head in supplication. The stripes across her back had been scourged so deep with the steel pen that the paper was torn. I was overcome with fear and disgust and, retrieving the bucket and cloth from the chapel, I hurried away without daring to glance again at the dying Christ.

I turned it over in my mind now as I replied automatically to Harriet's reminiscences. I suspected that the tortured girl in the drawing was Theresa, and that I had glimpsed the workings of a mind obsessed with cruelty – with a drive to inflict suffering that was as compelling as the universal human drive to find love and freedom. Yet I forced myself to endure Harriet's praise of Glyde. Her love for her brother seemed genuine and, after all, she could only ever have seen him acting with affection.

At Harriet's direction I brought one dress after another out of her wardrobe and she eventually chose a jade-green silk. The style was a few years outdated but it was barely worn and the material was as soft as new grass. I took it downstairs, freshened it with a damp cloth and painstakingly pressed every gather and frill with a flatiron. Then I dragged the weighty skirts back upstairs to Harriet, doubting that she would have the strength to walk in them. I laced her into a corset, which barely touched her wasted frame. A spreading underskirt of stiff buckram followed, then the dress.

She stood and regarded herself in the glass, finding fault: it made her look sallow, too old, too thin, it no longer fitted her.

I pulled in the loose folds at the back. 'I'm sure I could take it in, madam.'

But she whirled about, exasperated.

'Take it off me,' she said, tensing her shoulders as if something about it were paining her. 'Take it off. *Take it off, I said!*'

I tried to turn her around so that I could help her.

'I'll undo the buttons,' I said, as though to a child. 'Keep still for a moment longer, if you please.'

But she started to struggle, her arms flailing as I tried to extract them from the sleeves, and there was a ripping sound.

That upset her all the more.

'Take it off me!' she cried.

She was half in and half out of it, her bony elbows rigid. It was hard to calm her and encourage her to relax and stay still. In the end I managed to ease the dress away.

'The hateful thing!' She snatched it, threw it to the floor and trampled it underfoot.

Two hours' work was reduced to a crumpled heap. To my dismay, Harriet cast herself forward on her bed, still in her corset, and started to roar, her thin shoulders quivering and her cries muffled in the bedclothes.

Quelling my irritation at my wasted work, I watched her for a while, unsure what to do and what lay at the root of her agitation.

'Madam …' I touched her shoulder.

She kept up her roaring, giving way as she grew tired to deep sobbing breaths.

I unlaced her corset at the back but she would not get up for me to remove it. I brought her satin dressing gown and covered her over with it, and at the touch of the cold heavy fabric she quietened down.

'Dr Doughty will be home soon,' I told her. 'He will not like to see you so upset.'

'Damn him!' she muttered, without lifting her head. And then: 'He hates me … how can I continue … I am going to kill myself. *I will! I will!'*

'But your brother is to be here on Thursday,' I pleaded, afraid to dwell upon that last comment. 'You were so looking forward to his visit.'

'What if he sees me like this?' She turned her wild-eyed face to mine. 'An ugly creature, sallow, ruined?'

'I imagine he will wish to see you better.' It was hard for me to imagine Glyde acting charitably but I could only hope that he would be kind to his own sister. 'But you will be better. You are a beautiful lady, madam. Delicate … exquisite …'

She started to pay heed to me then, and I wondered if flattery offered a chance of calming her.

'Your hair, madam, so fair, your eyes so violet, and your figure so slender and elegant.'

'Do you really think so?' She started to sit up.

'Oh, yes. I think if you might allow me to help you, you would be looking your best when Reverend Glyde comes to visit.'

'Yes, I must look my best. He should not see me like this.'

'Come to the mirror, madam,' I coaxed, and sat her in front of the dressing table with her dressing gown over her shoulders. 'Your hair, you see, if you allow me to brush and braid it, can be in the latest style – and, as to your complexion, a little powder and rouge will soon bring it to perfection. I was once in the theatre, you know. And your teeth …'

Harriet's teeth were scaled with a brown layer, making her mouth like an old woman's, though fortunately none were missing.

'I have some charcoal paste,' she said, 'but …'

'While I repair your dress, madam, perhaps you might work on your teeth? May I use your sewing box?'

I set her up with a basin of water and a brush and found the charcoal paste amidst her shelf of bottles.

Then I threaded a needle and, having turned the dress inside out and spread it out on her bed, I began to repair the seam in the sleeve that had parted during her struggle. It would be possible to add some darts to reduce the waist.

I kept up my patter. Occupied with her teeth, she could not gainsay me. I painted a picture of a mass of blonde braids and curls above a slender neck, of huge and beautiful eyes emphasized with kohl, of soft coloured powders creating a peach-like bloom. As I spoke, she rinsed away the charcoal and I saw the brightness of her smile, like a will-o'-the-wisp, a ghost-light floating above a marsh of despair.

I thought it strange that she was so animated by her

brother, when she was content for her husband to view her in whatever state.

Indeed, that same night Doughty was at her bedside, wakened by her cries and the furious clamour of her bell as she woke in a state of panic.

He had taken his candle in, and around its flickering light it seemed that the shadows that she had feared were gathering. Her face glistened with tears, her hair had become matted, and as she wept she dug her fingernails into her own cheeks.

Despite her distress, she did not reach out to him and he kept himself aloof, concerned only to see that, like a patient, she had her laudanum and a drink of water and needed nothing further.

Only as her eyelids started to droop, and she gave him a wan smile, did he bend to kiss her brow.

'Goodnight, dear,' he murmured.

Her eyes closed. He faced me across the bed, across the quilted coverlet that shrouded the thin limbs of his wife. I looked at the lips that had kissed her. He was capable of gentleness.

Mrs Doughty started to snore.

'She is taking more laudanum than she is allowed,' I said. 'It's impossible to stop her.' The sound of my voice did not disturb her. She was falling into a deep slumber.

'She needs to sleep,' Doughty said. 'It is her refuge. God knows I cannot comfort her.'

His eyes lingered on me, and at the spot where my night wrapper overlapped my bosom.

'I think that Dr Astley-Scrope should be sent for again, in view of her agitation,' he added wearily. 'It can wait until the morning.'

Mrs Doughty's arms were limp, straight down at her

sides like tasselled ribbons, and he laid a hand over hers. There was no response. I saw him curve his fingers into the spot where her pulse beat between the tendons of her wrist. Her chest rose and fell with her breathing and a little pinkness remained in her pale lips. His eyes were still on me.

Satisfied that she was fast asleep, he returned to his room.

I crept as quietly as I could back to my own and locked the door behind me. I dozed uneasily, startling at the contractions of floorboards, at mice scuttling in the walls. Within a couple of hours I was wide-awake again. I had heard a voice.

I froze beneath my blankets, straining my ears to capture the faintest sound. The voice came again … a sob. It was Harriet.

I crept softly to my bedroom door and unlocked it. I turned the knob ever so slowly and edged it open. The sob came again, from below. I crept softly down the stairs and paused part-way. The door to the nursery was ajar and a faint light burned within. I slipped across the landing and peered through the crack between the nursery door and the architrave.

Harriet was there, standing quite still, looking down into the empty crib and holding a candle aloft, stroking and patting a bundle of blankets, disturbing the cobwebs so that spiders scattered away from the circle of light. Her hair lay long and loose over her shoulders, and the candle lit her face from beneath, so that her tears glistened as they fell.

'Agnes,' she moaned to the empty crib, 'don't cry, my little lambikin. Mama loves you. Don't cry, my little one.'

At once I felt Nathan's wasted limbs, heard his fretful cry – and my own bereavement rebounded upon me. I longed to go to Harriet and comfort her, to weep with her, to hold her – but at the same time I was afraid of intruding on her private grief.

She placed her candlestick on a tallboy and lifted a bundle of blankets out of the crib as though cradling a ghostly baby in her arms. She rocked it from side to side, her cries muffled in the blankets, but as the candle burned down she calmed herself and placed the bundle back in the crib.

Smiling down at it, she said: 'One day we shall be together again, my little Agnes, you and I, and your darling papa, together again in Heaven ... without pain, without shame, united in God's forgiveness and our love for each other.'

As she turned away and approached the door with her light, I retreated swiftly to my room. I heard her descend the stairs.

She rang for me then, and once more in the night, and I went quietly back and forth to her, calming her quickly to sleep with her laudanum without waking Doughty. It was tiresome, but I pitied her distress. Despite her adoration of her monstrous brother, I resolved to endure her, partly because it was my employment, and also because I intended to understand her better, in case I could discover a way of getting her back to health. After all, she could never have seen that drawing, or known of Theresa's terrible death.

14: Aethereal Balsam

Dr Astley-Scrope was a long, angular man, white-haired, with steel spectacles.

As I followed him up the stairs, I ventured that my mistress might manage with less laudanum, as the more I gave the more she seemed to crave it.

'Her condition is unstable,' he snapped. 'If you reduce her medication you will find she deteriorates abruptly.'

'But the laudanum, what does it do?' I persisted. 'It is only a sedative, is it not?'

The physician stopped abruptly on the landing and turned around. He drew himself up to be as tall as he could be and craned his neck downwards in its high white collar, jolting as if impelled by some mechanical device. His lower lip sagged in a sneer.

'How do you be so bold, young woman? I, not you, am the physician. Your mistress's condition is vulnerable to any imbalance in her medical regime. It is of the utmost importance that the prescribed treatments are taken exactly as advised. Any attempt at precipitate withdrawal may seriously weaken the patient. She is in an extremely delicate state of nervous debilitation.'

He rapped at Harriet's door, and then went straight in without waiting for a reply.

She greeted him effusively, but he did not respond.

I followed him in.

'You may instruct your servant not to harass me with impertinent questions, madam,' was all he said.

'Perhaps you may leave us, Jane,' said Harriet, who lay in bed, draped in a bed-jacket of Brussels lace. 'Dr Astley-Scrope is a highly esteemed member of our church. I am sure I shall not need a chaperone.'

'I shall be just outside the door, ma'am, should you require anything.'

I perched on the stairs until, after a few minutes, there was the tinkle of her bell.

'I have written a prescription for Mrs Doughty,' Dr Astley-Scrope indicated a couple of scraps of paper on the dresser, 'and there is my invoice for the last month, for which I should appreciate prompt settlement.'

'Jane,' crooned Harriet, 'you must take the prescription down to Bright's Pharmacy straight away. You may use my reticule basket – there is a little money in it. And get a large bottle of the Emerald Soap Solution, please. I shall settle directly, doctor. I have asked my husband to go to the bank today, and you may collect your fees on your next visit.'

'You may ask him to come straight to my rooms with the payment, madam, to avoid yet further delay.'

After ordering me to follow his instructions to the letter, Astley-Scrope descended the stairs smartly and was gone. He had not been in the house above ten minutes.

Going to Bright's was a chance for me to take my letter to be franked at the Post Office on New Street. By Friday at the very latest, it would arrive at the Theatre Royal. Perhaps there would be a delay before Edmond received it – to Saturday perhaps. Then he might send for me, or even come himself to Birmingham. Within a fortnight even, he might knock on the door of 49 Newhall Street and demand that the Doughtys surrender me up. My heart fluttered like a sparrow at the thought.

Emerging from the Post Office, I paused to gaze across the street at the colonnades of the Theatre Royal, where *The Imprisoned Contessa* had brought Edmond such success. I remembered how I had first seen New Street from the window of a hansom cab, as Edmond and I were driven from Curzon Street Station.

He had slipped his hand beneath the sable of my pelisse, and though I protested my resistance seemed to pique him.

'You shall pay me for this later,' he teased.

'Be careful you don't become one of your characters,' I replied, but I was smiling now.

Outside the cab I watched the real world go by: the shops with their canvas awnings, a broad thoroughfare thronged with people and carriages. Edmond had said that the dressmakers and milliners of New Street rivalled the best in London, at half the price. When I asked him how he knew so much about dressmakers and milliners, he replied that he had once had a young friend who was interested in such things, but would say no more. A shadow had crossed his face.

Now I hurried along New Street in my servant's dress, glancing at the shop windows. In the milliners', the summer hats were like bouquets of flowers, and new fashion plates were on view in the dressmakers'. I would never again be beautiful, wrapped in luxuries, hearing Edmond vow his adoration, and burning with desire for him. What a universe lay between that life and this. I had become dowdy, swollen-handed from menial work, with the dull weariness of the poor ingrained into every movement. I paused outside the stay-maker's and a shop-girl stared at me with arrogant distaste.

I passed by the Midland Hotel, remembering our first few nights in Birmingham. Inside the grand building the foyer was lined in Carrara marble. The personages who came and went were affluent, quietly respectable, elegantly dressed in dark colours. When we had first arrived the hotel manager himself had greeted us, bowing, directing a group of flunkeys to conduct us to our first-floor suite. Now the doorman viewed me with disfavour as I craned my neck to see the window of what had been our room.

With Edmond standing behind me, his hands at my waist, I had looked out from there at the town, wondering when, and how, to tell him the true reason for my increasing size.

To some extent I could sway him, especially if he was in the mood for pleasure or comfort. But, at the same time, he insisted on being my master. I understood and accepted it – it was part of his obsession with me. He chose my clothes, sometimes sending me to change my dress upon a whim when I was nearly ready to go out. Rather than following my own appetites, he instructed me on what I should eat, and in what quantities, directing me to eat more if he felt I should, or less, according to his fancy. He decided what I should drink, what skin creams I should use, how I was to style my hair. He told me how to conduct myself in the presence of his friends. Under his regime I became more beautiful: my hair glossy, my figure voluptuous, my dresses the height of elegance.

But he'd had no means to control the new life in my womb. And I had been unable to discuss it with him until my pregnancy could no longer be concealed.

In truth, my life with him had been a poor preparation

for motherhood. After Nathan's death I could not properly grieve. I could not allow my guilt to haunt me or I would have been destroyed by it. In admitting that guilt I would have to allow Edmond a share, yet he was my one dream and my one hope for the future.

I should not have been dawdling, and quickening my pace soon arrived at Bright's Pharmacy on Cannon Street. Behind mullioned windows were a polished mahogany counter and rows of shelves with gilded jars of chemicals.

Mr Bright studied the doctor's writing through his spectacles.

'Aethereal Balsam contains opium,' he said. 'He has also prescribed elixir of laudanum separately. It will not sort well.'

It took some effort to persuade the pharmacist, but I knew better than to go back to Harriet without the medicines. I described her distress, Dr Astley-Scrope's visit, the urgent need for the increased medication. After producing a violet flask of laudanum, Bright fetched one bottle after another from his shelves. He measured and mixed ether, menthol, Friars' Balsam and opium into a blue-ribbed glass bottle. The harsh aroma of ether spread through the air. Bright stoppered the bottle and, as he shook the mixture, it turned cloudy and seemed to boil.

'Shake the bottle first, then no more than five drops, mixed with a little milk,' he said, 'and she must try to refrain from her old medications at the same time.' He corked the bottle and sealed it with wax, then wrote the same instructions on a label and gummed it to the side. 'Is there anything else?'

'Emerald Soap Solution,' I added. 'A large bottle, please.'

Bright said he was trying to discourage the use of that, but took a dark-green bottle from the shelf and checked the label.

'It is just a five-per-cent solution of arsenic. But women swear by it, that it whitens the complexion like nothing else.'

Still grumbling, he wrapped the bottles in brown paper. 'If I refused to stock it, then they would buy it from Mr Ascham on Summer Lane.'

Although my meagre salary could buy little on New Street, there were shops in the side-alleys that were for the lower classes. In a clothier's trunk I found old shifts of fine cotton, embroidered and inset with handmade lace. They were stale and yellowed around the arms and neck, but they would bleach, and come up like new. I examined the seams and pin-tucks, formed with tiny stitches, half the size of my own sewing. It was so long since I had felt the smoothness of fine fabric against my skin.

'Sixpence each,' said the shop woman, and I chose one.

But then there was a baby's bonnet, of linen, neatly worked, with white silk ribbons. I picked it up and held it. It filled me with dark despair: Nathan would have been two months old.

'Beautiful,' said the shop woman fondly, 'lovely for a babby.'

Smiling while my eyes filled with tears, I pushed the things back into her hands and fled.

I had been wasting time. I hurried back, hoping that Harriet would not yet have woken needing assistance.

I caught up with Doughty returning home at the top of Newhall Street.

'Jane!' he exclaimed. I had taken him unawares. 'How d'ye do?' He raised his hat and offered me his arm, as if I had been a female acquaintance and not his servant.

I smiled, assuming he was in jest, and kept my distance. 'Thank you, sir, but it would not do, if your neighbours were to see.' The windows in the tall brick houses were right beside the street. I bobbed him a little curtsey.

He wanted to know where I had been and, as I explained

about Dr Astley-Scrope's visit, I fell into step beside him.

'Aethereal Balsam and laudanum together? Are you sure?'

We were in the hallway and he opened the study door. He ushered me inside.

'Let me see.'

I produced the bottles from Harriet's reticule basket. Doughty unwrapped them on his desk and studied the chemist's labels.

'Aethereal Balsam is opium, and with enough ether at these doses to render a carthorse insensible. How could Bright dare to supply all that?'

'Mr Bright warned me that it would not sort well. But Dr Astley-Scrope insisted on the medicines. He said her condition was highly unstable and I was to follow his instructions exactly.'

'She should not be using the Emerald Soap either. It is a solution of arsenic.'

'I know,' I said, 'but, if she sends me for it, I have no option but to do as I am told. Perhaps you could speak to her?'

He shot me a glance, his eyebrows raised, which implied that he had no more agency than I in the matter.

Perhaps woken by our return, Harriet started ringing her bell.

'Opium.' Doughty sighed. 'Ether. I'll go up to her.'

He left the bottles behind. I gathered them back into the reticule-basket and trailed him up the stairs.

'Is everything all right, my darling?' He was at her bedside.

'Where is Jane? I thought she had returned. Where are my medicines?' Harriet sat up in bed and looked around, but I was watching them through the gap along the doorjamb.

'Harriet, Jane has obtained from Mr Bright enough opium and ether to kill you. I cannot allow you to consume such a quantity.'

'Please, William, don't interfere. Aethereal Balsam is a new medication. Dr Astley-Scrope insisted upon it. We are to follow his instructions precisely. Where is Jane?'

She rang her bell again.

'The active ingredient is opium,' insisted Doughty, raising his voice over its ringing. 'There is enough ether to end your life and the rest is quackery and flim-flam.'

I hesitated on the landing, reluctant to interfere between them.

'If you spent less time with the dead and more with the living,' countered his wife, sounding her bell again, 'then I might trust you more with my care. But, as it is, you will have to defer to a more experienced physician. Where is Jane? Is she not back?'

'Do you question my knowledge?' Doughty bristled. 'Do you not know how many inquests I have performed? Indeed, many of my cases would not have been so, had it not been for the misdirected efforts of their doctors. Physicians should treat according to the best interests of the patient, rather than out-worn traditions, old-wives' superstitions and their own financial gain!'

'And yet, when we were in London, your practice was so unpopular no one would consult you. It was said to me that you lacked heart, that you were cold, and people wanted sympathy, not scientific lectures. We were near-bankrupt and Vernon had to help you.'

She sounded her bell again, but yet I hesitated to go in.

Doughty was silent, although he looked as though he were near the end of his self-control.

His wife, oblivious, continued her outburst. 'You were an utter failure! Dr Astley-Scrope, on the other hand, is highly successful, and a pillar of our church. Everyone – not just Vernon – says how good he is. He understands my case – I should have been long dead, were it not for him. I will not hear you gainsay him!' Harriet's voice was squeaking as though she was close to tears. 'Now, you must go and make the payment for his invoice! Take it directly to his rooms.'

I stood back from the doorway as Doughty strode out onto the landing with Dr Astley-Scrope's bill in his hand.

Harriet rang her bell again.

'Go in to her,' he muttered. 'Damn her!' He was tense with anger, his face stony hard.

'She is not well,' I said. 'I'm sure that she does not mean to offend you. She becomes agitated when she is in need of her laudanum.'

'Look at this!' He thrust the paper in front of my nose. His hand was quivering. 'Two guineas! He's a charlatan!'

He was ready to tear it up.

I took it from him and glanced it over. Half-a-dozen home visits were listed.

'I can run over with the payment when madam is settled down,' I offered, 'to spare you the annoyance of the errand. I am sorry, sir.'

I looked up at his stern profile, waiting for him to respond. I was not saying sorry on his wife's behalf, but I had seen that she had stabbed at a tender spot and wished to ease his pain.

'You're very good, Jane.' He calmed down as he met my eyes. 'So patient, and thoughtful. I wish that I understood my wife as well as you do. Go in to her, take your time. I'll go over to Astley-Scrope.'

As he pocketed the invoice he heaved a sigh, his glance still lingering on me, his mouth pressed shut as though there was much more that he wanted to say, but would not. Sidling past him into Harriet's room, I was conscious for a moment of his hand at the back of my waist. I heard him clear his throat and then clatter down the stairs. After a moment the front door slammed shut.

Harriet eagerly took her new medicine and soon afterwards subsided into sleep. She was unrousable for her broth at teatime, and unaware of me as I brushed her hair so that it lay neatly across her pillow and wiped her face with a flannel and warm water. I sat beside her bed and watched her for a while as she slept. She was deathly pale, but her breathing was steady, and her face in deep repose. I pitied her: the grief for her long-dead Agnes was as sharp as if the child had only just passed, and the love of her husband, that should have comforted her in her bereavement, had turned to bitterness.

Yet there was something else. Bending over the empty crib, addressing the bundle of blankets, she had spoken of 'your darling papa'. Perhaps, in her heart, she did truly love her husband, and it was only her illness and her dependence on medication that made her spiteful.

Doughty did not return until late at night. I was already in bed and, as I heard his footsteps pause on the landing below, I got up and checked that I had locked my door. But he went on into his own room.

15: A Vile Mouth

On the day of Glyde's visit Harriet, taking ever-increasing quantities of Aethereal Balsam, was not well enough to get up, despite all the effort expended on the renovation of her green dress, and said she would spend the day in bed.

'You may show him up here when he arrives,' she said, and then made a great fuss of setting me to look for her prayer book and her Bible, saying that her brother's prayers for her health were better than Dr Astley-Scrope's medicines.

I avoided her eyes, letting the babble about the Reverend Glyde's virtues drift like dust motes in the air as I helped her perform her toilette, washing and perfuming with the greatest of care, as though preparing to meet a lover. A fresh dressing gown of pearly silk and swansdown was required and in it Harriet lay back on her pillows, her white leather-bound Bible in her hand, waiting, praying.

I was dismissed to wait downstairs for the doorbell to ring.

'You must not keep him waiting,' insisted Harriet. 'He dislikes being kept waiting.'

I waited, longing to hide myself away in the privy, for my bowels were turning to water with fear. My last sight of Reverend Glyde had been his cruel grin as he ordered Theresa to remain behind, while I supported a weeping boy as we filed away.

But as he introduced himself on the front step, in his black coat and white preaching bands, he presented a face of pious concern. His eyes slipped across mine; he had a slight squint, which made it hard to identify the direction of his gaze, and he betrayed no recognition of me as I ushered him nervously indoors. He was a man in his prime, high-coloured, well-built and finely tailored. He dropped his cane into the stand and removed his tall hat to uncover thick red-gold hair that ran down into a dark beard. He placed the hat on the hall table and turned his back to me so that I could help him off with his coat. I began to feel reassured.

'Now, you must show me up to my poor dear sister, bless her.'

His next action belied his pious tone of voice for, as soon as he was free of his coat, he pounced. He spun round, grasped my waist with both hands and held me there. I gave a yelp of shock and, letting go of the coat, tried to prise his hands away, but only felt his grip tighten as his mouth widened into the grin that I remembered. He leered, close to my face.

'A workhouse girl, indeed,' he said through his teeth. 'Idle and vicious, like the others. I remember you at the Sunday Penances.'

Afraid that Harriet might hear, I stifled my cries, but I twisted in his hands and pushed uselessly at his chest. Still gripping me, he pushed me backwards and wedged me against the front door, holding me there with the weight of his body. In the narrow entranceway there was no escape for me to either side.

'Your employers may yet send you on Sundays for the Penances, if you displease them.'

His fingers came up to my throat and squeezed so that I could not breathe and felt that I would faint, that I would die. I could not get a grasp on them to pull them away. As I started to lose consciousness I felt his mouth crushing mine, the scour of his beard, and a slimy tongue cutting off my remaining air. Then I was released, and he was shaking me awake.

'Conduct me to my sister, and look lively about it, girl,' he said, as though nothing had happened and I had merely been idling.

Gasping for air, I struggled to rebalance myself and retrieve his coat from the floor. I could still taste the sourness of his breath.

The whole episode had lasted perhaps less than half a minute, so brief a time that afterwards I had to examine the tender bruises on my neck to be certain that it had happened.

Satisfied with his cruelty, the Reverend's attention was now elsewhere, and I followed rather than conducted him up the stairs to Harriet's room. My face was smarting. I felt soiled and dishevelled and dared not do more than put my head around the door, in case she noticed something. I would have died of shame if she had. But all her attention was on her brother. Glyde sat down on his sister's bed as though nothing had happened, declining her offer of tea, and asking only that I left them to their devotions. He watched me closing the door.

I rushed down to the scullery and washed out my mouth with fresh water. The shock of that assault and my instinct to keep a calm face wore off. But even in private I fought down my tears, with a pulse throbbing in my head. I knew that my hatred of Glyde had deepened a hundredfold and I was intensely angry, not just for myself, but for Theresa.

Although his attack on me had been fleeting, I was doomed to relive that moment time and again: the entrapment, the lack of air, the inescapable contact with his vile mouth. He had opened my eyes, providing me with a new lens through which I could view Theresa's suffering and experience the disgusting nature of her treatment. Now I understood her shame and her withdrawal from those who could have consoled her. I clenched my fists until my nails dug into my palms, vowing that I would kill Glyde with my bare hands if he were ever to touch me again. I would not allow myself to fear him.

Despite my fury I was unsure how I would actually overmaster Glyde, but fortunately Doughty came home shortly after that for lunch and rang for me. I composed myself before going up to the study, so that he would not suspect that anything had happened.

Nonetheless, he subjected me to his usual close inspection and wanted to know if anything had upset me.

'Not at all,' I replied. 'I am perfectly fine, thank you.'

'You seem … distressed. And your cap is awry.' He had been seated at his desk, and now stood up. 'Can I do anything to assist you?'

'No, thank you.' I put my hand up to straighten my cap. 'What was it you rang for, sir?'

'I wanted only to know if Reverend Glyde was here with my wife.'

I said that he was and suggested that he could go up, but he shook his head.

'Please make sure that he speaks to me before he leaves.'

I felt apprehensive about dealing with Glyde again, but I would have to find a way, as he was likely to be a frequent visitor to the house. If he attacked me and I called for help, would my employers protect me? He could easily twist the situation to make me appear at fault. It would be my word against his.

An hour later, as I was dusting the parlour, I heard him coming down from Harriet's room. She had not rung for me to show him out. My heart sank. As I hesitated, the study door flew open.

'Vernon, I wish to speak with you.' Doughty's voice was reedy with tension.

'Good day, brother,' replied Glyde, still descending the stairs. 'And how are we today?'

I kept completely still – they were unaware of me behind the open door of the parlour.

'The Court of Petty Sessions – I am summoned to appear before them tomorrow morning to explain my fees. They have not paid my invoices. Nor reimbursed me for the surgeon's fees for post-mortem examinations.'

'As you know,' replied Glyde, pausing in the hallway, 'the Town Council is much encumbered at present in its finances.'

'But you yourself are a magistrate there – can you not do something? I should not have to justify every case carried out as part of my routine work.'

'I think you should be careful though, William.' Glyde's voice was unctuous. 'You see, there's precious little money to pay for your inquests. Don't go adding to the costs with extra this and that, you know, surgeon's reports and such like.'

'Post-mortem examinations are already restricted. Often I cannot command them when needed. They have to be agreed by my jury – if the jury refuse then the post-mortem is not done, even when it's obvious that it's essential.'

'William –'

'I had a case only yesterday where it was clear that a woman had been fatally poisoned by her servant.' Doughty's voice rose. 'The Beadle even saw the vials of turpentine in the bedchamber. What was their verdict?'

'But –'

'What was my jury's verdict? Death by Act of God! May He give me strength! You knew that I wanted to improve the inquests with forensic science. You knew it when you told me, you instructed me, to put myself forward for this post. But I'm blocked by procedure and superstition, ignorant jurymen, and now this from the magistrates! My fees!' Doughty heaved out a long breath of frustration.

There was a pause. I remained motionless, realising that Glyde must have helped his brother-in-law to obtain the position of coroner, and wondering if this had been for his own purposes.

'For the poor people, we are the authorities in this town, sir, you and I,' Glyde said in a level tone. 'I, as the guardian of the workhouse, and of the souls of the parish; you as the agent of the Crown. Let there be harmony between these functions, let religion and justice walk hand in hand, and there need be no public wrangling, no imputations of scandal, no –'

'No restrictions set upon my inquests and my post-mortems, and the fees that I rightfully claim, as being my due, and set by statute?'

Glyde dwelt at length on the scarcity of the Borough's finances and the need for economy, but Doughty persisted until he obtained reassurance about his fees. Glyde maintained that he had little influence on the Borough's income. But he did hold some sway with his fellow magistrates and it might be that some money could be found somewhere. He would do the best he could.

'You might help yourself by working for the authorities in the town, rather than against them,' he added. 'Now, the suicide: the case at the workhouse. She hung herself, we knew that, so what benefit did it confer to have her dissected? Why did you order that?'

'The jury entirely supported it.'

'But the verdict was obvious from the start: suicide. Self-murder. It was up to you to guide the inquest proceedings to reach that verdict in the most efficient manner.'

'It was not how she died, but why. There was a concern that this inmate had been subjected to extreme suffering and her agonies had driven her to end her life. The post-mortem examination found evidence of severe beatings over a prolonged period of time.'

'A delinquent, as I am sure Mrs Siviter would have clearly testified. Only the worst of delinquents would defy the birch to such a degree.'

'There was, in fact, far more in the post-mortem report than could at that point decently be made public.' Doughty lowered his voice. 'I won't offend you with the details. Suffice it to say that the deceased was pregnant.'

I now knew what was in Graves' report that Doughty was guarding so closely. My hatred of Glyde reached a new level. He had proven the vileness of his nature by his attack on me. I had no doubt who was responsible for this pregnancy.

Now he uttered a glib dismissal; he saw sin in everyone, except himself.

'Alas, that the depraved little trollop should so brazenly flout the workhouse rules!'

'She had been brutally violated. Mr Graves documented appalling injuries of which you shall be made aware in due course. I am to present a confidential report, including the whole of his findings, to the Workhouse Board of Guardians next Thursday.'

'You know what the workhouse girls are like,' Glyde said

sharply. 'There is no end to their deceit. I myself have kept watch in the dead of night to witness them climb over the back wall into the rookeries – they will perform the lewdest of acts for a farthing. Indeed, you have procured yourself such a one to work in your house, have you not?'

'I –' Doughty was brought up short, and then recovered himself. 'On the contrary! Jane's a good girl, and has proved most helpful, particularly in caring for Harriet.'

'Jane?'

'Verity.'

'Beware of over-familiarity with your servant, sir. Should I remind you about the use of the cane?'

Doughty was slow to reply. 'I threatened her, but in truth ...' He cleared his throat. 'I could not bring myself to do it. But she has nonetheless settled well to her work. We ... we are well fed and the house is kept clean.'

'A man who looks at a woman with lustful intent has already committed adultery with her in his heart.' Glyde's voice had the sharpness of a razor blade.

'Certainly not! I –'

'She is a pretty little thing who has tasted the forbidden fruit, and having found it agreeable, is hungering after more,' sneered Glyde. 'If she tempts you, or causes you any trouble, simply send her back to the workhouse and I will personally see to it that she is corrected. There are many men who would stray from the path in your situation; do not place your mortal soul in danger. I would remind you that it has been six weeks since I last saw you in church, and much longer since your last confession.'

'I have been very busy. You know the nature of my work.' Doughty laughed nervously. 'But there can be no question of any transgression of the bounds of holy matrimony, and as the girl's employer – and, I must emphasise, I have taken her on as an act of charity – to take advantage of her would in any case not be proper.'

'You are too impetuous,' said Glyde. 'Reflect upon yourself, and do not obey the first impulse that enters your head.'

There was a pause, then Doughty started to apologise for troubling Vernon about his fees, and the post-mortems, and he hoped Vernon would forgive him but he had much to prepare for tomorrow's inquest, and so forth, until Glyde was out of the house.

Doughty exhaled a puff of relief after the front door had closed and shut himself up in his study. He rang and asked for sandwiches, averting his gaze from me.

After taking up a tray, I crept back to the kitchen where I sat at the table to think. Glyde had had ample opportunity to assault Theresa after the Sunday Penances, and now I had heard his excuse for visiting the workhouse at night. I recoiled from the ugly thought of Theresa following him in silent terror through the dark corridors.

It was another half an hour before Harriet rang. I had thought that she at least would have been made happy by Glyde's visit but I found her in disarray, the white books closed upon the bedside table, and seemingly forgetful that she had wanted me. I straightened her bedclothes and asked if she would like anything. She said that she felt already the absence of her brother's dear company, and only wanted her laudanum.

As I brought her the violet flask she said that wives should submit in everything to their husbands, as we do to the Lord.

I stopped and stared at her. Her lips were parted and her cheeks greyish pale.

'I have been remiss. I must be a better wife to him,' she said sadly. 'If he loved me as he used to, then he would not go against Vernon.'

'But, madam, you are ill.'

'I remember the first time William saw me. He was reading with Vernon in the long gallery at Malton Hall – my parents' house.' She sat up in bed with an effort, pawing her hair into place as I arranged her pillows at her back. 'It is a beautiful room, a library … with gilded books behind gilded grilles. Vernon nudged him and he turned to watch me as I went towards them. He smiled at me. "Who's this little wisp of thistledown?" he asked … as if I had been a child … Vernon had to introduce me …'

Her lips twisted into a half-smile and she seemed for a moment to drift off into her memories, but then her eyes snapped open.

'It is through mortifying the flesh, through cleansing away our sins, that one finds God's true blessings.'

I shuddered, still unable to rid myself of the vileness of that fleshly contact with Glyde. Had Glyde married his sister off to Doughty, invoking religion to urge her to submit to her wifely duties?

'I need my laudanum, Verity. My Aethereal Balsam. You cannot imagine the pain I suffer. Here, in my heart.' She grasped the neck of her nightdress with trembling hands.

'I am sure your husband loves you, madam.' I did not really know what to say.

'The pain of my dead child – the shame – I cannot forget. Vernon says we should forget and have another. I should make my husband come to my bed.'

'Dr Doughty would not want you to … to make your condition worse.'

'I have my medicines.'

'He would want you to be well, madam,' I insisted.

As I dropped the laudanum on her tongue I could not envision Doughty desiring her. Did he make demands, which she was unable to fulfil? He could be harsh, that aggression no doubt nurtured by Glyde's counsels: I had seen it in the study. But I had also had kindness from him, and an informality that did not suit my present humble situation. I knew his desires had shifted to me; Glyde had sensed it too.

It would be better for both of us if Harriet were restored to health.

16: An Expression of Disbelief

Later I sat at Harriet's dressing table as dusk fell, watching her until she slept, and straining in the fading light to discern the faint pink marks at the base of my throat where Glyde's thumbs had blocked the air. He was a dangerous man, dangerous to me and to others. I winced as I thought of those women and girls, admitted to the workhouse on the brink of starvation, powerless, voiceless, and completely at his disposition.

What to do, when I too was powerless?

I remembered a phrase my father had used, of his appearances in the courts of law: *My voice is my power.*

I had a voice. I might have the ear of the coroner. And if Glyde had expected to bind Doughty to him through Harriet, it seemed to me that that bond had grown weak, indeed was strained to breaking point.

Doughty had not gone out. I closed Harriet's green-velvet curtains, went softly down the stairs and knocked on the study door.

'Enter,' he said.

He sat with his coat flung carelessly over the back of his

chair, the lamp on his desk illuminating the contours of his pale face, his frown etching out the vertical brow-lines above the bridge of his nose. His dark hair was in disorder, his cravat loose and his shirt-neck open above his velvet waistcoat.

He regarded me, his pen still poised in his inky fingers. Irritation at being interrupted gave way to a faint smile.

'Sir, I …' I stood there, not knowing how to begin. 'I must speak to you. It is about the workhouse.'

The smile faded and the way he looked at me, his eyes like dark pools, made me tremble. He too had seen horrors which he kept pent up inside him. He put down his pen.

'Very well,' he said.

I closed the door behind me and stood facing him across his desk, the pewter inkstand between us like a miniature fortress. In the hallway the long-case clock chimed the half-hour.

'Well?'

I hesitated again, wondering if he would believe me.

I put my fingers into my collar and pulled it down an inch or two, baring my throat.

'This is what Reverend Glyde did today.' I ran my fingers over the skin. It was still tender. 'He said I was idle and vicious and seized my throat to choke me.'

I leant forward into the lamplight. Doughty rose and, as his fingertips explored where mine had been, I shivered at his gentleness.

'Let me see the back of your neck.'

I bent my head forward. My hair was tied up under my cap, but there must have been a little free at my nape, which he brushed away. I thought that he might have found the marks of Glyde's fingers there, but he said he could see nothing amiss.

He sat back in his chair, pondering me.

'Did you provoke Reverend Glyde in some way?' he asked.

'I did not.'

'You're claiming that he strangled you? For no reason whatsoever? Are you sure this happened?' His voice was gentle and exploratory, but he was frowning. 'It is impossible for me to believe it.'

I felt deep shame as I met Doughty's eyes, but I willed myself to tell him, to go through with it, to use my voice.

'I thought I was going to die.' I put my hands to my neck where Glyde's had been, reliving the assault. 'He pushed me against the front door, his thumbs here, on my windpipe so that I couldn't breathe. And then …' my hand came up to my lips as if trying to wipe away what I had already scrubbed and rinsed, 'I felt his mouth, his tongue, his beard. I fainted away.'

'It is impossible,' he repeated. 'I know that I was out when he arrived, but Harriet was upstairs. Why did you not cry out?'

'He choked me so suddenly – I did not know that he was going to do it. And then – afterwards – I did not want to upset Mrs Doughty. And I felt so ashamed.' I looked down at my hands, twisting a corner of my handkerchief. 'As if I had done it, and not he.'

'So, if you are ashamed, then why are you telling me?' He was still weighing what I had said and motioned me to sit down.

'You are the coroner.' I took a chair and sat beside the desk, thinking again of my father. 'It is about Theresa Curran. I could not help but overhear what you told Reverend Glyde today. I was in the parlour and dared not interrupt you, in fact I was afraid to come out in case he saw me.'

He protested at my eavesdropping on his conversations – these were strictly confidential matters – and I apologised until he fell silent.

Then I continued. 'I have something else to say.'

He bowed his head in acquiescence.

'I believe that he –' I blurted out, wondering how I could decently express myself.

'What?' he said quietly, his head still bent to the desk.

'Reverend Glyde. He forced her. I was certain it was him after he assaulted me today. If he would harm me in that way, he would do the same to others, and worse. To any female with whom he was alone, and unobserved.'

He looked up at me, incredulous, his dark eyes wide with shock.

'What are you trying to tell me?'

I had twisted my handkerchief into a cord and now wound it around my fingers. It went against my upbringing to say it.

'I am telling you …' I held his stare, composing the sentence in my mind, 'that I believe that Reverend Glyde violated Theresa Curran. She was … pregnant, was she not? I overheard you telling him. I know I should not have listened and I do apologise, but I could not help it. So was her pregnancy the reason for her suicide? After all, she had been ill-treated for all the time that I was in the workhouse.'

For a moment, looking into the depths of his eyes, I thought that he believed me. But at the same time I knew that I was working against a friendship that stood at the heart of his domestic life and his career.

'What evidence do you have?' he asked, at length.

'She was always kept back after Sunday Penances. The penances – we used to go to Glyde and he would whip our hands for punishment. He dismissed everyone else and kept her for the last. For prayers, he said.'

He shook his head. 'I heard that she was a delinquent, wild.'

'That's untrue.' My eyes started to mist over. 'I was watching her die long before she made away with herself.'

I told him how passive and self-denying Theresa had been, going silently to her unmerited punishments, and following Glyde away in the night.

'It's impossible – Vernon would never behave in such a manner.' He frowned, trying to make sense of it. 'You are asking me to believe too much. What if you have a motive to speak ill of the workhouse? I myself saw the workhouse master ill-treating you. I suppose that Reverend Glyde may have punished you himself in the past. What if you have a score to settle? If you are hoping for revenge, let me assure you that I am not going to be your instrument.'

'But I believe he raped her!' It was out, I had used a word that my upbringing had taught me not to utter. 'I'm sorry, but I'm certain of it.'

Doughty still wore an expression of disbelief.

'He is a highly respected clergyman, a leader of our community. What possible proof can you have for this awful allegation? Come now, you are a lawyer's daughter. You know your father's profession. Could you stand up in court and say what you have just said to me?'

My fingers went to my throat. 'I know I have no evidence.'

'It is not possible.' Doughty shook his head. 'I'm sorry, Jane, but the Reverend Glyde is my brother-in-law, he is a trusted friend, he is a man of many virtues, of strong Christian principles. He has been a mentor to me for much of my career, keeping me on the straight and narrow. I cannot believe this of him.'

'But it happened,' I pleaded. 'And Theresa, I believe, no – I *know* – I am certain that Glyde mistreated her, that he forced her, I could tell it from the way that he put his hands on me. He must have used her cruelly. Heaven only knows how deeply she must have suffered. Think of the details of your surgeon's report!'

He assessed me in silence, the lines on his brow and at the corners of his mouth slowly deepening, his hands resting on the edge of the desk and the fingers drumming up and down. Then he shook his head. His fingers stopped and his expression hardened.

'You've been reading my papers. I told you these matters were confidential.'

'No,' I said. 'I heard you speak to Glyde of details that could not be made public, and I can well imagine what they were, but I have not read your papers. I only know what I have seen and overheard. Yet, if my suspicion is supported by your reports, is that not proof? Don't you believe me?'

He was obdurate.

'You cannot expect me to take you at your word on this matter. Your evidence is as non-existent as the marks on your lovely throat.' He folded his arms. 'If you harbour ill will against the Reverend Glyde it is going to become a barrier to you remaining in this house. I may have to ask the Beadle to return you to the workhouse.'

That was like a thunderbolt. If he sent me back to the workhouse with the information that I had spoken out against Glyde, what would they do to me?

'They would beat me to death.' I cupped my face in my hands and closed my eyes. 'You yourself saw Siviter beating me. Now you may imagine the reason.'

He sighed. 'Your assertions, if you persist in them, could not go unpunished.'

'They will put an end to me.' I felt nauseous. The bleak walls of the workhouse courtyard towered up in my mind, the rotting bones, my blood trickling between the cobblestones … I looked up and met his eyes just as I had on that first day. *'Don't send me back.'*

I could see that he feared for me, and that I could at least persuade him on this point.

'Haven't I worked hard in your house, and taken good care of your wife?' I realised that I was fingering the base of my throat as I spoke, feeling for the places where Glyde had hurt me.

Doughty watched me do it. His mouth became soft and tender and I knew well that there was a further reason that he would not send me away.

He heaved a sigh.

'You must say nothing further of these matters. Reverend Glyde's goodwill is as important for me as it is for you.'

17: An Ill-Matched Pair

That night, having at length finished the chores, and washed myself in the scullery, I retired to bed long after Doughty and his wife had bid each other goodnight.

I felt that I was alone against Glyde and Doughty would not support me. Yet I hoped that I had sown in him the seeds of doubt. If there were further cases at the workhouse, he might be more alert to suspicious features. But even if he found clear evidence against Glyde, I was not confident that he would act on it. There was clearly an issue about the inquest fees over which Glyde held some sway. And Glyde himself had discouraged the post-mortem examinations.

I changed into my nightgown and combed out my hair. The comb was one that Edmond had bought me, the day after I had eloped with him, and had lain in my bundle at the workhouse during all those weeks of misery. My thoughts turned to him. By tomorrow at the very latest my letter should have arrived at the Theatre Royal. It might even be in his hand at this very moment. I was sure that it would not be long before he would send for me and rescue me from this difficult situation.

For a moment I attempted to recall Edmond's caresses, hoping to forget the vileness of Glyde. But my present situation pushed my memories to the back of my mind. I could not conjure up Edmond's face and suddenly doubted myself. Were I to pass him in the street, would I know him again? I was ready to weep, but it would not do. The hour was late and I knew that Doughty had to attend the magistrates' court in the morning; I would have to be up early to prepare his breakfast and his hot water.

But as I turned back my bedsheets I heard noises and sat on the edge of the bed to listen. There was someone on the landing downstairs, a tap upon a bedroom door. It was Harriet's voice in the corridor, then the door opened, there were two voices, low and murmuring, Harriet's voice pleading.

There was a silence.

And then, quite distinctly, I heard him say: 'You've been talking to Vernon about this, haven't you? My God, you have!'

Harriet was pleading further, but he was having none of it. She started to sob, then the sound faded into her room. Her bell tinkled out. I suppressed my annoyance, knowing I must go to her, however awkward the situation, and however late the hour, so I put on my night-wrapper and went down the stairs barefoot.

A candle burned on the night-stand and in its dim light I saw Harriet as she climbed back into bed, still trying to cling to her husband, in his nightshirt, who was trying to soothe her and detach her clinging arms at the same time.

'Madam, what is it? Sir?'

'Jane,' she croaked, 'I can't sleep.' But her eyes were losing focus now, with the glassiness of laudanum. She collapsed back on her pillow, releasing her husband. Her hands collapsed at her sides, the fingers still twitching. Her fair hair was in chaos around her face, tears running back from the corners of her eyes, her mouth falling open in unhappy gasps.

'Shall I stay with her, sir?' I stroked Harriet's hair into place with my fingers, looking up at Doughty.

'Yes, if you would be so good, Jane. I have the Court of Petty Sessions first thing in the morning.'

He was suddenly intent on me – my eyes had strayed to where his open nightshirt revealed curling dark hair. Instead of covering up, he stood still, his muscles on display like a racehorse in a painting. He maintained his gaze and it was only when I looked down at Harriet that he switched his attention to his wife.

'Dearest,' he said, with deliberate gentleness, 'you need to get a better physician.'

'But Dr Astley-Scrope is so kind,' she whispered. 'He comes whenever I send for him. And a good Christian, so devout.'

I dabbed at her tears with a handkerchief.

'He is an old charlatan,' said Doughty, still standing like a thoroughbred, 'and doctors of his ilk keep my inquest juries busy. I know that he does not keep abreast of medical endeavour. If you had a better physician and took less laudanum, we might …'

'I'm sorry, my darling,' she pleaded, 'I'm sorry. Oh please …' Her eyelids fluttered half-shut.

'Sir, please, don't disturb her,' I said. 'She will sleep if you let me mind her.'

Doughty pulled his nightshirt closed and folded his arms over it, as though suddenly cold.

'I shall leave you in peace then, my dear.' He leaned forward and kissed the top of Harriet's head. 'Sleep and you will feel better in the morning. And you must please consider a change of doctor. Jane, look after your mistress, but don't forget my hot water at seven.'

I nodded acquiescence and he left, closing the door behind him.

'My Aethereal Balsam, Jane,' said Harriet at once, even though she appeared drugged already.

'But, madam,' I objected, 'you have already had your bedtime dose.'

'Dr Astley-Scrope has said that I may increase the dose if I need to. He said I could go up to twelve drops and I have only had eight, so that means I can have another four. It brings quietude. Otherwise, I have much on my mind: my responsibilities as a wife, and a chatter of secrets and memories that keeps me awake.'

I duly gave her the four drops and sat wearily watching her silent face, thinking about her husband. He should have covered himself. I should have looked away, but there is only so long that a woman can resist. We are not as different from men as they would have us believe.

I wrenched my thoughts instead to Edmond, and imagined what happiness we might once have had, unlike this ill-matched pair. A house up in Islington perhaps, away from the noise and clamour of London, with a garden where Nathan might have run, and I would have been free of this life of drudgery to amuse and instruct him, and to work on my music. In the gloom beside Harriet's bed I struggled to maintain my hopes and allowed bitterness to overwhelm me. In truth, Edmond had always had the ability to assist me, had he but devoted a small portion of his extravagances to keeping me from the workhouse.

After a while Harriet started to drowse. I watched her eyelids droop and the eyeballs roving underneath. Harriet's secrets and memories, whatever they were, had fallen like snow to the bottom of her mind. Why did she marry, I wondered, and I felt again some pity for Doughty in his loneliness.

I put out the candle, and went up at last to my own bed, passing as silently as I could outside Doughty's door.

It was past the hour when I could sleep deeply, exhausted though I was, and I found my eyes opening at every creak of the floorboards, although I had checked more than once that my door was locked. I must have dozed towards morning, and dreamt of Theresa Curran, mutely comforting me as she had never done in life, mingling her sorrows with mine as I wept bitterly for my son.

I woke, exhausted, feeling that my heart had been hollowed out.

18: Glyde's Letter to Harriet

Friday 10th April, 1840

The Rectory
St Michael's Church
Birmingham

My Dearest Sister,

If it does not inconvenience you, I should be most grateful if you would do me the favour of allowing me to call upon you again later on this morning? I am most anxious to be appraised of your state of health and to join with you in prayer for your prompt recovery. There is also a further matter for me to discuss with William, assuming that he is returning home for his luncheon.

Kindly advise me of the same by return. My servant will bring me your reply.

Yours most affectionately,
Vernon

19: A Dangerous Vote

Harriet was determined to appear well, so in the morning after Doughty had left to attend the court, she made me dress her and braid her hair and help her to move slowly downstairs clinging to the banisters. By the late morning, which was early for her, I settled her in an armchair in the parlour with her embroidery. The church kneeler was half-completed.

My morning chores were done so I offered to play the piano for her again and felt my fingers regaining their suppleness as I played from memory a simple melody. She seemed to enjoy it, and as she stitched away I wondered whether she was starting to accept me as her companion rather than merely as a housemaid. I might have helped to lift her out of her depression.

But I soon had to stop, for there was someone at the door and I found the Glyde's maid, Mary, with a note. I had her wait in the hall and took the note in to Harriet.

She opened it and clapped her hands with glee.

'Tell him to come at once,' she said, 'and that I am feeling better and out of bed. And, as he wishes to meet William, he will be able to do so at lunchtime.' She told me to get things ready in the kitchen.

I relayed the message to Mary. Her hands were hidden in her shawl, and to me she appeared drawn, and much thinner, but she insisted that she was well.

As Harriet waited for her brother she became anxious that he would not come. Then her mood plunged into despair and dark thoughts. She talked, half to me and half to herself, of death and the little that she would leave behind. Her secrets would die with her and Doughty would not mourn her when she was gone. I tried to draw her out of her melancholia, distracting her with her embroidery, taking over the work as she wearied and dozed. I stitched in half an hour what Harriet would have taken half a day to finish. The blue kneeler in Berlin wool-work was going to be for St Michael's Church: its flying cherubs bore, not a crucifix, but a golden sword. It was now nearly complete.

She woke in a better mood, pleased by the progress in her sewing, for which I gave her the credit even as I replaced the embroidery in her lap.

'Go quickly!' she exclaimed, at Glyde's knock at the front door. 'Do not keep him waiting.'

Was she afraid of him too? I left the parlour door ajar, so that as I admitted him Harriet called out. As I backed swiftly along the hall he had to give me his hat and coat and greet her from where she could see him.

They sent me for tea, and I was unable to overhear any conversation, but later as they were drinking it I heard Doughty come home for lunch. I went up to wait on him. He was clearly in an ill temper, with a face like a thundercloud, divesting himself of his hat and coat as if he hated them.

He stopped still when I told him that Reverend Glyde had called upon Mrs Doughty.

'I believe there is also something that he wished to discuss with you.' I indicated the parlour door.

'Is there, indeed?' He flung it open and stood in the doorway. 'Vernon?'

Glyde responded with a cheerful greeting but Doughty merely pointed at him, not even troubling to close the door.

'I understand that you put a vote to the Magistrates of the Bench on whether to remove me from office! And I saw you only yesterday, and you said nothing of it!'

Harriet gave out a gasp of shock.

'He promised,' Doughty jabbed his finger towards Glyde, 'that he would always support me, you know it. And now this!'

'*But he has!*' cried Harriet. 'You would not even have your position, had it not been for him. It must be a mistake.'

'A vote – it will be in the newspaper for everyone to read – a vote about removing me from office! Not only have my fees have been disallowed, but a vote?'

'Vernon?' came Harriet's pleading cry.

'Brother!' Glyde's reply was musical, his tone placid and sweet. 'My dear brother, you have misconstrued my intentions – I merely thought to clear the air. They were so unhappy about your fees, particularly for the surgeons. I only asked them if they would have preferred a legal man.'

'Legal?'

'But, fortunately, they still supported your tenure. It has cleared the air, although there were some who voted against. It was only a show of hands.'

'I'm overwhelmed with gratitude,' Doughty snorted.

'But what of William's fees?' Harriet interrupted. 'I did not know about this. He said nothing. How will we meet our expenses? My physician's bills? Vernon, you must do something.'

'I will speak in his favour,' replied Glyde evenly, 'but there must be a move away from post-mortem examinations. The magistrates do not support them.'

'But how am I to fulfil the responsibilities to which I was appointed?'

Glyde replied that Doughty's responsibilities did not include ruining his own career. He should remember that there were a number of members of the Board of Workhouse Guardians who were also Magistrates of the Bench, and that if next week Doughty was intending to present to them certain information that was too disgusting for the public to hear, then he would advise him to desist for the sake of his own professional reputation.

'I am on the verge of completing a lengthy report,' protested Doughty, 'and how can the Siviters be allowed to continue in their posts?'

Glyde said at once that the Siviters were of the highest integrity. He would be hard pressed to replace them if they were forced out of their position. Doughty should not interfere in matters of which he had no experience and which were not his responsibility, when he had already developed a reputation in the town, and amongst the magistrates, for exceeding his remit.

'For the future you need to relinquish your interest in paupers and concentrate on the more normal duties of a coroner.'

Doughty advanced into the parlour, slamming the door behind him. I heard raised voices but thought it prudent to return to the kitchen as sooner or later one of them might emerge in a fury and find me listening behind the door.

Then the parlour bell rang.

Unwilling to move, I watched it quivering on the end of its spring until it fell silent. It rang again. When I went up to them, the men had fallen quiet. Doughty sat in an armchair, gripping the arms and scowling at the floor.

'I am feeling faint,' said Harriet. Her eyes were half closed. 'I think it must be the heat. Would you help me, Jane, to go upstairs and lie down for a few minutes?'

Doughty glared at Glyde and informed him that it was time for lunch.

'Perhaps I should return home,' Glyde replied.

Harriet's eyelids fluttered open.

'No, not at all, I shall be recovered, and back downstairs in a very short time. Jane, please.'

I helped Harriet to her feet and across the parlour floor. She stumbled as she got to the door, hanging on my arm. Doughty remained where he was but Glyde sprang up.

'Allow me.' He was at Harriet's elbow immediately, supporting her into the hallway and up the stairs.

I made to follow them, but he shooed me back from the foot of the stairs.

'I can manage. Here, Harriet, dear, hold the banister – there you are – steady now.'

They progressed slowly upwards as Doughty emerged from the parlour.

'I shall eat at the Dog and Duck,' he said, and grabbing his hat and coat he marched out of the house, slamming the front door.

I turned back towards the kitchen.

Then I heard a strange noise on the stairs. A sigh. Silence. Their footsteps had stopped. Feeling an ugly suspicion, I slowly tilted my head around the architrave.

They were on the half-landing beside the tall window. Harriet was no longer clinging to the banister, but stood upright, her head arched back. Glyde held her waist in his hands, and was savagely kissing her lips, her ears, her throat, her chin, her bosom.

'I love you, Vernon,' Harriet whimpered. 'I love you. I am so sorry for everything. Only believe that I love you …'

They were oblivious of me.

'Seraph … evil ... beautiful … seraph …' he hissed between kisses.

I drew back into the kitchen stairway and retreated as quietly as I could, creeping slowly down the treads so that they did not creak.

I closed the kitchen door and leaned back against it.

'How could she!' I whispered. *'How could she!'*

This, then, was Harriet's disease.

For how long had they deceived the world? And Doughty? No wonder Harriet was so cold to him, and he ready to look elsewhere. Yet he could have no idea. He was deliberately blind to the monstrous nature of his brother-in-law. Would this new rift between them yet open his eyes?

My instinct to disabuse Doughty was checked by consideration of my own position. What if he refused to believe me, or worse, he challenged Harriet and received, as he must, a denial? They would say that I had seen something that I had misunderstood, an expression of innocent affection and nothing more. Doughty would say that it was a further expression of the grudge I held against Glyde. How could I prove otherwise? I might be returned to the workhouse to face a cruel retribution.

I should have moved myself. I should have been cleaning the kitchen floor, black-leading the grate in the dining room, and checking the rat-traps in the back yard. But I stood with the door at my back, staring ahead of me, and wondering how I would conduct myself when it was time to see Glyde out.

In the end I shut myself in the scullery with the laundry, trying not to think of anything. I must behave as though I had seen nothing. It was some hours before Harriet's bell rang.

I went up to her room. Thankfully Glyde had gone.

She lay on her side with her face to her pillow, her full skirts crumpled, and the bedcovers in disarray. One of the pillows was on the floor, and I picked it up and put it back on the bed.

'My Aethereal Balsam, Jane, please,' she said quietly.

She had been crying, for her eyelids were swollen. Her vices did not make her happy.

I fetched the medication and dosed Harriet. Twenty drops. She retched on the bitterness.

'You will need some more of this in a few days, ma'am,' I warned.

'Dr Astley-Scrope says he will issue a new prescription whenever I send to ask for it. You only have to apply to his surgery, you know, on Bennett's Hill.'

'I know,' I said. 'I went there the other day to fetch him.'

'Oh yes,' said Harriet. 'I had forgot. Thank you.' Her face became vague; she belched out ether.

'Shall I help you with your nightclothes, ma'am?'

It was only six o'clock, but Harriet acquiesced, and I helped her rise and change into her nightclothes.

She flinched as I brushed her hair down over her shoulders.

'I'm so sorry, ma'am.' I lifted the curtain of fair hair aside. There was a red mark at the angle of Harriet's neck, no, a pair of red semicircles, making an oval the size of a plum. 'You're bleeding, I'll get some liniment.'

In Doughty's dressing room there was a lotion he used when he cut himself shaving: Rowland's Kalydor. I paused there, inhaling the familiar, reassuring scent of Low's cologne, and for a moment I closed my eyes. I had seen the same mark on Theresa, more than once; sometimes she had several of them.

Harriet winced at the touch of the liniment and wrinkled up her eyes.

'I'm sorry,' I said, and I felt truly sorry for her.

I stoppered the bottle of Kalydor and returned to gently stroking the silver hairbrush through her pale hair. I met Harriet's eyes in the mirror: sad, violet eyes.

'I live for my brother,' Harriet said. 'I am only happy when he is here, and when he leaves I am bereft. I live for the time when I will next be able to gaze on his dear face.'

I brushed through the fine, fair strands, watching them lie against each other and then separate with each stroke of the hairbrush. I had once, in another time, another world, felt that for Edmond.

'All my life, since I was a small child, I have lived for him. I was his special, sweet sister, ever since he first sat me on his knee to read the Scriptures to me. He is devoted to me and deserves nothing less than my total love and obedience.'

'Naturally, ma'am,' I said, resisting the thought of the young Harriet sitting on her brother's knee.

'Although nothing improper has ever occurred between us, you must understand.'

A denial that was almost an admission of guilt: why else would she feel the need to mention such a thing with regard to her brother?

'It is the purest of passions.' A tear quivered at the edge of an eyelid and trickled down her cheek. 'It is so lonely to be away from him. Especially now that I feel my life is ebbing away.'

'Ma'am,' I protested, softly, 'if you were to find a better doctor you might recover. Your husband often says so. You should obey your husband.'

'No.' Harriet frowned. 'He knows only of the dead. Ask him why my baby died. He could not save her. What help can he be to me?'

'He is still a medical man. Perhaps he can find you another physician?'

'Vernon says that Dr Astley-Scrope is the best physician in Birmingham. He has no confidence in anyone else. I dare not change.'

I knew that my advice would not countermand Glyde's.

I helped Harriet get back into bed, smoothing the covers.

'You will play the piano for me, Jane,' said Harriet. 'You play very well.'

I thanked her. 'I once had hopes of playing professionally, madam,' I said. 'But it is not easy for a woman in the theatre. Is there a piece that you would like to hear?'

'Can you play a nocturne? I have the folio down there in the bookcase, but it's too difficult for me. I would like to hear it. I am sure I could hear it from my room.' Her bedchamber was directly above the piano in the parlour downstairs. 'It would console me.'

Doughty was back in his study when I went downstairs. I knocked at his door and put my head around it to tell him that Harriet had asked me to play the piano for her and that I hoped it would not disturb him. He acknowledged it with a nod and continued writing.

I paused for a moment, looking at his head bent to his work. I could have told him what I had seen. But I closed the door quietly, went into the parlour and sat down at the Broadwood piano. I knew that I could not say anything. He had not believed me about Theresa. I would just be adding to his disfavour.

I found the nocturne on the shelves and read through the once-familiar staves. It was one of Chopin's that I had practised many times in my former life. My own melancholy, and regrets for all I had lost, rose up in my heart as I started to play the delicate notes.

As the melody strengthened, I hoped that Harriet was still listening and that the music would help her to find some resolution for herself, to lessen her unhealthy attachment, and with it reduce her dependence on her medications. But I sensed also that Glyde had her in thrall; he had a chokehold on her spirit.

I concluded to applause: a series of steady, loud claps came from the direction of the study. I smiled to myself. Despite a long absence from the piece, I had not misplayed a single note of it, and had infused the music with the subtleties it merited: with echoes of wasted love, of fading memories and of nostalgia for past times.

When I went back up to Harriet she was snoring, curled up with her secrets like a lizard in its egg.

20: Court of Petty Sessions, Birmingham

From the *Birmingham Gazette*,
Friday 10th April

THE CORONER FOR BIRMINGHAM, Dr William Doughty, appeared before a bench of seven magistrates, in regard to his claims for reimbursement.

The Chief of the Bench, Sir Thomas Pountney, stated that coroner's fees, particularly in respect of post-mortem examinations, had doubled since Dr Doughty's appointment and had now increased beyond the means of the court to pay them. Under the new laws, Dr Doughty received a guinea per case. The surgeon was paid a guinea for his dissection, and a guinea for his evidence, two fees for the same post-mortem, which could not be countenanced.

The post-mortem examination was moreover an unnatural, grotesque, and indeed barbaric practice, which desecrated the deceased and created a burden, not only on the public purse, but on the bereaved, who must endure the mangling of their beloved dead.

Sir Thomas Pountney rejected Dr Doughty's claim that the post-mortem examination was a scientific investigation into the cause of death. There were far too many inquests where the verdict was merely Natural Causes such as apoplexy, fever, or a death in childbirth. Dr Doughty asked the Court to consider those who were killed by poison or by stealth, or medical mistreatment. Without an inquest with a medical man, they would go unchallenged. Sir Thomas Pountney countered that unnecessary post-mortem examinations had been held that did not alter the verdict. One recent case had even been a pauper who had taken her own life in the workhouse. These unfortunates were beyond the help of a doctor, yet Dr Doughty's surgical associates had pocketed generous fees.

Dr Doughty maintained that the surgeon's report had identified certain details, which he did not want to make public, but which were of a very serious nature in regard to the welfare of the inmates and would be discussed with the Board of Workhouse Guardians in due course.

A further obstacle put to Dr Doughty, however, was the case of Rutter v. Chapman. Mr. Rutter, the Lancashire Coroner, had raised a dispute with Mr Chapman, the coroner for the newly incorporated Borough of Manchester, over who had the right to take a certain case. This dispute has remained unresolved and is now before the Court of the Exchequer Chamber in London.

Like our Borough of Birmingham, Manchester was incorporated by Royal Charter, two years ago. While Her Majesty had granted the Charter, she did not compile the list of ratepayers. The dispute in the Exchequer Chamber had come to this: was it lawful for Her Majesty to empower the Town Clerk to decide which inhabitants must pay the rates? If not, then the newly incorporated boroughs: Manchester, Bolton, and Birmingham, might in law not exist. Mr Chapman's appointment in Manchester, and by extension, that of Dr Doughty as Borough Coroner for Birmingham, would then have no legal basis.

Sir Thomas Pountney observed that at present the churchwardens were refusing to collect the rates in case they had not the legal right. The whole business of the Borough, including the Law Courts, was supported by Treasury loans from London. Even these loans may be illegal: the Government cannot lend money to an entity that has no legal right to exist.

Dr Doughty expressed incredulity and stated that in his opinion if lawyers could prove a falsehood to be true they were happier in their cleverness than if they upheld an obvious truth, and that no profession was so devoid of reason and common sense.

At this point Dr Doughty was reminded that his position was dependent upon the goodwill of the same lawyers. Indeed, at the suggestion of the Reverend Vernon Glyde, the magistrates had on the previous day debated the power of the court to remove him from office and call a new election for his successor. As Dr Doughty's appointment was in doubt and in view of the high cost of his services, it was arguable that his post might be better fulfilled by a legal man.

The magistrates' bench would however have had to petition the Lord Chancellor in London and, after a vote, this step had not been agreed. For now Dr Doughty was requested to be more circumspect and consider the condition of the borough's finances before embarking upon post-mortem examinations. His invoices were disallowed for the remainder of this quarter.

21: Pride and Humility

'Pride is the progenitor of all of the Seven Deadly Sins. In believing the self to be superior to others, lacking humility to God, the sinner sinks into gluttony, greed, lust, envy, accidie, and wrath ...'

Gluttony. It must have been lunchtime by now, and I was fretting to get back to the kitchen. I had left the range lit, in the hope that it would be at the right heat for the Sunday roast on our return, but the Reverend Vernon Glyde's voice still resonated through St Michael's Church. He had described at length the Passion: Christ's Entry into Jerusalem, His Cleansing of the Temple, His Anointing, the Last Supper, His Agony in the Garden of Gethsemane, His Betrayal by Judas Iscariot, His Trial before Pontius Pilate and His Suffering and Crucifixion. Glyde was now elaborating on the sins which we had only a week to expurgate before arriving for Easter Communion in a state of grace.

It was Palm Sunday, the last Sunday of Lent, and a bare wooden cross stood on the altar where a wrought silver one ought to have been; the altar cloth was of brown hessian and Glyde's robes were of a severe black relieved only by his white preaching bands.

For the first time since my arrival in the house Harriet had felt well enough to attend church. So on that Sunday morning, instead of the usual routine of Doughty writing in his study while I saw to Harriet and prepared the lunch, we had all issued forth at the ringing of St Michael's bells, myself following my employers at a discreet distance. It was a dry, cold day and Harriet had lent me a worsted cape to cover my servant's clothes. She wore a black silk pelisse, with the wings of her poke bonnet keeping her face in the dark.

I had not been to a service since the Evensong that was held on Sundays in the workhouse refectory. Nor would I have chosen to go, knowing that Glyde would be conducting it. Around us were all the good souls of the neighbourhood. In this congregation everyone knew everyone else and the wives kept up the flow of gossip: if you slighted the butcher, the baker would know of it within the hour and it would be reported back to you by the candlestick-maker the following day.

'Therefore, never forget that you are Adam's children, and merely dust in the eyes of Our Lord. Be humble and, in your humility, respect those who are in authority and who deliver unto you the word of the Lord!'

Damn him, I thought, allowing myself a moment of Wrath. Let him be damned to the dust, with his vile face bulging as he preaches the self-sacrifice of Lent yet indulges in secret his cruelties and gross appetites to the full.

The church was packed and I was sitting at the far end of a pew beside Harriet, who, held erect by her corset, followed every word of the service, quietly chiming in when her brother intoned a biblical passage and muttering *'Amen'* under her breath. Doughty on her other side was hunched forward, his arms folded. His black-silk top hat was upturned on the floor in front of him, and he had jerked his head awake, and seemingly read the maker's label twenty times.

'Thus it was, and is, and shall ever be … and through our pain, and suffering, and grief, and sacrifice, we shall find the Holy Spirit. We shall shed our blood, and tear our hands in toil. Our sins shall be washed away, as though exposed to the ravages of the wild ocean. Then, we shall find our Lord Jesus, and we shall kneel, and abase ourselves before the might of our Lord God!'

Glyde spread his arms wide, and his black sleeves hung like lifeless wings.

'Father, the hour is come! Glorify Thy Son, that Thy Son also may glorify Thee!'

Somewhere up above, a cloud must have drifted aside from the sun, for a window brightened, illuminating Glyde's red-gold hair, and his red face, and the Palm Sunday branches on the pedestals on either side of him, as though Heaven wished to lend him some glory.

I made a bitter face, as though my mouth were full of gall.

'Let us rise and sing hymn Number Eighty-four.'

The organ started to drone obediently and the congregation rose, shuffled and coughed, stretching limbs that had stiffened on hard pews for the length of a sermon.

Above the brass eagle of the pulpit, Glyde led the hymn, his voice soaring, his chest puffed out, pushing his lips proudly around a note, his forehead veins engorged.

Harriet nudged her husband.

'You're not singing!' she hissed.

He sighed and joined in, putting a penny in the offertory plate, and no doubt waiting for it all to be over.

'Lord, now lettest Thou Thy servant depart in peace, according to Thy word. For mine eyes have seen Thy salvation!'

I felt my belly rumble as Glyde led out the churchwardens and choir with stately slowness.

There was a queue to get out.

Doughty supported Harriet on his arm, as they proceeded down the aisle.

Glyde stood at the church door, receiving the respects of his congregation.

'A good sermon, sir,' said Doughty. 'Very good. Humility. We must all of us be humble, all of us Adam's children. Very important, eh, to treat the lower orders well? *Inasmuch as ye have done it unto one of the least of my brethren, ye have done it unto me.*'

Harriet plucked at Doughty's sleeve, as if to pull him away from where the sour tone of his comment hung in mid-air like an unwanted body smell.

But Glyde displayed no reaction to the remark.

'Coroner Doughty, my dear Harriet.' He radiated a vague warmth. 'You appeared quite fatigued this morning, sir. The heavy burdens of a medical man? Working long hours, and late into the night, writing your post-mortem reports? Ah, Mrs Edwards, Mr Edwards …' Passing over me completely, the rays of Glyde's smile illuminated the next in line.

We crossed the churchyard and walked along Colmore Row very slowly, with Harriet struggling breathlessly against the slight gradient like a bird flying into a gale. There was less soot in the air on a Sunday, and it ought to have been easier as they turned the corner into Newhall Street, and started to descend the hill, but she dragged upon his arm.

'Please, William, do not walk so fast!' she gasped.

'I'm sorry, my dear,' he said, and slowed to a pallbearer's pace.

I came to a virtual stop behind them. Newhall Street was busy and the bells of St Michael's faded under the clatter of horse-carts.

'Not far now,' he said. He looked down at her, but his view of her face must have been impeded by her bonnet.

They walked on with infinite slowness. Now he was the one with an upright back, while she was the one who slumped. I found myself watching the set of his shoulders in the fine black wool of his frock coat, and dropped behind a little, so that instead I looked down the hill and beyond the canal and the foundry chimneys, across to where the estates of the wealthy lay upon the rising ground to the north-west.

Doughty walked on patiently at his wife's side.

I wondered at his quoting the gospel at Glyde today: was it a chance remark, or had he begun to believe me?

22: Quarterly Meeting of the Board of Guardians of the Poor

From the *Birmingham Gazette*

A meeting was held at the Birmingham Parish Union Workhouse, Lichfield Street, at 9 o'clock on Thursday 16th April 1840.

Accounts were prepared and read by Mr Adrian Eggington. Expenditure in the last quarter has almost doubled particularly on inmates' diet, and on outdoor relief. Mr Madden, Relieving Officer of the Parish Union, noted that the number of inmates has increased from 215 to 269 and of those in receipt of outdoor relief from 186 to 349, due to an influx of paupers from outside of the parish. He makes every effort to turn them away but it is almost impossible as they arrive in a desperate situation.

The Birmingham Coroner, Dr William Doughty, attended the meeting at this juncture and begged leave to present a report following the inquest held on 5th March regarding an unfortunate female inmate who died by her own hand. This report contained details of the surgeon's post-mortem examination, which were not suitable to be made public.

Reverend Vernon Glyde, as Chairman of the Board, advised the Guardians that he had privately read the coroner's report, which gave details of a most gruesome dissection and were of a revolting and disgusting nature. He was of the opinion that it did not increase understanding of the case of the unfortunate deceased, which had already been concluded some weeks previously and, time being short and other pressing matters requiring the attention of the Guardians, he advised that the Board need not concern themselves further with the details.

The Reverend Glyde further advised there was no reason to question the integrity of Mr and Mrs Siviter, the Master and Matron of the Workhouse, who carried out their disagreeable duties with the utmost alacrity, and in whom he reposed complete confidence. In this he received the unanimous support of the Board of Guardians.

Dr Doughty accordingly withdrew from the meeting and there ensued a review of dietary arrangements in conjunction with a report from the Workhouse Medical Officer Dr Wright. Dr Wright reported that over the last quarter the commonest cause of mortality was frailty, the average age of inmates having increased from fifty-three to sixty-two years. A greater proportion of inmates were now excused from manual labour due to feebleness and poor health and therefore their nutritional requirements were smaller. Therefore it was agreed to reduce expenditure on dietary items by 100 L for the next quarter, as it was imperative for economies to be made.

Meeting concluded at 10 o'clock.

23: Worlds Apart

I had suspected that the meeting with the Board of Guardians would not go well for Doughty and was not surprised to hear the front door slam as he returned at lunchtime. He thundered down the back stairs. I had been baking that morning and I supposed that he found the smell of food a consolation. When I emerged from the scullery, drying my hands on my apron, he was already sitting down at the kitchen table with a slice of chicken pie in his hand.

'I would have brought that up to you, had you rung, sir,' I protested, fetching him a plate and fork, and a glass of water.

He licked his fingers noisily before taking them.

'Your pastry is improving,' he said, while his eyes seemed to appraise my waist.

I thanked him. 'I never made pastry before I came here. But I have noticed that you enjoy your pies.'

He deliberately wiped his mouth with the palm of his hand.

'You play the piano very well, Jane,' he said.

'Thank you, sir.' I straightened up and stood still, hands folded together, watchful.

'Mr Graves told me that you became a theatrical pianist,' he mused. 'I was at medical college in London – Bart's. Not far from you perhaps. He told me that your father has his chambers at Gray's Inn.'

I nodded. 'My parents lived near there – on Bedford Street … just a short walk from St Bartholomew's.'

'Lived? Are they dead?'

'Live. They still live there.' I felt a flush overspread my face. 'They will always live there.'

'You miss them. And you are so young.' He studied me with renewed interest, as if a hen-sparrow had hopped in from the street and a gilded feather had flashed beneath her dusty wing. 'Will they truly not take you back? Why do you not write to them, instead of to that … to your …' He made a kind of grimace; he did not want to mention Edmond's name.

'They will not admit me to their house. Even Papa has asked me not to write. I am what they call "ruined".' I turned away, my throat tense. 'And, there it is, I shan't see my parents again. I have entered a world apart.'

I waited for my eyes to clear, staring at the dresser with its brown clay jugs. They were dusty again: soot from the range outlined their crudely moulded hunting scenes. I would have to clean them.

'Lawyers cause more problems than they solve, in my experience,' he said eventually.

I turned back to him and repeated something my father used to say: 'We must have the law, we must have justice, how else should we live?'

He raised his eyebrows. 'Perhaps we will have to live without: I'm told that the town of Birmingham cannot afford to run its law courts.'

I could not resist. 'I read about Rutter v. Chapman, sir, in the newspaper. Are the churchwardens still refusing to collect the rates?'

'Indeed, and the Council has the law courts to fund, and the prison, as well as my services. The town is scraping by on Treasury Loans which may soon have to be repaid.' He looked straight into my eyes. 'So there is no money, and at present the magistrates are withholding my fees, much to my wife's disgust.'

He had finished eating and now rested his elbows on the table, staring into his water glass with his shoulders hunched.

I placed my hands on the chair-back opposite. 'You work too hard, sir, with your hours too long, and too little time at leisure.'

'Too little payment, that's the concern.' He hesitated, with his gaze lingering on my fingers. 'My wife regrets that I am a coroner, rather than running a fashionable practice. I should have a list of wealthy manufacturers, but instead I am the physician to the dead.'

'But yours is a respectable position, sir. Do you truly regret taking it up?'

'Presiding over such a court, Jane? Do you know where I hold my inquests?'

I shook my head.

'Your world apart, as you term it, is not so different to mine, Jane. My court is a ragged court – held in the back rooms of public houses, in the prison, in the workhouse. There are no strutting barristers and anyone may attend, so that even the meanest beggar may testify before me. My cases may be those of the poor, the helpless or the insane: the workman killed by machinery, the woman killed by her husband, infants exposed and left to die – *the least of these my brethren*.' His face was alive, and he spoke of his work with passion, barely registering my response. 'The pauper in the workhouse, the murdered and the merely unfortunate, the ruined and the damned; in death they are all one. I delve into the secrets of their lives, Jane, and what I find has no place in polite conversation, nor indeed, it seems, at the Board of the Workhouse Guardians.'

He spoke those last words bitterly and I dared to draw him out.

'What happened today?'

'The report about Theresa Curran, that Graves and I had spent so much effort to prepare, that was for their eyes only, was not discussed.'

'May I ask why?'

'Glyde.' Doughty leant back in his chair with his arms folded and glowered at the table.

I waited for him to say more, but his mouth was now clamped shut.

'Sir …' I ventured.

'I have said too much.' At that he pushed his plate away and got up. 'Thank you, Jane.'

He went into the scullery to rinse his hands and emerged, wiping them on a tea towel.

'I appreciate your honesty,' he said. 'I may continue to argue against it, but I have not forgotten what you told me. Our problem is a lack of evidence that would stand up in court. It will not be possible to take the matter any further.'

With that he went upstairs.

I sat down on the chair that he had vacated. My heart was thumping.

Our problem …

He had, perhaps, started to trust me. But how would I ever dare to tell him what I had witnessed on the stairs?

In the days that followed I was somewhat relieved that we avoided further discussion. Doughty had no more inquests at the workhouse and his cases seemed to be mostly accidents and industrial injuries.

Even though it was Easter, Glyde did not visit, and I was increasingly occupied with Harriet and her ailments. From time to time, I was still able to sit at the piano. I purchased sheet music in the town on my way back from Bright's and played for Harriet, dreaming all the while that one day I would return to a wider audience.

24: Theatre Notice

From *Bell's Life in London & Sporting Chronicle,*
Saturday 2nd May 1840

AT THE THEATRE ROYAL, Drury Lane, London, in its 10th week by Overwhelming Public Demand: Mr Davenant presents THE PURPLE ROBE. Mr. Edmond Verity terrifies as the Turkish Tyrant, and Miss Maud Frith (soon to be Mrs Verity!) as the tragic Odalisque, enchants the audience with her voice and beauty. Performances at 7 p.m.

25: An Inconstant Love

So Doughty had been right to say that I should not have written to Edmond, who had truly abandoned me, and forgotten me just as though I had never existed. The notice in the newspaper was two weeks old. I had found it beside the coalhole. No news had come from Edmond; I had written to him that the flame of my love had never burned out, but in truth that flame was now anger, not affection. My heart was riven by a stone-hammer of jealousy. Edmond would not return. No doubt he had held my letter up to the catcalls of his drunken friends, whilst enjoying a new love.

Maud Frith, of course. In *The Imprisoned Contessa* she had played the title role, with Edmond in the role of the evil but dashing baron, attempting to seduce her and possess himself of her fortune. Undeniably, a tension had existed between them on stage that made the audience hold its breath.

I had watched her flirting with Edmond on the train the previous October, as the theatre company travelled from London to Birmingham. Our trunk was heaven-knew-where, and I had been wedged between Edmond and the sooty window, in a first-class compartment gleaming with brass and red velvet, with Maud sitting opposite us, and beside her Mr Davenant. I had never been on the railway before and had heard that one could be injured by travelling so fast – at thirty, some said forty, miles per hour. As we had left Euston Station, the train had at first creaked slowly along, but then shrieked and bumped to a halt. A monstrous clattering and banging made me startle and cry out, fearing an accident, but Edmond said that the train had been hauled up an incline by a rope and a static engine, and was now being coupled to the locomotive. He had explained it kindly enough, but I felt foolish, like a child, and Maud smirked.

There was a noise as of grinding metal and then the vehicle seemed possessed of a new life, a humming vibration, and I heard the harsh panting of the engine as we started to move again. We rolled past streets where the ends of terraces had been torn down to make way for the new iron road, then after an expanse of market gardens we were into the countryside proper, the fields and water meadows of Hertfordshire, the trees gilded with autumn colours and glowing in the sun.

My dress was tight around my widening belly and my bosom was barely covered by the gaudy cloth. Over it I had a travelling pelisse lined with sable and I pulled it close, feeling the fur brushing my skin.

With a loud clattering, the train entered a tunnel, plunging us into complete darkness that seemed to continue forever while coal smoke filled our compartment.

I coughed and gasped. Edmond laughed.

'Nothing to be frightened of, my dear.' His hand slipped under the sable, inside the neckline of my dress.

Perhaps he had meant a tender caress, but it felt intrusive. The clattering of the train lessened and a faint light grew in the carriage as we neared the end of the tunnel. The smoke was clearing. Edmond withdrew his hand and pressed his lips briefly to mine, breaking away from me as the train once again entered open countryside.

Maud was watching us, her lovely mouth curled in amusement.

'Are you enjoying the ride, Jane? Stimulating, is it not?'

I gave her a half-hearted smile and turned to watch the landscape slide past the window. She turned her attention to Edmond, and began entertaining him with some sort of anecdote, enlivened with arch looks heavy with innuendo. She was a dazzling woman, tall, with red hair and white skin, huge blue eyes, and dark eyebrows and eyelashes. I had listened to her voice filling a theatre and reducing the most rowdy audience to a hush, but now I could not hear what she was saying above the clatter of the carriage. Edmond's attention slipped away from me entirely as he leaned across. He and Maud were soon chuckling together. I knew that it was better not to show jealousy, but to smile and be complaisant, for Edmond could not tolerate what he termed my 'vapours'.

The train then entered a deep cutting, the rock-face bearing thousands of scratches made by labourers' picks. Edmond settled back beside me but, against his pressure was another, the tiny flutter within me of his child. I had not yet had the courage to tell him and feared what he would say: I had heard him speak of women being *in the family way* with disdain.

I had leant against the sooty glass and pretended to sleep, but between my lashes I had watched Maud with her slender erect figure, her cold white skin, and the sharp angle of her mouth as she sweetened her smile for Edmond.

Now, as I stared at the newspaper with futile hatred, for a moment I wished them both dead. I imagined Maud glittering with false diamonds and with her red hair glowing, in a gorgeous ball-gown, and her gloved hand resting on Edmond's arm. A ballgown of rose silk, which did not become her. Maud, who had long desired to steal Edmond from me, triumphant in her victory. Maud with her coquettish ways and her sharp tongue, without whom Edmond would have remained true, and Nathan might have had the chance of a life. As for Edmond, the '*Turkish Tyrant*', I wondered if he perceived any boundary between his characters and himself. I had been fooled by his playacting; he dazzled, but there was no substance to him.

There was no help for it now, no point in blaming either of them. I devoted myself to my work. As they had said in the workhouse: it was the only path to salvation.

I gave up the piano and day after day, with my jaws clenched in anger and despair, I scrubbed the kitchen and scullery with washing soda. I mixed turpentine and beeswax and polished to a mirror-finish every wooden article in the bedrooms, the dressing rooms, the reception rooms and the hall. I washed and wrung out piles of linen – some of it not even soiled – and hung it in the yard to dry. When not cleaning the house I fussed over Harriet, feeding her, drugging her, dressing her, undressing her, washing her, changing her bed linen and emptying her pot, as if caring for the baby I had lost. Late in the evenings I stood in the scullery ironing, too weary to consider the bitterness that blackened my heart.

I had meant to maintain a distance from Doughty, but after a week of this routine the study had to be cleaned and he did not like me working in there when he was out; in fact, he had taken to locking the door. I made a start in there one afternoon, although whenever I glanced up from my work his eyes were on me.

He pushed his chair back from his desk and lifted his feet

so that I could sweep into the kneehole and around him, protesting mildly that it was unnecessary. I replied that I was spring-cleaning and that there was dust in there from his boots. He stopped me, placing a hand on my wrist.

'Show me your hands,' he said.

I winced as he examined them. They were cracked and broken, with deep red splits at the bases of my thumbs.

'This won't do,' he said.

He sent me to fetch the bottle of Rowland's Kalydor from his dressing room. When I brought it he took my hand in his and rubbed the lotion in with his forefinger and thumb. His fingertips were smooth and warm. Then he paid the same attention to the other hand. When he finished, he released me so slowly that it was almost a caress.

'Don't do any more cleaning today. Leave the lotion on your hands and rest.'

'I still have the study and the hall to finish,' I insisted. I was at that level of exhaustion where it is no longer possible to stop.

'The house is perfectly clean as it is. And these are your piano-playing hands.'

He looked at me from under his eyebrows, holding me still with his gaze. His lips were pursed – warm and red. He was in the dishabille of a waistcoat, and his shirt open at the neck. As we studied each other the scent of his cologne sprang up and mingled with the balsam smell of the lotion.

'What's the matter, Jane? You look fraught.'

I did not reply. He considered me, and my sore hands, as though forming a diagnosis. Two frown lines deepened at the bridge of his nose.

'Have you heard from your actor?' He had gone straight to the heart of the matter. 'You sent your letter – what – a month ago? Six weeks? Where is he now?'

My eyes stung with the tears that I had suppressed for weeks.

'He is in London. In a play called *The Purple Robe*.' I could not bring myself to say it, that Edmond was engaged to Maud Frith.

'He has deserted you,' sighed Doughty. 'A fine young cock.' With the click of that last word his mouth twisted into a wry smile.

'Please, don't talk like that. You think me loose because I was in the workhouse. We were so in love.'

'What, both of you?' A thick eyebrow flicked up for a moment.

'We were going to get married when we got back to London. He often talked about it. He promised me so many times.' I could no longer control my expression and I brought my hands up to my face. I inhaled Rowland's Kalydor. I felt so utterly weary. 'I shall never play the piano again ...'

I heard him get up. He stood before me, his hands came up to my shoulders and I drooped my head to cry.

He mumbled a few words of comfort. As his arms folded around me, my strength ran out. I leant my head against his waistcoat, my tears running into its dark damask. When I was quiet I looked up and found an expression of great tenderness in his face. He dabbed my cheeks with his handkerchief and I took it and blew my nose. His hand lingered at the back of my waist, and then he drew me close again.

'Don't be sad,' he murmured. 'An inconstant love is worse than no love at all. You will recover.'

'But my baby!' The cry escaped me, and he loosened his arms. I stepped back from him. 'My son is dead. He died in the workhouse. You cannot imagine ... you have no idea ...'

As Doughty peered at me through narrowed eyes I recollected the abandoned nursery upstairs and apologised. He had a bereavement of his own.

He shook his head.

'What was your son's name?'

I rubbed my eyes with the heels of my hands.

'Nathan,' I said. 'But he was never baptised. The day after he was born I was put to work sewing sacks. My milk never came in. He was put into the care of a simpleton who recited the Bible over him but did nothing to keep him alive. He lies in the cesspit beneath the workhouse: there was no funeral, no prayer, no inquest.'

'I am sorry. That is a far greater grief than the loss of your lover.' He sighed, and gave me a sad smile. 'I suppose that, in the course of my work, I have become accustomed to dealing with the bereaved. I know that I cannot console you. People may tell you that you will forget, and start anew. But you never forget. Eventually you become stronger, that is all.'

He fell silent then, perched on the edge of his desk, looking down at the floor, his hands interlaced over his waistcoat.

'I have seen the nursery,' I said, and after a while added: 'What was the matter with your child?'

He answered without looking up.

'Agnes was born prematurely, and did not survive. She had various … abnormalities. So our house is as you see it: empty. Perhaps Harriet still grieves.'

'Mrs Doughty is very close to her brother,' I replied, wondering whether to say it, how to say it.

'Yes, Vernon's presence, and his prayers, bring her some comfort.'

He suspects nothing, I thought, studying his open expression. *Your darling papa.* I wondered which of them was the father.

'She put herself to great trouble to prepare for his visits,' I ventured. 'It seemed to … exhaust her.'

'She is not well,' he replied. 'Her melancholia is getting

worse, and she is taking more and more of her opiates and ether. I have seen how much time you spend attending to her. Thank you for that.'

I regarded him evenly. 'I fear for her life, sir.'

'I know. There was a point when –' he hesitated, as if willing himself to go on, 'when she tried to take her own life.'

I asked him what had happened.

'Three years ago, not long after Agnes died, I found her. She was lying on the floor in my dressing room, bleeding from the wrist, very pale, but mercifully still alive. She had cut herself with my razor – fortunately she missed the artery. That was when I called in Astley-Scrope. After that I watched over her as much as I could, but I did not dare to treat her myself. I did not want to have the loss of her life on my conscience.'

'I know it has been very difficult.'

'I hate her for it!' he exclaimed, all of a sudden. 'I know I should not, but whatever I do is futile, there's no helping her and she will not help herself. There's nothing wrong with her and yet she lies in bed as if she were eaten up by cancer and the best physicians in the world were not equal to the task of treating her.'

'She has an ailment, sir, but it is an ailment of the mind, and it impairs her just as much as any illness or injury.' I was almost on the point of telling him what I had seen, yet I dared not. 'We can only be patient.'

'I have no more patience. Do you hear how she speaks to me? I have a mind to dismiss Astley-Scrope and throw the Aethereal Balsam down the privy.'

'It will not do,' I said. 'She is unable to live without it now. Her internal agony is too great, it overwhelms her.'

'What do you know of the matter?' he snapped, then apologised for being too sharp.

I pitied Doughty, for his losses and suffering were as deep as mine: his child dead, his wife a stranger to him. I accepted his apologies and waited for him to calm down. He had to be told. I took a deep breath.

'I will tell you what I have witnessed,' I said, 'but you must listen to me, and try not to deny it. There is something I ought to tell you about Mrs Doughty.'

My eyes slid past him to the leather-bound spines of the books on his shelves. I hesitated, realising that I had not prepared myself to make this disclosure, that I had not yet devised a way to mitigate any consequences.

'Well?'

In the silence I watched dust particles dancing in the window light.

'It is, I think, the source of her malady.' I had his interest, and had to say something. 'Perhaps it is not my place to say this. But I … saw Reverend Glyde … kissing her.' I felt ashamed to say it, as though I had committed the sin myself.

But the information instead of affecting him seemed to bounce away as though a sword had glanced off a shield.

'They are brother and sister. They have always been close,' he said, with a shrug. 'Why should they not kiss?'

'I saw them together as they went upstairs. They thought no one was looking. They kissed … like lovers …' I forced myself to continue. 'She loves him and she is in agony over him.'

'That's preposterous!' He looked at me aghast, as if I had lost my wits, and was offering him a dead rat on a porcelain plate. 'What on earth has possessed you to say that? What evidence do you have?'

'I can only tell you what I saw.'

'But is it not possible that you were mistaken? That you misinterpreted what you saw?'

I hesitated, realising that I was unable to convince him, and that to proceed would damage the trust that he had begun to display.

He stood up. He was very close to me and lowered his voice.

'You must have been mistaken. I have never known my wife to display anything other than pious virtue. She finds consolation in her brother's company, to be sure, but it is of a profoundly spiritual nature. You could not possibly have seen what you describe.' His hand rested on my shoulder, then brushed my neck and tilted my face up to him. He studied my confusion with a half-smile. 'Why did you wish me to believe that?'

At the warm touch of his hand a shiver spread across my body.

'I was not seeking to attract your attention, sir, nor to deceive you. I was merely telling you what I had seen … what I thought I saw.'

I drew myself up and took a step backward to free myself.

'You were mistaken, at the very least, Jane, I am sure of it.'

'Perhaps I was.'

'You had best return to your duties.' Doughty was frowning at the fireplace, as if he had not entirely dismissed my claim. 'Please, watch her closely, and ensure that she does herself no harm.'

26: Emerald Soap Solution

By now, Harriet was starting to look forward to her Aethereal Balsam, counting the hours between the doses, waiting for the moment of release when the drug dissolved through her mind and a smile blossomed on her face, her eyes half closing, like a cat whose cheek was fondled.

One morning in early June the medication ran out sooner than it should, and I answered Harriet's bell to find her agitated, sweating and crying out that her whole body was racked by pain. I had to run down Bennett's Hill to summon Dr Astley-Scrope in haste, and then was sent straight out again to Mr Bright's shop with the prescription.

'How long will it be?' Harriet demanded, her eyes overflowing with unwarranted tears and her nose streaming into a handkerchief. 'Please – I can bear it no longer!'

I returned to find her in a state of high anxiety, retching and vomiting. With great effort she swallowed the double dose of medication that the physician had advised. I sat by her bed, cooling her face with a soft flannel refreshed in cologne water, hushing her like a child.

Summer had begun early and, in the evenings, languor embraced the city. Long before bedtime, we drifted like wraiths in the heat. I had to accede to sleep, quelling my private thoughts, forgetting proof, causation, evidence. Anger might heat the skin, and ultimately its restless burning would lead to exhaustion.

Even though I bathed her in cool water and dressed her in thin muslin, Harriet could not settle at night. From my own bed I heard her raving. Her voice, keening, moaning, rose from the floor below.

One night I struggled awake from deep sleep and gazed through the window at the velvet-blue sky, illuminated by a full moon. My head was aching. The warm air was stifling; my sheets were damp with sweat and I pushed them back. I heard Doughty's door open, the stumble of his weary feet along the landing, the low rumble of his voice. She did not calm. Surely it would be only a moment before her bell rang.

He tried, nobly I suppose, but I could hear the frustration and sadness in his tones. I knew what she would gush forth. She would have seen the monstrous spirits of the dead and mutter of secrets. A disguise for her own lies, her guilt, the dead infant. I could see why Doughty resented her: she was no wife to him and yet enjoyed the privileges of a spoilt child, cossetted and pampered when he should have cast her aside. She had no need to work, she did nothing for the household, nothing to lighten his life. He worked long hours for his fees, seven days a week, returning late in the evening to the house to sit up at his desk with his reports. But I also pitied her, for her destruction at the hands of her brother, and for her self-loathing and deep unhappiness. She loved Glyde with a kind of love that I recognised: a love that consumes the soul.

I would go to her, I decided, even though the bell had not rung, and with the sound of her misery keeping me awake it was not so hard to rise and don my night wrapper before descending the narrow staircase. A patch of moonlight from the back window made rectangles on the landing. Her wailing grew louder.

I craned my head around the open door, curious to see them together. The curtain was open a little in her room, admitting a dim luminescence from outside. Doughty sat on the edge of the bed but separate from her and making no move to embrace or console her. If they had once loved each other, all that was past; there would be no going back. In his hand glistened the bottle of Aethereal Balsam. He gave her the drops and stroked her hair. Her sobbing died away. It must have been after midnight, for the street outside was quiet, but as always the low grinding of the factories rumbled in the distance.

'Sleep now.' He rose and put the bottle on her dressing table. 'There are no more spirits, no more secrets, be at peace.'

She quietened with the drug and, as she started to snore, he left her. Closing the door, he startled as he saw me there on the landing. We looked ghostly in our pale nightclothes, our faces and hair silvered by the moon.

'I heard her cry out. I wanted to see if I could be of service, sir.' I flattened myself against the wall for him to pass.

He stopped, but said nothing, and I heard him inhale slowly and exhale. He put his hands up to my shoulders, pressing them back to the wall.

'Yes, I suppose that you may, but not as you thought.' His voice came out as a low rasp, but he cleared his throat, and continued more gently. 'Would you like to?'

So the inevitable was happening, as Clara had said it would. I should have been prepared, but I did not answer. I felt the pressure of his hands. He stepped closer, bringing his knee into my skirts.

'Your smell,' he murmured, 'you smell of violets. Your sweet body, abandoned, beaten, ruined … let it be caressed again, let yourself be adored, loved …'

I raised my hands reflexively, and they came up against his chest. I felt its rapid rise and fall and his heart beating under my hand. He took my fingers in his own and raised them to his lips. I trembled; my limbs tingled as if overfilled with blood.

'I too can be ruined,' he continued. 'You have opened a trap-door beneath my feet. Now, let me fall from grace, let me plunge, like the angel Lucifer, into darkness …'

He drew my hands to his hips. I brought them up against the solid mass of his body and, as I gasped, inhaled his cologne and his warm breath.

His mouth was near to mine.

'You want me … oh, say you want me!'

He was passionately aroused: he pulled up our nightclothes, and soon would have been in full possession of me. His skin felt like velvet. I felt myself beginning to ache for him, but I jerked my face away.

'*No.*' Even in a low voice, my tone was sharp. If I was tempted to encourage him, if my body was rebelling against my mind, I knew better than to show it.

I might as well have burnt him. He let go of me and stood still, as if struggling to master himself. Then, stepping back, he allowed me to pass him and begin to climb the stairs.

'Jane.' There was a creak of longing in his voice. 'I'm sorry.'

I paused and turned around to stare down at him. Momentarily, I pitied him; I pitied myself. Both of us were lonely, and each might have comforted the other.

'Jane.' He stretched out and touched my fingers, where

they were tense on the stair-rail. 'I'm sorry. I shouldn't have done that. You're so beautiful. Forgive me.'

I took a deep breath. I fought down the urge to reach out to him and drew my fingers back.

'Did you think to seduce me?' I said. 'As my employer, a married man, within earshot of your own wife?'

'A mad impulse. I'm sorry. I thought you might … such temptation … any man would …' He bowed his head.

I pursued my advantage. 'Do you understand now, how temptation may corrupt the most respectable of men?'

He did not raise his head at that, and I returned to my room.

I locked the door behind me, looking up at the brilliance of the full moon and hoping desperately that what had passed between us would not be mentioned further. When he had uttered my name something in his voice had caught me, a pleading sincerity that shot straight to my soul. For a moment I had felt as if I were again desirable, and Doughty my suitor.

But what a suitor! Twice my age, with his black suits and his penumbra of death – a Charon guarding the netherworld. And yet, strong and well-made. I sighed, allowing myself a little pleasurable regret, imagining myself creeping back downstairs to his divan. How delighted he would have been to see me! Yet, how quickly would he have taken control of me for his own satisfaction. Alas for womankind: what our instincts lead us to admire in men, in our heroes of history and literature – their virility, their muscularity, their boldness – are precisely those qualities that enable them to overpower us.

I contemplated instead a vision of Edmond in his glory: a youthful Apollo radiating desire, a light blinding me to all others. Yet it grieved me all the more, for I had never heard that depth of longing in Edmond's voice … indeed we had lived barely any time together before I had noticed periods of coolness, like a cloud drifting across the sun. And now, it seemed that he had consigned me entirely to the shadows.

The following morning Doughty had no inquest until eleven and stayed with Harriet. I was glad that he seemed more attentive towards her, feeding her a bowl of porridge that I had made.

I went out to Dr Astley-Scrope's to get a repeat prescription for Aethereal Balsam and then to Bright's to get it dispensed. Mr Bright was even slower and fussier than normal, keeping me waiting to be served then reciting his list of objections to Dr Astley-Scrope's prescriptions until I informed him that I was merely an ignorant maidservant and could not possibly offer an opinion in the matter – however, if I returned back to the house empty-handed I would surely be dismissed by my mistress without a character and with no future other than to rot in the workhouse. At that point he grudgingly made up two small bottles of the mixture, refusing to hurry himself, even though I said that my mistress needed me and I had to be back.

Finally I rushed back to Newhall Street, perspiring with the effort of it all. The hot weather blazed on; the city was lifeless in the over-bright sun. Smoke rose from hundreds of furnaces, mingled with the sulphurous smell of burning coal and the vapours of steam engines, creating a choking heat that filled the senses with lassitude. Coal smuts landed on the washing that drooped from the tenements and the screams of fractious children, scolded by their mothers, issued from the open windows. My eyes stung.

It was after eleven. Doughty was no longer in the house, and I found Harriet in her dressing room, coughing and retching, with the Emerald Soap Solution open in front of her. I was horrified; she could not have been alone for more than half an hour.

'Madam, that is not to be drunk,' I protested. 'It contains arsenic! It is only for your skin!'

She made no reply, but bringing her hands to her throat, heaved forth onto the floor a large quantity of green liquid, in which porridge was mingled. I cleaned her up as best as I could and got her back into bed with the bowl from her washstand beside her. She continued to vomit until it was just dry-retching and there was nothing left in her stomach. I checked the Emerald Soap bottle. She must have taken half the contents, and vomited them back.

'You must not take your medicines without me to help you,' I said. 'Or you will make mistakes.'

Her face, eyes puffy from weeping and mouth sagging, betrayed her despair.

'I wanted to end my life,' she said. 'It was not a mistake. I have done what I ought not to have done, and there is no health in me.'

Oh, my Lord, I thought, and wondered what had passed between her and Doughty while I was out of the house.

I fetched some milk from the kitchen and told her to drink it to settle her stomach; eventually the spasms of nausea eased and she lay back on her pillows.

I sat beside her as tears welled up in her eyes.

'I am unworthy to live – everything is black before me – and all that is past – I cannot endure the day. The pain of it is unbearable.' She was sobbing. 'I must sleep, and if I cannot sleep then I must die. I cannot answer questions.'

I reached out and held her hand to comfort her, and turning it palm upwards saw the faint white line across the inside of the wrist. I could not help but run my fingers over it.

'I am sorry, ma'am,' I said. 'I am here to help you if you feel bad. You have only to ring your bell.'

But she knew I was looking at her scar.

'Yes,' she murmured. 'This is the second time, and again I failed. The third time … the third time …' She fell silent, interrupted by her own thoughts, as if she had formed the intention and were already planning its execution.

'Please, ma'am,' I begged. 'You have only to ring and I will do what I can. I will keep you company, play music, I will get you whatever you want.'

She made no reply but lay back against her pillows, staring at something I could not see. She belched and complained of nausea but kept the milk down.

I scoured my mind to think of a way to persuade her against self-destruction. What could I say? What did this woman have to look forward to in life? An unhappy marriage, an incestuous liaison, the constant mourning of a dead child. There was only religion to rely upon.

'If you have faith in God,' I attempted, 'then you must surely believe that it is a sin to harm yourself. God would not want you to do this.'

'I have faith in my brother.' Her mouth formed each word distinctly as her hand swept from her brow back across her pale hair. It rested on the pillow behind her head; the gauntness revealed where the flesh had deserted the tendons so that it resembled a skeleton held together by wire. 'Vernon is the only one who has helped us. It was he, it was our family connections, that obtained my husband his practice in London. Vernon was his friend from his early days as a medical student. Then when he came to Birmingham … Vernon must come to see me – I must speak to him. Tell him that I have taken a turn for the worse, that it may be the last time.'

'I cannot leave you alone,' I protested, feeling that Glyde would in all likelihood make her worse, but she would have none of it.

'Give me my medicine and I will sleep until he comes;

and if he does not come I will sleep forever. Go now.'

I gave her a dose of Aethereal Balsam, and on the pretext of finishing the embroidered kneeler, sat and observed her until she seemed to be asleep.

Then I hastened, as fast as I could in the heat, to cover the half a mile or so to the Rectory. I delivered my message to the unhappy Mary, and went straight back to Harriet without awaiting a reply.

I heard her ringing as soon as I had come in.

She sat bolt upright in bed as I put my head around her door.

'Well?'

'He is coming directly,' I lied – I was sure he would not fail to respond to the message. 'It would be best, madam, if you had a little more of your medicine, so as not to appear discomposed.'

She was happy to take a half-dose of the Aethereal Balsam, enough to blunt the edge of her agitation without rendering her asleep for when Glyde should arrive.

And arrive he did, frowning at me as he pushed past from the doorstep and took the stairs two at a time.

I dared not follow him and waited in the downstairs hall, listening to his tone – upset and angry rather than kind – and to Harriet's high-pitched whimpers that subsided into sobs. I should have gone to her, but I was more afraid of him than sorry for her.

There was quiet. Eventually he came down the stairs, slowly, and glared at me again. He held out a letter. It was from Harriet's escritoire; the wax bore her seal.

'Give that to your master when he comes in. And keep her medicines locked up. If anything happens to her you will answer for it.'

Then he was gone and I leant against the front door, glad

to have that thickness of wood between us. The letter was sealed up and I had no business to examine it further. I put it on Doughty's desk in the study.

As the evening drew on Harriet became fretful at Doughty's lateness, like a child denied its mother. She refused supper despite my coaxing her, telling her that it was only a little fresh bread and ham. I managed to get her to take a glass of milk, then brushed her hair and dabbed her eyes and face with cool water. I dosed her with Aethereal Balsam. I read her a long passage from the Bible of the nature of '*And Jehosophat begat Japheth*', until I saw her eyelids close and her mouth fall open.

I guessed that Harriet was now in a desperate situation. '*I have done what I ought not to have done … I cannot answer questions …*' My disclosure to Doughty should have led to him questioning Glyde, the perpetrator of all this mischief. Instead I suspected that he had served her, the victim, with an inquisition along with her morning porridge.

27: Glyde's Letter to Doughty

Monday, June 15th, 1840.

The Rectory
Birmingham

My Dear Brother,

I came today to see Harriet at her urgent command and found her much distressed by some bizarre and eccentric questions which you asked her, over what is no more than an entirely innocent expression of a natural affection between siblings. This is not one of your inquests, but your own wife, who suffers an extremely parlous state of health and must not be subjected to such an obnoxious inquisition.

I understand that her anguish had been compounded by your brutish manner and your callousness, so far that she had been on the verge of taking away her own life.

I see that you are no longer disposed to be kind towards my sister; it behoves you however to consider the teachings of the Church and the vows that you made when you wed, and to care for her in sickness and in health.

At the very least, if you do not want to be faced with an inquest of your own making and all the scandal and damage to your reputation and professional standing that would ensue, I would advise you in the strongest terms to be more circumspect.

I remain, Sir, your brother,
Vernon

28: A Love that Destroys Everything

Doughty must have been much occupied that day; it grew late, and I was on edge for his return. We were not far from midsummer and the evenings had lengthened, yet it was dark outside. Downstairs, at the front window, I watched as the lamplighter brought his ladder, and on the pavement outside a yellow circle was cast by the hissing gas-flame. The evening was calm under a Prussian-blue sky, the noise of the factories reduced to a slow murmur. A couple of horse carts passed, then a chaise, and finally Doughty appeared in the circle of light.

He tipped his tall hat as though to an acquaintance across the street but turned immediately back; perhaps his gesture was not returned. I went to open the front door for him.

'Jane.' He looked weary. 'It's late ...'

I was resolutely efficient: taking his coat, asking him if he had eaten, telling that Mrs Doughty had been very unwell and I had helped her to bed.

'She took Emerald Soap.'

I told him that Harriet had taken it deliberately, and not

in error, and that I had moved the bottle into his dressing room.

'There may be further symptoms: stomach cramps, diarrhoea, convulsions,' he said, his brow furrowed with concern, and betraying no sign of the desire that had seized him the previous night. 'There is no treatment for arsenic poisoning, unfortunately.'

'I think she vomited it all up,' I said. 'After that she asked me to send for Reverend Glyde, which I did, and he left you a note. She is desperately upset.'

'Headaches, and blood in the urine, those are two other symptoms,' he said, evidently still thinking about the arsenic. 'No, I hadn't time for supper. It was late when we concluded the evidence; the inn had stopped serving.'

There was no energy in him; he went into the study, glanced at the seal on Glyde's letter and let a bundle of papers fall upon the desk.

'I was not sure what had upset Mrs Doughty,' I ventured. 'She was extremely distraught when I found her, not long after eleven this morning. Had she said anything to you?'

'No.' He frowned. 'She has virtually refused to talk to me. Now, if you don't mind, I'm very hungry.'

I said I would fetch him something to eat and perhaps he could go up to her afterwards. He nodded as I reminded him about Glyde's note.

Doughty dined alone on a cold collation and a glass of claret. When I returned from the kitchen to clear the table, I hoped that he had gone into the study, but as I peered past the half-open door I saw him still slouched in the dining chair, with his shirt collar undone, and staring at his empty plate.

I began to hope that he would not mention what had passed between us the night before.

'You may come in.' He had sensed me in the corridor.

I asked him if he had been up to see his wife; no, not yet, he answered. Quite possibly Harriet was still asleep, so I did not say anything further.

As I reached for his plate, he put his finger on it to keep it there; I jerked back my hand as though from a hot coal.

'I was wondering, Jane,' he said quietly.

Was this to be another advance? But his demeanour was sad and calm.

'My inquest today.'

I breathed again.

'Sit down,' he said, gesturing to a seat across the table.

'Sir.' I perched on the very edge of it, keeping my eyes on my folded hands.

'A young woman found in the canal, bearing the marks of violence. And her lover was seen running away.' He was caught up in his work and wanted only to talk.

'A handsome youth – he was a draper's assistant before his love put him into distress. When the police took him to see her body he had called on God to forgive him, and said he'd always thought he would be hung for her. At today's hearing he pleaded his innocence, he told me he loved her and he believed that she had drowned herself from her own distress. He had spent all his wages on her; he could no longer properly work and had been sent to the House of Correction. I couldn't believe him to be guilty. And then he asked me if I'd ever known a love which created a disorder in the mind, an insanity, sweeping everything away to its destruction, like a wildfire burning everything that stood in its path.'

He was silent, and I glanced up. His dark eyes brooded upon me. I studied the contours of his face: strong bones, deepening frown lines above the bridge of the nose, a passionate mouth. Just below his collarbones he was as hairy as a beast.

'I thought of you, Jane.'

I tensed, unable to breathe or swallow, as he continued.

'Was that what you experienced, a love that destroys everything? A love after which you are bereaved of your old life and everything you thought that you held dear?'

Was it Edmond, I wondered, who had destroyed my life? Or the destructiveness of my passion itself, that had eaten away my spirit? With an effort, I recovered my voice.

'I am ruined, as I told you, and all my former life is at an end.'

'And would the lover then destroy the beloved? This youth, could he really have hurt his sweetheart? He seemed so deeply in love.'

I stared at a point behind his shoulder, my memories black. I thought of my own situation, and of Harriet's, and a darkness descended in my mind. I remembered Edmond in his angry, jealous moments, and my own hatred of him when I discovered that he had forsaken me.

'For some, love and cruelty are one,' I said.

'There is too much cruelty: the world loves to see cruelty and we are too much in awe of it. If it were not so, my work would be cut in half.'

'In awe of it, sir?' I was startled. 'Surely it is repugnant?'

'If you read a work of fiction, or see an opera, or a play at the theatre, is it the hero or the villain that triumphs?'

'The hero, naturally. Good triumphs over evil. It is the natural order.'

'But our prejudices of the natural order corrupt our view. What I have found at inquests is the difficulty in persuading the jury that the deceased are not villains, but victims. The woman who is cruelly violated and murdered is argued to have provoked her attacker. The abandoned infant is deemed illegitimate, unbaptised, it has no place in society.

We withhold pity from the weak and the defeated, and instead we forgive their abusers. I blame the scribblers of novels for this pernicious state of affairs.'

I wondered whether his mind had been running on what I had told him but could not ask. He was too caught up in his own argument.

'Why, some ladies are only content when reading romances about brutal men!' he said.

I rose to put the dishes and the empty decanter on the tray; now Doughty did not impede me. I was determined to keep my hand steady but the claret glass wobbled on the plate.

He continued to voice his thoughts.

'But do people truly find love like this? Love mingled with cruelty? Love that brings one to the point of self-annihilation? With no notion of duty, or honour? Of consequences?'

'They think only of their own pleasure.' My eyes were drawn to his for a moment too long. 'Like children, they build their castles of cards, and ruin them with their own breath.'

'And perhaps they truly love? They taste the bloom of youth before it fades; they sacrifice what little they have at the altar of Eros.'

'They are not of your world, sir, as I have said before.'

'My world, as you term it, is as dark as yours, Jane, and my ears full of the voices of its inhabitants.'

There was a creak in the corridor and my tray jolted in a betrayal of guilt as Mrs Doughty entered the dining room. I could not exit the room without pushing past her.

'Harriet. My dear!' Doughty rose and held out his arms, but no response was forthcoming. 'I am sorry to hear that you were indisposed.'

He sat down awkwardly.

'I heard the door, and you did not come up to greet me.' She stared at his desk. 'Another inquest, then.'

'I had a difficult case today. A young woman, dead in the canal,' he said, hastily sifting through his papers to find Glyde's letter. 'It took a long time for the jury to reach their verdict.'

'No doubt of her own doing.'

'There was a murder verdict. A young man was committed to the Assizes for trial. Half the people of the town were there to watch.' He broke the seal on Glyde's letter and scanned its contents briefly.

Harriet pulled her night-wrapper tightly around her, a thin wrapper of white lace, hunching her shoulders as though cold. Her pale hair was loose; streaks of it had dried against her scalp.

'I hope, then, that you will be prompt in claiming payment,' she said. 'Our savings are dwindling and Vernon informs me that Papa cannot continue to support our expenses. It is most awkward, especially after what he has already done for us.'

'If we could spend less on quack medicines, perhaps? Or make fewer donations to your brother's charities? I am sure that my income would then suffice.'

Doughty would have still more bills today, for the physician's prescription and the pharmacist but he did not yet know.

'You would starve me of physic for the sake of economy, then? I suppose then that our world is as dark as a servant's, as you said yourself. When I was given to you in marriage, it was not intended that I should live as one of the lower orders.'

'I merely meant that …' He paused, perhaps wondering how much she had overheard. He tried again, with a rueful smile. 'I do not intend us to live like servants, Harriet. Whilst pursuing my profession, I learn how other people live. To enter the world of the dead, I must make myself smaller.'

Harriet was repulsed, as if his corpse were leering at her.

'I cannot tolerate a husband from the world of the dead. And as for your questioning of me: my brother has written to you about it.'

Doughty glanced down at Glyde's letter which lay open on the blotter.

'Very well,' he said, his face suddenly cold. 'You cannot tolerate me. You may inform your brother that I no longer consider that the matter to which he alludes is any of my business. You may act with him as you please.'

She looked so shocked then that I wanted to comfort her, but I had the tray in both hands. In any case, it was not proper for me to be present during their conversation and I gently cleared my throat.

'Yes, Jane.'

Doughty gestured that I might leave, but Harriet remained in the doorway, her eyes fixed on her husband.

'Good night, William, and pray do not disturb me again.' Bringing their conversation thus to a full stop, she shut the door behind her even as I made to follow her out with the tray.

Doughty and I exchanged glances, mine alarmed, his full of anger. Then he shrugged.

'Allow me.' As his wife's footsteps receded, he got up to re-open the door for me, but slowly enough to detain me and to resume our interrupted conversation. His face changed as he became intent on me, and he lowered his voice as if Harriet were still listening.

'The verdict was Wilful Murder. Yet he pleaded his love, Jane. A desperate love. *"You can only be happy at her whim,"* he said. *"If she intends you to suffer, then there is no rest or peace for you in the world. You are walking around yourself, you cannot work."* And although he denied it, I could understand that in the grip of his passion he might have lost his self-control. I could not help then but think of you,

Jane. My heart twisted on its axis.' His mouth became soft and sensual and he almost whispered the rest: 'I shall never find rest or peace ... it is a wildfire love, that will burn everything else away.'

I stared at him, trapped by his intense gaze. He really was on the brink of abandoning his marriage; and it would be his undoing professionally. He remained there, his hand paused on the doorknob, making no move towards me.

'It cannot be,' I said. 'Please reflect, and be careful of yourself, and of your wife. These emotions are merely dreams – once you make yourself a victim of them there is no remedy.'

He opened the door and bowed me out with a flourish like a footman. I took the tray down to the kitchen, hoping that I could extinguish the spark that he had ignited.

29: Horrible Murder in Birmingham

From the *Birmingham Gazette*

The town of Birmingham has been thrown into confusion. The body of a young woman, Roseanne Meakin, having been found in the canal, below Walmer-lane Bridge. An inquest, held yesterday, 15th June, excited universal interest. It would appear that a boatman was walking along the banks of the canal early in the morning. He saw a woman's bonnet floating on the water; and fearing that a body was in the canal, he used his boat-hook and aided by his brother, dragged the water. They soon pulled up the body of the deceased, and having conveyed it to the Navigation Public House, searched the pockets and discovered the following letter:

'Dear Roseanne – I hope you will still read these lines with as much affection as they are sent. It has been six weeks, and my imprisonment must be grievous to you, but I shall be released from here on Friday next. You will please let my mother know that you have heard from me, and ask her to send me some money to come out with, to the House of Correction, as I dare say that you have none to spare, and a clean shirt also I want. I am sunk low, my darling, yet if you think it proper to come to meet me, I shall be very happy to see you where we used to walk out. Whatever your feelings for me now, Roseanne, I send my best love to you, and shall try to be content with hoping that you will attend to what this contains. I am yours as ever.

Written by JOSHUA SEFTON'

Suspicion fell upon Sefton, and information having been despatched to the Stationhouse, Constable Clay went to the residence of his father and apprehended the youth. Sefton exclaimed, 'Good God, is she dead?' adding 'I always said I should be hung for her.' He admitted meeting the deceased upon the towpath, where they were wont to walk out in the past. Constable Clay reported also that, on taking the prisoner to view the deceased he cried aloud 'May God forgive me!' which he (Clay) took to be an expression of the prisoner's guilt in the matter.

Coroner Doughty then asked the prisoner whether he had drowned the deceased. He replied 'I do not know: I could not stay with her – she had turned mad.' This was, he claimed, due to her father's cruelty. 'He would drive her from his house if she spoke to me again. He did not care that she loved me. We swore true love, to the death, and beyond.' He claimed that the deceased had destroyed herself. 'She asked me for a token. Give me your handkerchief, she said, for a keepsake, for I cannot walk out with you again. I said I would not, for if you break with me now, I shall never be complete again. She insisted again on my handkerchief, and, when I said no, she was on me like a fury. She had turned raving mad. A raving, delirious fit. I fled.' The prisoner repeated that he would be hung for the deceased and vowed that he loved her.

The father of the deceased, Thomas Meakin, demanded to know the truth. He claimed that Sefton was a wastrel who was forever taking his daughter's earnings and idle himself. Sefton, he said, was not above raising his hand to the deceased; she had a few months previously had marks around her throat that she had admitted to him were inflicted by Sefton during a fit of jealousy.

Certain members of the jury objected that the evidence against Sefton proved nothing and, after some discussion, Coroner Doughty requested an adjournment in order for a post-mortem examination to be performed.

The surgeon, Mr Stephen Graves, however, was unable to state that the deceased had not drowned; the absence of water from the lungs in his view proved nothing. The cause of death in drowning was not the entry of water into the lungs. It was due to the obstruction of the windpipe by water, leading to an increase in the noxious properties of the air within the lungs. He had found a fracture to a small bone in the throat of the deceased, which led him to suppose that she had been strangled. (At this information, Mr Meakin cried out that his daughter had been murdered, and had to be restrained.) There were numerous external bruises on the deceased however, and on further questioning Mr Graves admitted that it could not be proven that these injuries were not occasioned by the retrieval of the body by the boatmen.

Despite this lack of clarification, Coroner Doughty directed the jury to consider a verdict, based upon the scientific facts.

The jury having retired at nine o'clock in the evening shortly returned with a verdict of Wilful Murder against Joshua Sefton.

Even at that late hour the room was packed to suffocation, and the most deathlike stillness prevailed. The moment the verdict was announced, the prisoner, who throughout the inquiry had preserved the greatest firmness, suddenly fell back insensible. On recovering, the countenance of the youth presented the most piteous appearance; and during the signing of the deposition he wept bitterly.

At the direction of the coroner, the prisoner was committed to the County Gaol at Warwick to await trial for the offence. It is to be noted that the magistrates will be sorely vexed to find the cost of this incarceration, the funds of the Town Council being gravely depleted due to the continuing case in the Court of the Exchequer Chamber, as previously reported in this newspaper.

30: Heat

Harriet's life from then on would be strictly timed by her Aethereal Balsam, a routine that came to determine mine. In the first hour after a dose Harriet was drowsy and nauseous, by two hours she might be alert enough to talk and eat, by three hours she was becoming anxious about her next dose, and by four hours she was in despair at her entire life situation. I was afraid of another overdose, and so I gave her Aethereal Balsam every three hours, day and night, regulated by the clock. By this means, I kept the dose stable. I was assiduous with Dr Astley-Scrope's prescriptions, to avoid the risk of running out. I cleared out the myriad of bottles from Harriet's dressing room; the remainder of the Emerald Soap Solution was discarded into the privy. Only the Aethereal Balsam remained, and I kept it on the side-table outside her room, so that it was convenient, but still out of her sight.

July arrived, still infected by the stifling heat of summer. It was the cruellest of months, with relentless sunlight scorching all it touched. The air outside the house was as hot as the air inside; there was no breeze, almost no point in opening the windows. Beggars died of thirst in the streets, paupers collapsed in the workhouse. The men in the foundries went mad with the heat and brawls broke out when the public houses closed at night. Babies burned with fever, their high-pitched shrilling adding to the temperature. Browned patches of grass and weeds were ready to take fire from the cinders that were the only rain. At night people lay prostrated, slippery with sweat, gasping for breath.

The heat sapped Harriet's energy; she lay in bed in a thin wrapper of white lace and fanned herself when she could muster the effort. It was hard to get her to eat but I made her milky tea and she nibbled on biscuits. From time to time, unbidden, Glyde visited her, sweeping past me as I opened the door, going directly upstairs, and invariably leaving without requiring to be shown out. We made up the embroidered kneeler and he left with it under his arm. Harriet seemed to be no better for his visits although her regard for him was as high as ever.

The smell of fermenting refuse permeated the basement kitchen. Clearing it out and mopping the floor with warm water was almost unbearable; I was soaked. After my morning chores were over I washed in a little cold water and changed my chemise. The effort of washing the cast-off brought the sweat out of me again.

The heat made me remember the summer before. I had been with Edmond in London and for a whole week, when it had been too hot to dress, had lain idle with him in bed, with nothing but a sheet tangled around us. The windows had been thrown open but the humid air did not stir; our room smelt of candlewax and wilting lilies. Edmond had read aloud his lines, with our heads throbbing with desire and champagne. Doughty was right: that love affair had been a wildfire that had destroyed everything in its path, leaving me with nothing but ashes. Yet, despite everything, I felt the renewal of hope. I was still young and able to make a new start. I could still play the piano. A phoenix might yet arise from such ashes, with a life of itself, independent of what had gone before.

When at home, Doughty took refuge in his study, and worked at his desk in shirtsleeves, his feet and throat bare in the heat, writing the report on Roseanne Meakin's murder for the July Assizes. I knew what drove him: I had read the newspaper article. The post-mortem examination had in fact proven nothing. I feared that the grief-stricken appeals of the father, the lateness of the hour and Doughty's abstraction, his head filled with what he supposed was our love affair, might have led to a wrongful charge against the youth. Doughty wrote until it was too dark to write any longer and delayed the lighting of the lamps as long as possible, preferring to stumble about in the gloom than to add a flame's heat to the summer.

At one o'clock and four o'clock each morning, I crept past Doughty's door to give Harriet her laudanum. If he heard me, he ignored me. Retreating into formality, he had courted me no further and we maintained a mutual avoidance. I hoped that, having had the opportunity to reflect on the destructive power of his emotions, he had seen the damage that lay ahead and drawn back from the edge of the abyss. But it was to last only a few days.

It became my habit that when Harriet was having her afternoon nap, to escape the heat of the kitchen I put a chair out in the shade at the back of the house. There was a small patch of hard earth here; its moss had dried out but a few clumps of grass remained green. One afternoon the sheets had dried quickly on the washing lines, and I should have taken them in for ironing, but I was too hot and weary. I was curtained by them, and nearby a wild honeysuckle had grown over the side wall. I put everything from my mind and read *The Housekeeper's Guide*. A peacock butterfly toyed with the honeysuckle flowers, and a bee droned past my ear. My eyes became heavy.

I heard a footstep and woke to find that my head had lolled uncomfortably and my neck was stiff. The book was still open in my lap.

Doughty was holding a glass of lemonade.

'I've been ringing for you,' he said reproachfully. 'I suppose you didn't hear it out here.'

I sat up, massaging my neck, and apologised. 'What was it you wanted?'

He raised the glass. 'I had to fetch it myself. But I am unharmed by the experience, and I must allow that it is quite agreeable out here.'

'What time is it?'

'Half past three.' He stood still, watching me. The fine cotton of his shirt was unbuttoned at the neck. 'How pleasant and cool it is in the shade, Jane. Your hideaway is the best spot of all.'

'Shall I get you a chair, sir?' I offered, though I needed to rest. There was still half an hour before Harriet's next dose.

'I can get it myself,' he said. 'Here, hold my glass?'

He came back with a chair, which he placed companionably beside me, and sipped at his lemonade, glancing at my face.

I was quiet; I had nothing to say.

'You seem weary,' he said.

'I have not been sleeping well. Since …' I knew that I did not need to explain. 'And in the heat.'

'And you have been ministering to my wife at night, have

you not? I have heard you creeping past my door. I do not sleep well either. But kindly note that despite being stung by temptation, twice every night, I have not intercepted you.'

'For which I must thank you, sir.'

'I am sorry that I disturbed your nap. Close your eyes, I will sit quiet here. I shall not molest you, I promise.' His voice was a comfort. He offered me his shoulder. 'Come, what harm is there? Rest your head on me.'

I should not have, but I knew that I was half-seduced already. I was empty with loneliness and too exhausted to protest, and sank upon the white cotton of his shirt. The hair beneath my ear crinkled if I stirred. I could hear the slow beat of his heart. He took a sip of lemonade and I heard him swallow; his stomach gurgled.

I lifted my head.

'I should not sleep. Mrs Doughty must have her Aethereal Balsam at four.'

'I will wake you then. I have my pocket watch, and I will keep the time and swat the wasps away. Close your eyes. Admire me for my forbearance. You are safe.'

Doughty smelled of his familiar cologne, his chest was a pillow of muscle, and I sank back into sleep upon the rise and fall of his breathing.

When he nudged me awake I had been dreaming that a pack of wolves chased me across a burnt wasteland, and yet I ran exulting in my freedom, crying out and laughing. Now I opened my eyes to the dreary confinement of the backyard, with its walls of blackened brick, the lines of dry washing that were gathering smuts, and the dull eye of the stairwell window with the sun catching its film of soot.

'You wanted me to wake you.' His hand rubbed my shoulder, and then he released me. Where my head had rested, his shirt clung wetly to his skin.

'She needs her Aethereal Balsam.' I sat up straight with an effort. 'She suffers if it is late, and then the dose goes up. I have kept her to twenty drops for the last week.'

'Twenty drops.' He raised an eyebrow. 'And two doses during the night?'

'At one and four. She cannot reduce it.' I stood up and stretched my aching neck.

'Shall I give her the one o'clock dose in future, and leave you to give the other? It will enable you to have a longer sleep, and halve my nocturnal temptations.'

I accepted gratefully.

He leaned forward, resting his elbows on his knees, tilting his chin up to look at me.

'I suppose I should be more attentive to my own wife.'

'She suffers.' I hesitated. It was the briefest of words to describe Harriet's outpourings of anguish and self-hatred. 'Her spirits are extremely low. I think she did not mean to slam the door in that way. She often asks me how she should speak to you.'

His face darkened. 'Tell her that she should speak to me with love and respect. Tell her that I work day and night to keep her provided for, while she lies in her bed. Tell her that I get not one iota of happiness from her –'

'Those are harsh words, sir, and not likely to improve her. Would it not be better if you sought a reconciliation?'

'She will not improve!' he burst out. 'She has always been thus, from the early days of our marriage. I think it was her brother's wish that we should marry, rather than her own. I never treated her ill, but after six months of marriage she delivered our child, and she has never returned to health. She still blames me for the death.'

Six months. Did he still not suspect the origin of this infant? He had fallen silent, staring down at his clasped hands. Time was running on, and Harriet would be in need of her Aethereal Balsam.

'I must go and see to her. Thank you for your – your kindness to me, sir, for minding me while I slept.'

'My name is William. Call me by it. And, Jane, forbearance is no quittance.'

I hurried up the back stairs with a glass of lemonade, knowing that I had permitted an intimacy in which there was no innocence, and which did not deserve any thanks. Doughty's moment of gentleness had soon passed, and once his passions were aroused I doubted that he could be relied upon to master them. If he lost his self-control it would be up to me to retain my own.

As I reached the ground floor, I heard that my footsteps on the stairs resonated with the footfalls of my mistress.

'My medicine. I rang for you, Jane, I rang …' Harriet was in a panic, her voice tremulous, wandering the parlour, the dining room, back to the parlour. In the hot atmosphere the exertion had made her red-faced, and beads of sweat streamed down her neck and across her bosom. 'Where is it … my medicine?'

'Please, ma'am, do not agitate yourself.' I kept my face calm, denying even to myself the husband's intimacy. 'I shall fetch your medicine straight away.'

'You do not know the burden I suffer.' Harriet opened the study and stood in the doorway. 'Only my medicine can ease it. A secret is a terrible burden to bear. We are eaten away by secrets. All of us.'

I murmured reassurance and went quickly for the Aethereal Balsam. It was on the little side table on the landing, where I had left it. For some reason Harriet had not seen it.

I was well aware of her secret and wondered how long she could maintain it in her confused state.

31: Trial of Sefton for Murder

From the *Birmingham Gazette*

WARWICK ASSIZES

CROWN COURT, Monday 6th July, 1840

Mr Justice Littledale opened the court this morning at nine o'clock.

CHARGE OF MURDER

Joshua Sefton, a young man of respectable appearance, aged 17, was charged with the Wilful Murder of Roseanne Meakin, at Birmingham, on the night of 14th May last.

The prisoner, who was defended by Mr. DANIEL, pleaded Not Guilty.

Mr. CLARKE and Mr. MELLOR conducted the prosecution.

Mr CLARKE stated the case and called witnesses in support of the charge.

The evidence went to prove that the prisoner and the deceased were upon intimate terms and on the evening of the 14th of May were walking together.

They were seen to speak angry words and to go towards Walmer-lane Bridge, about nine o'clock in the evening. After that, the deceased was never seen again. About eleven o'clock a person was observed to be running from that direction but could not be identified as the prisoner. Two watchmen of the names of Taylor and Evans, whose beat is close to the bridge, had heard a moaning noise several times, proceeding from the direction of the canal, but saw no-one about, and had heard no cries for assistance.

Two boatmen, named Thomas Morris and Josiah Morris, stated that on the morning of 15th May they saw just under Walmer-lane bridge a bonnet floating upon the water, and, suspecting that a woman had drowned herself they dragged the canal. They pulled a body from the water, which was then taken to an adjoining public house and identified to be that of Roseanne Meakin, from a letter in her pocket, which had been written by the prisoner.

A police officer, named Clay, proceeded to the house of the prisoner's father, and found the prisoner in bed. Clay told him he came to apprehend him for drowning a young woman, to which the prisoner replied, 'Good God, is she dead!' and added that he always thought he would be hung for her. He was subsequently taken by the police to see the body and appeared very much affected, calling on God to forgive him.

The evidence stated that the prisoner was formerly an assistant to a draper at Birmingham and had formed an intimacy with the deceased. In consequence of this attachment he neglected his master's business and was committed to the House of Correction; while confined there he wrote to the deceased the said letter, requesting her to tell his mother to send him some money, and asking the deceased to meet him on his return home. The girl's father, disapproving of the prisoner as a husband for his daughter, was anxious to break off the attachment, and consequently forbade the deceased to visit him.

The prisoner in his defence maintained that he had not drowned the girl, but he considered himself as bad as if he had, for that when they were together by the canal she asked him for his handkerchief, and upon his refusing to give it she went mad, saying that she would drown herself. She ran in the direction of Walmer-lane Bridge, and he left her and went home.

There were no marks of scuffling on the towing-path; but according to the coroner's report, numerous bruises on the body of the deceased and a fracture of a small bone in the throat suggested strangulation rather than drowning as the cause of death. However, the absence of water in the lungs of the deceased did not preclude drowning.

Mr DANIEL, in defence of the prisoner, said, that it was pleasing to find that no satisfactory evidence had been adduced in support of the charge. His Learned Friend had observed that the proof of the prisoner's guilt would be that he made statements which did not tally the one with the other; he hoped before a prisoner's life would be despaired of, they would remember that the lad was unexpectedly disturbed from slumber and charged with the grave crime of murder. The statement by the prisoner that he was as bad as if he had done it corroborated what he said afterwards, namely that he considered himself so because when he parted from her she had expressed her intention of committing self-destruction.

He (MrD) thought the jury would be of the opinion that no murder was committed at all; if any strangulation attempt had been made the deceased could have offered a strong resistance. It was well known that a strangle-hold could be broken by the simple means of lowering the chin, which protected the throat from occlusion and enabled the victim to pull down the attacker's hands. The watchmen had not witnessed any evidence of such struggle. The boatmen had testified to considerable exertions made to recover the deceased from the water; there was no evidence that the injuries seen upon her were not the product of these efforts; the coroner himself had stated that the absence of water from the lungs did not preclude drowning. The surgeon's post-mortem report therefore proved nothing.

His Learned Friend had said there was no motive for the deceased committing suicide; that he (Mr D) denied. She was threatened by her father with utter destitution, and, while he had acted properly in endeavouring to break off the connection existing between his daughter and Sefton, she affectionately loved the prisoner; and those circumstances formed a sufficient motive. What was more probable than that, in her excited state of mind, she had rashly destroyed herself?

HIS LORDSHIP said that the case was of an extraordinary nature and must be sifted by the jury with the greatest care. It was true there was no evidence that the prisoner had been seen to take away the life of the deceased; but in cases of murder it generally happened that no human eye witnessed the act, and upon circumstantial evidence only was the offender brought to justice.

In the present case, the parties appeared to be affectionately attached to each other. The prisoner in the heat of his passion had certainly made violent expressions; but the jury must not take these into consideration unless they corresponded with the whole of the case brought by the prosecution. His Lordship considered the post-mortem report was unsatisfactory and an important circumstance in the case was that no evidence of struggling existed, or anything else which could satisfy them that the prisoner himself did actually strangulate or cast the deceased into the water.

The jury, after a short consultation, returned a verdict of Not Guilty.

The court was adjourned, the case having occupied the whole day.

32: Glyde's Letter to Doughty

Friday 10th July 1840

The Rectory, Birmingham

My Dear Brother,

I received no reply whatsoever from you to my last letter, although Harriet informs me that you have desisted in your unpleasant behaviour, and now I am forced to read the conclusion of the Sefton case in the Birmingham Gazette.

You will remember that, when you put yourself forward for your post, it was I who argued for you. Many here thought you too young for the post, lacking experience, a doctor rather than a lawyer, and I assured them of your keen interest in medical jurisprudence.

Now Sefton's acquittal has thrown a grave doubt upon whether you had conducted your inquest correctly, and whether you acted properly in committing him for trial.

I have listened to countless objections from my fellow

magistrates as to the expense of this case. They are indeed furious about the money which they perceive as wasted, both in the costs attaching to the inquest and the post-mortem examination, and in the imprisonment and prosecution of the accused. They are planning to discuss again the possibility of your impeachment. I will speak in your support, provided that I see a sustained improvement in your behaviour, in both the domestic and the professional spheres.

I should not have to remind you about the parlous state of the Borough Council's finances. In fact, the Earl of Warwick has just blocked the bill in the Lords, which would have allowed a Treasury advance of £10,000 to the Borough Council. He does not want the borough of Birmingham to be independent of his jurisdiction, and so he questions its right to exist. But if the Borough Council does not exist, then it cannot be made to pay for the maintenance of a prisoner in Warwick Gaol. The County of Warwickshire can foot the bill for that. We are preparing a case on precisely that question, for the County Justices Sessions in October.

In the meantime, the magistrates, unless they are County Justices as well as Borough Justices, do not have the right to commit prisoners to the County Gaol. And nor do you, as a Borough Coroner. You have grossly exceeded your jurisdiction in this case, I am afraid.

I advise you, that you must, at all costs, tread carefully. Allow the worker ants, upon whose toil the institutions of this town depend, to go about their daily business unmolested. Do not poke the ants' nest with a stick, lest the occupants, disarranged, come boiling out to bite you.

– Vernon.

33: Clara

'Clara Scattergood!' I startled, as though stung by a wasp, as I held the front door ajar. A draught came in from the street, and with it the racket of the rain, pelting down outside.

'Well, Jane, you never thought you'd see me, did you?' Beneath a broad umbrella, Clara looked immaculate in a plumed bonnet. It was late July and the fierce summer heat had given way to thunderclouds the colour of tarnished silver.

'Merciful God! Why in heaven's name have you come here?'

'49 Newhall Street. That's what Dr Doughty told me. He gave me this, see? A half-a-crown, in earnest.' She held out a silver coin. 'I saw him on my beat the other night.'

There was a flash of violet light and a rumble of thunder from outside. The pavements were steaming and the rain was making swans in the puddles.

'But I can't disturb him – he's working!'

'So am I, darling, so am I. Now, are you going to stop staring and let me in, or do you want the passers-by to hear us? I'm getting wet.' In she waltzed, folding and shaking her umbrella and casting it with a clang into the umbrella stand. She left a trail of muddy water across the floor.

'I'll tell him you're here,' I said, but she was already peering into the rooms.

'In there?' Before I could stop her, Clara was in the study in a cloud of fragrance and a beautifully cut walking outfit, brushing raindrops from her person with gloved hands.

To my utter shock, Doughty greeted her courteously, rising from his desk.

She took a chair and perched neatly on the edge; as I paused awkwardly behind her I saw him eyeing her dainty boots, wet with rain.

'Would you bring us some tea, please, Jane?' He showed me a face of innocence, as though it was nothing for him to entertain a prostitute.

'Two sugars,' added Clara, 'and knock on the door before you open it.'

I did not exactly slam the door, but it was very close. Thunder hammered the sky outside. I told myself that there was no reason for me to care whom Doughty consorted with.

When I went back up with their tea I heard them fall silent as I tapped on the door.

Then, *'I'm just finishing!'* yelled Clara, and I heard her chuckle.

'Come in!' Doughty called out.

Clara, still sitting facing Doughty across his desk, her hands in their black kid gloves folded in her lap, let out a giggle as I put the tray down so sharply that the crockery jumped.

'Oh, darling,' she said, raising an eyebrow at me, 'you've got a face like a smacked arse.'

'Clara came here to give me some information about the workhouse,' Doughty said, flushing, his voice ragged. He cleared his throat; there was a look of anguish in his eyes. 'I have heard something I did not wish to hear.'

Clara stood up, elegant in her midnight-blue sateen, and slapped the half-crown down on Doughty's desk.

'I don't want any tea,' she said, 'and you can keep your money, thank you.'

She stepped out into the hall and I closed the study door.

'What's happened to you, Clara? When did you come out?'

'Want to know what I told him?' she said in a low voice, folding her gloved fingers around my forearm. Her face was very close, and I could see how much powder and paint she wore and smell a rank undertone to her perfume. 'Everything he needed to know about Glyde. Who has been visiting me, once a week. A vicious man with some vile requirements, I can tell you. But at least he pays me for it now.'

Clara let go of my arm and started to adjust her bonnet in the hall mirror, fluffing its ostrich plumes. I had to lean forward to hear her words, muffled by the wings of the bonnet.

'After Theresa died, I was the one kept behind at the Sunday Penances. He would take me into the chapel after everyone else had gone. He made me strip to the skin and tied my hands under the cross. He said I should be cleansed by suffering, I should suffer for my sins, just as Christ suffered.'

I remembered the sketch in Glyde's journal and the paper broken by his pen.

She turned her face to mine, her eyes dark in the shadow of the bonnet.

'And you are so desperate to be untied, to be released from that torture. You could not stand up with the pain, only the cord at the wrists holds you up. So you will promise anything, and when he releases you, you know you must go to the bed, crawl to the bed, and you know you have to put up with it. He asks for what the most vicious of men will ask in the whorehouse; but here there is no pimp, no madam to watch out, and you fear for your life. You fear for your sanity. You fear that you will never be whole, never be clean again. And all of it … Reverend Glyde, he takes pleasure in it.'

'Clara.' I reached out to hold her, not knowing what to say.

She stepped backwards, out of my reach.

'Then there was the lock-up. I couldn't work properly, I was in so much pain. So then I had Siviter on my back. If I didn't work I'd be in the lock-up for twenty-four hours, with no bread or water.' Clara drew her umbrella from the hallstand. 'Siviter used to fetch me to the lock-up at night. He'd leave me there and Glyde would come in. He had a heavy rope with a knot in it the size of a fist. And an iron poker.'

Clara gripped her umbrella like a weapon, making me flinch.

'And what about Siviter?'

Clara's mouth curled in a sneer of contempt. 'I'll tell you about Mr Siviter. He is not able to do anything to a woman, which is why he is so free with his use of the cane. He hates us for it.'

But she had at least got out. I asked her how.

'I tried to be discharged from the workhouse but Mr Siviter said that Reverend Glyde had ordered that I could not go out unless I had a respectable employment. In the end I went to Mrs Siviter. I told her she had to do something. Either I would kill myself, or Glyde would kill me, and there would be another coroner's inquest. I stripped off and showed her my wounds. How would it look if I were found dead in the lock-up like this, I asked her. She didn't really know what to say. I think she knew – she knew about Theresa – and just lied to protect her husband and Glyde – and herself of course. She knew I was telling the truth. Early one morning, she let me out of the side-door and I went to Mrs Graham.'

I remembered Clara telling me about Mrs Graham, on Suffolk Street.

'You're living in her – house – then? And Glyde is still …' I could not bring myself to say it.

'She knew me from before and she took me in and nursed me. I owe her a lot of money now, but I'm paying it back. Her girls are no more to her than working animals, like pretty horses, but at least we get food and care.'

'And Glyde?'

'He can't do so much to me now. At least at Mrs Graham's her son keeps an eye out for me. Johnny's not afraid of roughing up the clients if they cross the line.'

Clara smiled, and then jerked her head towards the study door.

'I was right about him all along, eh? Do you know what – he wouldn't go with me the other night. He said he was saving himself, that he was in love.' She winked. 'It's not often I'd hear that, from any man. But he said he hadn't seen me on my beat for a while and when I told him I'd been in the workhouse he wanted to hear more. Well, I must be on my way – duty calls.'

I told her to watch out for herself and reached out to embrace her. She returned my gesture briefly then shrugged me off with a teasing smile.

'No more now, or you'll have to pay.'

After she left I hesitated in the hallway, looking at the study door. I tapped on it and went in.

Doughty sat at his desk with his head in both hands.

'I know what she told you,' I said.

He raised his head slowly, and with his shoulders hunched over and elbows on the table he looked as if he had not the backbone to act.

'How do I know that her claims are not malicious?' He sucked in his mouth, studying my face.

'That was what you said of me.' I turned his question back at him then. 'Are you going to say that to everyone? Clara thought she was going to die under him. How many girls have to suffer dreadful abuse before you confront the abuser?'

He shook his head and bowed it back down towards his papers.

'There is no evidence,' he said. 'Who will believe a female who lives in a house of ill-repute?'

'She has no need to make such a claim. If that is how she must earn her keep, then what will she gain by slandering a regular customer? In any case, do you not see that her information corroborates mine?'

'You must have spoken to her about this before. How do I know that you did not agree on this story?'

I drew myself up with my hands on my hips.

'Do you really think that I have spoken to her? It was you that invited her here, without even warning me.'

He pondered that, now intent on me, a half-smile softening his lips. My initial reaction to Clara's presence had been something rather like jealousy.

'I will send Vernon a letter,' he said. 'Will you take it over there for me?'

I nodded and left him to write it. I was surprised at myself, at my instinctive resentment of Clara and at my relief when she had told me that Doughty had refused her.

34: Doughty's Letter to Glyde

July 20th, 1840

49, Newhall St.

Vernon,

My position – this Coronership that you were so insistent that I should occupy – and for what? – is becoming untenable. The magistrates regularly debate my removal from office. I have been refused my fees, and the surgeons' fees that I pay out of my own pocket are not being reimbursed. And now I have no jurisdiction over murder suspects. I cannot go on like this. At times I find myself cursing the entire legal profession to hell, begging your pardon. Never mind your damned ants.

I fear that I shall have to resume medical practice or face financial ruin. But who will want to consult the physician to the dead? Even my own wife does not trust my professional judgement. I am selling off my investments to pay the bills. My four-per-cent Consols are nearly depleted. After that I shall be but a month's salary from the workhouse myself, sir, like any working man.

I do not believe that you are defending me to your fellow magistrates. I rather fear that you have been stirring up hostility against me, for reasons I cannot entirely fathom, and using the case of Sefton as a pretext.

If I am to be disgraced, however, I may bring you down as I fall.

You cannot imagine how much it pains me to write what follows.

I regret to inform you that I am receiving numerous allegations from various informants of misbehaviour on your part, both towards my wife, and towards certain young female inmates in the workhouse.

Today for example I spoke to a young prostitute who claims that you used her cruelly in the workhouse and continue to do so; in fact that you have also availed of her services in a brothel on a regular basis, and that, according to orders drawn on a bank in the name of a certain Mrs Graham, the Fund for the Relief of Distressed Gentlewomen is being misused for that vicious purpose.

My instinct is to believe that these allegations are malicious. If, however, they continue, I must feel bound to initiate an investigation. It is only my concern for my wife's parlous mental state that holds me back at present.

Perhaps we should arrange to meet and have these matters out, man to man.

— *William*

35: Harriet Declares Her Love

'I am to wait for the reply.' I handed over Doughty's letter.

The housemaid at the Rectory was a new girl – white-faced, with pale hair strained back under her cap.

'Is Mary still here?' I asked.

'Who?'

She made me wait in the front hall and went upstairs with the letter. After a while she came back and showed me into the drawing room. I took a seat on a hard leather wing chair. The room was large and chilly, with varnished oak floorboards and a dull crimson wallpaper which was not enlivened by the sun filtering through tall muslinned windows. Glyde was evidently from an old family, with portraits of his ancestors alternating grandly with baroque paintings of martyrs, the largest being St. Sebastian with arrows impacted in bloodied flesh, his eyes piously fixed on Heaven. Across the room in a gilt frame hung a smaller painting, another saint, a woman with her pearly breasts exposed to her tormentors, her hands clasped in prayer. I wondered if that went through Glyde's mind as he inflicted the Sunday Penances.

I heard the creak of floorboards as someone moved upstairs, but otherwise the house was silent.

Glyde was taking his time to reply to the letter. I guessed that the contents, written immediately after Clara's departure, were unpleasant.

The pearly-breasted woman was St Agatha and her bosom was outlined in exquisite detail by iron pincers. My stomach turned; Glyde must delight in the image. The horrors of the workhouse, the suffering of the inmates, their powerlessness in captivity, their terror returned to me in all their force. I knew they would never leave me, long after my physical injuries had healed.

As I stared at the picture he was there in front of me, his black robes blocking my view.

'How dare you bring this!' He thrust the letter in front of my face.

Doughty's handwriting, normally an orderly copperplate, was large and angry.

His housemaid put her head round the door and withdrew it hastily.

'Sir,' I replied evenly, 'I have no knowledge of its contents. I was to wait on your reply to my master.'

His slap caught me across the ear and my head rang. *'You dirty little harlot, bringing a prostitute like that into a Christian household!'* Then he cast the letter aside and with both hands pulled me up from the chair by my throat.

He had nearly killed me before and he was not going to do it again. As he tried to tighten his grip, spitting insults through clenched teeth, I ducked my chin, relieving the pressure on my airway. I grasped at his wrists and tugged them down, bringing my knee up smartly into his robes. He was, I supposed, unused to encountering resistance. My life at the Doughtys', combining daily drudgery with a good diet, had strengthened my arms.

'*You may keep these to yourself,*' I said. I tightened my grip on his writhing wrists, watching the veins bulge in his pale hands and his fingers begin to tremble. It was no harder than wringing out the washing; I should have liked to have crushed his bones. '*And as to prostitutes, I believe that you are better acquainted with them than I am.*'

As I released him he began to bluster: it was outrageous, I was no better than she was, dishonest, impertinent, immoral. He was very pale in the face.

'If you have no reply for Dr Doughty as yet,' I said, 'shall I return later?'

'How dare he challenge me, Vernon Glyde, the Rector of this parish, with the vile slanders and lies of a common whore?' He rubbed his wrists where I had hurt him. 'It is preposterous. I will not meet him. You may tell your master that.'

I saw myself out, but as I was closing the front door I heard him shout after me that he would have me fetched back to the workhouse, for he did not want me looking after his sister. I almost wished I had not heard him. I surmised that the letter had contained a question framed in some form, about the embrace I had witnessed, or about Glyde's conduct with Clara. If Glyde suspected me of providing information to Doughty, then by removing me from that house he would silence me. In the workhouse he would find a way to finish me entirely: with a death certificate from the workhouse doctor I could easily vanish unremarked.

For now I was at least out of that house, and free in the church square, which the locals called Pigeon Park. The storm had blown over and the baroque martyrs were replaced by blue sky and the sooty walls of the terraces. The leaves of the churchyard trees fluttered in the sunlit air. In this bustling town there must be a way to evade the workhouse. If I could only obtain some other employment. Everyone here was making something and it did not seem that pianists were much in demand. I might have to work in a shop, or perhaps a factory. Heaving a sigh, I called in at the draper's for Harriet's sewing materials: she had asked for a length of white muslin and several spools of white cotton thread.

We had no dramas for three weeks. Doughty told me that there was no legal way by which Glyde could have me readmitted to the workhouse. He took no further action against Glyde and an uneasy atmosphere prevailed in the house.

I played the piano to divert Harriet and keep myself in practice for when an opportunity should arise: if Davenant ever returned to Birmingham, for example. I had soon exhausted her few non-liturgical pieces and mourned the loss of the sheet music that I had bought to go with my piano; it had been sold at auction for a couple of shillings and I did not know to whom, or else I would have repurchased it from my earnings.

There were four or five music-sellers in the town, but my favourite was Samuel Flavell, of Bennett's Hill, who specialised in importing music from the Continent, including the editions of Schlesinger from Paris and of Breitkopf and Hartel from Leipzig. He was highly musical, was able to pick out for me the orchestral works that had a substantial piano solo and knew of publications that were forthcoming. He shared my enthusiasm for Chopin and had in stock four of his waltzes, four polonaises, and four nocturnes. Nine of these works were not in Harriet's collection and I was in the process of purchasing them one by one from my salary.

Harriet sometimes was well enough to come downstairs to the parlour and lie on the chaise longue as I played, and it usually calmed her. On one of her happier days she asked me to clean the nursery. When I had done, she spread white muslin over the table and cut the panels for a baby's white-work robe. Marking out and embroidering the delicate pattern absorbed her for a while. She said it was for one of her brother's charities. But at times her agitation required increasing doses of Aethereal Balsam, often with additional laudanum when she could not settle.

Then one night her bell rang, waking me in an anxious sweat. It echoed in the corridors and the dark stairway. I was still tired. Surely it was not time yet for her four o'clock dose? I lit a candle, put on my night-wrapper and went down. The clock on the landing read just after one, and I cursed Doughty for not keeping his promise to give her medicines. But then I heard his voice raised, hers too.

I paused outside the door; something was afoot.

Within all was chaos: she was pacing the room, her bedclothes were thrown on the floor, the curtains were half torn down. She was breathless, her hair was wild and she muttered and wailed. He took her by the shoulders, trying to calm her, but after aiming a few feeble blows at him she twisted away and started to fumble with the window.

'What are you doing?' he demanded, beseeching her with his outstretched arms.

Amongst her agitated mutterings I heard it distinctly and crossed the room to her.

'She intends to throw herself out,' I said.

I caught hold of her shoulders, even though she tried to wrestle herself out of my grip and positioned myself between her and the window. She looked at me as though she did not recognise me, and wailed that she should be let go, that I was cruel, that I was obeying the orders of her cruel husband.

'Did you give the one o'clock dose?' I asked Doughty.

He shook his head. 'She was like this when I came in … I tried to calm her.'

'Harriet,' I said firmly, 'you must take your Aethereal Balsam.'

Still attempting to resist, she repeated that I should let her go, asked me who I was, and before I could answer pronounced that I was cruel.

'It's time for your medicines.' I kept my voice calm and steady.

Doughty stepped up with the Aethereal Balsam in his hand but she shook her head and again tried to escape my grasp.

'Get him away from me! He has no heart! I want Vernon! You must send for Vernon!'

'At this hour!' exclaimed Doughty. 'It's half past one in the morning.'

'Vernon is the only one,' she said. 'And I must finish my embroidery for him.' She started to babble about a sale of work at the church for the relief of the Distressed Gentlewomen, and how wonderful it was that her brother did so much for the many charitable causes which she proceeded to enumerate. As she did so her arms relaxed and her face lost its agitated frown.

'He is a muscular Christian,' she sighed, 'a muscular Christian … you must fetch him …'

'Take your medicine,' I cut in, 'then we shall see. Maybe you will finish your embroidery first and we will fetch him when it is done.'

She had started work on the second panel of the baby's robe earlier that day.

'Jane,' she said, recognising me now, 'will you look for it? My needlework bag – my white-work – I don't know where it is, and I must finish it.'

'I'll look for it once you've had your medicine,' I said. She had forgotten that the needlework bag was in the cupboard of her night-table.

'Now, then.' Doughty held the dropper from the Aethereal Balsam out to her tongue. She took the drops – I counted twenty – and allowed me to lead her to her bed.

She climbed in; I picked her pillows up from the floor and arranged them behind her.

'Vernon,' she said, as I spread the bedclothes over her and put the needlework bag on her lap. 'Vernon must be sent for.'

'You love Vernon, don't you?' Doughty sat on the edge of the bed, studying her face.

She rummaged in the bag and unfolded the piece she was stitching from around its hoop frame. The needle was paused at an angle in the embroidery. She glanced up at her husband, then down at her work. She fumbled for the needle and began, with shaking hands, to sew.

He put his hand on her blankets and she glared at it, her needle pulled up to the end of its thread, as though she meant to lean forward and spike him with it. He drew back and she jabbed the needle down into a spray of white flowers.

'You love him,' he repeated.

That word, love, might mean anything: a chaste affection, a romantic longing, a destructive passion – a frenzied, obscene coupling. In the pause that followed, I wondered what I had felt for Edmond.

Doughty watched Harriet's face. She remained intent on stitching the centre of a flower, very slowly overcasting a tiny edge around a tiny hole.

'But you are only a sister to him, aren't you?' he said quietly.

I imagined him in his black coroner's robes, questioning a witness. But he should not have probed her so, in her parlous state.

Her needle paused and she looked up. Even in the candlelight I saw her pallor intensify, blood leaving her lips and cheeks. She was as white as the muslin in her hand. The Aethereal Balsam was quieting her, but she parted her lips as though she had something to say.

'What is it, Harriet?'

She stared at him.

'I will not.' Her lips moved silently at first and then she drew a breath. 'I cannot keep it secret.'

'Go on.' He sat very still, clasping his hands together in his lap.

'I can't bear it any more. At first it is easier to lie, is it not?' She put her needlework aside. 'Because the truth is too hurtful to tell. But that untold hurt builds up, until it becomes an agony that no medicine can cure.'

He waited for her to speak again, his head and shoulders bowed.

'Vernon and I ...' she began, then faltered.

I wanted to comfort her. Doughty remained motionless. She seemed to be in great pain. There were deep furrows in her brow and around her mouth. The words would barely come.

'Vernon loves me. We have always been in love.'

I could not say anything. Doughty put his elbows on his knees and cupped his forehead in his hands. For Doughty, his mentor and his marriage, the two certainties of his existence, were but a slippery slope of lies flowing like black oil.

'No,' he groaned, his hands muffling his mouth. 'I should not have asked you.'

It was too late.

'Lovers ... we are lovers. From my earliest memories, before I even grew up.' Now, the words started to spill out; she could not hold them back any longer. 'When I was a little girl, his was the only love I had.'

'No. That is a natural affection between siblings. It is no more than that.' He looked up, desperate for her to agree.

'*O God*,' she continued, her eyes staring, her pupils constricted, '*we have offended against Thy holy laws. We have done those things that we ought not to have done. And there is no health in us.*'

'I will find you a better doctor,' he said, 'a decent medical man. When you are feeling better, when you have had time to reflect ...'

She looked past him as if he was no longer there, and through the gap in the curtains at the blackness outside. Her voice rose.

'*But Thou, O Lord, have mercy upon us, miserable offenders. Spare Thou those, O God, who confess their faults. Restore Thou those who are penitent.*'

'It is not true.' He seemed to barely hear her words. 'Oh, I wish that it was not.'

She quivered, her shoulders hunching as her hands clawed like thorns at her face. 'God will forgive us, because we have repented and prayed for mercy. If we believe in God, then the blood of the Lamb will wash away all sins.'

'It cannot be true.' He stood up.

Please, I thought, just hold her, comfort her in her agony. But he was unable to be near to her. His revulsion pressed him back as through swept by an undertow.

'Please say that it is not.'

'I love him,' prayed Harriet. 'O God, dear Lord, only Thou knowest the agony of my love.'

'*No! No! No!*' His shouts filled the house, the street.

Harriet continued, now mumbling prayers.

'You should have lied to me,' he said eventually. 'I cannot stand to know this. My house is not my house. My wife is not my wife. My brother is not my brother.'

She brought her hands to her ears. Her tense fingers caged her head.

'I tried. You do not know how many times the words have formed on my lips, and I have opened my mouth to speak but no sound has come out. A secret is a burden, it is intolerable, and after a time it is a burden that can no longer be borne. Is it not, my husband?'

She spat out that last question, still staring down at her skirts.

'Anything I have done is as nothing, compared to this!' He stood over her, his arms folded. 'How could you be so shameless?'

I supposed that for him it was easier to blame her and conceal his own failings. His pursuit of me was not half as shameful as her crime. But he forgot that her crime was in the greater part her brother's, and so had to watch while her spirit died, like the last moments of a sinking ship, when the hull tilts up out of the sea and then slides backwards, down into the deep water.

An incoherent scene developed then, she weeping, half swooning on her pillows; he claiming the moral high ground for himself. With a growing awareness that he had been deceived, he taxed her with one occasion after another. She denied some and admitted others, seemingly at random, and at length was hysterical again, her words reduced to indistinct gasps. He, his arms folded tightly around his body, was unable to calm her, or himself. Her face was red, wet, and ugly.

'*What a mess!*' He repeated it to himself: '*A mess, a mess, a mess!*'

How would he be able to work? His reports, his inquests, how could he face them? And the infant, the dead, deformed infant, worst of all … Agnes.

'*She was Vernon's child!*' squeaked Harriet.

Doughty was silent in utter shock.

Her head lolled back on her pillow, her face turned away from him, and she closed her eyes tight to keep tears from spilling. I pitied her and Doughty; they were dupes. Each blamed the other for their misery, but what of Glyde?

'Is there no end to this?' Doughty choked the words out, bowing his head and folding his arms around himself, burying his fingers and gripping so tightly that he must have bruised his own flesh. The spasm passed. He leaned across the bed and shouted in her ear. *'Yet you blamed me for the death, why me? Why me? How could the child of such a union be healthy?'*

'Oh, my little Agnes … my lamb … how much longer, dear Agnes, must I go on alone, in such pain, in such torment?'

As Harriet started to weep, the words that she squeaked out with her tears were of death and destruction and anguish.

I pitied her: she had been her brother's prey, and now was helpless. The more she wallowed in shame, the more she drew condemnation.

Eventually Doughty's anger burned out to a grey ash of despair.

He exhaled a long, weary sigh and shook his head.

'It's nearly two in the morning. I have reports to write tomorrow.'

We exchanged a glance: his was an appeal for help. Mine said: *her state is desperate.*

'Leave me with her,' I said. I wiped her eyes and nose with her handkerchief. 'I'll sit with her.'

'Medicine,' she said.

'No,' I said, 'it has been only half an hour. It's too soon. Lie still and try to sleep. Try not to think of anything.'

Doughty leaned down to place his hand on hers.

'Whatever is in the past, is in the past, Harriet. Don't

brood over it.' He forced a smile. He spoke of comfort but his voice was cold. 'We are still husband and wife. Whatever bitterness we have, we must try to forget, try to make a life for the future.'

She pulled her hand away.

'I need my medicine.'

Doughty's smile faded and he took the Aethereal Balsam from the nightstand.

'Sir –' I said.

He cut me off. 'Four drops then.'

'Six.' Her mouth opened like a baby bird's.

He stood, considering. 'No.' He took the bottle and went out. I heard him bang it down on the hall table.

She gave a cry of alarm. I sat down on the bed beside her and put my arms around her, for I did not know what else to do.

'My Agnes, my dead baby, he killed my Agnes,' she whispered.

'Hush, madam.' I stroked her hair. 'I'm sure it was not so.'

She did not reply and lay still, her puffy eyelids drooping closed. I felt weary, impatient for her to sleep. Surely she must sleep, from sheer exhaustion. Sleep would silence her pain.

At last she shut her eyes. I left her my candle and crept out onto the landing, shutting her door softly behind me. In the darkness I started to trace my route with my fingertips towards my staircase. My hand skirted the little table and encountered another.

'Jane.'

I startled. Doughty was there beside me and his words hung in the void of the stairwell.

'I can't suffer this on my own. Please. Come to me. Help me.'

I felt at that moment that I also had been alone and hungry for too long, and that the enormity of the chaos around us both could not be borne in isolation. As we collided against each other in the darkness we tangled into an embrace. At first it felt more like a challenge than a comfort; through the thin fabric of our nightclothes I could feel that every muscle in his body was as tense as a piano-wire. We kissed shamelessly, scouring each other's mouths with an emotion that was almost like anger.

'I love you, Jane,' he murmured, his body relaxing as he withdrew his lips from mine.

I did not reply, and wondered if I truly felt anything for him, yet my heart was thudding and heat sprang from his hands wherever they roamed. Mine were on his shoulders; I slid them up his neck, cupped the back of his head, and gave him my kiss again. I could gladly have gone to his bed.

'Let me come to your room,' he said, as our mouths parted. 'And never lock it again.'

I groaned as his hands slid down my back and rested on my hips. But I took a deep breath and drew back.

'Sir,' I whispered. 'Your wife is on the other side of that door.'

'I will be quiet,' he pleaded, but the moment had gone.

'No,' I said.

He exhaled a long, long sigh, and turned away from me to his own room, every step seeming to be a conscious effort.

I should have gone straight to my attic, but stood there, still full of arousal. I did not know how I would be able to sleep and feared that I would regret my firmness and go to him. On the side-table at my hand was the Aethereal Balsam. I took four drops before going upstairs. It burned in my mouth like strong spirits, the ether invading the back of my nose, and almost as soon as I entered my room I felt it occupying my head.

I locked the door behind me and cast myself on my bed, falling into a profound sleep.

36: I Cover the Mirror

I woke to a pounding headache and the clatter of carts in the street outside. I must have been oblivious to everything and had not heard the chimes from the clock downstairs. Sun shone down through my skylight. Harriet had not rung, but what had happened with her four o'clock medication?

I got straight out of bed and ran my fingers through my hair. There was no time to wash. I dressed in haste and went straight to her, although by now I was afraid of what I would find: agitation, anger, jealousy.

But the room was still in darkness and she was quiet. I smelt the tang of ether. I drew back the curtains and opened the window to let in fresh air. She lay still, staring, her pupils tiny pinpoints in her violet irises. The green walls and drapes reflected an algal light upon her pallid face.

'Ma'am!' There was no response.

For a moment Harriet seemed dead, but no, she was taking tiny, rapid breaths like those of a mouse. I lifted the hand that lay upturned on the green silk coverlet. It was warm and soft, but the fingernails were a dusky blue.

'Harriet!' I grasped her shoulder and shook her gently. Silence hung in the room like a pall. The violet eyes continued to stare.

I went and banged on Doughty's door, yelling out for help.

When he entered the room he took two great strides towards the bed.

'Good God.' He felt his wife's wrist, then over her heart, and stooped to listen at her mouth. 'Her colour …'

Her lips were dusky in her pallid face. She blinked once, but her staring eyes did not move or focus on him. Her fair hair flowed like twisted wire across her pillow. On the floor by the bed lay the Aethereal Balsam bottle, empty. I picked it up.

'I forgot to dose her in the night,' I said. 'She must have wakened.'

'Go at once for Dr Astley-Scrope,' said Doughty. 'Tell him to bring his stomach-pump.'

Heart thudding, I pulled on my boots and shawl.

I hurried along Newhall Street and towards the doctor's house on Bennett's Hill. The streets were full of carts and carriages and thronged with pedestrians; the shopkeepers were opening up and the costermongers were uncovering their fruit barrows and calling out their wares. I pushed and dodged and sidestepped my way through the crowd.

I hammered on Dr Astley-Scrope's door and a manservant showed me in. I said it was urgent and was told that the doctor was not yet up. It seemed a good twenty minutes before he made his way down the stairs with his bag of instruments.

'Dr Doughty says you must bring a stomach-pump,' I said, relating quickly what had happened.

He balked at that. 'Well, my girl, I won't be told my business by the likes of you. I shall see the patient first and make my own mind up what's to be done.'

It took several minutes to persuade him, but eventually he went upstairs and returned with a varnished wooden case. It was then a struggle to direct his angular frame through the early morning crowds to Newhall Street; he seemed to bump into everybody. I took him by the elbow, steering a path.

Doughty, still in his dressing gown, was kneeling by Harriet's bed, his ear resting on her bared bosom, his hand at her wrist, trying to detect a heartbeat. Her violet eyes slowly rolled upwards, unblinking, the whites visible between the eyelids, the irises nearly vanished.

'Why's it taken you so long?' he demanded. 'She's nearly gone! Did you bring the stomach-pump?'

Astley-Scrope *humph*ed by way of an answer, pushing up Harriet's eyelid with his thumb to examine the staring pupil beneath.

'For God's sake, man. Look!' Doughty indicated the empty bottle.

Astley-Scrope examined the Aethereal Balsam, reading the date on the label. He jutted his chin forward, peering at me through his wire-framed spectacles.

'This was only dispensed two days ago. It should have lasted for a fortnight. Have you given it all at once?'

I shook my head and launched into a description of Harriet's regime.

'There's no time for this. She is barely breathing. A bucket of water, Jane,' commanded Doughty, 'and an empty one beside.'

I dashed down to the kitchen and when I returned I found they had inserted a red India-rubber tube into Mrs Doughty's mouth. Fumbling with a brass tap, Astley-Scrope drew up into a syringe then expelled a brownish liquid into the empty bucket. A harsh smell rose up: vomit and ether.

He instilled fresh water into her stomach, then drew it back out, continuing until the water ran clear. Mrs Doughty remained motionless, unaware of the tube in her throat. He shook his head and withdrew the apparatus, dropping it into the bucket. A long red coil lay in the turbid liquid.

'She's failing,' said Doughty. 'Her pulse is very slow, less than thirty.'

Astley-Scrope wiped Harriet's face with a towel. Her lips were darkening and a film covered her eyes.

'Have you an antidote?' asked Doughty. 'You must have brought something: caffeine, atropine, permanganate?'

'It is too late,' said Astley-Scrope. 'There is nothing that will overcome so powerful an overdose. The poison is already in the system. When did you last administer Aethereal Balsam?'

'She had twenty drops at one o'clock. The bottle was three-quarters full,' I said.

'Twenty drops! And did you administer any further dose?'

'No, she did not ring.'

'And yet the bottle is empty,' said Astley-Scrope. 'You must have overdosed her.'

'She took it herself,' I said. 'I have not been in to her all night. The bottle was not even kept in her room. She must have crept out to the landing to get it.'

Astley-Scrope scowled.

I looked at Harriet from the foot of the bed and saw that the rhythm of her breathing altered, and she gave two slow, deep sighs. I hoped that she might be awakening, but her chest became immobile. Her skin turned greyish-blue. We watched her in despair as she heaved another couple of deep sighs, and then ceased breathing again. The sighs resumed after a while, but shallower, and failing; the interval between them grew ever longer.

'She is dying,' said Astley-Scrope. 'If you claim that this is suicide, young woman, you are making a rash statement, indeed. Be careful what you say. A suicide requires an inquest, as Coroner Doughty will confirm.'

'I never agreed with your prescriptions,' said Doughty bitterly. 'She is addicted to ether and opium. Everything you ever prescribed for her was a form of it.'

'I cannot be blamed if the medicines I supply are misused by the patient.' Dr Astley-Scrope glared at me. 'Or by their attendants.'

At that moment I was sure that Mrs Doughty had ceased to breathe. Her black mouth gaped.

'Does she yet live?' I asked.

Doughty felt her pulse, and laid a hand on her heart, then knelt by the bed and listened again with his cheek against her skin. Then he stood, pulling his dressing gown tight around him, wiping his face with his sleeve. He went to the window and looked down at the street, arms tightly folded, shoulders hunched. He was silent.

Astley-Scrope placed a stethoscope over Harriet's heart for a few moments, and then shook his head.

'Cover the mirror, and close her eyes,' he said to me.

I draped the dressing-table mirror with Harriet's shawl, averting my gaze. It was said that an escaping soul could become trapped in the silvered glass and be enslaved by the devil, lingering to create mischief; a glance in the mirror might reveal her dead face, heralding madness and death. Her eyelids were soft and cool, and though I pressed them gently closed, they did not stay shut, leaving visible a rim of white. I would have to find some pennies.

On the nightstand beside Harriet's bed was her needlework bag. The baby's robe would never be finished. She had said it was for a sale of work, but I thought of her trying to bring her husband to her bed and wondered if now the baby who would have worn it would remain unborn.

Doughty remained by the window with his back still turned, shoulders tense. He regrets it, I thought. He taxed her with what I had told him, and now he hates me for it.

'A grievous situation,' said Astley-Scrope, to Doughty's back. 'May I offer my condolences?'

Doughty turned around to him. His face was cold.

'I told Harriet to dismiss you.'

'I am sorry for your loss, sir, but you can hardly blame me for it.'

'She wouldn't listen to me. Oh, God.'

'Dr Doughty, you have had a profound shock. You are barely aware of what you are saying, and I am sure do not intend to question my professional judgment.'

'You made her an addict. You prescribed her lethal quantities of ether, of opium. She took it constantly.'

'But it was not I who emptied the bottle. You should have supervised your servant more carefully.' Astley-Scrope looked at me contemptuously from across the bed. 'You must have attended her during the night.'

I shook my head, and an untidy tangle of hair skeined out of my mobcap and hung down my cheek. I pushed it back. I was on the edge of an abyss of disgrace.

Astley-Scrope's mouth tightened.

'You can't put the blame on her,' Doughty said.

'Your servant may well have poisoned your wife.' Astley-Scrope stared at Doughty over the top of his wire-framed spectacles. 'Accidentally, through her own stupidity or, indeed, deliberately. She is the obvious culprit. In fact, I would suggest that she be reported to the police.'

Doughty could have vouched for me then but was silent. My spirit sank: these men might sacrifice me to preserve themselves, concealing the shame of Harriet's suicide and protecting Astley-Scrope's practice from scrutiny.

'The police will soon get the truth from her,' added Astley-Scrope.

Doughty startled at that. 'It's not Jane's fault!'

'How can you be certain?'

'She hasn't been into my wife's room!' Doughty hesitated, colour rising in his face, then met Astley-Scrope's glare with his jaw outthrust, enunciating clearly: 'She spent the night with me.'

I stared at him in shock.

Astley-Scrope clamped his beaky jaws together and pushed his spectacles upwards with his forefinger.

'Good Lord!' he said eventually. 'A servant!' He peered at me with a new curiosity and I averted my gaze, hoping that he could not see my confusion.

A sheet of paper on the escritoire caught my eye: a letter.

'We tended Harriet together last night,' Doughty insisted, as though daring Astley-Scrope to object. 'My wife was … unwell … agitated, in a distressed state of mind. She had her usual dose of Aethereal Balsam, and eventually settled to sleep. After that, I persuaded Jane to allow me to her bed. I besought her for comfort, she pitied me, and I lay all night in her arms. She did not, therefore, give further medication to my wife. She is innocent.'

'Innocent? Innocent?' spluttered Astley-Scrope, thinking no doubt that no-one could have merited the description less.

'Certainly. It was I who acted dishonourably, it was I who seduced her. She would have resisted me, had we been in a better situation. She's innocent of any wrongdoing. I'll gladly swear to it in a Court of Law.'

'Well now,' said Astley-Scrope at last, 'that throws a different light on this sorry business, does it not? But even so, you are blinded by your little love affair, sir, when there is a simple answer. You are making the situation unnecessarily difficult for us both.'

'What? I should hang her, to preserve myself?' Doughty shook his head. 'It's taken me all my life to find her; if I lose her now, I'll spend my remaining years in hell. Whatever price there is for this, it's I who must pay. I'm the one that married Harriet. Jane is blameless.'

'Are you mad, Dr Doughty, with your infatuation for this servant?' Astley-Scrope looked again at me, as if unable to believe that I was worthy of such regard. 'You are surely besotted.'

'No, sir, merely truthful, in a world accustomed to convenient lies.'

He said it with such conviction that even I started to believe him, wondering if I had surrendered to him while drugged with Aethereal Balsam. But no, my door had been locked from the inside, and I knew that my body was untouched.

Astley-Scrope was thinking. He stared down at Harriet's corpse, and then at each of us in turn.

'Or have you both conspired together to end this life?'

Doughty opened his mouth, and looked about to return an angry answer, when I indicated the escritoire.

'She has written something.'

The candle had burned down in the night, and its beeswax formed runnels down the silver candlestick and a honey-coloured puddle on the green leather inlay. The pen was still in the open inkwell. There was an envelope addressed *'To Vernon'*, tucked behind the inkstand, and another letter, which Harriet had not troubled to fold.

'Read it out, then,' said Doughty, scowling at Astley-Scrope.

The doctor craned over the paper, his face shrivelled like

dry-rotten wood as his eyes zigzagged from line to line.

'It is addressed to you – a suicide letter,' he said, tight-lipped, handing it to Doughty. 'Most unpleasant. Distressing.'

The paper trembled in Doughty's fingers.

I drew close to his elbow. Harriet's copperplate script wavered, the lines collapsing at their ends as they ran down the page.

37: Harriet's Letter to Her Husband

11th August 1840

To Dr William Doughty – Farewell!

I no longer know who we are, nor want to set eyes on you again. I am in despair, and you have shown me no kindness, only utter contempt – even hatred. I did not choose this path. I was destined to receive the extraordinary power of my brother's passion. He loved me before I learned to speak, forming me into his perfect creature, driving out my sins with the force of his love. Vernon has been my only guiding light, without whom I would long have terminated my darkness. I obeyed him in everything, even consenting to marry you, a husband of his choice, whom I could never love. It was Vernon's greatest sorrow that someone else must provide for his child, and it so grieved him that Agnes did not survive.

Suicide is acedia, the worst form of sloth, the deadliest of sins. But I have faith that, through God's infinite mercy, Vernon and I both shall be forgiven, and reunited with our little Agnes in Paradise.

I will be buried in St Michael's churchyard, beside the path that leads from the rectory to the church. Vernon will pronounce my burial rites, and each day his footsteps will pass where I lie, and from the rectory windows he will look down upon my tomb and repeat his prayers.

And, my so-called husband, although I know I have earned your hatred, it is your deceit which has dealt me the fatal blow. It is you who should be ashamed. You thought I knew nothing, but it was that hot afternoon, when I had rung for Jane and she did not come, and I wanted water. I stood on the landing and looked down through the window, between the washing lines. You had put your chairs out in the shade at the back of the house and thought yourselves concealed. You sat side by side with her – a mere servant! Her bare head lay upon your shirt, and as she slept, you caressed her shoulder, and pressed your lips to her hair. Then you turned up your eyes, and closed them, and you sighed. I never had such tenderness from you.

Tonight, you thought I slept. My eyes were closed, but my ears were open and I heard you both, murmuring on the landing outside my door. And now it is a night of horrors, and although I have rung and rung for Jane to help me, she does not, and you do not, and through the wall I can hear you, crying out her name. You did not even notice me when I went to find my medicine. You have cruelly forgotten me, forgotten how much I need help. I cannot stand it another moment. How can I remain any longer in this life, washed and clothed and drugged by tainted hands, while you deceive me under my own roof?

So I bid you farewell, and it is not truly a parting, for we were never truly united.

– Harriet.

38: The Death Certificate

I looked up at Doughty in horror. 'She saw … she heard us,' I murmured.

He laid the letter on the escritoire, still staring at it, but no longer reading, the shadows darkening beneath his eyes. His fingers remained on its edge, undecided.

Astley-Scrope pursed his mouth as if he had eaten bitter aloes.

'In my experience, this sort of thing is best burnt. Else it will open a Pandora's Box of miseries. As I said, a suicide requires an inquest. Would this perhaps fall to the Warwickshire Coroner? As things stand, Birmingham is no longer within his jurisdiction, but then, you can hardly do it yourself.'

'Truth will out,' said Doughty, shaking his head. 'It can't be helped. I am disgraced. I was already in disfavour enough with the magistrates.'

'The letter proves self-murder,' said Astley-Scrope, 'and thus exonerates your servant and yourself, although it bears witness to adultery upon both sides. But as to Vernon, a most odious offence is laid to his charge, which can scarcely be credited. He is a dear and trusted friend.' He stood in a questioning attitude with one hand cupping the opposite elbow and the other hand laid to his cheek, tilting his narrow face toward Doughty.

'I could not believe it myself,' muttered Doughty. 'She confessed it last night. We quarrelled. It has forced her to this act of despair. If only … but it is too late …'

We stood contemplating the dead face. If only … what? The seeds of Harriet's self-annihilation had been sown in her from her earliest years. If only Glyde could be brought to account – but how could that ever happen?

'As a suicide, Vernon will not even be able to bury her in his own churchyard.' Astley-Scrope started to rummage in his bag. 'I think I had best issue a death certificate. A sudden illness has evidently overtaken her. And then I will take and destroy those letters.'

'How can you write a false certificate?' Doughty looked up in alarm. 'Do you hope thus to help me? Or do you try to protect yourself?'

'It is neither you nor I,' said Astley-Scrope. 'It is Vernon. There is no committee in the town that does not have him at its core. If he is brought down, there may well be others who will fall. It will make an immense scandal, more than the town can bear, at a time when it is fighting for recognition, indeed for the survival of its Royal Charter, and for its right to self-determination.'

He sat down at the escritoire, laying the death certificate on top of the letter.

'May I use this pen?'

Doughty gestured to him to go on. I supposed that he saw no alternative.

'Diphtheria,' said Astley-Scrope.

He completed and signed the death certificate and

handed it to Doughty.

'Take this to Mr Madden – well, I need not tell you. You know the system. He will advise you about an undertaker. And then I suppose that you had better inform your brother-in-law of his sister's death. She wished for Vernon to conduct the burial service.'

Doughty wiped his palm across his brow and hooked his fingers in his hair.

'It is an impossible situation. I scarcely know what to say to him.'

'I would advise against going into excessive detail.' Astley-Scrope plucked Glyde's envelope from behind the inkstand and put it into his bag with the suicide letter. 'You may tell him that you thought it was no more than a chill and a sore throat, and so did not think to summon him. He will be severely distressed that he was not here at the end.'

'He has always been here,' I said softly.

'Have a care,' said Astley-Scrope, his tone suddenly scalpel-sharp. 'Think yourself fortunate, young woman, that you are being protected from the consequences of your shameful conduct. A tittle-tattling tongue will destroy that protection.'

'Her shameful conduct, as you term it, was at my behest.' Doughty was quick to defend me again, but only irritated Astley-Scrope further.

'Even with those letters destroyed, sir,' he snapped at Doughty, 'you face professional ruin if you do not remove her from your household. Others may not know what I know, but even so, society will not stomach the two of you living here alone. You a widower, sir, and she a fine-complexioned young female. It won't do. You must put her out of your house.'

'What, send her away? She stays here!' insisted Doughty. 'I am her employer and I wish to retain her here. I cannot be expected to shift for myself, without a servant.'

'It is not seemly,' said Astley-Scrope, 'for the two of you to continue cohabiting. And if rumours get out about the nature of your alliance, then, irrespective of my death certificate, suspicions will arise as to how your wife met her death.'

'He is right,' I said. What I had felt for Doughty the previous night was growing stronger. I was ashamed of it. 'Dr Doughty, I had better not stay with you.'

'Jane, please take the stomach-pump and wash it for Dr Astley-Scrope,' said Doughty, in a low, angry voice.

I took the buckets and the stomach pump down to the scullery, hearing their voices growing louder upstairs. When I returned they had come down to the study, still arguing.

Astley-Scrope demanded whether I had purged the tubing with clean water and said I clearly did not understand the process. He said he would clean it properly when he returned home, stuffed it away without properly closing its case, and left.

Doughty's eyes locked with mine.

'Do not leave me, Jane,' he whispered. 'You cannot leave me now. Say you will not.'

I shook my head. 'You are overwrought, sir. It is a dreadful situation.'

'William,' he said, 'my name is William.'

'You are overwrought. We will discuss this another day.'

'You will stay until then?'

'Long enough to settle things,' I said. 'But, I am sorry, Dr Astley-Scrope is correct.'

Yet I permitted him to take me into his arms and leaned my forehead into his neck.

'Do you not regret what you have said?' I murmured, the sudden comfort of the soft velvet of his dressing gown beneath my lips making my head throb. My shame evaporated; I desired him. 'You told a lie; you harmed yourself to save me.'

He hesitated. 'I do not understand my own feelings. I did not think that I loved Harriet. I realise now that I did not even know her. And yet there is something numb in my heart, as if a part of it has been erased. I did not want her to die: you saw how I quarrelled with her over her medicine.'

His arms were trembling at my back. I drew away and looked up; his eyes were moist and red. I put a finger up to his cheek and stroked away a tear.

'*A man who looks at a woman with lustful intent has already committed adultery with her in his heart.*' He tightened his embrace. 'I do not regret what I said to Astley-Scrope. Nor do I regret our kiss. If I lose you, I will hold that memory in my mind until my wits become feeble. But no one will take you from me, Jane. I will keep you safe.'

He wanted me, his mouth was close to mine, and my heart was leaping, but I could not allow it.

'I am grateful that you protected me, but …' I extracted myself, 'your wife is still lying on her deathbed, her body not yet cold.'

'Harriet's spirit is extinguished on earth, and has gone to another world, Jane.' He had let me go, but still sought to persuade me. 'She is no more. Believe me, I have seen innumerable dead, and their spirits are no longer here. There have been many inquests where I have longed for the departed soul to return and provide the answers I sought, but they never do. Once they are gone, there is no return, however ardently we may wish it.'

'You will mourn her,' I said, wishing that I had not disengaged myself.

'I wish that I had been more patient with her,' he replied. 'I always thought of her melancholia as a conceit, a charade by which she sought to escape the duties of a wife. Now I know it was an unbearable anguish, the symptom of a severe disorder that one day would take away her life. And I suppose that I am glad that what I said to Astley-Scrope was in part a deception, and that we did not lie together last night, for her sake. I thank you for that.'

'And I you.'

His face became grave. 'But you will see now that we will be judged as though we had.'

39: Garrett & Sons

Doughty went out to register his wife's death, saying he would also inform Glyde. I started to put the house in order; the daily chores were much the same, death or not. Doughty returned after a couple of hours and not long afterwards Garrett & Sons, the funeral directors, arrived with a cart, bringing a coffin and other paraphernalia. I showed them up to Harriet's room. Mr Garrett said I should wash Harriet, which I did, and then a sheet was draped across her.

Doughty watched Mr Garrett as he twisted a large needle into Harriet's neck and another into her heart.

'The funeral arrangements we discussed,' said Doughty. 'Could they be made, perhaps, less expensive?'

Mr Garrett, who was running a tube down to a bucket beside Harriet's bed, looked at him in a doleful manner that he had no doubt practised all his professional life. He raised his undertaker's eyebrows, and said that Dr Doughty was no doubt still in a state of considerable distress, and that perhaps when Dr Doughty had had the opportunity to reflect on how such things must appear to the neighbours, he would see the propriety of the recommendations.

'Please do not omit to avail of the opportunity to examine our excellent collection of monumental masonry.'

Mr Garrett held up a funnel, slowly emptying a bottle of embalming fluid down a tube into Harriet's chest. Her face was like alabaster and bloodless veins bulged in her neck, strangely lucent. Dark liquid oozed into the bucket.

'Of course, you need not choose exactly at this moment, but I would like to draw your attention to the very favourable rates we charge for monuments ordered within a fortnight of the burial. Pray be assured that Garrett & Sons offers a great advantage not elsewhere to be obtained, by providing every requisite used in the business, thus avoiding the inconvenience and uncertainty of using a smaller establishment.'

As Doughty started to protest, there came a loud rapping on the front door and I excused myself.

Glyde was on the step, his face red, hatless and without his walking-cane. He passed me as though I had not been there and I followed him as he swept up the stairs and marched straight into Harriet's room.

'But why was I not told before?' he demanded, his voice shaking. 'I would have visited her. I would have given her the last rites. She has died unshriven.'

'It was all too sudden,' said Doughty. He regarded his brother-in-law coldly. 'A little fever, a cough, a sore throat. I expected it to resolve in a day or two, but her constitution was frail and it carried her swiftly away. It was no more than a few hours. She died during the night.'

'Did she not ask for me? I would have come at once, at any hour.'

'I thought it only a chill, and she did not want to trouble you. Astley-Scrope diagnosed diphtheria.'

Glyde's misaligned eyes shifted quickly to scrutinise Doughty's face.

'He saw the membrane in her throat,' said Doughty, maintaining his gloomy expression unchanged.

I swallowed back nausea as with a groan of despair Glyde crouched beside the bed. I thought of them lying together, a fragile child violated by a brutal brother, a lost childhood perverted away from innocence.

Glyde's arm went around Harriet's corpse; he rested his head on her belly and sobbed.

Mr Garrett intervened. 'I would avoid touching the flesh, sir, if I were you. Due to the employment of white arsenic. A fly landing on the skin might be dead within five minutes.' A shrunken man, himself of a pallid and cadaverous complexion, he placed a restraining hand on Glyde's shoulder. 'In our firm, and I assure you that Garrett and Sons are the most reliable and best-established undertakers in the town, we cannot recommend embalming too strongly, for reasons of health and hygiene. Else the vapours and liquids issuing from the deceased who awaits burial may prove fatal to the living. In some instances, people allow the remains of their dear departed to remain exposed for several days in the very room in which they dine – and I have known every single member of a family to perish, one after the other, young and old, for the want of this precaution. Or a closed coffin may explode with mephitic gases, bursting in the night, sir, like cannon fire, the resulting exhalations bringing disease and death.'

Glyde was oblivious to Mr Garrett's philosophising.

'Let me gaze upon my sister, my angel, my seraph, just for a moment longer, just one moment more …' He rose laboriously, his eyes streaming tears, then retreated to stand at the window, his shadow falling across the bed. 'My sweet seraph! We shall be reunited in Paradise.' He blew his nose into his handkerchief.

Mr Garrett indicated the pennies on the bedside table. 'I have sewn her eyelids shut over the pads, so you may reclaim those back. The jaw has been supported in place with small sutures.' He selected a small brush from a canvas instrument roll and applied carmine to Harriet's lips and cheeks. A curved needle ran through the lapel of his coat.

I brushed out her hair. The blonde strands separated and rejoined on the white pillow.

Glyde's wet eyes lingered on the frail, cold, poisonous cadaver, and he mumbled prayers through his handkerchief.

'She who has been baptised into Christ Jesus is baptised into His death and is buried therefore with Him by baptism into death. Just as Christ was raised from the dead by the glory of the Father, she too will walk in newness of life.'

Mr Garrett ignored him, disconnecting the tubes and packing up his instruments and his bottles of solution. His sons came to move Harriet with gloved hands and I changed her stained sheet for a fresh one.

'Be careful, miss, wash your hands well afterwards.' Mr Garrett picked up the bucket of waste fluid. 'I trust that I may be permitted to dispose of this in the privy? I presume it is outside in the back yard?'

The sons shrouded Harriet in white satin, then carried her downstairs to her coffin, which rested on trestles in the parlour. I smoothed the satin folds straight; a border of paper lace was glued to the margins of the casket and, plumped by the embalming fluid and enlivened by carmine, her peaceful face was more beautiful than it had been in life.

I went to wash my hands and when I returned the late afternoon sun sent a brave beam of light through the gloomy air; the throb of the distant manufactories beat out a march of death. A brass-ornamented lid leaned against the wall and a black velvet pall was folded on the settee.

'Do not cover her yet!' begged Glyde, hovering tearfully beside her. 'I shall never see her dear face again!'

Doughty watched him in silence, disguising his emotions.

Mr Garrett came in with his invoice.

'Fifty pounds, nineteen shillings and sixpence,' he said, 'with the inclusion of a medium-sized monument from our selection in the manufactory, which, Dr Doughty, I believe you viewed earlier.'

Doughty's protests were cut short by Glyde. He went through Mr Garrett's invoice: the horse-drawn carriages, the embossed memorial cards, the mutes, the coffin-bearers, and criticised every arrangement.

'Tear that up and start again, Mr Garrett. I have recourse to funds within the parish,' said Glyde. 'She shall be buried with all due dignities.'

'She wanted you to perform the burial rites,' Doughty muttered, reddening. 'I am sure you will compose a fitting eulogy.'

'Indeed,' said Glyde, 'for no-one knew her innumerable virtues better than I or loved her more deeply or for as long a duration. And it falls to me to oversee the order of service. You may be certain that our entire congregation will attend.'

40: Invoice

JOSEPH GARRETT & SONS
UNDERTAKERS TO THE GENTRY
ALABASTER – SPAR – & PETRIFACTION
WAREHOUSE
BIRMINGHAM

12th August 1840

Embalming services with attendance of Mr J. Garrett & Sons

A strong elm Coffin, lead-lined

White sattin Mattresses to sides, head, foot & lid.

A Shroud of white sattin & a Sheet of the same.

A very strong Oak Coffin Case covered with superfine black cloth & finished with Japanned nails, four pair of large fancy handles, & two brass lid ornaments

Engraved bevelled brass Plate inscribed: REQUIESCAT – HARRIET ANN DOUGHTY

7 days use of silk velvet Pall & Coffin trestles.

Eight Coffin-bearers

Two Wand-bearers

Four Mutes

Feather-man bearing a rich Plume of black Ostrich Feathers, 4 feet high & 3 feet across.

Best Hearse drawn by six horses

A Set of best Black Velvets & a Set of Ostrich Feathers

Two Processional Coaches with four horses each

Two hundred embossed Memorial Cards

Large Monument of best pale Alabaster on Pedestal of black Basalt, with gilded letters, winged Mourners & Acanthus leaves.

TOTAL L. 200. 0. 0

41: Requiem

The bell at St Michael's began to toll, and a procession climbed up Newhall Street under an overcast sky. Everything was in black. We were led, one step every two seconds, by four sombre-faced mutes, ancient men with long overcoats and silk gloves, with hats swathed in crape, silk stoles and ebony staves draped in cloth. Behind them walked the feather-man, balancing on his head a lid of black ostrich plumes. Four sable-coloured mares, as glossy as jackdaws, caparisoned with plumed heads, and with their hooves muffled with sacking, were driven by Mr Garrett himself, drawing a great hearse topped with ornate tracery and a crown of plumes. The glass sides revealed Harriet's coffin draped with a velvet pall, and four coffin-bearers walked on either side. Behind, in a mourning-coach with its blinds drawn, rode Mrs and Mrs Glyde, Harriet's parents, who had been staying at the Rectory. They had not acknowledged Doughty and had not been to visit, not even to view their dead daughter. I wondered if Glyde had given them some twisted account of Doughty, and his treatment of Harriet.

Doughty and I were in the second carriage, enthroned in black-velvet damask upholstery. It creaked with infinite slowness up the hill and we stared ahead, watching the coachman through the glass. Doughty had refused to travel alone, and I was grateful not to walk the short distance to the church. I had become conscious in the last several days that as I passed through the streets I attracted attention. Evidently rumours had spread. Neighbours glanced at me, looking away as I met their eyes. Young working-men gave me insolent grins. In the butcher's shop, they no longer greeted me, and merely discharged their business. I reassured myself that it was of no consequence; in time they would forget.

Doughty wore a knot of black ribbons in his lapel and a crape hatband; his face was gaunt, drawn tight over his cheekbones. Down beside my black skirts, his hand gripped mine; I tolerated this discomfort, hoping it would sustain him. At his expense I wore full mourning, as though every piece of my clothing, from my petticoats to my silk gloves and veiled bonnet, had been dipped in ink. I suspected it was his way to make me purchase new clothes. He had been most specific about black silk stockings.

The cortege drew up at St Michael's churchyard. Doughty helped me down from the carriage and offered me his arm, but I gave him a tiny shake of the head and retreated to stand behind him. The bearers lifted out the coffin and turned it towards the church gates, Mr and Mrs Glyde taking precedence over Doughty as we followed behind.

The sexton and the parish clerk followed Reverend Glyde as he stepped forward, robed in black.

'I am the resurrection and the life, saith the Lord.' Glyde's expression was set, his slightly squinting eyes making it unreadable.

With his head and shoulders held high, he led us all in

stately procession towards the church, the coffin with its mutes and coffin-bearers and feather-man following the churchmen, the mourners walking behind, our paces in time with the corpse bell that tolled from the tower above.

The gravestones stood crooked in the churchyard, as though loosened by the unquiet spirits of the dead. In this overpopulated town the graves were close-packed, and each burial place undermined its neighbour. The sexton's spade might cleave through rotting wood in an unmarked grave and toss a bone into the air.

'He that believeth in Me, though he were dead, yet shall he live,' intoned Glyde at the church door.

As the coffin entered the church, the high notes of the boy choristers floated on the air, the deeper notes of the men resonating beneath: *Requiem æternam dona eis, Domine, et lux perpetua luceat eis.*

I had intended to sit at the back, but the church was full. Doughty beckoned me forward and I followed him. I could not see the faces of the mourners either side of the aisle, and could only imagine their disapproval as he ushered me ahead of him into the front row. I glanced sideways under cover of my veil and saw Doughty was standing with his hands not held in prayer but clenched at his sides. On the low shelf at the end of the row was Harriet's Berlin wool-work kneeler, with its cherubs and its golden sword and its pattern of bars. I looked at it again, seeing something familiar about the angelic faces: if my eyes did not deceive me they were Harriet and Glyde.

After Harriet had been closed into her coffin and everyone had gone, Doughty had asked me to clean her room and change the bed linen. Conscious of the silent coffin in the parlour, and nervous of looking in the mirrors, we had returned to our own orbits: he to his coroner's duties, I to the care of the house, eating separate meals. He worked until late at night while I sat at the piano playing melancholy nocturnes to Harriet's coffin. At night I lay awake and alone, sensing that it was only a matter of time before we collided again. There was much that we might have discussed, but I dared not risk that intimacy; we had spoken with a formality subverted by the hunger and fire in his eyes.

I had scrutinised the newspapers for suitable vacancies, without finding anything for which I wanted to apply. In any case, Doughty would not countenance talk of my departure.

Now the coffin rested before the altar. A wreath of evergreens lay on the black velvet pall and a huge white candle burned at its foot. Glyde, at the lectern, stood with bowed head. The exquisite sorrow of the echoing requiem crushed me to my heart. My mind filled with my own distress: Nathan's miserable little life, my estranged parents, Theresa's suicide, Edmond's desertion, and now Doughty and I had created a scandal. I prayed to God that I would escape and make a new life. From the airy voids of the church I imagined the answer came back: *This is a problem you have caused; do not ask Me to solve it.*

The requiem ended; the church was silent. Someone coughed. Doughty was motionless at my side. If there was to be no help from religion, the will to leave him must stem from my own strength. But against my better judgment I had begun to love his lonely pride, to be moved by the strength of his passion and his battle to control it, and I yearned to feel the imprint of his body upon mine.

As Glyde delivered the eulogy he paused and struggled to maintain his voice. Red-faced and quivering, he drew the congregation in sympathy. His grief was sincere, but his words contained a barb.

He praised Harriet for her charitable works and her

support for the church, he spoke of how the delights of motherhood were swept away by the cruel hand of Death, of how the frail flower of womanly beauty had been corrupted by the worm of disease, how feeling herself *forsaken* – he emphasised that word and a shudder of dismay swept through the congregation – 'by those who should have been faithful, despair consumed her spirit, and despite all the medicines prescribed by her excellent physician, her soul was surrendered into the more worthy keeping of our Lord'.

Glyde was staring at me, compounding my anguish. Then he looked upwards and his expression softened.

'*It is sown a natural body, it is raised a spiritual body.* Corinthians, one, fifteen. Our sister has entered upon another state of being, completing a journey which we must all one day follow. We will undertake it strengthened by our faith, as our Christian souls plunge into the death-agony, the furnace of which will burn away our evil. As we change worlds, we leave our mortal sins to be buried with the body in the grave, while the purified soul escapes to the regions of holiness and peace!'

Glyde's rising voice conveyed the earnestness of his faith. I wondered how he could ever leave his own sins behind and be purified. Surely he must enter Hell, or there would be no justice for the poor creatures he had defiled.

'*That new existence is achieved through faith in Jesus Christ, our Lord and Saviour. Who for us men and for our salvation took flesh, and was crucified, and rose from death, and ascended into heaven, and has pleaded incessantly at the right hand of the Father for us, the weak and erring children of the Fall. For the eternal God is indeed our refuge, and underneath are the everlasting arms of the Church.*'

At that, Doughty's grunt of disgust resounded in the air.

After the reading and the prayers, the sacred polyphony of the 'Agnus Dei' filled the church and Glyde consecrated the host for Holy Communion.

'Agnus Dei, qui tollis peccata mundi, miserere nobis. Lamb of God, who taketh away the sins of the world, have mercy upon us.'

I turned to Doughty; he gave a barely perceptible shake of the head. We remained in our places, refusing to take the wafer and the chalice from Glyde's tainted hands. The rest of the congregation filed past us and knelt in turn on the altar steps. From behind my veil, I watched them return to their pews, their faces either turned away or glaring at us in cold disapproval. Astley-Scrope gave us a wary glance as he passed.

After the committal, the coffin-bearers bowed to the Cross and turned, shouldering the coffin in slow procession out of the church. I followed Doughty down the aisle, through the stares of the congregation. They seemed to be studying my body, some of the men leering, their wives' mouths set in contempt. Doughty's head was lowered and his hands clasped together behind his back, like a prisoner in chains.

We stood at the foot of the grave as a soft rain began to fall, like the tears of the sky. It was a cold day and a breeze rattled the leaves in the plane trees, whose edges had started to brown. Summer would soon give way to autumn. The pall was removed and, as Glyde recited the burial prayers the coffin was lowered into the muddy oblong at our feet, the coffin-bearers gripping the ropes.

'Suffer us not at our last hour for any pains of death to fall from Thee,' intoned Glyde, holding his prayer book like an amulet.

He paused and gestured to Doughty. It was time for the earth to be cast upon the body.

Doughty pulled the ribbon knot from his coat lapel and touched it to his lips. Then it fluttered down into the grave, landing on the coffin lid with a thump. He stared at it, tears standing in his eyes. What did he see? Perhaps the death of a hope he once cherished, or something he had lost years ago? He stooped to gather soil and let it drop, small stones striking the polished brasses on the coffin. The sexton started to shovel in the earth.

Glyde prayed on, tears streaming down his face, wiping his nose from time to time on his sleeve. Of all of us he was the only one who openly grieved her. Her parents stood stiffly by. I imagined Harriet lying below in the darkness of her coffin, her livid face upturned to the wood, her hair streaming over her shroud, and her eyes sewn shut.

Glyde closed the prayer book and looked up. It was over.

The mourners dispersed. Mr Garrett shook Doughty's hand, and the empty hearse clattered away over the cobbles, its black plumes tangling in the rain. As if primed, Glyde's relatives retreated and waited at a distance while he faced Doughty across the grave.

'You have lost your good name in this town,' said Glyde. 'Ever since the Sefton case your conduct has been the subject of much discussion amongst the magistrates. They will now make a requisition to the Lord Chancellor to remove you from your position of coroner.'

'What, I have lost my wife, shall I also lose my employment?' Doughty drew himself up, his shoulders set tense in his mourning coat.

'You cannot live in sin.' Glyde sneered, and his oblique stare settled on me. 'Nor may you flaunt your vices at my sister's funeral.'

I glared at him through the black lace of my veil, then as my hatred of him welled up I cast the veil up over the peak of my bonnet.

'And what of your own sin? Your many vices!' I stepped forward to Doughty's side, unable to remain silent. 'You have a heart of cruelty. How you tortured me! Theresa Curran, remember her? Clara Scattergood? And your own sister – rest her poor soul – why do you imagine that she was the way that she was?'

The sexton beside us must have heard every word, but he continued to shovel earth over the coffin regardless.

Glyde grew pale and his fingers tensed around his prayer book as though to crush it.

'How dare you? You, of worthless character, a trollop rescued by the workhouse from a life of vice, to which you have clearly returned. *When lust hath conceived it bringeth forth sin; and sin, when it is finished, bringeth forth death.* James, chapter one, verse fifteen. Are you so ignorant that you have forgotten your illegitimate child? Who are you to speak to me of cruelty, of vice?'

'It was you who you denied my son a Christian burial!' I hissed at him. *'I can never forget that!'*

Glyde's scowl passed from me to Doughty. 'Put her aside, if you wish to be able to look the good people of Birmingham in the eye. Let her return to the workhouse.'

'Jane told me of the cruelty she encountered from you,' said Doughty quietly. 'She told me of your behaviour towards the workhouse girls, and of her suspicions about Harriet. To my shame, I did not believe her at first. But I have learned the truth. As you said yourself: lust conceives sin, and sin brings forth death.'

I glanced at his profile, strong and determined, and felt my breath catch in my lungs; he had again declared his loyalty to me, careless that he was ruining himself in the process. The sexton continued his shovel cuts, alternated with the thump of dropped earth.

'William.' Glyde glanced over his shoulder at his relatives then came closer, skirting the grave hole. He lowered his voice, his lips stretched in a mirthless grin. 'You should not believe the vile lies of your servant. She required correction in the workhouse and she hates me for it. She intends to corrupt and manipulate you. Do not let her create an obstacle to our brotherhood. There is still time to make amends.'

'You are no longer my brother,' said Doughty, stepping back from him.

'So, I am too late. Your little harlot, whom you procured from the workhouse for your own immoral uses, has poisoned your mind,' sneered Glyde, still advancing. 'You are too weak, too easily corruptible. You should have beaten her as I told you to, or better, sent her to me, for the Sunday Penances.'

At that, Doughty grabbed at Glyde's chest, shoving at him with a fistful of robes.

'It is you whom I should beat. My wife confessed the truth.'

'And what is the truth?' Glyde tensed with fury and he spat out his words. 'That she was interrogated and humiliated by you and your whore?'

I cringed inwardly, but Doughty was not to be stopped.

'I discovered the truth from Harriet herself. You befouled her from her earliest childhood.'

'My poor sister.' Glyde did not even hesitate. 'God rest her soul, but she was not right in the head, her mind befuddled by her illness.'

'And why was she not right in the head? Because you had corrupted her when she was too young to know what she was doing!' Doughty stepped forward, shoving Glyde's jaw upwards with his robes. 'If that is not a mortal sin, then your Church is a temple of evil. Why do you think I refused the Communion from your hands?'

'Because you were not in a state of grace to receive it!' spat Glyde.

Behind him, his family was glancing anxiously. Mrs Glyde's hands were raised to her mouth. The sexton had stopped in the middle of a shovel-cut, and was watching. I tried to stay Doughty's arm, to remind him of where he was. But it was too late.

'I abjure my faith.' He shoved Glyde violently away. 'I cannot worship in a Church where virtue is evil and evil is good.'

'Hey!' shouted the sexton, dropping his shovel, and there was a murmur of horror from the watching relatives.

Glyde teetered at the edge of the part-filled grave as the sexton held him up.

'I shall press charges for assault!' Glyde snarled, as he recovered his balance. There was a look of murder in his face.

'Do you want the truth to come out in Court?' I retorted.

Glyde stood very still, his black robes still swaying around him, his jaw thrust out.

'As for you – vermin – if the Beadle finds you on the street he will bring you in, and I will see to it that a spell in the lock-up will cure your impertinence for good.'

I was ready to reply further but Doughty cut in.

'Jane!' He offered me his arm.

I took it and, thus joined, in front of Glyde and all the onlookers we marched away down the path that led past the church to Colmore Row, as the rain started to rattle down. The mourning-coach awaited and we clambered in, as though divorced from that church and united in a dark marriage.

42: Consolation

As we returned to Newhall Street, the shower was passing and sunlight starting to creep beneath the clouds. Doughty lingered by the hallstand as I removed my veiled bonnet and shook the raindrops from my shawl.

'Thank you for remaining with me,' he said at last. 'I couldn't have borne it without you.'

'It would have been better if I had not been so much on display beside you. They are all against us.'

'Nor could I have faced up to Vernon afterwards.'

'Reverend Glyde will avenge himself a hundred-fold,' I said, remembering how he had fixed his cruel eyes on me as he spoke of the Sunday Penances. 'It is only a matter of time.'

Doughty started to unwind the funeral crape from his tall hat.

'Without his support, I am finished,' he said. 'I only occupy my position through his favour. The magistrates will soon have me dismissed.'

He opened the parlour door but I hesitated on the threshold. There was an empty space where the coffin had lain on its trestles.

'What in Heaven's name will you do?' I was filled with dismay that he should lose his position.

'There's a post I intend to apply for in Dublin, at the Meath Hospital. Graves will vouch for me; he has a family connection there.'

'I fear that I have damaged your reputation.' I followed him into the parlour.

He gazed out of the window into the street, handsome in his black coat. A shaft of sunlight reflected in and formed a pale circle on the floor. I shivered, recalling Harriet's pale face.

'You comforted me when I was broken. Was that wrong?' He came a little way towards me. 'And now, I am a free man.'

'But if I had never said anything about Glyde, if you had not questioned her about it – if Harriet had not seen us together – she may not have destroyed herself. So, how can we say that it was right? Do you not even regret her death?'

'She's better off now.' he shook his head. 'Her agony is at an end. May God forgive her, as she believed He would.'

'Better off dead? But as a physician, do you not believe in the sanctity of human life?'

'Yes, but there are times when we can no longer strive for it. How could we have changed what happened that night? I shall forever hold this inquest, to order the chaos of causation that was Harriet's life. It was her brother who brought her so low. He made her his creature before her young mind had taken form.' Doughty broke off and looked down. 'If he had respected her innocence; if Harriet or I had been able to have existed away from her brother's orbit. If I had not asked her – but how could any man not ask his own wife?'

'If she had not suspected a liaison between us she might still be alive,' I said. 'You saw her letter.'

'What was there to suspect? God knows how I fought to control myself.' He came and put his hands gently to my elbows. 'We will never know how we could have kept her alive, or for how long, or to what purpose. What is certain is that I loved you the first instant I saw you. Your beautiful face, like a perfect petal amidst your life-blood. I knew at once that I was doomed. I regret nothing, except that you have withheld yourself from me.'

I allowed him to draw me closer, sensing his heat, the aroma of his cologne.

'We cannot – you know that I must leave you. Or Glyde will find some excuse to return me to the workhouse.'

'I will never permit it.'

His arms were around me, and my heart quickening, but I did not lift my face to his and he had to be content with kissing my hair.

'You desire me. It is the same for you, only say it is!'

He had felt the compliance in my body and I could not deny it, but I turned away from him and deliberately descended to my domain in the kitchen. I heard him go into the study.

I tidied the kitchen and started a stew.

After a while I heard his feet on the stairs and glanced up from chopping onions to see him leaning in the kitchen doorway and gazing at me. My eyes were watering.

He stepped forward, fumbling for a handkerchief. He dabbed gently at my face.

'Let me be the one to dry your tears,' he murmured.

'Onions.' I shrugged him away. 'Don't get underfoot, or your supper will be late.'

He was not to be so easily dismissed. He crumpled his handkerchief into his pocket and took the knife, testing the blade with his thumb.

'Not if I help you. I was six months a surgeon, and should be able to use a knife, even this blunt thing of yours.'

Ignoring my protests, he found the sharpening steel and whistled it along the blade. I watched sceptically as he cut up the onions, then allowed him to bone and chop the mutton.

'In here?' he asked, tipping the pieces into the pot.

I took over at the range and he sat at the table as I got the stew to a simmer.

'It will be an hour yet,' I said, carrying the dirty board into the scullery.

'But I'm hungry now.'

'You can have a slice of bread.'

'Not that kind of hunger.'

'You're incorrigible.' I rolled my eyes. 'Now, I will sit by you, for there are things that should be discussed.'

I rested a hand on the table as I sat down; he trapped it with his fingers.

'Life has been cruel to us, dear Jane. Tragedy has been heaped upon tragedy and you say that we must each bear our separate burdens alone. But for now, in spite of everything, I am a free man. Let us steal just one evening from the remainder of our lives. What do we have to lose?'

I left my hand in his, regretting my folly. Once the lock-gates have swung open the water must flow out and can no longer be pent up.

'What would you most like to do with this hour?' he murmured. 'The world already thinks the worst of us, so may we not do exactly as we please?'

'I would like to play the piano again.'

He cocked an eyebrow at me; it had not been the answer he wanted.

'It has been a sombre day,' I said. 'It will be a consolation.'

So we returned to the parlour and replaced the furniture that had been pushed aside for Harriet's casket. Then he lit the candles and I played the 'Venezianisches Gondellied' and 'Licht und Liebe'. After a while he joined my soprano with a fine tenor voice. He complimented me on my playing.

'What did you want, when you were a young girl, to do with your life?' he asked, lounging with an elbow on the piano-back.

I played an arpeggio and paused to recollect that previous life. 'My first disappointment was that I was taught as a girl that I could not follow my father's career, and become a lawyer. Nor was I to be permitted to play the piano professionally. My ambitions must be those of my husband's. Perhaps I could have been a missionary's wife – at least then I would have travelled. I suppose that my looks were my downfall. I was considered a beauty then –'

'As you are now,' he murmured, but I shrugged his compliment away.

'I could not appear in society without being surrounded by suitors. I was therefore judged a flirt, and this discouraged the more thoughtful, quieter gentlemen, those with whom I might have had a life of the mind. And then I met Edmond. Or rather, he sought me out, and would brook no refusal. He offered me the chance to play the piano for the theatre company. He convinced me that I had found true love. So I left home.'

'An elopement. Did you actually marry?'

I shook my head.

'I took his name, when we were living as man and wife. I was born Jane Ayliffe.'

Doughty smiled. 'So, Jane Ayliffe, you are a free woman?'

Instead of answering, I played another arpeggio, my fingers stroking the black keys. I muttered something about being rusty, and then sorted through the sheet music and played a nocturne of Chopin, the low notes murmuring like a running stream, the high notes cascading like petals fluttering down from overhanging branches. In the exquisite melancholy of the music I heard the echoes of those whom I had lost.

He turned the sheets of music for me with a pensive face. The nocturne ended, the final notes ebbing away into silence. I closed the lid over the keyboard.

'The last time I played this, I did not know how much I was to lose,' I said, leaning my elbows on the lid and resting my forehead on my palms.

'Jane.' He held out his arms, offering a dangerous refuge.

I rose and was held there against him, with his hands in my hair and at my waist, his lips finding mine. His mouth was sweet, my body warmed to his and our hearts were thudding against each other. We tried to kiss away each other's memories, to obliterate the griefs of the past with the present: the reality of existence and the powerful sensations of arousal.

We kissed until we were out of breath, then broke apart. Dusk was falling; the night lay ahead.

'Supper,' I said, and led the way down to the kitchen.

He ate slowly, as if replete with looking at me.

'Marry me,' he said.

I told him that I must leave him and he knew it as well as I.

'You should not be put off by our neighbours,' he said. 'They will forget in a few months, once matters are regularised between us. And if we were married, you might be able to –'

'It is not that,' I interrupted. 'There is something not right.'

'It is my age, then,' he said, pushing his half-finished plate aside. 'But I am from a long-lived family, and am yet in my prime.'

'No,' I said, 'but we are master and servant – how can we love as equals?'

'But I will make you my wife, I will raise you up.'

'I want to raise myself up. I will not be beholden to any man.'

'But you have nowhere to go, my darling Jane ... only see how kind I can be to you ...'

'You must write me a reference. In any case, I will find another situation. It is not decent for me living here. People look at me when I go out. I cannot stay here. I will go somewhere I am not known.'

He twisted his mouth in a bitter frown. The sweetness of our embrace had turned sour.

'So, you will leave me, then. And I must write your character reference. Well, what would you like me to write about? Your chastity? Your morality? Or your generous and accommodating nature?' He paused, and softened his tone, but could not entirely silence his anger. 'Shall I write about your exquisite beauty, and the fragrance of your skin, the delicacy of your soft neck, about how sweet your voice is and how divinely you play the piano? Shall I describe your reading habits: *Bell's Life in London* and *The Pickwick Papers* and *The Housekeeper's Guide*? Or the methods you employ to shoo me away when you are busy with your work, and how I have learned to evade them? Shall I write about what a wonderful wife you will make for a man of intellect, for a life of the mind?'

'You see,' I replied, quelling my own anger, 'you are mocking me, for you mean to entrap me here. You are cruel to me, after all.'

'Jane,' he pleaded, 'where will you go? To the abuses of the workhouse? To work in a factory until you fall into the machinery from sheer exhaustion? Or to the household of a lecherous old man? There is no refuge for you. For God's sake, stay here, where you are loved. The storm will blow over, and we will marry. You will be safer within these walls than outside them.'

I fell silent and he watched me across the table. It was true that I had few options. If only I could find work as a pianist.

'You are loved,' he repeated. 'Stay with me, for I love you dearly.'

He rose and walked around the table to stand behind my chair, rested his hands on my shoulders and then stooped and stroked his mouth along my neck. I did not evade him, and my head drifted back. My sigh was silenced by his lips. He ran his fingers over my face, down my throat, inside my dress, and knelt beside my chair.

'Come to my bed,' he whispered. 'I want you so desperately.'

'But I must leave you.' I was breathless.

'You cruel beauty! Leave me tomorrow, if you must, but only stay with me tonight. For I would sacrifice everything that I have for one night with you. What harm can it do, in any case? If you fear ruin, we are already ruined.'

He drew me up and held me, pressing me hard against the table, infecting me with his desire; I trembled within. He murmured endearments: a beautiful angel, a sweet creature, a darling girl. He took me, unresisting, to his divan.

By the time we were naked, it was completely dark. There was no candle and no moon, and his bold caresses seemed to come from nowhere, surprising me with the imprint of lips, the dry warmth of a palm, the firm touch of fingertips, the slip of a tongue.

'Trust me,' he murmured, 'lie still. Forget your concerns, forget about me. Sense only your body. Ignore all else, think only of what you feel ... here … forget everything, do not think, only feel …'

He caressed me, calm and languorous, coaxing me to let thought drift away, to allow sensuality to invade, until heat radiated from me and my breath was trapped in my throat. Then my whole body seized and my lungs filled and emptied in long slow sighs.

He lay down alongside me in the bed. I was panting and

my heart was drumming.

He kissed me deeply. 'Sweetheart.' He pressed against me.

'We should not,' I sighed, but I moved to embrace him closer. Almost as if Harriet were still in her room, we moved slowly, hesitating if the bedstead creaked the floorboards or bumped against the wall, muffling our whimpers and grunts in each other's flesh.

After he was spent he slept; I rested half across him, my pleasure mixed with regret, wondering for all his ardent avowals how long his passion would last. It was a cataclysmic love, he had said, an earthquake that would sweep his world away and change him from his former self. But as it changed him, would it not change the man who had fallen in love with me? Nothing could be counted on to stay the same.

Edmond's adoration of me had once been as powerful. He had lavished attention on me, insisting on the best of everything. He bought me extravagant luxuries, advising me what to wear, what to eat, what to drink, how to conduct myself. My hair had become glossier, my figure fuller, and I was radiant in silks and jewels. He praised and flattered me and vowed his love was never-ending.

Yet after that first intensity of passion I had seen his cruel side. One evening, playing cards in another actor's apartments, he had insisted on staying late, although I was tired. And our host, Martin Hellbronn, took my part.

'You should go home, Edmond, for you are on a losing streak …'

He winked at me and I smiled; it was only a joke.

Edmond stayed on, draining his glass and raising the stakes until he had no more money.

Once home, he rounded upon me.

'You laughed up your sleeve at me!' he hissed, his face red with drink. *'While I was losing money to Hellbronn!'*

'But I tried to get you to leave!'

'You set your cap at him,' he said. 'I was watching you.'

'How can you –'

Edmond stopped me with a slap.

'If you ever make eyes at another man, it will be the last time.'

I put a hand up to my face. It was not possible. Pain stung me. His face was tense with rage. My lips became cold and my heart gave a few slow thuds. Darkness obscured my vision.

When I came to, I was lying on the floor. He was staring down at me.

'Oh my darling, I thought I had killed you!' He dabbed my face with a handkerchief, his hands shaking. 'I thought I had broken your neck ...'

He soon mingled his apologies with reproach.

'Be a good girl now, and don't make me lose my temper with you.'

Edmond had persuaded me that he was jealous because he loved me, and so I must resolve not to upset him. It had never happened again, and his neglect during my pregnancy was in some ways a relief, until I realised that I had been deserted. I wondered if a man's love was truly something to be desired even though it was so hard to live without.

Now as I lay with Doughty's arm beneath my neck and my thigh across his, I felt the rise and fall of his chest and the slow beat of his heart under my breast. His sleep would be brief, and as soon as I dozed I would awake, quivering, to the soft teasing friction of his tongue and his fingertips and we would enravel each other in a lascivious embrace.

Yet I knew that the lonely road was the path I must take, and that I must find completeness in my own self and from my own art.

43: Pious Betty

It was almost certain that our time together at Newhall Street was finite. Perhaps Doughty was less in demand for inquests, for he spent more time at home, and my chores were often interrupted by his attentions. In the evenings I played the piano and he turned the music for me, or joined me in song. I asked him innumerable times to write my character reference. He in return tried to persuade me to marry him. He swore that he deeply loved me, and I believed him, but I always said no, arguing the scandal that would ensue, and asking him how he could be sure that he would be able to support me, given that the magistrates were petitioning London for his removal. He was certain of the Dublin post, he said, although it might not pay well.

For nearly two weeks we continued as lovers, and as we became bolder we moved into the large bed that had once been Harriet's, after I had aired and cleaned the room. The nights were exhausting, harrowing in the intensity of his ardent passion. During the days, when I was apart from him shame flared up in my mind, which filled with cruel voices. *A life of vice. A trollop. A worthless character. Little harlot.* We were behaving with the amorality of wild beasts, and I worried about the consequences. What if I fell pregnant again? Yet he was so in need of me, and for my part I could not look at him without a longing that came from my own loneliness. Whenever he touched me my heart leapt to meet him just as my conscience recoiled.

One morning, the first day of September, as we lay in a shambles at dawn, stained and sore, our skins sealed together with sweat, he spoke breathlessly between kisses.

'This is a love that is changing the course of my life … I have found my fate in you … do you not feel as I feel?'

For an answer I softly caressed him; he quickened under my touch.

'Obey your instincts,' he whispered. 'Listen to your heart.'

'I have learned to mistrust those emotions,' I sighed. 'They cannot decide my fate.'

'Let me teach you otherwise,' he murmured, his voice catching in his throat. 'Learn again to be loved … and to love in return …without love, we have nothing …'

We dozed, only to be woken by someone battering on the front door. Doughty's limbs were knotted around me, and my arm had gone numb. He disentangled himself with a groan, and got up. Daylight filled the room as he folded back the shutters. Still naked, he threw up the sash window and leaned head and shoulders out over the sill.

'Hey!' he shouted; the knocking stopped.

'Put on your dressing gown!' I sat up in bed, pulling the sheet up over me.

'When that door needs repainting, I shall charge it to the magistrates!' he called down.

There was an answering shout from the street.

'The Beadle.' Doughty closed the window. 'I'll go down to him.'

'What if the neighbours saw?'

He stroked my bare shoulder with his fingertips.

'No-one saw me. And what if they did?' Putting on his slippers and dressing gown, he went downstairs.

The men's voices echoed in the hall, and faded as they closed themselves in the study. I dressed and went down to the kitchen to start the day. It was past eight o'clock; the Beadle must have wondered at Doughty's state of undress.

The *Birmingham Gazette* had arrived so I glanced briefly through the list of vacant positions, wondering about Doughty's warning about the households of lecherous old men. Stay here where you are loved, he had pleaded, although at that I frowned; I had already seen Edmond's love turn bitter.

The Beadle left and Doughty came down to the kitchen with a grim face. He leaned against the dresser, bolting down a slice of bread and jam.

'The workhouse, again. A woman found dead yesterday morning in the lock-up. Betty Marshall. Do you know anything of her?'

'Pious Betty!' My first feeling was that she was repaid; I had not forgiven her over Nathan's death. But no-one deserved to die in the lock-up, trapped behind the iron door, fading into darkness to join the ghosts that must haunt that vile place.

'She was a strange woman,' I replied, 'but I had never known her to get into trouble. She was deeply pious. And the lock-up …' I faltered, imagining Betty, terrified and alone.

Doughty drained his teacup in two gulps and set it back on the saucer.

'Someone, one of the casuals, reported to the Beadle that he heard from the lock-up the terrible screams of a woman, as though beaten, or terrorised, and pleading for mercy, over and over again.' The casuals were vagrants who slept in the workhouse overnight and were out in the morning. 'Yet Dr Wright has certified the cause of death as an epileptic seizure.'

I felt faint. Doughty must have seen me blanch; he asked if I was all right.

I recovered myself, and said that Betty must have a proper inquest.

'Do you believe Dr Wright?' I asked.

I was answered by his look of horror and went to him. He rested his chin on my head.

'Dr Wright is beholden to Vernon – we all are,' he muttered into my hair. He held me gently, as though trying to derive strength to face what he must go out to confront: the death of a helpless captive, a pauper woman beneath notice and beyond protection; the ignorance and obfuscation of the authorities.

'What if Betty had angered Vernon?' I said, pulling back and looking up at him. His hands lingered on my waist, but the furrow reappeared between his eyebrows, darkening his face. 'He would have treated her brutally. There will be something hideous concealed.'

'If there is the slightest thing, I will challenge him.' His voice was low and lethal. 'This is my only opportunity. He will soon have me removed from my position. I was not worthy to occupy it in any case.'

'You are trying your best,' I said.

'Vernon expects an easy life,' said Doughty bitterly, 'the freedom to do as he pleases under a false scrutiny. I am ashamed of how ineffective I have been in the past.'

His voice softened and he traced my chin with a fingertip.

'But you, you have shown me that the truth must be upheld, even if it damages us. You see how unworthy I am:

I, in a prominent position of responsibility, am shamed by you. Beaten down though you were by misfortune, and at whatever risk to yourself, you still could not let a lie go unchallenged.'

I said I had done little, and that it was he who had committed himself to carry out his duties to the best of his ability, but he demurred.

'You have restored my hope, and my faith in myself.'

I saw an opportunity. 'Then I hope you will be good enough to write something of your appreciation in my reference?'

'But you will not leave me.' Tenderly he repeated his arguments: the depth of his love and the way it had altered the course of his life; my charm and beauty; his health, vitality and willingness to faithfully provide for me.

I remained firm.

Then he leant forward, his face close to mine and whispered, 'What if you were carrying my child? Would you marry me then? I would be a devoted father.' He had guessed that my monthlies were due; my breasts were tender and heavy.

His words sent a tremor through me, but I shook my head.

'Do you not appreciate the irregularity of our situation? You saw the faces of the congregation. Everyone in the neighbourhood has guessed that we are lovers. Even if we were to marry we would not be accepted into society. You must write my reference, even though it pains me to leave you.'

'Not yet.' His frown deepened. 'What if we were to leave Birmingham together?'

'I need the reference now, if I am to have any chance for the future. My reputation will suffer further for every day that you delay.'

It took me some time to persuade him but in the end he left me with a bad grace and went upstairs to the study.

What if I proved to be carrying his child? As I tried to begin my daily chores, I was assailed by memories. The cruel reality that I had shut away came back with such power that I stood still in the kitchen with my eyes closed and my heart pounding. Nathan's birth, the nightmare of his constant crying, cursing him and weeping, exhausted by lack of sleep as I struggled to get him to suckle on my breast. My milk would not come at all and when my patience ran out Betty had been given the task of feeding him with thinned gruel, for there was no milk to be had in the workhouse. He had been feverish and listless when she had bathed him in cold water, thinking no doubt to revive him, but the shock of it had ended his life. His cries had stopped, his eyelids part-closed revealing a sliver of white, and I had watched in anguish as his tiny limbs grew grey and cold and the rapid grunts of his breathing stopped. My howl of grief turned to fury: I had blamed Betty. But at heart I knew that my failure to feed Nathan had been the cause. I did not deserve to be a mother, and Betty deserved justice.

After a few minutes Doughty returned and dropped a letter on the kitchen table. He ignored my thanks, retreating into formality to protect himself.

'I must wash and dress. The inquest starts at ten. Please bring my hot water up as soon as possible.'

For all that he professed to love me, he did not seem to realise that to provide his hot water I had to fill the copper from the pump, light the fire under the copper, wait for the water to heat, fill a water jug and carry it up the stairs. After he had finished, I would have to dispose of the waste water into the privy. Fortunately I had started the task while he had been in his study. As I lifted the heavy jug I reflected that if I chose a life with him it would always come to this: even if we took on another servant the chores of the household would be my responsibility and done at his bidding.

44: The Character Reference

I had my character reference at last. Now I was ready to make new plans. But later that morning, closely studying the newspaper, I saw that it would not be so easy. Most of the 'Wanted' advertisements were for men:

WANTED … a Youth of sober and industrious habits as an apprentice … a clerk with general knowledge of the iron trade … a young man as porter in the grocery trade … an active persevering young man … a journeyman who understands the manufacture of printing ink … a coal master who can command the consumption of nearly 200 tons of coal per week.

The few advertisements for women demanded virtue.

WANTED … immediately, a pious, active, and respectable Female Assistant who has a thorough knowledge of the Fur Trade and who has been accustomed to serve behind a Retail Counter … an assistant in a Ladies School of the highest respectability, who can undertake the music and French departments as well as assist in the usual routine of School duties.

I studied my character reference. Doughty had written that I was hardworking, capable of performing all household tasks, a good cook, well educated, and of the highest degree of honesty and integrity. But he had limited himself to the truth and said nothing about piety or respectability.

A notice requiring *'A thorough Servant of all work, apply at 133 High Street, Bordesley'* specified very little.

It was a long walk to High Street, Bordesley. I crossed the upper town, passing the churchyard where Harriet was buried, looking across to the patch of freshly turned soil, where we had challenged Glyde at the graveside. Doughty was uppermost in my thoughts. Was he protecting me or taking advantage of me? Was his behaviour, that he perceived as love, merely driven by desire? Indeed, was it not heartless self-interest that perpetuated all human relationships?

Past the ancient church of St Martin's in the Bullring, the High Street was full of shops, some on the main thoroughfare and others in cobbled courtyards. Every building was occupied by businesses, some twice or three times over. Aproned shopkeepers stood in their doorways, bidding the public a 'Good morning!' An affluent couple passed me, the wife's gloved hand supported on the husband's arm. Two handsome top-hatted gentlemen, apparently with nothing else to do, sauntered and conversed on the pavement. I glanced at at their faces and then away, reminded of the rumble of Doughty's murmured endearments, of the tight embrace of his arms, of the voluptuous touch of his caresses. I paused at a shop window. My eyes fluttered closed for an instant, then I suppressed an upswell of craving and went on. Was I a heartless creature myself, I wondered, animated only by lust?

I passed the premises of tea dealers, basket-makers, bookmakers, cheese factors, bottle merchants, hardware men, woollen drapers, printers, chemists, brewers' hop merchants, seed and corn factors, hatters, confectioners, auctioneers, wine and spirit merchants, glovers, hosiers, lace manufacturers, jewellers, engravers, tobacconists …

There was a notice in a window: *Help Wanted. Drinkwater's. Apply in Court House Yard.* It was not the address I sought, but I thought I might as well enquire.

The adjacent alley was packed along with baskets and boxes of apples and vegetables. Drinkwater's was a fruiterer's shop alongside the crumbling pilasters of the Court of Requests. Under a striped canvas awning were more fruit baskets, and weighing scales on a trestle table. But there was a stench here, not of rotting fruit, but rather that of a pigsty. I startled as cries of '*Remember the poor debtors!*' rose from cellar gratings at my feet. Begging hands were raised up beneath the bars. I jumped back, relieved they could not reach me. My shadow must have fallen across them. It was the debtors' prison: after the hearings in the small claims court above, the poorest captives were incarcerated down there, packed in and starving. I was afraid of working in the vicinity of these wretches, but it would have to be borne.

Mr Drinkwater wanted to know if I had a character reference. He said he needed someone trustworthy to mind the shop.

'I work for the Borough Coroner.' I offered him Doughty's letter.

Without taking it, he glanced up sharply and pursed tobacco-stained lips.

'I wouldn't call that a respectable household, miss. Magistrates have applied to the Lord Chancellor.'

He sucked again on his pipe and handed the letter back. I stared in horror. The gossip had spread through the town, it seemed. Doughty was discredited.

Drinkwater said that in any case he was looking for a young man.

'I need someone as can lift these here baskets about,' he explained. 'Sorry, miss. You might try at the dairy, Mr Powers, on Long Bridge Lane. Just over the road there, keep walking and you can't miss it. He's always in need of milkmaids, respectable or not. You need to watch him, though.'

Drinkwater tapped the side of his nose with a dirty finger.

I continued instead on my original course, along the High Street towards Digbeth and Bordesley, passing the clothier's shop where I had sold off my ballgowns to pay the landlord. The rose silk still hung in the window, grey with dust. This was the oldest part of Birmingham, the parish of St John's, and between new brick buildings the ancient half-timbered structures lingered crookedly on: the Golden Lion Inn, Smith's Tripe House, and the Old Crown. There was a foul odour from the cattle market and the slaughterhouses. Rows of split carcases hung from hooks outside shops, and in a side street I heard the bellowing of an animal as its butchers yelled out to each other. An excited babble came from a gang of urchins, crowding around a slaughterman's wooden shed and trying to peer between its planks. Blood streamed from beneath the door.

Just short of Bordesley Prison was Number 133, with Isaac Averill's name above the door, a tailor's shop. Behind the windowpanes a dummy displayed a '*Suit of Best Quality, New Colours and Patterns, £3 12s 6d*'. I opened the door and a bell tinkled above my head. Shelves were stacked with bolts of cloth, a stout gentleman stood in his shirtsleeves, arms outspread, and Mr Averill, a pencil behind his ear and a tape measure in his hands, stared at me above his steel-framed spectacles. I explained I had come in response to the advertisement. Raising grey eyebrows he appraised me briefly, and smiled.

'Catherine!' he called, in the direction of the back of the

shop. 'My wife will attend to you, miss.' He resumed his measurements and scribbled them in a notebook.

The tailor's wife was stoop-shouldered from years of seamstressing and wore the same make of spectacles as her husband. She adjusted them on her nose to read my letter of reference.

She looked up again in alarm.

'Servant to the Borough Coroner,' she said, her voice as sharp as scissors.

'Yes, madam,' I replied, my confidence already deflating.

'I heard that he is about to lose his situation.' She handed the letter back. 'We have no need of a servant. The position has already been filled.'

'Catherine!' protested Mr Averill, as I opened the shop door to leave and the bell tinkled out again.

As I stepped outside I overheard Mrs Averill's reply.

'A scandal. People say they killed his wife.'

I should perhaps have stopped to protest my innocence, but suspected it already to be futile. I would not be believed. Instead, I pretended I heard nothing, and walked on. At Deritend Bridge I paused. The thumping of foundries vibrated the ground and the air was filled with the noise of forging hammers. Factory chimneys rose on either side of the main road behind sooty terraces of houses where women sat on their doorsteps and dirty children played in the gutters. Sulphurous coal smoke combined with the stink of tanneries: leather and rot. The River Rea ran between banks choked with refuse, with its water brown and curdled with the filth that flowed into it from the town above.

I turned back.

There were vacancies at '*Mason's Pin & Needle Makers*', advertised on a signboard, which pointed to a courtyard off Coventry Street. The ground floor was a small workshop crammed with rows of dusty children turning grindstones, sharpening points. Some looked to be no more than seven or eight years old. At a far bench, women worked on rolls of steel wire with tools I had never seen before. I asked for the offices and was directed up a wooden stair from the courtyard outside.

Mr Mason read my reference, then fixed me with a bold stare and asked me what I could do. I admitted that I had never worked in a factory.

'We've no places in the manufactory, but we need out-workers. The needles to go on to cards and the pins to be counted into boxes. Needles, we pay a farthing for two gross of cards, pins a farthing for two gross of boxes. Where do you live?'

'Newhall Street, but I must find another place.'

'It's a long way. We'd take off an ha'penny for the work to be dropped and collected.'

'I'll see if I can find a lodging.'

'Come back when you have.'

I doubted that I could earn enough to pay for a room in a lodging house, together with the candles that I would need to work by. I would try the dairy. I asked for directions to Long Bridge Lane.

I crossed the High Street and, skirting the livestock market, entered a slum district. The miserable dwellings were lightless; broken windows were closed with boards, rags stuffed into crevices to keep out draughts. There was a smell of sewage. In the narrow streets I edged past shrunken people who were pale and haggard in the face, prematurely aged, their tattered clothes blackened with grease, bound to their wasted bodies with twine. They moved listlessly, or sat or lay in doorways, their energy drained away. A withered arm trailed across my path and I stepped around it, unable to look at the face. If only there were a way to help them; but it was beyond my power. A beggar wrapped in muddy sacks lay in a bundle beside a pile of refuse, too exhausted to ask for alms. I dared not offer him anything; to produce a farthing from my pocket would draw down a horde of the starving. I was uncomfortably aware of my neat dress; a housemaid's clothing was as misplaced as a rose-silk ballgown in these desperate streets.

Powers' Dairy was no more than a large cowshed, the cattle crowded in semi-darkness, roped by the neck to posts, with their heads bent to troughs of brown sludge. They were fed on brewers' spent grain; there was nowhere to pasture them. The atmosphere was warm and fetid, the place awash with the smell of sour milk and the effluent of the animals.

'What you after?'a milkmaid challenged me. Her head in its brownish mobcap was buried in the grey flank of a cow, and as she looked up at me her dirty fingers were still working at the teats, squirting milk into a rusty pail.

'I heard Mr Powers is looking for milkmaids,' I replied.

For a moment the girl's hands paused and she lifted her head. The cow shifted and I took a step back. The milkmaid grinned. A couple of her front teeth were missing.

'He's always on the look-out for girls. You can go and ask him. He's in the next house along.' Her eyes were sly, and her expression became a leer as she turned back to her work.

The next house was a tenement as grim as all the others; from within came coarse male laughter. I lifted the iron knocker and let it fall with a dull thud.

After a while the laughter stopped and Mr Powers answered the door. He was in his shirtsleeves, sticking his thumbs into his waistcoat pockets where the velvet trim had worn to thread. Above an unkempt beard his florid face, still smiling, betrayed a stupid lechery. His hair had been combed back with grease, the trails of the comb's teeth still visible.

'Well, well, my little beauty, what can Josiah Powers do for you?' He lounged against the door jamb, one leg crossed over the other, belly thrust out.

'I …' I hesitated.

'Want to work for me?' He withdrew his hands from his waistcoat and made a milking action, his lips spreading into a grin. He might only have been expecting a saucy reply, but his meaning was unmistakable.

Without a word, I turned to flee. I stumbled forward on the slimy cobbles and a passer-by grasped my arm.

'*Up-a-daisy, bab!*' he wheezed, as though to a child.

Though he stopped my fall I pulled away from his calloused hand in horror.

Mr Powers' ribald laughter pursued me as I hurried through the narrow alleyways, echoing in my mind long after I was out of earshot. Once back in the upper town I wandered, hardly aware of my surroundings. I felt indifferent to the contemptuous glances; I had sunk so low in despair that nothing could worsen my situation.

Outside the Theatre Royal, the playbills announced Davenant's Theatre Company in a new play, *The Hostage of Barbary*. It was shut, and dark inside, but I stopped and studied the names of the cast: Edmond Verity had returned to Birmingham. And Maud Frith, it seemed, had not.

At last I returned to Newhall Street, and closed its door behind me with a feeling of reaching sanctuary. I was loath to leave its protection again.

The postman had left a letter from London and, eyeing its grand seals with misgiving, I put it on Doughty's desk. I hung up my bonnet and shawl and went down to the kitchen to brew a cup of tea. The range needed blackleading, the floor to be scrubbed, the linen to be ironed, and it was already late in the afternoon. These were the limits of my world.

Yet I will not be able to stay here, I thought, and then a longing started somewhere at the base of my throat and spread, half-paralysing me. Doughty. How soon would he come home?

But a series of knocks on the front door echoed their impatience through the house. No one knocked like that. Doughty had a key. The knocking continued as I hastened up the stairs. The Beadle would be at the inquest. The butcher's boy always came down the area steps to the kitchen. I stood behind the front door, wiping my palms on my apron, wondering who was on the other side, to knock with such force. Was it one of Glyde's subordinates, come to return me to the workhouse?

I opened the door.

It was Edmond Verity, grinning.

I stared at him, wordless, and started to tremble.

'My dearest Jane.' He was in a coat that must have cost him twenty guineas, and lifting his hat to display his golden hair. 'Do you not recognise me?'

Behind him, a coachman in a ridiculous scarlet livery waited beside a carriage and a handsome pair of horses.

I swallowed, my mouth suddenly dry, my tongue rough against my palate.

'Edmond,' I whispered.

He was holding a letter that I remembered writing, months ago, at a different time in my life. He was still smiling.

'I had your note. Constant love and devotion – most affecting. Of course, I would have come sooner, but … we have only just arrived …'

45: Disinterment of Bodies by Coroners

From the *Birmingham Gazette*

An inquest was scheduled yesterday, 1st September, at the Birmingham Parish Union Workhouse, Lichfield Street, to take place before Coroner Doughty, and a respectable jury, to inquire as to the death of Betty Marshall, an inmate. The workhouse doctor, Dr Wright, considered the cause of death to be apoplexy but a witness had made representation to the Beadle that he heard screams from the lock-up in which situation Miss Marshall had been found deceased. The coroner having sworn the jury, they expected to view the body but were told it had already been committed for burial. The coroner issued his warrant for disinterment to the churchwardens and overseers of the Parish but was told that it could not be complied with.

The inquest therefore could not proceed, but the following heated discussion, which lasted for two hours, took place:

The Rev. V. Glyde, Rector of the Parish, entered

the room and, addressing the Coroner, asked him whether he had yet received a letter of dismissal from the Lord Chancellor, a recommendation having been made by the Magistrates of the Bench to remove him from office.

The Coroner: I have received no such thing.

Mr B. Huntly (Foreman of the Jury): The jury have accepted the Coroner's authority and are minded to continue the inquest.

The Rev. Glyde took the oath, identifying himself as the Rector of St Michael's, Justice of the Peace, Chairman of the Workhouse Guardians of the Birmingham Parish Union, Trustee of the Asylum for the Infant Poor and of the Reformatory for Penitent Females, and Treasurer of the Benevolent Fund for Distressed Gentlewomen.

The Coroner: Tell us what you know of the death of Betty Marshall.

The Rev. Glyde: I must first protest, sir, that even if your tenure of office continues, your warrant to disinter this body is not legal, and nor is it merited in this case. This inmate died of apoplexy. What need is there for an inquest to be held, when a death certificate has already been issued by a medical gentleman? None of the Guardians of the Parish consider this to be necessary. You are acting a charade.

The Coroner: I have reason to believe the information on the death certificate to be incorrect.

The Rev. Glyde: Do you call Dr Wright's opinion into question? That is a clear insult to him, indeed to the medical profession.

The Coroner: The Beadle was informed that screams were heard from the lock-up in which Miss

Marshall was subsequently found dead. She was heard to beg for mercy.

The Rev. Glyde: The screaming was doubtless part of the apoplectic seizure. The cause of death has already been determined. The Master of the Workhouse, or the Parish Guardians would be surely better placed to inform the coroner of any deaths occurring under their notice than an ignorant Beadle?

The Coroner: There must be an objection to my being informed of deaths by the route you suggest. What if the master of the workhouse, or one of the Guardians of the Poor were himself the cause of death of one of the inmates? Where then am I to get my information? The Beadle's informant heard the deceased to beg for mercy from an assailant.

The Rev. Glyde: Preposterous. Your inquisitions are already notorious for their excess and expense, and this one provides a further example. You cannot expect the magistrates to pay for this, this travesty, this unnecessary and illegal proceeding.

The Coroner: You have not got the right to tell me when I can and cannot hold an inquest. It is my duty to investigate this death, whether or not the magistrates elect to pay the fee, which is rightfully mine.

The Rev. Glyde: In any case your warrant for this disinterment is not legal.

The Coroner: Through your innumerable offices, you know the law, and you know your Church. How can you say that I have no right to issue the warrant?

The Rev. Glyde: The law does not give you the power assumed in the warrant.

The Coroner: If we begin a legal discussion about each and every power in Law which my office confers upon me, we shall never finish the business of this case; I act under statute law and custom and precedent, and I shall see the body, as otherwise there can be no inquest.

The Rev. Glyde: If I obeyed your so-called warrant, and allowed that grave to be disturbed, I should consider myself subject to ecclesiastical censure.

The Coroner: Ecclesiastical censure? A complete fabrication. There has never been censure from the Church to any disinterment ordered by a coroner. You must reflect that I am a sworn officer of the Crown. You will obey the warrant.

Mr. Huntly: On behalf of my brother jurors I beg that we may go on with this inquest, or else abandon it.

The Rev. Glyde: Coroner Doughty, I offer no resistance to you recovering this body. But you cannot legally compel me to order a disinterment that amounts to grave robbery and a desecration of holy ground. It would be a scandal. Consider the effect upon members of the public of the exposure of the coffin, of perhaps the very person of the deceased, in the churchyard, doubtless in the most indecent manner. Consider the effect on bereaved relatives who might be attending the funeral rites of their beloved. It is after all only a short time since you yourself were in that position. Have you no fellow feeling for those that mourn? Do you not grieve?

The Coroner: I have no wish to distress those who have lost their loved ones, but when I must exercise the powers of my office, to overcome obstruction, I will do so.

The Rev. Glyde: I am not obstructing you.

Mr. Huntly: The sexton said you forbade him to assist in digging up the body, or even to go into the churchyard without your leave.

The Coroner: Reverend Glyde, as vicar of this parish, as Chairman of the Board of Guardians, and as a magistrate, highly conversant with the law, and moreover holding custody of the body, you alone can assist me with this case. But instead, you are deliberately hindering me. May I ask the reason why?

The Rev. Glyde: I would further argue that no minister has the power to disinter a body without a faculty from the Doctors' Commons. I will send to London and obtain written legal advice on the matter from Dr Addams, or some other eminent ecclesiastical lawyer, and if I am wrong, I will order the disinterment of the body.

The Coroner: I beg to state that I do not consider myself bound by the legal opinion you mean to bring forward. I shall issue warrants ordering the disinterment of the body to both churchwardens.

The Rev. Glyde: You know where the churchyard is. The law gives you the power to go and disinter the body. No impediment will be thrown in your way. But you cannot compel the churchwardens or procure the assistance of the parish sexton.

The Coroner: At all events, I shall go on until I see the body, as I have no grounds to act otherwise.

The Rev. Glyde: Well, you may dig her up yourself. No man in my parish will dare to desecrate holy ground in such an un-Christian manner, at the whim of one who is clinging to his office as to the last spars of a shipwreck. So, dig her up! '*In the sweat of thy face, till thou return unto the ground, for out of it wast thou taken: for dust thou art, and unto dust thou shalt return.'*

The inquest was adjourned until 10 o'clock on the following day.

46: Edmond

'I cannot accompany you to London,' I said.

I sat at the other end of the sofa from Edmond, edging away from him and hoping that he would be gone before Doughty arrived home.

I had been completely taken aback by his return. He was if anything more magnificent than ever: success had brought a bloom to his cheeks and his blue eyes were all the more startling for the trace of black kohl that he never bothered to properly wipe away. But I did not warm to him and he sensed it. Once inside the house I had turned away from his open arms and shown him into the parlour, engaging him in small talk about the theatre.

'Ah, London!' sighed Edmond, dropping his voice into velvet tones and shifting towards me. 'Don't you remember how we danced at the Vauxhall Gardens? You were in that wonderful rose silk … we drank champagne and watched the fireworks glittering in the dark ... I thought my own heart would explode that night. You were as exquisite as a princess, nay a queen, with jewels and feathers in your hair.

Don't you remember the tender passion we enjoyed?'

'I cannot dwell on it,' I said in a low voice. 'We cannot speak of the past. You betrayed my trust and you betrayed your own son. Nathan might have survived …'

'I am sorry for that, but … I meant to write …'

'It was inexcusable.' I was close to tears and turned towards the arm of the sofa, shrugging Edmond's hand from my shoulder.

I thought I heard a noise in the hall but Edmond continued regardless, resting his hands on my waist.

'But, my dearest Jane, I've returned to you now, have I not? Just as I promised I would. To the sincere and undying devotion which you professed in your letter. And you are looking better than I expected, radiant, even. But you could at least spare me a few gentle words, another kiss from those lustrous lips, some token of the fond love that we had for each other, as you so sweetly wrote. I did not expect to encounter so cold a reception.'

'And I did not expect you to become engaged to someone else,' I hissed. 'I do read the newspapers, Edmond.'

Doughty had returned: I heard the rattle of his cane in the hallstand and a deliberate clearing of the throat.

Edmond heard it too and his protests faded into silence.

'You must go …' I was half-sobbing.

'You should not be living like this, in any case, abasing yourself as a servant,' said Edmond. He drew back; his hands trailing across my skirts as Doughty opened the parlour door. 'You could at least audition again for Davenant.'

Doughty's face was a mask, his jaw tight. He looked as though he wanted to wrench us bodily apart. I wondered what he had made of Edmond's carriage outside. He found his voice with an effort, and brought out something half-civil.

'I do not recollect inviting guests.'

I could not meet his eye and mumbled an apology, while

Edmond rose, bowed, then adopted a straight stance, unperturbed by the hostile audience, his chest up, his fair hair and his face in the light.

'Edmond Verity, of Davenant's Players.' He extended his hand. 'I don't believe I've had the pleasure.'

'Humph!' Doughty snubbed the handshake, arms tightly folded, containing himself on the edge of fury.

'It seems I am unwelcome, somewhat de trop, perhaps.' Edmond made a moue at me and seemed to be waiting for me to speak.

I felt a crimson blush spread across my throat, my cheeks, and invade my whole body. I was not yet cured of him.

'I trust, madam,' Edmond placed his right arm across his midriff and inclined his head at me with mock formality, 'that you will condescend to allow me the exquisite delight of waiting upon you again.'

'No, Edmond. Please, you must go.'

'Go – I do not want you in my house.' Doughty held open the parlour door.

'I can see that you think me an Undesirable.' Edmond shrugged, with a half-smile on his face, and proceeded regally past him into the hall. 'She wrote to me of your respectability – and your being somewhat advanced in years.'

Doughty made no reply. I heard the front door open.

'She won't stay here. Not after I've given her the proof of my affection,' was Edmond's final comment.

Doughty slammed the door and came back into the parlour. He propped his elbow on the mantelpiece and stared at himself for a long time in the pier-glass.

I heard Edmond get into his carriage, the coachman stowing his bucket, and cracking his whip. The urchins squealed and scattered. The horses' hooves echoed, and the whole equipage drew away.

'Well,' Doughty said.

'I did not ...' I hesitated.

He turned from the mirror, setting his back against the corner of the mantelpiece.

'I loved you so much that I gave you my complete trust. I allowed you to invade my thoughts; my eyes saw nothing but your beauty and sweetness. I came to believe everything you told me about Glyde, about Harriet. I protected you at my own expense. I allowed my belief in you, my heedless passion, to overturn all I had. And now? Last night as you lay in my arms I had the bliss of believing that you were mine. This morning you told me to write your reference. And now I find you with him!'

'It was not like that!'

'How long has this been going on, this flirting behind my back?'

'I have not been flirting! I refused him. I might never see him again.' I glared at Doughty. 'And you are too hasty.'

'Hasty? You're the one, it seems, who can brook no delay.' He had grown very pale and despite his harsh words he trembled.

'Edmond arrived here unexpectedly. He asked me to go back to London with him, and I said no.' I knew that Doughty was in pain, but he had angered me and I felt a cruel desire to make him suffer. 'But now – now I wish I had gone with him, if this is how you are going to behave.'

'I behave? I!' His voice shook. 'And what of your behaviour, making love to him under my roof?'

'I permitted him no more than what you saw.'

'I saw enough! And you've written to him, pleading your love – your undying love – and complaining of me, and my cruelty.'

'I wrote to him once, and once only. It was months ago –

you saw the letter yourself. He never replied, until he came here today.'

He paced the room, then returned to the mantelpiece and sank his head into his hands, digging his fingers into his skull.

'Lustrous lips! Damn you both!'

'I thought he would never come back. He was engaged to Maud Frith.'

'And?' He lifted his head again to look at me.

'She broke it off.' I rose and crossed the Turkey rug.

'So you are running back to him as if nothing had happened. Do you imagine that he has changed?'

'I have been everywhere today.' I caught the smell of whisky as I stood before him, hands on hips, chin lifted. 'Our affair has harmed me far more than it has harmed you. You would not believe the squalid places where I sought employment, to no avail. The filth, the disease, the lewd ways of the men. That is where I must go, when I leave here, if I can find any place at all. Edmond may be able to get me into Davenant's company again as a pianist. If not, he is wealthy enough to support me. And yet I said I would not go back to him.'

'But why not? He is young, handsome, wealthy, a fine catch for you.' He uttered the words with venom, his voice constricted by his resentment, choking in his throat. 'So, why not, I ask? Why not?'

The question hung between us. I almost told Doughty that I loved him. My eyes met his and my lips opened to speak, but I hesitated. Then his anger propelled him on.

'Just go to him, then!'

I protested and he raised his voice.

'No – don't lie to me! It's not over – he still moves you, he still excites your desire. I saw his hands on your skirts – and the heat rising in your face like any common slut. I will not stand for that –'

I spoke over him with my head held high.

'If you truly loved me then you would not speak to me like that. I have done nothing against you, and I permitted Edmond nothing. You envy him, because you are losing the power to help me.'

Doughty's eyes widened.

I felt again the impulse to be cruel.

'A letter came for you today, from London.'

It was as if I had cut his legs from under him at a single blow.

'It is on your desk.'

'Oh Lord.' He half slumped against the mantelpiece. 'They have sent it so soon. And the inquest is not yet done, it is barely started …'

He went into the study and touched the red wax seals of the letter.

I watched him from the doorway.

'I can't …' He turned, and held it out with a tremor, as if it was chilling his hand. 'Please.'

'No. Open it yourself.'

'Forgive me,' he said. 'I so dread you leaving. I am jealous. Jealousy and my stupid, wounded pride.'

I took a deep breath and let it slowly escape.

'Please,' he said, the letter in his hand still shaking as he stretched across the gap between us.

I took it, cracked the seals and unfolded the paper, my attention flickering across the paragraphs. I separated the pages and found the final disastrous sentence.

'You are removed from office.' I did not read any more.

He stood silent with his head bowed, and his body sagging like an empty suit. Then he slumped into a chair, his elbow on the desk, his hand cupping his forehead.

I could offer him no comfort.

'What will you do?'

'I'm so weary,' he said into his sleeve. 'Weary of fighting, weary of trying to believe I am right. One can only make a finite number of mistakes before being overtaken by failure.'

'I suppose you have tried to do what you thought best,' I said.

'I should abandon this inquest and save everyone a good deal of inconvenience and distress. Including myself. I must accept that my work's at an end. When they replace me, they'll elect someone less troublesome.' He lifted his head and looked to me for endorsement.

'Is that what you want?' I kept my tone neutral, neither accepting his surrender, nor encouraging him to persist.

He sighed. 'No.'

'Then what?'

He did not reply directly.

'This morning, when I opened Betty Marshall's inquest, she had already been buried. As if to obstruct me, for I could not proceed without sight of the body.'

I sat, facing him across his own desk as if I had been the coroner, and he the witness. He rested his fingers on the mahogany edge and interrogated the embossed border of the leather inlay with his nails.

'Tomorrow, her body is to be exhumed and cut apart, to satisfy a suspicion that rests on nothing more than my own prejudices and a few words from an untraceable vagrant. They will obey a warrant which I no longer have the right to issue.'

'Did you find out why she was in the lock-up?'

'She shouted abuse at Vernon during Evensong. Obscenities and blasphemy, according to Siviter, the workhouse master.'

I remembered Betty, swaddling Nathan, reciting the

Beatitudes over his screams. *Blessed are those who hunger and thirst …*

'She was so devout. Pious Betty. She would never blaspheme during a service. She had the entire Bible by heart.'

'I'd paid myself for gravediggers to recover the body at first light tomorrow. But now …'

'Perhaps she had a grievance against Glyde.' The letter from the Lord Chancellor lay on the desk between us, and I obscured it with my fingers. 'And what if I had forgotten to give this to you? If it lay amongst the newspapers for a few days, overlooked? If I had, in my foolishness, kindled the coals in the boiler with it?'

'The Lord Chancellor will have written also to Sir Thomas Pountney, the chief of the Bench. Pountney can be slow with his correspondence, or else he's yet to hear, but no-one said anything about it today. Until then – even if I have but a single day before they terminate me – I may yet conclude the inquest. I must find out how she died.'

Doughty reached across the desk and covered my hands, which I did not withdraw, with his own.

'Forgive me, Jane, stay with me. It has been a terrible day, and then I came home and saw you … I should not have said what I said. I saw my only comfort, my only strength, in the hands of another man. Please – stay until this case is over. Promise me you'll stay.'

I said I would consider it, just to quiet him down. But although I knew I cared for him, his behaviour had convinced me that I must leave. Whatever his gallantries, he would always expect to be the master and I the servant.

After supper I went to the piano, my haven, and allowed him to turn the music for me, lost as he was in his private despair. The melodies comforted us, while for me, as my anger faded, it was also a chance to practise in case I obtained an audition with Davenant. I went from Beethoven back to my beloved Chopin, and was still playing when Doughty went alone and exhausted to bed.

47: London Assurance

Doughty left early the next morning, with a grim look on his face and bidding me a terse goodbye.

The previous evening I had been unable to tell him, silenced by his anger, that he had rooted himself in my soul, and that when I left him I would leave a part of myself behind. What was said could not now be unsaid. *Just go to him!* he had shouted. He had seen my flush of embarrassment, and misread it as desire. *Any common slut.* A slut! How dare he, when it had been he who had been the seducer? I should never have yielded. His apology had come too late and I had gone to the piano for solace. Perhaps my music could yet be my life. But I hesitated to go to the Theatre Royal to seek out Mr Davenant, for it would bring me back into Edmond's orbit.

Was it true then, that I still loved Edmond? Who would not have been in awe of his eloquence, his voice and his talent? He had become more handsome; his face had lost its boyish softness and gained the strong lines of masculinity. But he had not regained my trust; I could not ignore his traces of paint. He was skilled at immorality: creating the villain with irresistible charm and making the audacity of evil a source of pleasure. His elegant language was drawn so much from the stage that it was hard to be sure of him.

Just go to him. Very well then! I climbed Ludgate Hill, crossed Colmore Row and skirted St Michael's churchyard, where a group of gentlemen in dark coats had formed in the corner by the paupers' graves. The constables were not letting anyone inside, and a few people lingered at the churchyard railings watching the gravediggers shovelling earth. It was a beautiful sunny day, at odds with the sombre scene.

'Graverobbers,' I heard someone muttering in the crowd. 'Desecrating the graves. Why can't they leave the dead in peace?'

I turned. An old man had spoken. His shabby clothes and unwashed state suggested he had recently been a workhouse inmate himself.

'It's to find out how she died,' I said.

'What?'

'They'll do a post-mortem,' I said. 'She was healthy when she went into the workhouse. She was put into the lock-up and never came out alive.'

'Aye, that evil place.'

'It is,' I said.

'He narrowed his eyes at me. 'And what would you know about it?'

I turned away to look at the graveyard scene. I did not want to admit that I had once been a pauper. It was as bad as confessing to having been in prison. But he was insistent.

'What would you know, missy?'

I regretted speaking to him.

'I was in there once. But I don't speak of it.'

'Aye, I've felt the whip there. But we don't speak of it, do we?'

I looked at the wizened, unkempt creature.

'You were beaten too?'

'No one goes through that place without a beating, 'tis said. Even though 'tis against the regulations. I were beaten for talking at dinner. Insubordination, they said it were.'

'Who beat you?' I asked.

'The chaplain, that vicar. I dursn't go to church now, in case he sees me.'

'You mean Glyde. I suppose there are many who have suffered at his hands?'

'Aye, there's some that have spoken of it, and others have passed on without telling their tale. They want us to fear the workhouse, see, so that we don't go in and make a burden on the parish.'

'But what else can people do?'

'I'd be better off starving in the streets than showing my face in there again. I were lucky to get out alive.'

The men at the graveside were craning their necks forward. There was a thump as someone jumped down into the grave. Ropes were carried to the edge of the hole, and there was shouting as they were secured. Eventually the four gravediggers took the ropes and hauled the coffin out. It came up feet first, sliding across the mud.

The men stood around the coffin and debated what to do with it. I heard Doughty's ringing tones as he demanded it to be taken back to the workhouse mortuary.

'This post-mortem examination shall be made, and the inquest properly conducted.'

The gravediggers shouldered the muddy coffin and passed in a grim procession down the cemetery path and out of the gate. Behind them walked the Beadle, Doughty, and the fifteen jurymen. Doughty's face was sombre, but he nodded to me as he walked past.

I went on. Temple Street took me to New Street and the Theatre Royal. From across the road I admired its facade: the huge arched windows, the columns, the statuary upon the roof. Drawn onwards by curiosity and nostalgia, I crossed the street and passed under the central arch of the portico, pushing open one of the tall wooden doors, and looking in. The evening's performance would not start until eight, and there was no one about except a clerk in the ticket office.

This was Edmond's world: of gaslight and greasepaint, playbills and posters, orchestras and audiences. He had spoken the previous day of rehearsing a comedy of flirtation; he had enthused over Lee Moreton and Madame Vestris and Charles Mathews. He loved to expound upon narratives, characterisation, genre. His illusion of himself was that he would become one of the greats: an actor-manager with his own theatre company.

I sighed to think that I had once belonged in Edmond's world, the novelty and excitement of it so intriguing after the quiet sobriety of my family. My father, cerebral and austere, and my mother with her modest piety, had faded to shadows beside Edmond's shining seductions: the fashion, the parties, the celebrities. My parents' preoccupations had been the welfare of the poor, the endowment of charities, the abolition of slavery, so their dinner-table conversation had concerned philanthropy, education, and public health. They believed that men should earn their income decently, by studying to enter a profession, and by hard work thereafter. The gambles of the theatrical world, its spectacular successes and awful failures, the debts and bankruptcies of the actors and the managers, its immorality and high living, its drinking and gaming, its affairs and intrigues, were decidedly not to their taste. Even if Edmond had courted me for a year and proposed for my hand in the traditional manner, they would have refused him whatever his wealth. They would in all likelihood have preferred Doughty as a son-in-law, perceiving him as educated and respectable.

For a moment the gilt and velvet of the theatre dissolved before my memory's eye and revealed the comfortable elegance of our house in London: the bookshelves, the music room, the garden. I remembered my own simple bedroom and the wardrobe where every knot of ribbon or swirl of lace, and every dress that was not grey or black, represented a victory over my mother at the dressmaker's shop. She never saw my rose silk, but I was glad to have worn that dress, even if only for a short time. I wondered if I would ever redeem it from the pawnbroker's dusty window.

As I hesitated by the door, two men approached the theatre, one whom I did not recognise, and the other was Martin Hellbronn, with whom Edmond had once accused me of flirting.

Hellbronn's face creased in a kindly smile.

'Why, it's little Jane!' The tall Swiss had that familiar lazy accent. He took my hand and bent his head to press his lips to my glove. 'I thought you had disappeared. I was asking Edmond where he had hidden you. Have you come to see him rehearse? They have started work on *London Assurance*. You can sit in the stalls if you like.'

I started to object that I could not stay to watch, and wanted only to speak to Mr Davenant about an audition, but Hellbronn took my arm.

'You have a sad face, my dear, come and amuse yourself for a moment. You will adore this jewel of the stage, this miracle of heartless flippancy!'

He waved at the clerk in the ticket office and ushered me across the red carpet of the stalls. On either side, three tiers of gilded, white-painted boxes rose up, separated by columns, like an inside-out wedding cake. Hanging in the dome of ceiling a gas chandelier gave out a constant hiss, its scores of bright glass globes branching out from circles of gleaming brass pipe. We settled on a plush-covered bench, which afforded a good view.

Edmond was on stage with a big bold girl whose voice boomed through the auditorium. The other players stood in the wings, conferring over their scripts. Mr Davenant was in the orchestra pit, leaning on the conductor's podium, holding a page of script up in his fingers like a dirty napkin.

'That is Mrs Nisbett, as Lady Gay Spanker,' said Hellbronn quietly.

I raised my eyebrows. 'Gay' implied a lascivious nature – and 'Spanker'…

'No!' I covered my smile with my hand.

Hellbronn winked at me and turned his attention to the stage, where Edmond wafted smelling-salts beneath the nose of Lady Spanker as she leaned back in a chair.

'I, the third daughter of an Earl, married him out of pity for his destitute and helpless situation as a bachelor with ten thousand a year. And – conceive if you can – he actually permits me, with the most placid indifference, to flirt with any old fool I may meet!' The plump underside of her forearm was revealed as she curved the back of her hand against her brow.

'Good gracious! Miserable idiot!' Edmond was playing the old fool.

'Sir Harcourt Courtly,' whispered Hellbronn.

'I fear there is an incompatibility of temper, which renders a separation inevitable.' Lady Spanker uttered her line in a powerful contralto, sitting upright and pushing away the smelling-bottle.

'Indispensable, my dear madam! Ah! Had I been the happy possessor of such a realm of bliss – what a beatific eternity unfolds

itself to my extending imagination! Had another man but looked at you, I should have annihilated him at once; and if he had the temerity to speak, his life alone could have expiated his crime.' Edmond caricatured Sir Harcourt's passionate baritone.

'Oh, an existence of such a nature is too bright for the eye of thought – too sweet to bear reflection …'

'My devotion, eternal, deep …' He knelt at her feet.

'Oh, Sir Harcourt!'

'Your every thought should be a separate study, each wish forestalled by the quick apprehension of a kindred soul.'

'Alas! How can I avoid my fate?' Lady Spanker's excessive alarm made the other players look up from their scripts.

I snorted with amusement.

'Edmond!' called Hellbronn. 'You have a very receptive audience!'

Edmond looked up, let out a laugh as he recognised me, and stood to deliver his line to the stalls, one hand on his chest, the other outstretched to me.

'If a life – a heart – were offered to your astonished view by one who is considered the index of fashion, if you saw him at your feet, beseeching your acceptance of all and more than this, what would you answer?'

The players whooped, and he ran to the end of the stage, then down to the stalls.

'My dearest, most adorable Jane! How wonderful to see you again, so soon!'

He advanced and, clasping my hands and drawing me to my feet, he leant forward. I drew my head back, reducing his kiss to a light brush with the lips.

'You suggested I might speak to Mr Davenant about an audition – whether I could play the piano again?'

I glanced at Mr Davenant, down in the pit, who raised his hand in greeting, but Edmond intervened.

'Jane's coming back to London with us on Saturday,

aren't you, my love? We shall have to go and buy you some finery and some fripperies. You shan't be in that awful bonnet and that black dress for much longer, eh?'

The players laughed as he threaded an arm around my waist and grinned back at the stage – now they were his audience.

'You will excuse me for a moment?' he called to Mr Davenant.

He was the star and he did as he pleased. Davenant shrugged his acceptance.

As soon as we were alone in the foyer I stopped.

'I am not coming back to you,' I said.

'What? Then why are you here?'

'I already said. I came to try for an audition with Mr Davenant and then Hellbronn saw me outside and marched me into your rehearsal. I did not intend to see you.'

'Indeed? But I'm delighted to see *you*!'

We were alone at the side of the foyer by the exit from the stalls. As I backed away from him, my movement was arrested by the wall. He pressed into my skirts, his hands coming up around my face, his fingers at the back of my head, and now he took his kiss. His eyelids, with their long lashes, fell closed, he smelled of bergamot and musk, his lips and tongue were as smooth as ever. There were hundreds of women who would have fought me for that kiss – but it felt wrong; he did not seem to notice that I squirmed to get away.

Edmond's hand travelled to the back of my waist and then he jerked his head back and grimaced.

'Servants' clothes! I'd dearly like to get you out of this hideous woollen dress, my darling Jane. How can you stand to wear it? I suppose you have those awful thick black stockings on, that servant girls wear. You look as if you're dressed for a funeral.'

He obviously did not know the gossip and I was not

going to enlighten him. I wanted to wipe my mouth.

'There are some tolerable dressmakers here – you'll be outfitted within a couple of days. Silk dresses, pretty shoes and stockings, and an elegant bonnet instead of that awful black.' He lowered his voice to a wheedle. 'Let's go along New Street. I should like to get you something. A pair of beribboned garters, and silk stockings, and then you'll allow me to adorn your pretty legs … do you remember how it used to be?'

'Edmond, I do remember how it used to be: you treated me abominably.'

He continued as if I had said nothing: 'And my hotel is close by. I should be delighted to resume our acquaintance, in a manner of speaking.'

'I have work to do. I cannot remain out so long, even if I wanted to.'

He gave me an incredulous smile. 'Why do you stay in that terrible gloomy place with that old gent? Just fetch your belongings and join me in my suite. I've plenty of room.'

I could not tell Edmond the truth, although it was stabbing me.

'I must give Dr Doughty notice, so that he has time to find – to find someone else.' The pain settled somewhere at the top of my stomach, and I wondered that Edmond could not see it. 'He has an important case at the moment and I do not want him distracted. I must cook and clean for him, and he needs fresh clothes and hot water.'

'But you wrote to me of a durance from which you desperately desired me to release you? And now, I'm here, and you will no longer leave?'

'We have grown accustomed to one another. I work hard, and he – he treats me decently.' I dared not look at Edmond as I said this.

'And what of his wife?'

'She was an invalid. She died recently, of diphtheria.' Over Edmond's shoulder I saw through the arched windows of the foyer, the bustle on New Street: the clerks going to their lunch and the horse carts rumbling past.

'Well, I am surprised he hasn't taken advantage of you, for dwelling with you would discompose any virile man. Does he lack the energy and vigour which he may have enjoyed in his youth?' Edmond made an obscene movement of his little finger, holding it up to my face.

'Edmond!' I protested, shrinking back.

He grinned. 'I know you. You have a weakness for men, Jane – it is a fault in you.'

That stung me like a slap, like the slap he had given me over Hellbronn. In the old days I would have lowered my eyes in shame. But now I bridled.

'*Weakness?* It is you who are weak, and faithless. How quickly you forgot about me, and about our child, and latched on to Maud! How dare you speak to me thus?'

'Well, you have developed some spirit, I see. But if you want me back, you'll have to temper it. I have no need of a shrew, although the taming can be most amusing.'

'Do not presume that I either want you back, or intend you to tame me, as you put it.' I said this slowly and deliberately but it was as if he had not heard.

'In any case, how much notice can he possibly need? A lovely girl like you shouldn't rusticate here. We return to London on Saturday, by the railway – I shall send my carriage on ahead. Don't you miss the Great Wen? London, the capital of fashion, of wealth, of celebrity, the monstrous metropolis of the Empire? You're more beautiful than ever, Jane, and together we shall take London society by storm.'

'Edmond, as I said yesterday, I cannot trust you. After I wrote that letter, your silence gave me a stronger indication of your character than any of your speeches. You did not even trouble yourself to write back.'

'Ah! There's fire in your eyes, Jane. I've offended you – I cry your pardon. But you will not be angry with me forever, and you'll forgive your Edmond, for I have an unbearable craving for your sweet company – and then imagine what a fashionable life you shall have. D'you know, I've rented a house in Devonshire Street that once belonged to none other than Mrs Cibber? Susannah Cibber, the greatest tragedy actress of the eighteenth century!'

'Edmond, let me hear no more of your empty promises. I am not the girl that you once deserted. I have known bitter longing, and grief and death. My son's life was no better than that of a captive animal raised in a shed. It is too late; the past is in the past.'

He laughed, but the look from his blue eyes was startling and severe.

'Are you saying that you no longer care for me? My adorable little Jane. Of course you love me.' He inflated his chest and stood straight. 'You are the most beautiful girl in England and I am the only man that can make you happy.'

'You sang my praises before, you made me promises, and nothing came of it. I imagine that there will be nothing better on this occasion. And then what, when you desert me again? What will become of me?'

'Why then, you shall have to take care to treat me better, to retain my attention.' Edmond grinned, and gripped my waist.

'What gives you the right?' I raised my hands to his shoulders, and held him away.

He was merely amused by my resistance. 'Only come to my rooms, the Golden Swan is only a short distance from here, and I shall prove to you how I love you!'

'Let me go!' I broke away from his grasp.

Still grinning, he made no attempt to stop me. I burst out of the theatre.

As I hurried along the pavement I heard Hellbronn and Mr Davenant calling me from the side door.

'Hey! Jane! Jane Verity! What about your audition?'

But I had to get away from Edmond. I barged through the passers-by. I had not gone two hundred yards when I found that the Beadle had caught me up. His hand closed solidly around my arm just as it had on the day he had conducted me to Newhall Street.

'Jane Verity, you are required at the workhouse,' he said, in a tone of command, adding that he was in possession of a summons, and propelled me away.

48: Mr Graves' Report

POSTMORTEM EXAMINATION OF MISS BETTY MARSHALL, aet. 26.

By: Mr Stephen Graves MD FRCS
Assisted by: Mr G. Ensor and Coroner W. Doughty
2nd September 1840

On initial inspection the cadaver appeared generally emaciated.

On the head were several injuries. The front upper lip was split, and front tooth recently broken. The largest head wound, covered by a scab of blood, overlay a palpable depressed fracture of the temporal bone on the right side.

Multiple additional bruises were observed, including on the left cheek, on both shoulders and both arms in a recurring linear pattern. Each injury comprised two small round bruises, a narrow weal or sometimes a cut, another small round bruise, and a number of angled marks. This pattern denoted the use of an implement. I have observed these patterns before, inflicted by a wrought-iron poker. When held by the shaft, the moulded handle makes a weighty club.

The external injuries extended beneath the elbows, to the wrists and the backs and palms of the hands. There was an obvious displaced fracture of the mid-shaft of the right humerus, causing abnormal angulation of the upper arm.

These injuries were too numerous to have resulted from a seizure. The distribution of injuries indicated that the deceased had attempted to defend herself against blows. Some victims reach a hand towards a striking implement and are wounded on the palm. Others attempt to cradle their heads and the blows fall upon the outer aspects of the upper limbs. The deceased appears to have done both. Apoplexy, with loss of consciousness, was therefore highly unlikely.

Though numerous, the external injuries were not the cause of death. The abdomen was swollen and blackened, but containing gas, rather than blood, likely to be the result of post-mortem putrefaction.

In the absence of significant superficial bruising the thorax and abdomen were less likely to be the site of fatal injury.

It was therefore necessary to open the skull to evaluate the area of the depressed fracture. An incision line was made from ear to ear, over the crown. The divided scalp was retracted and a saw-line was made in order to separate the skull-pan without breaching the dura or disturbing the cranial contents within. On taking off the skull-pan it was clear that the brain had been deformed by an extensive haemorrhage, a mass of blackish clot compressing the cerebral hemisphere aside.

A small incision was made in the dura mater and a flap of that membrane retracted to inspect the surface of the cerebrum. The cerebro-spinal fluid contained no blood and the folds of the brain's surface had the delicate pallor of stewed barley. In those who have died from apoplexy, the brain is dark and suffused with blood. This unfortunate woman did not sustain her death through apoplexy.

Further examination revealed that the skull fracture had breached the middle meningeal artery. The effusion of blood found between the thick membrane of the dura mater and the skull, and the external injury corresponding to that part, I conclude that it had been caused by the blow to the head, from the same implement as had been used elsewhere, and the resulting brain haemorrhage was the cause of death.

49: I Testify

It had been nearly seven months since I first took those same reluctant steps into the workhouse yard. As the Beadle brought me under that gloomy archway and across cobblestones stained with slime I felt as though all my freedoms and hopes were destroyed. There was no indication of how long I would be here or if indeed I would be released at all. The place filled me with dread: how I would walk upright and keep my voice from quavering, I did not know. I was terrified of Glyde, of the Sunday Penances, of the lock-up.

In the yard two old men were pounding bones, just as Clara and I had done on the morning I first met Doughty. The rows of empty windows stared down from the towering black walls, and the rank smell of the place rose up and choked me.

The Beadle left me waiting on a bench in the entrance hall. From far away in the building I heard a single scream echoing in the silence. I feared that at any moment I would encounter Glyde, switch in hand, or Mr Siviter with his cane.

I felt I would be plunged defenceless into the constant violence that prevailed in the institution.

Then I heard my name called out. Mrs Siviter had come to find me. I stood up at once, expecting her to slap me down for being slow, or to direct me to strip off my clothes in the stoving room, and don the paupers' uniform.

'Jane,' she said. 'What a terrible business.'

I stared at her: she stooped like an old woman and her face was drawn with pain, very different from the hard face she had once shown me.

'You're summoned to testify,' she said wearily. 'It's terrible, terrible –'

I let out a gasp of relief.

'The coroner sent the Beadle to look for you,' she said. 'I don't know why he wants you. It's all about poor Betty. A terrible business.'

'Do you think you will be called?' I asked her.

'I don't know what to say.' She sat down abruptly on the bench beside me and buried her face in her hands. 'What will they ask me?'

I turned to look at her, with her shoulders tense in the cheap stuff gown, and her powerful smell of sweat. She gave out a cry, a kind of shrill mewing, her hands clenched to her face as though to keep her from a louder outburst.

It took me all my strength to pity her, but I reached out and patted her shoulder. After all she was another woman like me, lied to and manipulated by the men.

'Speak the truth, if they ask you,' I said. 'It's easier that way. Then you will know all the answers, whatever they ask. If you don't know, just say so. After all, maybe you were not the one to blame.'

One of her hands left off its grasp of her face and closed around my hand that was on her shoulder.

'I'm sorry,' she whimpered. 'That's the truth.'

'You have a power,' I said. 'Your power is your voice. If you are sorry, then say so, and say why.'

'I'm sorry.' She stared at me, and I saw the tears that lingered in her lower eyelids.

'Don't cry,' I said, 'and be strong.'

Then she reached into her apron pocket and took out two keys linked by an iron ring.

'Reverend Glyde's here. The way he speaks about you – he means you harm. Let yourself out by the side gate afterwards, as soon as you can. Run, if you have to.' She put the keys, warm from her body, into my hand and closed my fingers over them. 'Lock it behind you. There's a loose tile on the floor at the side of the archway. Leave these underneath.'

I thanked her and briefly reached across and embraced her. I felt that the gesture meant more to her than it did to me.

'Come straight to the boardroom now, Jane.' she said. 'They're waiting for you.'

I had somehow expected a large crowd of people to be assembled for the inquest but there was just a line of gentlemen, fifteen of them, sitting along the far side of the big boardroom table. I had never seen Doughty at work in his black silk robes before. His familiar face, though sombre, was a refuge for my eyes; at the sight of him a poignant nocturne started playing in my mind. At his elbow was a clerk, scratching at a ledger with a steel pen. At one end of the table a man in a jaunty yellow waistcoat pencilled notes in a book, perhaps the reporter from the *Birmingham Gazette*. At the other end sat Mr Siviter; his wife took a chair at his side. The oak tabletop had been polished to a glassy sheen, perhaps by Betty herself.

Facing Doughty across the table, where he sat in the

middle of the long row of jurymen, was a single chair, and after swearing me in he told me to be seated.

'Some of the foregoing evidence touches Betty Marshall's character, about which certain statements have been made to this inquisition.' He inclined his head towards me to indicate that I should speak. 'When and for how long did you last see her?'

I thought back. Since I had heard of Betty's death I had reflected about her but more as a series of images than as dates and times: her frizzy dark hair, her sallow skin, the freckles on her nose and her fondness for liturgical quotations.

'I have not seen her since I left the workhouse in March this year,' I said. 'Before that I saw her regularly for a few weeks.'

A couple of the jury made as if to protest at this, feeling perhaps, as I did, that it was too long ago, but Doughty held up a hand to silence them. As he spoke I studied the row of impassive male faces, wondering which ones were in thrall to Glyde.

'It has been alleged that the deceased was of an uncouth and blasphemous disposition, and last Sunday interrupted Evensong with appalling obscenities. This was adduced as evidence of habitual insanity. It had been thought that while in the lock-up her inflamed nature led to a fatal attack of apoplexy. We now find that the surgeon's post-mortem report indicates numerous injuries, the principal one being bleeding from the brain occasioned by a blow from an implement, probably a wrought-iron poker.'

I shuddered, trying to overcome my revulsion. Clara had spoken of Glyde in the lock-up with a knotted rope and a poker. But I had to compose myself, to speak. As I hesitated some of the jurymen stared at me, while others looked down at their folded hands or gazed out of the window. I thought of Betty's abruptness, her clumsy ways, her Beatitudes.

'We called her Pious Betty. I do not believe that she was insane. She was a devout Christian, and could recite entire chapters of the Bible, that she had memorised word-perfect. I never saw such an outburst as you describe, and would not think her capable of blasphemy.'

'Yet Mr Siviter, the workhouse master, has testified under oath that she had to be forcibly removed from Evensong. She insulted Reverend Glyde most improperly in the middle of conducting the service.'

'She was virtuous enough,' I replied, 'but in some respects, she was deficient. She always spoke her mind, and did not know how to conduct herself easily, or when to be silent. She could not meet your eye, nor read your expression, and she was unable to lie, even to save herself. You gentlemen should try to discover what it was, exactly, that she said, and whether there was a reason behind her outburst. Often what we women say is dismissed, but if you listen more patiently you will hear the truth.'

Out of the corner of my eye I saw Mrs Siviter nodding, while Doughty gazed at me with such hunger that I was unable to look away. The memory of his embrace overtook my body, and I blushed, hoping that the gentlemen of the jury had not heard the gossip about us.

'Tell me then the truth. Tell me anything you know of this institution, that you feel may be relevant,' Doughty said. 'We are ready to hear the truth.'

A wizened old man at his left side sat upright at that.

'I fear that this will lead to greater procrastination and delay in a hearing that has already –'

'Let her speak, Mr Huntly,' Doughty cut him short.

Where shall I start, I thought. One of the jurymen leered knowingly at me. I kept my head up and brought Theresa back into my mind.

'In March, just before I left here, a girl hanged herself – you conducted her inquest. Theresa Curran. She bore many cruelties in silence: beatings, violation. Her post-mortem examination found innumerable injuries from severe beatings, from vicious rape, and that she was pregnant. Death was her only means of escape. She was blamed for her own dreadful suffering and no-one was held responsible; it was all covered up.' I heard a sniff, and glanced to the end of the table. Mrs Siviter was holding her handkerchief to her eyes. 'Evil has been brought into this institution, to be unleashed against the poor and defenceless. A man who calls himself a priest, but has no religion save the gratification of his own perversities. A man who sends innocent babies into the cesspit without a baptism or a funeral prayer.'

Another juryman started a cascade of protests but was silenced by Doughty.

'Mr Handcock!'

He waited until the boardroom was silent even down to the stilling of the reporter's pencil.

'Let her continue.'

As I spoke I began to engage the jurymen's attention, even if it was only that they were willing to confuse beauty with virtue.

'I believe that I know who perpetrated that evil upon Theresa Curran. He has indulged himself in further cruelties since her death. I have myself suffered at his hands. I have witnessed his appalling behaviour towards other women. I suspect that he may have also murdered Betty Marshall.'

Mr Siviter darted me an anxious glance, but I looked away, into Doughty's dark eyes, holding his attention just as I had on that fateful day in the yard outside.

'And so I would ask, what, exactly, did Betty Marshall say during the Evensong that was so blasphemous and obscene? Reverend Glyde was conducting Evensong. What argument did that pious woman have against him? If she had suffered as Theresa had, it would have been impossible for her to remain silent. Nor would she have described it in a polite manner. What if that was the reason for her death?'

'You believe then, that Reverend Glyde had provoked the deceased with inappropriate behaviour of his own?'

I said that I was almost certain of it, but that more evidence would be required of those who had been present, as to what exactly had been said.

Mrs Siviter appeared to be studying the polished surface of the table.

The jurymen digested my remarks. They could not believe that I could say such a thing.

One darted his head towards another in consternation and they conferred. He turned back to me, a fat, purple-faced man with fair hair.

'How dare you speak in such a way of your superiors?' He turned to Doughty. 'I object to this witness. You are wasting the jury's time listening to this salacious speculation. Reverend Glyde is a devout churchman of the utmost respectability and who has been untiring in his efforts to assist the poor and indigent of the parish.'

'Mr Johnston! Let her speak,' repeated Doughty, though it cost him an effort to say it, 'and weigh her evidence without prejudice.'

'Theresa Curran,' I continued as Doughty nodded, 'was sent every week to the Sunday Penances. This was a punishment inflicted for trivial misdemeanours but Theresa usually did not know why she had been sent. For most of us the Sunday Penances meant that we knelt in line while Reverend Glyde whipped our hands. Perhaps that does not sound bad to you? In the workhouse, where we are employed constantly in hard manual work, that was a torment for days afterwards. In any case, after these cruelties were completed we were all dismissed, except for Theresa. She was kept back in the chapel to pray with Reverend Glyde. If we saw her afterwards she was silent, her face downcast, and shied away if we tried to speak to her. I suspected that it was during those times alone with Glyde that she was violated and that was why she was pregnant. I have since spoken to another girl whom he beat and raped there and I have also learned of his visits to the workhouse at night.'

'This inquest,' remarked Mr Huntly, 'requires evidence. Fact, not impertinent suppositions. Who is this other female to whom you refer?'

'Her name is Clara Scattergood,' I replied. My heart sank as I explained that she was to be found at Mrs Graham's on Suffolk Street.

'A notorious bawdy house,' Mr Huntly snorted.

Mr Johnston tittered.

'If the entire woman can be made to turn tricks for a shilling, why give any credence to the mouth?'

Led by Mr Handcock, a number of the jury now banged their palms on the table, protesting that they would not listen to such filth, that it was outrageous, irrelevant gossip, that Doughty should control the proceedings and that I should be made to keep a civil tongue in my head instead of producing this disgusting and impertinent nonsense.

Privately I wondered if any of these men, outwardly so righteous, had been clients of Mrs Graham. Doughty silenced them again and indicated that I should continue.

'So my testimony to you is mere gossip.' I met Mr Johnston's stare. 'I speak honestly and you call me impertinent. To you the truth is filth: you would take away the words that describe the crimes that were perpetrated. At the same time you deem Reverend Glyde devout and respectable, but I have witnessed his behaviour to be the reverse of that. He benefits by his authority; I am discredited because of my low position. You say Betty Marshall was obscene and insulting. Perhaps she was telling the truth? You should find out what she said, and listen to her words, without judging her first.'

I said nothing about Harriet, not wishing to publicly embarrass Doughty, and lacking the proof, for certainly Astley-Scrope had destroyed her suicide note.

In any case I had made an impact: Mr Johnston's gaze had shifted to his folded hands. The jurymen had resumed their seats and Mr Handcock glowered at me with pursed lips. Doughty leaned forward to look right and left along the line of faces. The Siviters exchanged glances. The court clerk and the reporter in the yellow waistcoat were each scribbling down their versions of what I had said.

The silence was interrupted by the blustering arrival of Glyde.

'You're late,' said Doughty.

50: Contempt of Court

Glyde was wild-eyed, and as he removed his hat his hair stuck up in spikes from his sweating head.

I rose hastily and retreated to a corner of the room as he planted himself in my chair. As soon as he had been sworn in he addressed the jury, his voice hoarse with emotion.

'Gentlemen, I can only advise you not to countenance these highly irregular proceedings, or to accept the jurisdiction of such a coroner.' He attempted a grin. 'On the verge of dismissal, Dr Doughty has acquired a zeal to ascertain the causes of death of all persons whom it may have pleased Providence to deprive suddenly of existence, no matter what sacrilege must be committed to that end, or what indignities be visited upon the corpse of the deceased by his surgical accomplices.'

The jurymen stared at him. Their mood had altered; they had been ready to defend him but now they were losing faith. They saw the outward appearance of a man of distinction at one moment but at the next it was as if the evil spirit that possessed him sneered at them from within.

Doughty remained calm.

'Reverend Glyde, your opinions exceed your remit as a witness, and may render you in contempt of court.'

'You exceeded your remit in desecrating this grave, sir!' Glyde's fists were clenched at his sides.

Mr Huntly intervened. 'If a workhouse inmate is arbitrarily deprived of her freedom, and thereafter is found dead, and is hastily buried, who then has exceeded their remit?' He rapped his knuckles on the table. 'Ought that not be investigated?'

'There was a time when the deceased were allowed to be conveyed to their last homes, and their remains to be left sacred and undisturbed. But, no. That practice, it would seem, is barbarous, and so, they must be dug up, and their innards catalogued to all, to form a means of increasing the fees of coroners and the circulation of newspapers.' Glyde snarled at the reporter, who, with a set mouth, continued to scribble.

Doughty would not yield. 'I should not have been forced to disinter the deceased, had you not conducted her burial, with a speed which was suspicious of concealment.'

'The burial was completely in order. Dr Wright provided a death certificate.'

'According to Mr Siviter, Dr Wright did not fully examine the deceased, and had never attended her previously. I can assure you that we will summon him in due course.'

'It was abundantly clear that her various injuries were the result of her violent and agitated behaviour during her apoplexy.'

Doughty raised his eyebrows. 'All her injuries? You were not here when Mr Graves gave his post-mortem report.'

Glyde hesitated, then his lips parted in a smile. 'But I witnessed her struggling. She struck herself in numerous places. It took three people to restrain her from violence.'

Doughty glanced down at the paper that lay on the table beneath his left hand.

'In Mr Graves' opinion, her injuries were caused by an implement, and were not self-inflicted, or due to manhandling. What have you to say about that?'

'What implement? Has he seen an implement?'

'A wrought-iron poker.'

'Has he seen such a poker? If not, his opinion is merely conjecture.' Glyde's eyes flickered over the jury. 'I will tell you what happened. This woman became violently disturbed and agitated, for no reason. Her language was terrible.'

'And what exactly did she say?'

'I cannot remember.' Glyde's stare flitted again amongst the jurors without finding a friendly face. 'It was obscene gibberish, nonsense. She was delirious, as though seized by a fit. She had to be silenced, for the sake of the other inmates. I therefore ordered that she be put in the lock-up.'

'Let the jury be mindful that the workhouse lock-up is the only means in this country by which a person may be held prisoner without recourse to the law.' Doughty studied Glyde as though seeing him anew. 'Nonetheless, she was silenced, and silenced forever. Let me make it clear: beaten to death with a wrought-iron poker. Was that also at your orders?'

Glyde gripped the seat of his chair, blood draining from his face.

'Certainly not!'

'Or by your own hand?' Doughty pronounced the startling words deliberately.

The jurymen looked at him.

'My God,' Mr Handcock muttered under his breath.

'Do you not know who I am?' The colour returned to Glyde's face as he rallied. 'What gives you the authority to question me in this presumptuous manner? And over what?

The death of a pauper, a feeble-minded woman, a raving idiot who met her end through the violence of her own uncontrollable agitation of mind! Your insolence is insufferable.' His spittle flecked the table and he wiped his mouth with the back of his hand.

'I am the coroner, elected by the freeholders of this town, and this is my jury of respectable and honest men, and it is our duty to enquire by what means Betty Marshall met her death.' Doughty kept his voice low and deliberate. 'Whether or not she was poor and feeble-minded, our purpose is the same.'

'Aye!' The jurymen were nodding; one man clapped the table.

Glyde ignored them now, turning and funnelling his venom towards me, his voice resonating with hatred.

'And you have paraded your mistress before this travesty of an inquest. You both should be flogged through the streets of this town!'

I was on my feet, up on my toes and pointing at him.

'What I have done is nothing as compared to you – I am not a rapist or a murderer.' I glared down my arm as though it had been a rifle aimed at his head. 'If I am to be flogged, then you should be hanged!'

Doughty merely crooked an eyebrow. 'My jury will be enlightened on your ideas on corporal punishment in due course. But for now, we must return to our primary purpose, which is to clarify the cause of this death. We know that the cause of death was a brain haemorrhage caused by a blow to the head with an implement. But we believe the blow was struck while the deceased was held in solitary confinement. Therefore the purpose of this inquest is not only to find the mechanism of death, but to discover how the deceased came to harm while imprisoned.'

Glyde now sprang up from his chair, which fell back with

a crash, and bellowed with his fists clenched against his hips.

'Your purpose is repugnant, sir, and shameful, and I will no longer endure your egregious malpractice!'

'Your outburst has not answered my questions.' Doughty maintained an unflinching calm. 'Must I remind you again of my duty?'

'Your duty? You – you no longer have any! When you are disgraced, we shall see then! We shall see then who has the authority.' He whipped out of the boardroom, slamming the door behind him.

Huntly cleared his throat, breaking the silence.

'Contempt of Court.' He pronounced the words with a hint of relish.

'Shall I go after him, sir?' asked the Beadle.

Doughty shook his head. 'I believe he has nothing further to contribute here.'

At that Mrs Siviter stood up. She tucked her handkerchief into her sleeve.

'I wish to testify,' she said.

Her husband looked up in alarm but did not stop her from advancing to the fallen chair, which she set straight before identifying herself and taking the oath.

'I have had many girls and women complain to me of the Reverend Glyde,' she said after she had sat down. 'I refused to listen to them, handed out punishments, sent them away with a box on the ears for impertinence. I will admit I have lost my temper with them, as has my husband. We have both been over-free with our use of the birch. There are nearly three hundred inmates here, in a building that was made for half that number, and with only my husband and myself to keep order. If we did not keep strict discipline they would rise up and overwhelm us.'

She turned and looked across the room, meeting my eyes.

'But I found the girl who hung herself,' she said. 'I'll never forget opening that door and seeing her hanging there, her eyes staring down at me. And I have asked myself a hundred times if I could have saved her. I may have struck her one time too many. I don't know. But rape, murder – no. And I don't agree with not baptising the babies. I've begged him to do it and he won't. I'm the one that has to lie awake in the night listening to –'

'Let us return to the facts of the present case,' urged Huntly.

Doughty intervened.

'Mrs Siviter, you imprisoned Betty Marshall in the lock-up after removing her from Evensong.'

'Yes, sir, according to the Reverend's orders.'

'And was there a struggle, to get the deceased into the lock-up?'

'No, sir. She was shouting and screaming, but my husband took one arm and I took the other and she went along between us like that. We just pushed her into the lock-up and shut the door on her, let her exercise her lungs.'

'The post-mortem examination found evidence of blows from a heavy implement. Her arm was broken and she died from a fractured skull, which caused bleeding inside her brain. Did you strike her?'

'No. Certainly not!'

'I remind you that you are under oath,' said Doughty. 'You are sworn upon the Bible. A man's life may depend upon your testimony.'

'I swear it upon the soul of my dear mother. We never struck her.' Mrs Siviter's voice was clear and firm. 'And she were in fine voice for a number of hours afterwards, screaming and swearing. The other inmates were complaining, especially with it being a Sunday. It got worse and worse and then she fell silent.'

'Had anyone else entered the lock-up?'

'Not to my knowledge, sir. But I wasn't nearby.'

'Does anyone else have a key?'

'Me and Mr Siviter have keys. There's one on the cleaning set, I keep that. And Reverend Glyde has a set of keys to the whole place. He's the Chairman of –'

'And you did not check on the deceased's condition? Even though she was considered to be having a fit?'

'I didn't want to set her off again, see. Especially at night when it'd wake everyone up. They all start work before seven in the morning.'

Without the vagrant's testimony, it would be impossible to define events further.

'What exactly did the deceased say at Evensong?'

Doughty was, I thought, now convinced that Glyde was guilty of the murder. He was searching for the motive.

'The Reverend was reading the lesson but she reckoned as he weren't reading it right. She got angry.'

'How would she dare to contradict him?' asked Huntly.

'*Oh ho!*' chuckled Mrs Siviter. 'She knew every word of the Scriptures by heart. There was something wrong with her, I think.'

'And what was the lesson?'

'From the Book of Job, sir. *He preserveth not the life of the wicked, nor giveth right to the poor.* And she reckoned he had got the words wrong. She said she knew the lesson. He said that she was an ignorant and illiterate woman, and would not be insulted by her. But she marched up to the front and she recited it and she had the whole chapter and verse by heart.'

Doughty beckoned to the Beadle. 'Beadle, pass me the Bible. The Book of Job, Mrs Siviter?'

'Yes, sir, Chapter 36, I believe.'

The Bible was bound in tattered black leather and had been sworn upon by thousands of witnesses. No-one ever read it; the gilt-edged pages clumped together as he searched. Doughty's eyes screwed up as if stung by the air, and he scanned the columns of tiny print until he read aloud:

'*He preserveth not the life of the wicked, BUT giveth right to the poor*. She was right – not so mad, then, Mrs Siviter. And then what?'

'She laughed at him. She said, "You call me illiterate and ignorant. But I read and I remember!" And I can't repeat what she said after that, sir. It was shocking. We had to restrain her.' Mrs Siviter looked down at her knees.

'Go on,' said Doughty.

'I cannot, sir. It should not have been said in the chapel.' Mrs Siviter's discomfort was genuine.

'But you swore on the Bible to tell the whole truth.'

'Yes, sir.'

'Then if you withhold evidence, not only do you hold the court in contempt – an offence punishable by a criminal conviction – but also you hold the Bible in contempt, for which you will one day answer to a higher authority than any here on Earth.'

I was sure I could smell smoke.

Mrs Siviter took a deep breath, and coughed, before replying to him in a low voice.

'She shouted out: "I read what you wrote in your office. I read your black book. It said: *Fuck, cunt, arsehole, prick!*" And continued in similar fashion. It was disgusting, like she was blocked up by these curse words and she was trying to spit them out. Please don't ask me to say more.'

There was silence, and Mr Sharp's pencil froze above the page. I had thought myself the only one to have disturbed Glyde's journal, but evidently Betty had somehow read it.

'How would she have got inside his office?' asked Huntly.

'She cleaned it,' said Mrs Siviter.

I supposed that Glyde had assumed that Betty was unable to read and had been unaware that, with her peculiar memory, she had memorised the Bible in its entirety. Betty would have expected the black book on his desk to contain some religious text, some new material to commit to memory. Finding it full of obscenities would have distressed her severely, and she would have been unable to expel the ugly words and images from her thoughts.

'I'm reluctant to interrupt proceedings, gentlemen, but I detect smoke.' Doughty was right – my eyes were sore.

'The town's full of smoke all the time,' Huntly replied. 'Foundries, engines, brassworks, glassworks, gasworks. The greatest manufacturing town of the world.'

'Allow me to investigate.' Doughty stood and crossed the boardroom to the door.

'The Birmingham Mint, the Soho Manufactory, Curzon Street Station,' continued Huntly. 'We live on metal, coal, and steam.'

Doughty opened the door. A faint haze of smoke came in. 'We'd best adjourn,' he said.

We followed him the length of the corridor. It was coming from the chapel. We went in through a mist of smoke, with the Christ crucified visible only through a haze.

Grey wisps were curling from under the door to the side of the altar.

'It's the Reverend's office.' Mr Siviter advanced and knocked, then tried the door handle. 'Locked.' He pulled a bunch of keys from his pocket and pushed one into the lock. He started to rattle it, cursed under his breath, and banged it with his hand. 'The other key's on the inside! He must be in there! *Fire! Fire!*' He hammered on the door with his fist, and shouted, but there was no reply.

An inmate came across the chapel – he'd been polishing

the floor outside.

'Don't just stand there, you daft bugger,' growled Siviter to him. 'Get a crowbar from the workshop!' He continued to pound the door, thumped his shoulder to it, but it held shut.

Eventually the inmate returned with the crowbar and a lump-hammer and Siviter broke the door open.

Heat blasted against our faces but there were no flames. The room was completely dark and filled with thick smoke.

'Open the shutters! Open the window!' Doughty took a lungful of acrid air and rushed in.

The rest of the group clustered outside, the jurymen straggling back along the corridor, some unwilling to approach too closely. Siviter sent someone for a bucket of water. We could hear Doughty banging about inside the little room.

Then there was a pause.

A cough, a grunt, and then nothing. Shutters banged back and a little light entered the haze within the room but still nothing could be seen.

I heard Doughty groan as though with a huge effort and then the slow creaking as he pushed up, bit by bit, a sash window. He gave out a long gasp and his breath heaved in wheezing lungfuls.

The air started to clear and I saw that Doughty must have stepped over Glyde's body to reach the window. The Reverend lay prone in front of the stove, a pile of books and papers strewn at his side.

Siviter was the first to venture forward, and knelt by the body.

'Sir?' He grasped the shoulder and shook it. The open mouth was a deep violet.

Doughty, still panting, stooped down and felt for a pulse. With an expression of loathing, he slid his hand under the waistcoat to where the heartbeat should be.

'Nothing. He's suffocated. Dead.'

'Why'd he shut himself in like this?' Siviter levered himself with an effort to his feet.

Doughty inspected the stove. Choked with ashes, it had been the source of the lethal fumes. Papers were piled up within it. Doughty dug out a half-burnt book with a poker. Its leather spine crumbled as it hit the floor; he stamped out the little flames. A charred fragment caught his eye and he picked it from the ashes. His look of contempt intensified as he examined it.

'Destroying his secrets. It was as Betty Marshall said.'

He looked at the wrought-iron poker in his hand, then turned it to hold it by the shaft and smacked the knobbed handle into his palm. It was the murder weapon.

I was no longer needed. The men returned in ones and twos to the boardroom where the hubbub of noise became unbearable. Nothing could be concluded, another inquest would have to be held, the Constabulary would have to be summoned, the documents – were they to be destroyed or preserved? There was talk of the Archbishop, of Lambeth Palace, and then in the midst of it all Sir Thomas Pountney the Chief of the Magistrates Bench arrived in haste with a letter from London and proclaimed that Doughty was no longer coroner and the inquest proceedings were suspended.

I slipped away, making use of the key that Mrs Siviter had given me, and concealing it under the tile as bid. No-one saw me.

I returned to Newhall Street and started to prepare the house for the evening, tidying the kitchen, lighting the fires, wondering whether to start a simple supper. It grew late in the evening and Doughty did not return. I supposed he had chosen to dine out with the other men.

Then someone was at the front door, and I went upstairs

to open it, drying my hands on my apron. On the step was Edmond's coachman, politely expressionless in his scarlet coat; in the street, the grand black and silver carriage, a boy minding the horses' reins. Above us the dusk had turned the sky grey-blue. The furnaces in the nearby manufactories rumbled and the horses shifted anxiously. The coachman spoke to them and they calmed. Then he turned to me.

'A letter, miss. I'm to wait for you.'

I recognised Edmond's writing.

'One minute,' I said, and shut him out. With my back against the door, I opened the letter.

51: Edmond's Letter to Me, with an Enclosure

At the Golden Swan – 2nd September 1840

My Dear Jane,

I have had the opportunity to reflect, and now keenly regret that my careless behaviour has occasioned you such hardship and distress. I would like you to think better of me.

In the hope that it will offer some recompense, you will be pleased to know that I encountered no difficulty in obtaining a position for you as a pianist in Mr Davenant's company, as per the enclosed letter of offer. No audition is required: he remembers you well.

Tonight is the closing night of The Hostage of Barbary, *and we depart for London tomorrow at 1 o'clock, by the Mixed Train, so I shall be expecting you to pack up your belongings – only bring what you absolutely need – and herewith send my coachman to fetch you to join us at the Golden Swan, where I have reserved a room for your use.*

I hope that you will be sensible of this means of removing yourself from your present degraded circumstances, and expect that surely you will not dare to delay, or to put me off any further, lest you forsake your only opportunity of elevating yourself from your miseries.

I cherish a hope that this action of mine may make some amends, that your sweet and generous nature will enable you to forgive me, and that we might renew our friendship.

– Edmond

Wednesday, 2nd September 1840

My dear Miss Ayliffe,

I was greatly pleased to hear from Mr Verity of your interest in rejoining our Company as a piano accompanist & would like to offer you a Contract for the Winter Season in London, running at the Theatre Royal, Drury Lane, until the 31st of January 1841. To include attendance at Rehearsals & Performances as required, payment being made at the rate of 2 shillings per Public Appearance & 1 shilling per Rehearsal.

As we depart for London the day after tomorrow, kindly acknowledge this letter by return, advising me of your Intentions.

Yours etc.
Geo. Davenant

52: Curzon Street Station

At Curzon Street Station the rain was falling, clattering like gravel on the station canopy, and passengers scuttled from hansom cabs and omnibuses to the shelter of the railway shed. Porters plied their barrows, the engine wheezed while men shovelled coal into its tender, and the train was loaded with goods and passengers. The stationmaster bellowed out names: *Coventry, Rugby, Wolverton, Harrow, London.*

I walked along the platform, in need of air. Being stuffed into a first-class compartment with Edmond, Davenant, Hellbronn and Mr and Mrs Nisbett was already proving uncomfortable and the train had not even started to move. Beyond the end of the canopy, sheets of rain poured down upon the iron road that led back to London. The engine hissed quietly; the driver and fireman were preparing for the journey. I imagined the train passing the green fields and water meadows, the cottages and the canals, and turned to look back down the platform. Beyond the station buildings the black tenements and the factory chimneys were shadowy hulks in the grey rain. I thought of Nathan's remains lying in the cesspit beneath the workhouse. I was leaving him behind, but now I imagined his spirit freed from his earthly body and soaring to heaven. One day I would build him a memorial, a winged cherub in white marble, and water it with my tears. Until then my grief could not be complete, or my guilt find forgiveness, and nor could I bear another child.

My mind turned to Newhall Street, imagining Doughty returning exhausted to an empty house, finding Edmond's letter where I had hastily left it on his desk. With the coachman waiting, I had bundled up a few belongings and what I had saved of my salary, and left in haste before Doughty could return and dissuade me.

A sudden hiss of steam startled me and the idling engine filled the air with a sulphurous mist. It dispersed to reveal a familiar tall figure, progressing slowly through the throng on the platform, barely glancing at the third-class passengers bundled up in their cloaks in the open wagons, and peering through the sooty glass of the first-class compartments, sometimes jerking his head away as though to avoid the occupants staring back.

Doughty saw me, and a cry escaped him.

'Jane!'

He strode quickly forward. He was bare-headed, wet through, his hair soaked flat. Rainwater dripped from the shoulders of his coat, and his trousers and boots were dull with damp.

'I went to the Golden Swan last night,' he said, 'but I could not find you.'

'Oh, why must you come here?' I groaned. 'I should not see you.'

His hands were on my arms, and then he clasped my hands together. He had been hurrying; I felt the heat of his palms and caught the familiar scent of his cologne. He looked as though he wanted to embrace me and I felt an answering pang. He might have been my shelter, even now, but I knew I must follow my craft.

'Why would I not come? You left your letter for me to read – I knew you'd be here for the train. Jane …' His face was drawn with fatigue. 'Jane, we have a chance … will you not stay with me?'

'It's too late.'

My reply made deep ridges above his nose; a grimace of pain. I could so easily have relented.

'How can it be too late?'

'It is impossible. Consider your position, your reputation – you cannot keep me, not now.'

'I can keep a wife,' he said. 'My reputation will recover, and I'll find another position. I have sent my references to Dublin already. And as for you – Edmond has already deserted you once. Surely you must consign him to your past?'

I told him that Edmond had merely prevailed upon Mr Davenant to take me back as a pianist, and I was obligated to him for it, as it was not possible for me to obtain any other employment in the town of Birmingham. I was determined to play the piano; it was my only opportunity of returning to the theatre.

'Edmond.' Doughty had divined my discomfort. 'Tell me, Jane, in truth, do you still care for him?'

'I have found it in my heart to forgive him.'

'Jane? Do you love him? Have you returned to him?'

'He has tried to make amends …' I would say no more.

'And what if … if our … if you are …' he faltered, a dark furrow of concern deepening between his eyebrows.

'I am on my reds, if that is what you ask,' I muttered. It had been a convenient excuse, the first of many, to keep Edmond out of my room the previous night.

'I see.' His shoulders slumped in defeat.

'In any case, you called me a common slut, if you remember, for merely talking to Edmond. Now I have spent a night in the same hotel, I am travelling to London in his company. You will not forgive that – how can I come back to you?'

'I know that, I am in despair with jealousy, and yet I stand here, abject, before you. I am destroyed … as if you had cut off both my legs.' His face wore a grimace of pain, his pride was gone. 'For, whatever he has imposed upon you, it's not him you love. I know it from my core. I see it in your eyes, I feel it when I touch you. It is me, isn't it? You cleave to me. For God's sake, come back to me … I'll always love you, even if my life is turned upside-down by it.'

'William.' My arms suddenly ached with the longing to embrace him. Perhaps I was making a mistake: I sensed his heart was true. But I kept to my resolve. 'I must go now. Edmond will see me talking to you, and make a scene.'

My eyelids were pricking and I looked past Doughty and along the platform, where the last few passengers were getting into the train, and their trunks and boxes were loaded into the goods van. My rose-silk dress, rescued that morning from the pawnbroker, was somewhere in there, in a new trunk. Steam poured out of the engine with an explosive hiss, and the scene was obscured.

Doughty raised a hand and fanned the fingers gently across my cheek, along my jawline. He studied me, and wiped a tear aside with his thumb. He turned my face to his and crushed his mouth to mine.

I gasped. His arms came tight around me and even through his coat I could feel that his heart was pounding. He was my true lover, my only home, yet he would never kiss me again; my head throbbed and I answered him with an equal passion.

We drew apart. The cloud of steam had faded and I saw that the platform was empty apart from the guard going along the train securing the carriage doors.

'They're leaving.' I was breathless. 'I must go.'

Then a door reopened, and Edmond leant out. He saw me, and started waving and calling.

'Do you still trust him?' asked Doughty. 'He won't marry you, Jane, I'm certain of it. He'll abandon you again.'

We watched Edmond climb out of the railway carriage.

'I suppose he'll soon give me up.' I gave Doughty a wry smile. 'But by then I'll have proven myself in London. I will always have my music.'

Doughty shook his head. 'Come home, Jane,' he said.

Edmond was hurrying towards us. The stationmaster put his whistle between his lips and raised a flag. The engine driver leant out and signalled back. There was a hoot that made me jump. A huge puff of smoke issued from the funnel.

'I've given my promise.'

'No,' said Doughty, 'he doesn't deserve your promises. Remember how he betrayed you? He'll cast you off again. Remember your suffering: remember the workhouse, remember your child who died. I've seen so many deaths of the destitute: frozen in the winter, parched in the summer, starved and wasted with consumption. Don't take that risk again, I beg you.'

Edmond confronted me, breathless and glaring.

'What are you doing here?' he demanded. 'The train's ready to leave. Davenant sent me to fetch you.'

I hesitated, steadying myself.

'Come now, Jane,' snapped Edmond. 'For heaven's sake, do as you're told.'

'You cannot compel her to join you,' said Doughty. He stood between us and I felt his grasp tighten on my arm.

'What is it to you?' Edmond glared at Doughty, then at me.

Doughty's eyes widened and he opened his mouth to reply but subsided as I spoke over him.

'He has just come to bid me farewell, and a pleasant journey, as it is the end of my employment. He knows that I still hesitate to follow you to London.'

'You owe it to me now,' Edmond said. 'If it were not for me, Davenant would not have taken you on. Don't waste it. Come on.'

There was a long blast on the station-master's whistle.

'I owe it to Mr Davenant, at any rate.' I started to move, but Doughty stilled me, his head drooping and grief lining his face. My heart ached for him, but also I thought of Davenant, of the rehearsals, the audiences, the concert halls. I put my hand on his fingers, that were white upon my black shawl.

'Let me go, William, please,' I said. 'I have a chance now, to support myself by my music. Whatever happens to me I must take that chance.'

As he released me there was a shout from the guard, and the train started to creak and rumble. The engine wheezed slowly past. Edmond had already turned back towards his carriage. Mr Davenant, calling out to us, was holding open the door. I hastened to follow and jumped up after Edmond, who pulled me inside the compartment.

'*Goodbye!*' I shouted back through the billowing smoke. '*Write to me at Drury Lane!*' I slammed the carriage door shut.

53: Doughty's Letter to Me

Wednesday, November 11th, 1840

41 Long Lane
Dublin
Ireland

My Dear Jane,

I am writing in the hope that this finds you at the Theatre Royal, Drury Lane, just as you once wrote in hope to your Edmond. I hope that my letters will find a more considerate reception than he afforded to yours, and that you might do me the kindness of writing back. And I pray that you are well and secure in your new position. I have read of the success of Mr Davenant's productions in the newspapers.

Since I arrived at the beginning of October I have been made welcome here, for the hospital is very busy and was in need of another physician. I earn sufficient for my needs, and have rented a good-sized house in the vicinity. I have been constantly learning since I took up the post. At present, I believe that Dublin outstrips London as a centre of clinical teaching. I regularly attend the meetings of the Pathological Society of Dublin, which aims to advance the treatment of disease by relating signs and symptoms to post-mortem findings.

I have heard a little from Mr Graves of doings in Birmingham since I came here. Dr Birt-Jones was elected Coroner, and Mr Muntz has assumed control of the Town Council and insisted that the rates are collected and that the town runs its own business, whatever pettifoggery the Court of the Exchequer Chamber might pronounce.

Vernon's journals were sent to Lambeth Palace for a Church inquiry, the outcome of which is as yet unknown. What I saw of them appalled me. Harriet, Theresa, and a further eight victims, had been violated, and their suffering written down in disgusting detail. Mr Welchman Whateley, the Warwickshire coroner, pronounced Vernon's death to be accidental. Much about Vernon remained concealed, his lies going unchallenged, while to myself there clung a taint, and offers to reinstate me were half-hearted. Dr Wright and Mr Siviter resigned their posts and left the town, but there are others, more important men, who stand to lose if Vernon's misdeeds are ever made public. I heard that Dr Wright also obtained a post in Ireland, but I have yet to encounter him.

You would find Dublin a pleasant place. It is true that there are many poor districts here, which supply the hospital with the majority of its patients. Arriving by the sea, however, one enters a beautiful bay set amongst verdant mountains where the city nestles like a jewel. The main thoroughfares are broad and tastefully laid out with many fine buildings and gardens. The hospital itself stands amongst lawns and flowerbeds, with a fruit orchard planted by Dean Swift himself.

I still cherish hopes that you will tire one day of the limelight of London theatrical life and make your home here. Would you consider coming here as my assistant? The skill you showed in nursing my late wife would be greatly valued here, and in this simple and industrious life you might regain the esteem and affection of your parents. There are lodgings set aside for the nurses, and we could perhaps walk out in the evenings and enjoy the slow development of an intimacy which the circumstances of our brief acquaintance cut short. We might arrive at an understanding which our previous lives as master and servant made impossible.

As it was in Birmingham, my desk is at the back of the house, and looks out on a pleasant garden, with paths among the flower-borders where children might run and play amidst the fluting of the blackbirds. The Broadwood piano, of which you were so fond, has survived its sea crossing and stands waiting in the parlour. Perhaps, in a time yet to come, your children and your grandchildren might grow up in this great city and the piano keys once again ripple like a river under the caress of your hands.

I am lost now, in a dream of you, which I have held in my heart ever since the day when you first opened your eyes to mine in the workhouse yard. Our time together began too abruptly and ended without a proper conclusion. If only there were a way for the chasm between us to be spanned and for us to speak simply, as one human to another, for me to meet your eyes again, to hold you in my loving embrace, we might yet be happy.

But, in reality, I must put down my pen before I render myself too foolish. After I take this letter to the Post Office, I have patients to attend in the hospital and to visit in their homes. Fortunately it is a crisp, calm morning, and the sun is bright for the time of year.

Yours affectionately,
— William

Acknowledgements

Poolbeg Press: Paula Campbell, for giving me the opportunity to realise a lifetime ambition, and Gaye Shortland, for her detailed, perceptive and constructive editing.

Fellow writers, especially: Joanna Orwin, Annette Liebeskind Berkovits and Jo Schaffel, Christine Cochrane, Kath Breen, Ruth Notestine and S.E. Adams and 'Christy' and 'Giselle' from Writers' Workshop for their fair and honest critique; Maggy van Krimpen for astrology and second sight; Wally O'Neill of Red Books in Wexford and Carol Long, who encouraged me to take part in the 'Meet The Publisher' event at Wexford Literary Festival.

Jericho Writers: Debi Alper, Emma Darwin, Louise Walters, for teaching me to self-edit and redraft.

Open University Creative Writing tutors: Kevan Manwaring, Tim Reeves, Gill Ryland, for starting me off.

Libraries: I thank The Wellcome Library, London, and the Birmingham Library and Archives.

While bearing the responsibility for all untruths, this being a work of fiction, I am particularly indebted to the following works:

Dion Boucicault. *London Assurance*. Samuel French, New York, 1860

Ian Burney. *Bodies of evidence: Medicine and the politics of the English inquest, 1830-1926* Johns Hopkins University Press, Baltimore, 2000

Pamela Fisher. *The Politics of Sudden Death: The Office and Role of the Coroner in England and Wales, 1726-1888*. PhD Thesis, University of Leicester, 2007

Conrad Gill. *History of Birmingham, Volume 1*. Oxford University Press, London, 1952

Ruth Goodman. *How to be a Victorian*. Viking/ Penguin Books, London, 2013

Peter Higginbotham. Workhouses.org.uk

John Jervis. *A Practical Treatise on the Office and Duties of Coroners: with an Appendix of Forms and Precedents*. London, 1829

Samuel Squire Sprigge. *The Life and Times of Thomas Wakley; Founder and First Editor of The Lancet*, Longmans, Green & Co., London, 1897

James Stevens Curl. *The Victorian Celebration of Death*. Sutton Publishing, Stroud, 2004.

Matthew Sweet. *Inventing the Victorians*. Faber & Faber, London, 2001.

Thomas Wakley. *The Lancet*. London, 1839-40

About the Author

Maybelle Wallis trained as a doctor in London and Birmingham and now lives and works in Wexford, Ireland. She loves the way her work always brings new patients and new challenges. At the same time, she is inspired by history and historical fiction and by the way that technology, politics, medicine, and civil rights have evolved over the last 300 years.

AUTHOR'S NOTE

Dear Reader,

Book reviews help other readers who are looking to discover the books they like. If you could please write a review – even a few words – about your responses to my book, on Amazon, Goodreads, or both, that would be much appreciated. Thank you.

Maybelle Wallis
HistWriter.com
Twitter: @DrMWallis
Facebook: @MWallisHistWriter

Printed in Great Britain
by Amazon